Earth Portal

A Novel

By Deb Kolbo Ellsworth

For more information about the Empathy Symbol, go to
https://EmpathySymbol.com

Printed in the United States of America

ISBN: 978-0-9884682-4-5

Version P1

CHAPTER 1

James Thompson had rehearsed the words he was going to say a hundred times over the last few days. Now, while those words were pounding inside his skull for release, he couldn't get them past his lips.

He shifted nervously in his chair, and scanned the bar they were sitting in, stalling. Garraty's Tavern looked the same as it did every Friday, full of people shedding their Minnesota reserve and getting a little freer and a little more raucous as the well-earned happy hour flowed into hour number two. The first time he'd set foot in Garraty's fifteen years ago, if the bartender had said to the waitress, "Bring this beer to the black guy," she'd have known exactly where to take it. Now he was one among at least a dozen, and there were many others in between his dark skin and the standard Minnesota pale. In fact, a couple of businessmen from India were at the next table over, giving the waitress a hard time about why there wasn't any Indian food on the menu. He had to agree with them; he'd developed a real taste for curry lately.

Pennants of every Minnesota sports team, even the defunct ones, adorned the walls. The lighted case behind the bar displayed autographed memorabilia: a Timberwolves jersey signed by Kevin Garnett; a Vikings football signed by the legendary quarterback Fran Tarkenton; a hockey stick signed by Herb Brooks, coach of the Olympic "Miracle on Ice" team; a basketball signed by the Lynx's

Maya Moore and Lindsay Whalen; and spotlighted in the center, like the Hope Diamond, a baseball signed by the entire 1991 Twins World Series team. Any sports fan would feel comfortable in this place. James watched the owner, Michael Garraty, wearing his standard University of Minnesota maroon and gold sweatshirt, laughing with a customer at the bar. He was probably telling another of his endless supply of Ole and Lena jokes in his mangled attempt at a Swedish accent.

James forced himself to look back across the table. He watched Danny drain the Guinness he always drank and slam the glass down on the table, the same table they always sat at, every Friday at five. They'd been talking sports, they'd been talking about their jobs, same as always. Yet everything was different.

Danny looked impatiently at James. "So c'mon, just spit it out, man."

James stuffed another French fry into his mouth and gave his best friend a carefully blank look. "What?"

"Ever since you came in here, you've looked like you're trying to say something." As Danny waited for James to respond, a mischievous look crossed his face. He rested his chin on his intertwined fingers and batted his eyes at James. "Listen, if you've secretly been in love with me all these years, just say so."

James burst out laughing. "Damn, Danny, I thought I was keeping it so well hidden."

"Yeah, well, I know I'm so pretty I appeal to both sexes. I can't help it." Danny puckered his lips and smacked them in an exaggerated air kiss directed at James.

James laughed again. "Now I'm gonna have to sue you for sexual harassment."

"Bring it on, my friend. But, seriously. What can't you say to me, your best friend since second grade? C'mon."

Yeah, he was right. An unlikely pair of friends they were, too. Even as a little kid, James was always a fairly quiet guy. Maybe it was because his father, a minister, was the opposite. His father sang louder than anyone in the church, not caring that he was off-key most of the time and preached enthralling sermons in a deep booming voice. He was renowned for the theatrics and gimmicks he employed in his sermons, like the time he actually pulled a rabbit from a top hat. His dad could walk up to any stranger, extend his hand, and make him feel like they were old friends within two minutes. When James was a young child, people were always saying things like, "Where'd you get this shy little rabbit, Reverend? You pull him out of that hat of yours?" His father would burst out with his rafter-shaking sonic boom of a laugh and say something like, "Oh, you just watch out. This boy's a thinker. One day this little rabbit will be standing in front of television cameras giving a brilliant acceptance speech for the Nobel Prize he just won."

Then Danny Friedman's family moved next door when James was eight years old, and within two hours, this wild, funny Jewish kid from New York had James flying off a bike jump they'd created from some discarded plywood and an old wedge-shaped snow shovel blade.

Danny was right. What couldn't he say to him? Well, maybe this: I'm pretty sure I was contacted by aliens. He'd said a lot of things to Danny over the last thirty years, but nothing remotely as bizarre as that.

James looked Danny straight in the eye. "OK…" He paused, working up his nerve. But his nerve went south. "I'm sorry to have to tell you this, Friedman, but that pink flamingo tie just doesn't go with that green shirt. Apparently, no one's mentioned it to you yet, but it's the truth. Better you hear it from me."

Danny laughed. "Coming from a guy who owns the exact same sweater in six different colors, I'll take that sartorial criticism with a grain of salt."

"What can I say? Emily said I looked so good in the yellow one, she made me go back and get all the others." James held up three fingers. "There are three important benefits to being a teacher. One, you get to mold young minds, sparking a lifelong passion for learning and possibly influencing the next Albert Einstein. Two, and no less significant, you get summers off. And three, you can dress comfortably for work."

Danny sighed deeply. "OK, I know that science teachers aren't renowned for their fashion sense—absented-minded professor and all that. But really, if you can't appreciate this striking flamingo tie set against the perfect shade of lime green, there's no hope for you."

James smiled, and chewed on another French fry. Maybe he'd let the thing go for now. Try to figure it out himself, maybe hash it over with Danny next week.

"So really, what's up? What's bugging you?" Danny eyed him suspiciously. "You got some parent threatening to sue you for failing her kid or something?"

Or maybe he'd have to deal with it now. James closed his eyes for a moment, willing himself to just say it and get it out there, on the table and in the open. He was disturbed to hear himself exhale loudly, nervously. He forced his voice to be calm and steady. "No, it's nothing like that. Nothing normal. That's the thing. I don't know how to say it 'cause I don't know how to say it. So you understand it, I mean."

"I'm not an idiot, James."

"I know, I didn't mean it like that. Listen, let me buy another round." James signaled the waitress. "At least I know you won't walk out on me if you've got a full glass of beer in front of you."

"You got that right." Danny pushed his empty glass to the edge of the table. "Man, I hate that in movies, when a guy is at a bar with someone and he's just ordered a drink, and then they have their significant one-minute conversation to advance the plot, and then he just walks out after taking one sip of his drink. Who would do that? I tell you, they lose all credibility with me at that point. Anyway, you were saying?"

All right, time to jump off the high dive. "OK. Here it is. I had a vision." James paused for his words to sink in, but Danny didn't look too impressed.

"A vision, huh? No, don't tell me." Danny held up his hand as James was opening his mouth to explain. "Let me guess. Knowing you, you probably had the revelation that you should sell everything, move your family to an island in the Pacific, and live a simple life at one with nature." He grinned. "Did I nail it, or what?"

"No. Not even remotely close."

"That's a relief. Although it would've been nice to have a buddy to visit in Tahiti."

"Tahiti's going to be under water in thirty years."

"OK, Montana then. High up on a mountaintop. Am I close?"

"No," James said flatly. "Look, you're not making this any easier for me. Here's the thing. I think I've had something really important revealed to me."

"Like, God spoke to you?"

"No, I don't think it was God," James said thoughtfully, "although I suppose it could have been. But it was like this vision was being given to me by someone. Like they were telling me something really important that no one in the whole world knows about, something that could change everything."

Danny leaned back, stretched out his five-foot-nine frame, clasped his hands behind his head of wavy dark hair, and said, "All right, enlighten me, O Visionary One."

James had come in here half hoping that Danny's usual flippant attitude would convince him that his experience was nothing, really. Now it was just pissing him off.

"It happened on Monday night."

Danny laughed, and raised his fresh glass of Guinness. "Oh, I get it. You had a few too many beers, maybe, while you were watching the Packers beat the crap out of the Cowboys. Did your revelation have anything to do with the Cowboys needing a new head coach? One time while I was watching the Vikings, I realized with absolute certainty that the Vikings needed me to be their idea guy. I actually called their fan line to tell them I had a great idea for tying in with that Norwegian Independence Day that Minnesotans love to celebrate, what is it, Sit-in-the-Mai Tai or something, right?"

"Syttende Mai, May 17th," James said, but Danny didn't pick up on the annoyed tone in his voice.

"How'd you know that?"

"Emily makes a traditional Norwegian Lutheran dinner every May

17th—meatballs, herring, green Jell-O and lefse."

"Oh, man, you poor guy. Anyway, I thought, the Vikings are from Norway, so everyone should celebrate the day with purple beer, like everyone drinks green beer on St. Patrick's Day, you know? I spent an hour messing around with food coloring trying to get my beer the right color of purple. You know what my problem was? Beer is kind of a yellowish-brown color, right? And when you mix in blue and red, you get this ugly greenish-brown color that looks like you just dipped the glass in swamp water. Anyway, the next day, I decided to lay off drinking for a while." Danny tapped his beer glass and grinned. "Maybe your vision means, switch to Coke."

This wasn't working. Most of the time, James enjoyed his friend's ability to pull out an amusing story to fit any occasion. Not now. "I had one beer. One. And this thing was way wilder than anything I could have thought of myself, drunk or sober. Besides, the last time I got totally hammered was at your wedding, and that was, what, seven, eight years ago? Look, I'm not just talking about a good idea here. I'm talking about something from so far out in left field, it's in right field."

"OK, OK. So, it came to you, what, when you were just sitting around your house watching Monday Night Football?"

"No, I was asleep. I'd just gone to sleep maybe fifteen minutes before."

Danny gave him a relieved grin. "Well, then you had a weird dream. Give me my hundred bucks, kid. I just saved you a visit with a psychiatrist."

"No, see, that's just it!" James leaned forward urgently, almost desperately. "It wasn't a dream. I know it seems like it would have been. But dreams are surreal, you know what I mean? This was hyper real. When it was over, I woke up drenched in sweat, even though it was freezing cold in the room. And I could still feel this... presence. Danny, this is the weirdest thing that has ever happened to me in my life, and if you can't cut the wise guy act and take me seriously, then just forget it."

"OK, sorry." Danny frowned. "The last time I saw you get all worked up like this was... Hell, I don't know when I've ever seen you get all worked up like this. Except over politics, of course. I mean, weren't you voted Mr. Reliable in our senior yearbook?"

"You know I was. You won't let me forget it."

"Right. So yeah, you ain't the kind of guy to have visions, my friend."

"That's my point," James said intensely. "This isn't me. I don't know for sure what it was, but I know what it wasn't. It wasn't a dream and it wasn't the beer talking. Look, don't get hung up on the word 'vision.' That's just the way I've been thinking of it, but we can call it an experience, if that helps."

James finished off his first beer, and started into the fresh one, trying to steady his nerves. "You know, I've been sweating this for four days. I haven't been able to think about anything else. And I've been looking forward to today, when I could unload it on you and get your take on it. But I'll be honest, I've been dreading telling you, too. Because it's so totally weird, and I'd rather just be sitting here having a beer and giving you shit about your wild ties and complaining about work as usual. But I don't know what else to do. So, I'm just gonna tell you the whole thing, and the hell with it. You believe me, great. You don't, fine, we just forget it and I'll try to deal with it in my own way. OK?"

For maybe the second time since James had known him, Danny was at a loss for words. He stared at James for a long minute. Then he said, "Tell you what. You've always been the rock for me, you know? I let the air out of the principal's tires, you cover for me. I tell you I want to propose to that sexy girl from Australia I only met two weeks ago, you talk sense to me. So OK, I owe you one time when you get to be the crazy guy and I'll be the rock. Go ahead. Shoot."

James sucked in a big breath and was flooded with the memory of the overwhelming experience. His voice took on a hypnotic quality as the story flowed from him. "It was a visual message—no words, just images. I could see the Earth floating in space, hanging there surrounded by billions of stars. It was so calm and peaceful and ancient feeling, and this incredible feeling of well-being just washed over me and filled me.

"Then, images of life on Earth started flashing—whales spouting in the ocean, insects crawling on flowers, kids running and laughing, trees growing, old people walking in a field in China, kangaroos hopping—just living thing after living thing, flashing in front of me, one after another, hundreds of images.

"Then... things got weird. The Earth started shimmering, and I could see these beautiful waves of color emanating from it, like a huge Aurora Borealis flowing from our planet into space. My God, it was so powerful, so amazing! Somehow—I don't know how, it just came into my mind—I knew this was emanating from every living thing, all the plants and animals and people. It was the Life Force of all living things on Earth.

"Then, picture it—the shimmering round Earth began darkening and getting silvery, so it looked like a big hole in space, but still with the Life Force flowing from it, radiating into space.

"Then I suddenly realized that the Earth's Life Force was attracting something. Like a magnet attracts metal, right? It was these... beings. These alien beings. They felt huge, but I don't know if they had any real physical size. They were definitely otherworldly. Way, way otherworldly. They kind of looked like giant white gossamer sheets, kind of undulating and flowing. But that's a really inadequate description."

James shuddered, mentally pulling himself out of the vision, and focused on Danny. "I wish I could tell you better what the picture in my mind was. It's really hard to put into words so that you get the full effect. Anyway, these beings were kind of flowing through space toward Earth. It's weird, but ever since that experience, I've been thinking of them as the Seekers. I don't know why, but that's what's in my head. I guess it's part of the vision.

"So anyway, I could see these Seekers streaming toward Earth, and kind of getting caught by the Life Force flowing from our planet. It was like they were riding in on the Life Force, kind of like surfing on it, and then they just disappeared into this shimmering dark hole that was the Earth. Suddenly, it all became clear, like I just knew. I understood that the Earth is a portal for these beings, these Seekers. Somehow, I just knew that they were passing into some other plane of existence, or some other dimension, or something that I can't explain because it is entirely out of my Earthly human experience.

But they're passing through, and the Earth is the portal that they do this through. Because of our powerful Life Force, you know?"

Danny hadn't moved a muscle. Now his eyes widened, and he said softly, "Holy shit."

James's voice became grim. "Yeah, well, I wish that was all there was to it. Because fine, they can pass through us all they want. We'd never know. We don't feel it, we don't perceive them. But... OK, this sounds stupid, but I think these Seekers gave me this vision as a message.

"See, they showed me one more thing. It was another Seeker coming to Earth, but this one was different. It was..." James paused as he struggled to come up with words to describe it. "It was all jagged, instead of smooth and flowing, and it seemed like it was writhing and fighting against the Life Force. This feeling of dread— of horror—filled me as I was watching this. Then it was like the picture was zooming in, like following this deviant alien thing as it got closer and closer to Earth—down through the clouds and toward a city and then into the city, you know? And then they showed this man who was killing someone, he had this knife and he was stabbing this other person, and there was blood flying everywhere." James shuddered and gave Danny a look of despair. "That awful alien thing got sucked right into that murderer. It was horrible. Then it was like they were pulling the view out again, back up through the clouds, and when it got back into space, there was this oily dark splotch on the Life Force radiating from the planet."

James drank deeply from his beer, trying to shake off the feeling of horror that had engulfed him again. He looked at Danny. "So, yeah. I think that was the message. I think they were trying to tell me that some of them are evil. Not just bad, but devastatingly, totally evil. And the thing is—the really, really scary thing is—some of those evil Seekers get stuck on their way through the Earth. They don't make it through the portal. They get stuck in people, certain kinds of people.

"It's like some people are predisposed to evil themselves, for whatever reason, maybe a genetic defect, I don't know. But there's something in those people that attracts the evil Seekers and accidentally catches them and holds them stuck inside. Which maybe ramps up their capacity for evil a hundred times."

James continued urgently, desperately wanting Danny to understand. "Like Hitler. It explains Hitler, how one guy could even think of trying to exterminate all the Jewish people in the world, not to mention the gays and the Gypsies. Or like Pol Pot, or Stalin. They killed millions, right? Hell, there was that Russian queen a long time ago who took baths in the blood of peasants. The point is, there have been a relatively few people, among the billions of us who have lived and died throughout history, who were completely, inhumanly, off-the-charts evil. Why? I don't know, but maybe I just found out."

James looked at Danny, holding his breath, waiting to hear his reaction. But Danny just sat there, beer poised halfway to his mouth, which was hanging open. James finally had to ask. "So, what do you think, Danny?"

Danny slowly lowered the glass to the table. And then he said the last thing James expected. He leaned forward, eyes lighting up with excitement. "So, do you think the really good people on Earth, like Mother Teresa or Gandhi or Martin Luther King, like they've been magnets for the saintly-type Seekers? Or like, maybe some people who've been super geniuses, and nobody's been able to explain why, because their parents were just ordinary people, maybe those people caught some of these Seekers, and maybe the Seekers are way smarter than us. Like Leonardo da Vinci."

"Or Einstein, or Isaac Newton," James added, relief washing over him like a cool shower on a hot day. The tension squeezing his muscles let go of its death grip. He relaxed and smiled at Danny with gratitude.

"Or Kurt Cobain!" Danny said.

"Uh, no, I think it was more the drugs with Kurt, man. I don't know. It's an interesting idea."

Danny suddenly laughed loudly. "Or hey, maybe there are really inane attention-seeking aliens who get stuck in our worst comedians."

"Yeah." James grinned at Danny. "That would explain you dropping trou at the fifth-grade choir concert. You've definitely got to be the magnet for any lame-comedian-sports-loving-flashy-dressing-can't-make-a-free-throw-beer-drinking Seeker types out there."

"Thanks. I'll drink to that." Danny raised his glass and drank. Then he frowned. "Hey, what do you mean, can't make a free throw?"

James snorted with laughter. "Ah, how soon they forget. My driveway, September, gorgeous day? You, for some unfathomable reason, challenged me to a free throw shooting contest. Me, sixteen of twenty. You, seven."

"Anyway," Danny said. "So, how did it end? Your vision, I mean."

"That was it. I was totally engulfed in this feeling of horror, and then I just woke up suddenly, and like I said, I was shaking so bad, and sweating, but cold, really cold. It seemed like it was twenty degrees in our bedroom."

"What about Emily? Did she sleep through this?"

"So that's the other weird thing. I must have yelled or something, 'cause I woke her up, too. Listen to this, Danny. She asked me why it was so freezing cold. That's the thing I can't get past. I've tried to convince myself it was just a nightmare. But then why did Emily feel the extreme cold?"

Danny took his time, sipping his beer reflectively. "You know what, James? I never told you this. I never told anyone this. Once I had a dream that was truly real, not just a dream. It was after my grandfather died, about a week later. He came to me while I was asleep, and he told me that he loved me. Which he had never said to me when he was alive. He said he needed to tell me. I woke up, and I could still feel his presence in the room. I absolutely knew he'd been there. So, I'm not going to be the one to tell you it couldn't be real."

"Thank you."

They sat there finishing off the basket of fries, both lost in thought. James wondered if he should turn the conversation back to the Gophers' prospects this year. He'd said this totally bizarre thing, and Danny was still his buddy. He felt a huge urge to get back to normal. Probably it was over and done with and nothing would come of it anyway.

But just as he was about to ask if Danny thought the Gophers' new point guard would be the key to their season this year, maybe even take them to the Sweet Sixteen, Danny spoke up. "The question is, how or why did you have this vision? I mean, was it actually given to you, by aliens or God or something, or did your unconscious mind somehow just find out this thing?"

"I don't know," James said thoughtfully. "It was such a bizarre experience—not just for the content, but for the way it happened. It felt like I was being shown a movie inside my brain. It felt like—OK, I feel like a total idiot saying these words, but it felt like the aliens were contacting me. Me personally."

Danny pointed a finger at James. "Hey, don't go getting abducted by space aliens, dude. Who would I have a beer with on Fridays then?"

James stuck out his fist in answer, and they did their elaborate handshake, tapping fists up, down, sideways, wiggling fingers, touching fingertips, hands gliding past each other, index fingers pointing at each other. The one they'd made up in ninth grade. "I'm not going anywhere. Not Tahiti and definitely not Mars."

"Good. So, what's the answer to the sixty-four-thousand-dollar question, then? Why do you think these aliens contacted you and revealed all this shit about the portal and the Life Force and the evil aliens getting stuck in people?"

James looked at Danny with a distressed expression and said hesitantly, "I don't know. But I think... well, I think maybe they want me to do something about it."

CHAPTER 2

Comfortable. It was a word that was highly underrated, James reflected, as he stretched out his six-foot-three body on the comfy old blue flowered couch in the family room downstairs and popped open a beer. He could feel the endorphins coursing through his body like his bloodstream was the River of Contentment.

But it was more than just physical comfort. He felt completely at ease in his world, in this home that he and Emily had created over the last thirteen years. The house had been listed as a "charming 1920's bungalow," which was realtor-speak for small but cute. Emily had fallen in love with it immediately. James had liked the park down the street, with the basketball courts where he'd play ball with his son one day.

Maybe ten blocks over, the elite suburb of Edina bumped up against their southwest Minneapolis neighborhood. James had no feelings of animosity toward the doctors and lawyers and business executives who lived there, whose streets were cleared of snow hours before James's street; whose sons played hockey with expensive equipment from the day they turned four years old; whose daughters were sent to expensive Lutheran colleges, where they wouldn't date anyone like him unless it was for a rebellious fling. But he wouldn't want to live there.

James liked his neighborhood. Down the block lived the guy, Ted Skinner, who wrote humorous columns for the Star Tribune about his car troubles and his dog troubles and his home remodeling troubles. Sometimes James saw him walking the dog, a little brown and white hairy thing named Mr. Stupendo, and it made James smile, remembering what Ted had written about how the dog stole a pie off the table or whatever. Next door lived a firefighter, who might any day put his life on the line to save James, or even one of the Edina lawyers, if they called in extra help from nearby cities.

James felt comfortable in his neighborhood. He liked that he wasn't the only one creating the diversity, the token interracial family. His son's best friend, Luis, who lived at the end of the block, had a Mexican father and a Japanese mother. At least a dozen African-American families lived within a few blocks. He'd heard that a Somali family had just bought the Arneson's house. A white lesbian couple lived a few houses down, in a purple house with turquoise trim, where they were raising their two brown-skinned sons, adopted from either Ecuador or Guatemala, he could never remember which. You couldn't get much more diverse than that. Unless maybe they were Buddhists, too.

The old couch had come from his first apartment. Upstairs, Emily had put Mission-style furniture in the living room to match the house, with simple lines and straight backs and wooden arms. Down here, a man could relax.

James pointed the remote at the TV and muted the commercial. The Broncos had just stopped the Patriots from scoring, and the Monday Night Football commentators were running out of ways to keep the viewers interested in this defensive struggle. Monday night: a week since the Vision. Thankfully, nothing unusual had happened since then. Whether it had been true, or just an incredibly powerful dream, it didn't matter. The vehicle called "James's Life" had skidded without warning, but it was back chugging along Ordinary Road, and James was happy.

To take his mind off that night a week ago, James scanned the family photos displayed on the shelves next to the TV. His eyes lingered on their wedding picture. Sixteen years ago. Amazing. College sweethearts, and he loved her as much as ever. No, actually, much more. Deeper. Truer. Sixteen years of life experiences together will do that, if you're lucky and you married the right person.

Emily hardly looked any different, he thought. She was still gorgeous, with her tall, athletic body and her long, auburn hair. He was glad she'd never cut it, like so many women did when they hit their thirties. And those alluring green eyes that pulled him in, and then softened as she smiled at him in a way that said he was all she would ever need. Maybe it was her unusual heritage: half Norwegian, a quarter Irish, and a smattering of Portuguese and Ojibwe. Whatever it was, she'd caught his attention the moment she sat down next to him in his freshman composition class at the U, and that was it.

On the shelf below their wedding picture were the kids' baby pictures, next to their current school photos. Why did school photos always look so goony? Well, even if those photographers took enough time to try to get a good shot, which they didn't, there probably wasn't much they could do with the material they had to work with. Trey's teeth were way too big for his six-year-old mouth, and his fresh haircut accentuated the ears sticking out like radar dishes set to catch all incoming signals.

Danielle was eleven, on the verge of adolescence, and that was always awkward. He knew she was self-conscious about that tiny mole on her left cheek, because of the way she always sat with a finger covering it. Of course, she hated her glasses. In the photo, she had that forced smile kids did so often for school pictures. Her natural smile was gorgeous, melted him every time. She had beautiful full lips, the kind white actresses paid tons of money to get. Her hair was a stunning combination of his and Emily's: a thick, wavy chestnut brown waterfall cascading onto her shoulders. "You are going to be one beautiful woman when you grow up, baby," James often told her. "I'm gonna be fighting those boys off soon enough." Of course, she always responded with a mortified "Daaad." But he hoped that a little part of her would believe him.

The game was back on. James unmuted the TV. Between plays, his eyes went back to the photos. Both sides of the family were well-represented. Emily's parents had had a studio portrait done of the whole extended family, with everyone dressed in denim. The photo of his family had been taken last Christmas when his sister Andrea was back from North Carolina and they were all together again. His sister Darlene's son Cory was at that age where boys feel compelled to mug for the camera. James chuckled inwardly, remembering Trey's delighted reaction to his cousin's funny face. He'd be trying to top him in the next family picture, no doubt.

That holiday photo reminded him: he should ask Emily if she'd called his mother yet about Thanksgiving. His folks always had it at their house, the same little starter house he'd grown up in, the one they kept saying they ought to move out of as the family grew larger, but somehow never did. Now it was just the right size for a retired couple. Emily had been bugging him about how they were almost forty and the folks were getting older, and really, they should be taking over the family holiday duties. She was right, he thought, looking at the grey hair his mother had allowed to show once she'd had a few grandchildren.

Another commercial? He muted the TV again and got up to stretch. The tee-ball trophy that was proudly displayed on the shelf above the TV caught his eye, and he picked it up, smiling fondly. That's what true happiness was. Screw the fancy cars. He'd never had more fun in his life than the summer before last when he'd helped coach Trey's tee-ball team. Who'd've thought baseball was so complicated? Before he tried to teach it to a bunch of five-year-olds, he'd thought of it as a simple game.

Smiling, he put down the cheap plastic baseball trophy and picked up the Destination Imagination Da Vinci Award Danielle's team had won at the regional tournament last year. His daughter was so creative she'd won an award for it. All right, she and the five other kids on the team. How proud he'd felt, watching those six girls standing up there in that gym, jumping up and down and screaming and hugging each other. They should watch that DI video again. When they'd watched it the first time, he remembered, they'd laughed at him, because for at least a minute all you could hear on the audio was him whooping and yelling like a maniac.

Emily came into the room. James smiled at her as he set the DI trophy back in its spot next to his own trophy, the student-voted "Best Teacher" award he'd received a couple years ago. "Man, we've got great kids, don't we?" he said.

Emily smiled back. "Yeah, we do. Although if you'd said that to me half an hour ago, I might have argued. Danielle was driving me crazy with the homework tonight."

James sat down, and Emily snuggled up next to him. "She's been working on this Hawaii state project for weeks, and it's due on Wednesday. She finally finished making the clay volcano for the diorama. But everything just takes her forever. You know how she daydreams. She just told me she wishes she could have been a Hawaiian princess who rode from island to island on dolphins."

James smiled. "That girl's gonna be a writer."

"Maybe, if she has unlimited deadlines. Could you just check the top of the news for a minute?"

James flipped to a local station. Two co-anchors sat behind the desk, filling the diversity requirements spelled out by the corporation that owned Channel 6. Julie Sjoding was blond, pretty, Scandinavian. Jason Yakimoto was Asian, affable. He was speaking now, in the middle of reporting something serious, it looked like.

"...as tension builds in the Far East today. President Scofield has ordered more troops to Japan, in response to China's support for the Southeast Asian Alliance. Japan has reluctantly agreed to take more U.S. troops, but the Japanese government is getting a lot of resistance from its populace."

Video footage showed Japanese demonstrators in the streets, carrying signs saying, "U.S. OUT OF JAPAN NOW" and "JAPAN IS NOT THE 51ST STATE."

Julie chimed in, as required by co-anchor law #12. "Wow, Jason, things are getting pretty tense over there."

Was Jason Yakimoto thinking, that vapid comment added no news value? Was he thinking, things in the country of my ancestors are going to hell? What he said was, "That's right, Julie. President Scofield has issued a warning to China that the U.S. will not tolerate Chinese military presence in Indonesia. What our country's response will be if China does not back down, we will learn tomorrow evening, when President Scofield is scheduled to address the American people."

"We'll be showing the President's address right here on Channel 6 at 8 p.m." Julie informed the viewers. "But don't worry, all you

Unnatural Disasters fans—we'll be showing the complete all-new episode of Unnatural Disasters right after the President's address, so you'll be able to see how the final four contestants survive the big storm."

Jason chuckled. "I'm betting Bob from New York City has a tough time with a tornado filled with pig slop."

"I can't argue with you on that one, Jason." Julie smiled, and then turned to the camera with an instantly serious look. "In other news, there was a deadly house fire in Minneapolis today that claimed the lives of three children and a grandmother. For dramatic footage of the fire, as well as the reaction of the children's mother, we go to Sam Barber in Northeast Minneapolis."

Emily picked up the remote and switched the TV back to football. "I really don't want to see that poor women tell us how it feels to lose your children and your mother in one day."

"This is bad," James said. "We've already got terrorists trying to wipe us out, and religious wars going on all over the planet. Now China's decided to get into the act. That whole part of the world is a pile of dynamite looking for a match, and I don't think Scofield's got the brains to blow it out if China lights it."

"I can't think about it anymore tonight. I'm going to bed."

"OK. If this game doesn't get any more interesting, I'll probably be coming to bed soon, too."

"Good. It's a school night for you, too, you know." Emily gave James a longer goodnight kiss than usual. "Anyway, maybe I'm not all that tired. I just remembered, I had a pretty interesting dream about you last night. It involved me being wrapped up in a big piece of black lace, and you unwrapping me. I know we've got those black lace drapes that we were going to put up in the dining room still sitting around somewhere…"

James hit the power button. "Let's give Danielle a few minutes to fall asleep."

———————————

The green numbers on James's bedside clock glowed: 2:23 a.m. James stirred, disturbed, but not awake. Something was pushing into his mind. Then, it felt like something was clamping onto his brain and holding it, forcing him into a strange state of awareness even though he was still asleep. Pictures began playing in his mind.

It happened as before. The Earth floated serenely in space in front of him. The Life Force emanated from the world, stronger and stronger. The Earth began to shimmer, transforming into a hole in space. The Seekers again were being drawn to the Earth, gliding on the Life Force and disappearing into the Earth Portal. Then James felt his mental state change from calm to agitated, like he'd been enjoying a peaceful canoe trip down an incredibly beautiful river, when suddenly huge, turbulent rapids erupted. An evil Seeker moved toward Earth. Where the other Seekers appeared smooth, flowing, moving in harmony with the Life Force and each other, the evil Seeker seemed jagged, discordant, and apart. James saw the Seeker get caught in a distorted part of the Life Force and get pulled in by it, writhing and fighting. Unbearable pain flooded James's mind, his body, every cell in agony. He desperately wanted this to stop. He struggled to wake up, but something wouldn't let him.

Then, something new happened: an image of the White House appeared next to the hideous evil Seeker. The evil one was raging, and James's mind was engulfed in the feeling of hatred that emanated from the horrible being. He could see the alien's ugly distorted Life Force extending out to the White House, battering the walls. Was it going to attack our country, is that what they were trying to tell him?

But no, suddenly the evil Seeker was being sucked into the White House, struggling vainly, as a hideous shrieking sound of protest split James's brain with pain. James saw flames erupting from the White House, and he felt the consuming rage, the desire to obliterate everything, his brain was on fire, and James was screaming inside his head in terror...

James woke up screaming. "No, no, no, stop, stop!"

Emily woke with a start. "Honey, what's wrong?" She put her arms around him, pulling him close, trying to soothe him. "James, honey, it's OK. That must have been some nightmare you had."

But James couldn't escape the vision. This was no nightmare. This was hell opening up beneath his feet. It possessed him and would not release its awful grip on his mind. He moaned in fear and horror.

"No, no, no, it can't be!"

"Honey, the nightmare's over." Emily stroked his head gently. "Wow, your hair's all wet, you're sweating. Poor baby," she said soothingly. "It's OK. You're here with me." She felt him trembling. "My God, you're shaking. It's OK. I'm here." She stroked his shoulders. "Breathe. Deep breaths. It's OK now. Relax."

James felt himself calm down slightly in Emily's arms, but he couldn't stop the violent shivers wracking his body.

Emily was concerned. "Do you want to tell me about it?"

"No, I want to forget it."

Emily kissed his forehead gently. "What's with all the nightmares lately? Maybe you shouldn't eat a snack right before bed anymore." Then she said softly, in a troubled voice, "You know what? I must have been having a nightmare, too. I just remembered. I was dreaming about an intruder in our bedroom." Emily pulled the blankets tighter around them. "Why is it so cold in here? No wonder you're shivering. Did you turn the heat down too far when you came to bed? I'm freezing."

"Maybe I did. I'll go check."

James sat up and swung his feet over the edge of the bed, but then he couldn't move. His brain was telling his body to stand up, but it wasn't responding.

Emily pushed herself up on one elbow. "You want me to come with you? I could sit up with you till you feel better."

"No, go back to sleep. I'll be OK. I'm just gonna check the furnace."

James forced himself to go downstairs, but each step took a conscious effort. He checked the thermostat, even though he was sure he'd set it to sixty-five. He felt like he couldn't warm up, he was chilled so deeply. Even though he told himself it was stupid, he turned it up to eighty. Then he went down to the basement to check the furnace, hoping it had gone out, that that would explain everything. He was dismayed to find it working just fine.

A cold November wind was blowing fiercely outside, giving him the strange feeling that he was living in a bad scary movie. He smiled slightly at the ridiculous thought. And then jumped when he heard a strange sound in the kitchen.

Good God, were they still here? Had they materialized in his house? If they were, there was nothing he could do. This wasn't a sci fi movie, and he wasn't going to be the hero who defeated the aliens with a baseball bat and a glass of water.

As James peered around the entryway to the kitchen, the dog looked at him guiltily, and pulled his front paws off the counter.

"Kirby!" He meant to sound stern, but it came out as relieved.

James picked up the cereal bowl by the sink. Kirby'd been drinking the last of the milk from Danielle's bedtime snack. He looked at the big shaggy black and white mutt sitting there at his feet wagging his tail ingratiatingly and spoke to him just to hear the comforting sound of a human voice. "Guess that's what I get for not finishing the dishes. But I had other things on my mind at that point. Dishes, or sex? What would you pick?"

There was no way he was getting back to sleep anytime soon. He could feel his heart still racing wildly from the overload of adrenaline that had been dumped into his body. James got a mug out of the cupboard, his favorite one, the one with Van Gogh's "Starry Night" on it. His Earth Science third period class had given it to him one year, after they'd studied astronomy. Elementary teachers often got presents from their adoring little students, but high school teachers? Once in a blue moon, so to speak. He smiled at his little joke, wondering how he'd managed to think of something amusing at a time like this. Probably it was just relief that a big furry dog had greeted him, instead of a bizarre creature with ten legs and eyes on the end of waving stalks.

Even though he knew it wouldn't work, even though he knew there was no way he was getting back to sleep tonight, he put a Sleepy Time herbal tea bag in the mug, filled it with water, and put it in the microwave.

James took his phone off the charger, tried to sit, but couldn't. He paced as he checked the New York Times. The top headline read: "China, Southeast Asian Alliance sign pact." Subheading: "U.S. responds with warning." Even though he knew it was coming, when the timer buzzed, he jumped. Talk about nerves on edge.

In the living room, James settled himself on the couch, tea on the table next to him. He tried checking Facebook but couldn't seem to process the words. His hand shook as he picked up the mug. He fought down the feeling of panic that was churning in his gut, resisted the urge to jump up off the couch and run around the room screaming. Every nerve in his body was on high alert, ready to run at the slightest indication of an alien attack. Every year, he'd taught his biology classes about the fight or flight response, so useful for the caveman faced with a charging mammoth. Now he understood what he'd been talking about.

He closed his eyes. He concentrated on taking deep, slow, even breaths. Then he prayed. Dear God, please fill me with your strength. I don't know what just happened to me. I need your guidance, Lord. If a being from another planet did just contact me, I know it is your child too. I believe you have probably spread life throughout this great universe you created, a universe which we are only beginning to understand. Heavenly Father, I need your help and guidance. Please fill me with your spirit and show me the way. Amen.

He opened his eyes and took another deep breath. Although he had doubts that he was communicating with a divine being when he prayed, he still did so sometimes. Like now. It made him feel better, and what could it hurt? His daddy always said, "God is listening, whether you believe it or not."

Kirby came in and lay down cozily across his feet. Maybe that would warm him up some.

"Hey, you idiot dog," he said to Kirby, who looked up at him with a devotedly eager expression. "What good are you, anyway? In every sci fi movie I've ever seen, the dog can sense the aliens. The dog always freaks out barking, even though the humans can't see anything. Lot of good you were." But he patted Kirby on his big furry head anyway.

He clicked on the New York Times article, reluctantly. A photo of President Scofield speaking to the press showed an old but determined man. How the hell can there be an evil alien stuck in this guy? But that was the message he'd gotten from this second visitation. That's crazy, he chided himself. There had to be a simpler explanation for this whole thing. Yeah, but that's not something I'd have ever dreamed up myself. And that was no dream. Something weird happened to me, for a second time. Am I going crazy? Is this how it feels to be schizophrenic?

What would Danny say if he told him an evil Seeker was stuck inside Scofield? Maybe he shouldn't say anything to Danny. This was on beyond. The first time had turned out OK, but Danny might have him committed after this.

But was that for sure what the vision meant? They showed him the evil alien getting sucked into the White House, clearly against its will. It had been trying to go through the portal, presumably; it didn't want to get caught by a human; it didn't want to be stuck here on Earth.

But it was, it is. That's the whole point of the visions, it has to be, to warn us that this has happened, that something terrible is going to come of this. So, President Scofield's been taken over by an alien? Right. God, that sounds totally nuts. Maybe it's someone else in the White House, like his chief of staff or something. So why didn't I see that, then? Maybe they couldn't show me more. Maybe there are limits to how much they can make me visualize inside my head. I don't even know what the Chief of Staff looks like. Maybe they couldn't pull that image from my brain, since it's not there, so they couldn't show me where the Evil One is specifically. But how the hell do I know how alien beings are going to communicate with me inside my head? Maybe in my brain, the President is synonymous with the White House, so they pulled that image to tell me it's in Scofield. My God, it has to be the President, doesn't it? He's the most powerful person on Earth, he's the only one who could cause enough world-wide damage to make them want to warn us. That has to be what they were trying to get across.

James's mind was reeling. He picked up the hot tea and took a long, slow sip, trying to calm himself enough to approach this rationally.

I'm a science teacher, James thought. I believe in a rational, knowable world. I know that the probability that aliens are coming to our planet is infinitesimal. I also know that there are likely to be millions of potentially life-producing planets in the universe, so alien species probably do exist. Somewhere. I know that life has appeared in the most unexpected places even on this planet. Frozen in deep ice. In super-heated thermal vents deep in the ocean. So, life on other planets does not have to be like life here. Probably wouldn't be. Although the basic building blocks of life are probably the same everywhere, regardless of the form.

James sipped the tea, letting the warmth soothe him. Get a grip. OK, what happened tonight? It makes no sense. But it has to make sense. I just don't know how yet. I'm an intelligent person. I can figure this out. I'm an intelligent person who has just possibly made the most amazing discovery in the history of science. This was simultaneously the most absolutely thrilling and completely terrifying thought he had ever had.

The pictures he had seen in the vision swirled in his head, of life on Earth in all its immense variety, of that unspeakably beautiful Life Force flowing from everything, from the largest whale to the tiniest spider. One of the reasons James loved science, one of the reasons he became a science teacher, was because the world, and the universe beyond, were so breathtakingly beautiful. Not just physically beautiful, but in the way it was all so incredibly intricate and interconnected.

He had a very vivid memory of a summer evening—he must have been about nine or ten—when his mother had sent him and his sister to the store a couple blocks over. The shortcut took them across the parking lot of the church. He remembered Darlene screaming as she stepped onto the blacktop and leapt back. The entire surface was moving, as though the tar had melted in the summer heat and was slowly boiling. Then, his brain adjusted to what he was seeing under the parking lot lights, and he realized that the entire lot was covered with June bugs, thousands of them, maybe. Darlene had insisted on taking the long way around, but on the way back, he'd stopped to watch the huge black beetles. He must have sat there for twenty minutes, watching them whir and climb all over each other, a black undulating sea of bugs. Eventually he'd ventured out among them, suffused in a feeling that he was in another world, a whole new mysterious world where humans such as himself were not important. The next day he'd gone to the library and checked out twenty books on insects.

So it was for him as a boy, and still as a man. There were always new, amazing things to discover: wonders beyond human understanding, although we could certainly try, and were getting closer all the time. Wonders to be appreciated and savored.

James deliberately let his mind wander from the alien encounter. He smiled, remembering the lecture he'd given to his Earth Science class last week about water. He'd gotten so excited, telling them about the incredibly unique properties of water. At one point he'd grabbed a boy's water bottle off his desk and exclaimed, "This, my friends, is a bona fide miracle! Do you realize that it is because of water's high specific heat that it allows the uniform temperature distribution on Earth, via the oceans which cover most of the world's surface, which therefore allows life to exist? It is unique among liquids. You will come to appreciate the incredible strength of the hydrogen bond. It should boil away into gas at a much lower temperature than it does, but H-2-O does not. It remains a liquid, a life-sustaining liquid. Why? That you will discover in the coming weeks. The fact that water expands rather than contracts when it freezes, as one would expect of a liquid, also helps sustain life on this planet. How? It is because…" Then he had paused and scanned their faces: some baffled, some bored, a few intrigued. He'd continued, "But no, I'll let you discover that for yourselves. Think about it and come back on Friday prepared to discuss the formation of ice and its impact on life here in Minnesota."

It had been a good discussion last Friday. A few of the kids, especially Anthony and Maria, made very insightful contributions. If he could just spark a genuine interest in science in a few students, he'd have done his job. Maria and Anthony had an exciting future ahead of them, should they decide to become scientists. He hoped they would be in his AP biology class next year, so he could share the excitement of the Human Genome Project with them. Unlocking the secrets of life—now that was thrilling.

He patted Kirby's head, resting on his knee. "You're pretty amazing, too. I wonder if there are alien dogs, huh, Kirby?" When they'd gotten the dog three years ago, the kids had won on the choice of the dog's name. He'd wanted to call him Einstein, although that would have been an ironic name for this dog, as it turned out. But Einstein was his hero. If only Albert had been able to complete his work and come up with the Grand Unification Theory, James often thought ruefully. The one ultimate, simple, and therefore incredibly difficult theory unifying all the forces in the universe. James had always thought of the Grand Unification Theory as the escape clause for religion. That which explained all, created all, was all, was God.

James was feeling calmer now, more normal. Calm enough to let the images from his vision come into his mind again, to be examined rationally. The Earth: one complex, interrelated web of life, giving off those gorgeous waves of Life Force. Who could have imagined such stunning beauty? He imagined himself as they might see him, with Life Force surrounding him. His cousin Freddie Mae popped into his head. She claimed she could read people's auras. She'd told him last summer that his aura was mostly golden, with green and rose colors shimmering in it. He'd always dismissed it as nonsense, but maybe Freddie Mae was telling the literal truth.

He pictured the Seekers again, riding on that Life Force. What were they? Where were they from? Were they non-substantial spirits, or did they have physical bodies when they traveled to the Earth Portal?

He let the image of the evil Seeker—the Evil One, as he seemed to now be thinking of it—come into his mind, and as it did, it aroused in him such a sense of dread and revulsion that it stopped his breath for a long moment. As he let himself feel the vision again, rather than think about it, he remembered what he felt like when he woke up, horrified and dead certain that an evil alien was stuck in the President of the United States.

What if it was true? Maybe the current news was evidence that something was manipulating Scofield's mind. The man had never shown such war-mongering tendencies till recently, but now it was almost like he was pushing the U.S. into a fight with China, the way he was rattling swords so dramatically and refusing to negotiate.

His mind felt like it was going to explode. He had to call Danny. He'd go crazy if he didn't talk this out with someone. And for some reason he couldn't quite put his finger on, he knew he couldn't bring himself to tell Emily. Not yet.

One thing was sure. Something had happened to him. Twice. And given that he showed no evidence of being in the throes of a mental breakdown at any other moment of his life except these two late Monday nights, he didn't really think he was going crazy. Although this could drive him over the edge. Yeah, he had to talk to Danny.

A long blue tentacle stretched toward James's face. He desperately pressed his body back against the wall, but there was nowhere to go. The alien's jaws opened wide, thick green mucus dripping from its sharp jagged teeth. The undulating tentacle wrapped itself around his head, and he jumped and screamed…

"Honey. Take it easy. Wake up."

"Huh?"

Emily ran her hand over his shoulders soothingly. "Poor baby, you must have fallen asleep down here. Boy, you just jumped a mile when I touched you." She kissed him lightly on the top of his head. "I'll go make coffee. That should help." Then she turned back to him. "Oh, by the way, next time it gets too cold in here at night, maybe don't turn it all the way up to eighty, huh?"

As she left the living room, James sat up groggily on the couch, trying to clear his head. Why am I sleeping on the couch? Did we have a fight?

Then, with a rush of clarity, the horror of last night came back to him and swamped his mind. And all he could think was, Aliens have taken over the President, and no one on this whole planet knows except me. What the hell am I supposed to do now?

Deb Kolbo Ellsworth

CHAPTER 3

Danny's shiny black pickup truck featured an elaborate customized paint job: running down the length of the driver's side was a metallic green, red and gold dragon breathing fire. The flames swirled into his initials, DF. The personalized license plate read TKARSK. Danny's personal motto was "If you're not living on the edge, you're just taking up space." He'd had it made into bumper stickers when he was in college and handed them out to all his friends. James put one on his car, but he'd done it with an acute sense of irony, since he was driving a beat-up Toyota station wagon at the time. It made a lot more sense on the back of this one-of-a-kind power vehicle.

They were driving north on Highway 169 and traffic was fairly heavy. The scenery was boring, just farm fields of beaten-down corn stalk stubble, interspersed with human ant hills: modern housing developments, indistinguishable one from the next, beige box houses with no trees and no style. And why those people wanted to plant themselves right next to a roaring highway, James couldn't fathom.

The radio was set to The Current, until a high-pitched wail shattered the atmosphere. "I can't stand Granite Waterfall," Danny muttered as he punched the button to 88.5, the jazz station. A voice as smooth as hot buttered rum poured from the speakers.

"Kevin Mahogany," Danny said. "All I have to do to get Jenna in the mood is put Kevin on."

"Yeah, he's cool. Emily would definitely like this. A man can always use new tools in his arsenal, right?"

"You think this is good, you should try this Cuban horn player I just discovered. Hey, I'll make you a list—the best, guaranteed love-making songs." Danny looked over at James and grinned. "What would you need? About seven minutes worth?"

"Very funny. Send me all you got, my friend. In fact, I can share a few of my favorites with you, too."

Danny laughed. "Did I ever tell you about that Italian girl, when I did my semester abroad? She only wanted to screw to one album— the soundtrack to Grease. Every damn time. That turned out to be a deal breaker right there."

"I tell you what, man," James said. "The anthem of the Sixties may have been sex, drugs and rock and roll, but they were a little off. It's sex, wine and jazz that really make life worthwhile."

"You got no argument from me on that."

Gene Harris came on next, and then the sultry Diana Krall.

"Mmmm, she is smokin'," James said.

Danny looked over at James. "Hey, I'm glad you decided to come hunting with me. Even though you don't want to shoot anything, I guarantee you'll still have a great time. It's worth the price of admission just to breathe that clean air."

"You're the only Jew I know who hunts, you know that?"

"Yeah, I'd start a Jewish hunting club, but I'd be the only member. My mother wasn't too thrilled when Gary Knutson's dad took me and him hunting the first time, you may remember. I had to promise to get straight A's on my report card the next semester for her to let me go. Only time I ever got straight A's. Too bad seventh grade didn't count for college admission."

"You really shocked me when you told me you were going hunting that first time. I never ever figured you for it."

Danny laughed. "I shocked myself. Honestly, the main reason I went is 'cause my mother so totally didn't want me to go. The more she tried to pull me close to her, with that 'Oh what if my baby gets shot out there?' and that 'What do you know from hunting, that's for rough boys, not nice Jewish boys like you' shtick, the more I wanted to go. Then I killed something for the first time, and it shocked me even more. Not because I'd done it and it was so horrible, but because I kind of liked it. I liked the power. Honest to God, I liked the thrill of it. That's when I first had that sensation that I immortalized on my bumper sticker back there. I was living on the edge, and it was amazing."

"Uh, Friedman, you're making me a little nervous here."

"Yeah, well now I justify it by telling people it gives me a lot of satisfaction to literally hunt for food for my family like primitive man did. I could go into the whole spiel about how it's important to know the food you're eating, to respect the animal like the Native Americans did, to know that it's been running free and wild instead of caged in a three by eight pen. And that's true. But I gotta tell you, you really feel alive when you're stalking a big animal. Every fiber of your body is awake and paying attention then. It's been a few years since I've gone deer hunting, though. I buy a license every year, and then get too busy. I was glad when you called, gave me the excuse to do it again. I still go duck hunting with Jenna's dad every year, but that's not as fun. That's how I first got him on my side when I was dating Jenna."

"Guess I'll still stick with hunting for my family in the grocery store. Tracking down the elusive mac 'n cheese."

Danny honked at a white truck that cut in front of him. "Looks like everyone wants to get themselves a deer," he commented. "I figured traffic might be heavy."

"That's OK." James grinned. "I like riding in your truck. It's such a macho machine."

Danny kissed two fingers and tapped the dashboard with them. "I've been through a lot with the Dragon."

"Come to think of it, you may be the only Jew I know who drives a pickup truck."

"Son, if you don't know by now that Danny Friedman is a one-of-

31

a-kind guy, you haven't been paying attention. Anyway, I'm not throwing a bloody deer carcass in the trunk of my Beemer."

They rode a few more miles, James relaxing as he listened to the superb jazz filling the truck cab. But finally, reluctantly, he had to bring the subject up—the reason he was here in the first place. "Well, I guess we might as well use this time to do some heavy thinking," James said. "I need your input here."

Danny glanced over at James. "So, it wasn't a one-time deal, huh? The aliens came back?"

"Oh yeah," James said grimly, "they came back."

"Same vision as last time?"

"Uh, no, not exactly. Apparently, they hadn't finished giving me their message the first time. There was more."

Danny glanced at James with concern. "That doesn't sound good."

"Yeah, it's not. They showed me where the Evil One is located. You're not going to believe this, Danny. It's… well, according to what I saw, it's… God, I can't believe I'm about to say this. Uh… it might be in the President."

"What? Of the United States? That can't be right. It has to be stuck in some terrorist warlord in the Middle East or something."

"There could be evil aliens stuck over there, too, for all I know. That's just what they showed me."

"Which brings up that question. Why you? I mean, no offense, but why, out of the billions of people on this planet, did these aliens put their finger—or their tentacle—on you?"

"That's what I keep asking myself," James said with agitation. "I'm just a regular guy. I'm a high school teacher. For God's sake, I teach at the same high school I graduated from. I coach my kid's Little League team. I'm nobody special."

"You did get close to perfect on your SATs, didn't you? Maybe they probed your brain and found out you're a genius."

James shot Danny a dubious look.

"Or maybe it's like the radio," Danny theorized, gesturing at his dashboard. "You just picked up their signal."

"What, like on my molars?"

"Yeah, why not? Maybe they broadcast that vision to a lot of people, hoping to hit someone who could help them." Danny's eyes lit up with the thrill of playing detective. "Maybe that's why it happened on Monday night both times! Maybe they sent a subliminal signal on the Monday Night Football transmission, and it went into the brains of a whole bunch of viewers, and then it got activated when those people went to sleep. Now, I watched the game, but I didn't have any weird dreams. But maybe a certain number of receptive-type people like you did, and maybe one of those people can do something about it. Assuming these aliens are trying to alert us that the President has gone nuts."

"That's so bizarre it just might be right. Maybe I better watch Dream House with Emily next Monday night, just to be safe."

The song on the radio ended, and the news announcer intruded on James's thoughts.

"It's five o'clock. In the news today, the showdown between the U.S. and China continues. With two nuclear-armed nations in a standoff, the world watches and worries. The Dow Jones today was down…"

James switched off the radio. "See, that's the problem, Danny. If an evil alien gets trapped in a farmer in Iowa, who beats his wife and kids and shoots stray dogs, that's bad, but not devastating. But if one of them gets caught in the body of the President of the United States, and its evil being fuses with the most powerful person in the world, then what?"

"Then we're in some deep shit. You sure about this?"

"I've gone back and forth on this a million times! It can't be real—but it was such an incredibly bizarre experience that it can't not be real, you know? It was so weird, and so intense. It felt like they'd clamped onto my brain and were forcing me to watch a movie—the most terrifying horror movie ever made, I might add—and when I woke up, I just knew that the message was that an evil Seeker had gotten trapped in the President."

"God, I hope they're wrong."

The truck sped down the highway, each of them thinking about the terrible shape the world was in. Possibly much worse than the average Joe knew.

"Maybe I am going crazy," James said slowly.

"If you were going crazy, I'd be the first to know. And the first to tell you."

Suddenly James yelled out. "Whoa! Hey!"

"What?"

"Did you see that? Pull over!"

"What?"

"Back there! Back up!"

Danny wrenched the truck across the right lane of traffic and onto the shoulder and hit the brakes. He backed up until James said to stop, pointing toward the highway median.

"There! I was right, it is a turtle. See it? Look, it's starting to crawl onto the highway. There's no way it's not gonna get squished!"

"What? A turtle?" Danny said with disbelief.

"Yeah, I gotta go get it," James said, getting out of the truck.

"James, you can't…"

But James was already slamming the door. Crap, there were a lot of cars speeding down the highway. How was he going to do this? He saw a bit of an opening in the traffic and forced himself to go, running flat out. His heart was pounding when he reached the median strip. He picked up the turtle, thanked his lucky stars it hadn't turned out to be of the snapping variety, and prepared for the return crossing. He could see Danny over there, standing next to the truck. He looked alarmed. And maybe pissed off. OK, there was a lull in the traffic. James scrambled across the interstate, holding the turtle out like a sacred offering.

Danny was definitely pissed. "What the fuck, man? What the fuck?"

"I couldn't just let it get killed, could I? Somebody had to help it. Good thing I spotted it. Just luck. I don't know how it could have gotten itself into the middle of the highway."

Danny shot him an angry look and got in the truck without another word. James got in and put the turtle on his lap as he fastened his seat belt. Then he held the turtle up for Danny to see.

"Look, isn't it pretty? It's a painted turtle. Probably a female, since it's at least seven inches, I'd say. The females are bigger than the males."

"Great," Danny said in an annoyed tone, as he pulled the truck onto the highway.

James held the turtle up to look into its face. "You're probably desperate to get somewhere to hibernate, aren't you? Most of your buddies are already sitting tight on the bottom of some lake. You should be, too. I bet some kid had you as a pet and just let you go."

James put the turtle on the floor of the cab, blocking it with his foot so it wouldn't crawl under Danny's feet. "We should be hitting Mille Lacs in maybe half an hour. We could stop and put this little lady in the lake and catch some dinner. I'm getting pretty hungry. How about you?"

Danny stared straight ahead. "Yeah. I could eat."

They rode in silence for several miles. Danny never went this long without talking. Finally, James gave it another shot.

"Once we get past Mille Lacs, the scenery should be better."

"Yeah."

"Too bad the leaves will all be down. I bet it was really pretty up here a month ago."

"Yeah."

James felt irritated now, too. "What's your problem, Friedman?"

"I don't know. It just seemed like a stupid thing to do, to risk your life for a stupid turtle. And mine, too. In case you didn't notice, I had to make a dangerous move to pull over so fast."

"You're a good driver. And I made it, didn't I? If I hadn't rescued this turtle, it would have stayed on my mind the whole weekend, you know? Look, what are the odds of someone spotting a little turtle when they're whizzing by at 70 miles an hour? Miniscule, right? But I did see it, and that morally obligated me to do something about it."

"God, you sound like Rabbi Bornstein and his moral arguments he used to throw at us in Hebrew school. The trouble with you, my friend, is you have an over-developed conscience. You know what my New York grandmother would call you? A mensch." But Danny smiled at James and gave him a little punch in the arm. "Hey, maybe that's why the aliens picked you. Maybe they know you can't say no when someone needs help."

"Yeah, well, they should've looked for someone a little higher up in the chain of command. Turtles, I can save. The whole freakin' world, not so much."

It was ten p.m. when James and Danny finally walked through the door of the cabin. The place was definitely a no-frills guys' refuge. James doubted Jenna had ever set foot here.

"Gimme your clothes," Danny said to James, reaching for James's bag.

"That's OK, Mom, I can unpack myself."

"No, I need to hang them outside to get some of the human scent off 'em."

"Won't that make them kind of chilly to put on in the morning?"

"Yeah, and that's a good thing. It'll help wake you up when I throw your ass out of bed at four in the morning."

"Four a.m.? You didn't tell me about that when you were extolling the glories of the hunting trip. Give me a break, huh? How about five?"

"Four-thirty. Those deer don't sleep in, you know."

James handed Danny his clothes. When he thought Danny wasn't looking, he took a bottle of pills out of the bag and popped one in his mouth. But Danny happened to turn back at just that moment.

"Got a headache?"

"No, I'm OK."

Danny walked over and picked up the bottle. "Sleeping pills?"

"It's kind of hard to relax when you think aliens might be showing up every time you go to sleep."

"Yeah, I bet."

"It's getting kind of bad. I couldn't even concentrate enough to do my job these last few days. I copped out and showed my biology classes Jurassic Park today. I told 'em it was because we're studying DNA. Of course, they didn't complain." He mimicked a teenager's voice: "Hey, Mr. Thompson, like, can't you give us a test or a lab experiment or something? We're not getting our educational value just watching a video, Mr. Thompson."

Danny laughed. "Well, if the fresh night air up here doesn't put you to sleep, nothing will." He opened the cabin door and stepped outside with the clothes. A moment later, he poked his head back in. "C'mere. Take a look."

James joined Danny outside the cabin. "Wow."

A vast array of piercingly bright stars filled the clear black sky, reminding James of the heavily-glittered pictures Danielle used to bring home from preschool.

"This is incredible!" James said, awed. "This totally beats the city night sky. I wish my class could see this when we study astronomy. They'd never tell me it was boring again."

Danny hung the clothes on the line, as James continued to gaze into the star-saturated night.

"I wonder where the Seekers are coming from," James said quietly.

Danny joined him, and they stood silently together for a while, the immensity and glory of the universe filling them.

"My God, Danny," James said softly. "I'm just one little guy among billions of people, on one little planet among billions of stars. I'm a speck. I'm no one."

Four-thirty a.m. came faster than James had expected, maybe because it had taken him a while to fall asleep, despite the fresh air and the pharmaceutical aid. He and Danny put on hunter's orange vests over their heavy clothing. Danny poured steaming coffee first into two mugs, and the rest into a thermos, and started packing some food in bags.

"We'll head out to the deer stand first, see if we get lucky. If nothing comes our way by sunrise, we'll catch a little breakfast in the truck, and then start walking. You'll like that part. Meadows, gorgeous woods. You'll never want to go back to the city again after a weekend out here."

They sat down at the scratched and banged up wooden table and sipped the hot coffee, feeling the energy flow into their bodies.

"You know," Danny said, "I was kinda hoping for some little green men to show up last night. So, have you told Emily about the 'woooooo' in the night?" he asked, wiggling his fingers and making ghostly sounds.

"No. I probably should, but I keep hoping it won't happen again. I mean, if I told her aliens were appearing in our bedroom, she'd either think I'd gone nuts, take the kids, and run. Or she'd believe me, take the kids, and run. I'll tell her when we're sixty-two and we've run out of things to talk about."

"Here's what I don't get," Danny said. "If these evil Seekers are supposed to be attracted to comparably evil human beings, then why Scofield? I mean, I don't like the guy's politics, didn't vote for him, but not because I thought he was Satan. But I suppose you never really know with a politician. Maybe he's just faking it. Maybe he's really stone cold ruthless evil incarnate."

"Maybe. I dunno. I think of him more as dumb than evil. Although he did make a really bad choice for running mate. God help us if Cambridge ever becomes President."

"Yeah. Who'd've thought Jack's brother would be vice-freakin' President of the United States?"

"No kidding. How the hell he ever got elected governor, let alone senator, I don't know. Well, yeah, I do. Lies. And money. Lots of money."

Danny took a long gulp of coffee. "Ahh, that hits the spot. Jack's whole family was messed up. Jack could be a real jerk himself. God, he could shoot three-pointers, though."

"I'll never forget that time I picked Jack up for practice," James said. "D'ante was with me. His dad made us wait outside, even though it was like twenty below. He didn't even try to hide his racism."

"Screw racists, dude," Danny said, setting down his empty coffee cup. "Let's go kill us a deer."

———————————

Danny was right. They were traipsing through a meadow of dead grass that glowed in the golden light of the rising sun, heading toward some woods. Sitting in the deer stand hadn't panned out, but the tranquility of those pre-dawn hours had seeped into his body, and James felt wonderfully relaxed.

A few oaks had some stubborn, crinkled brown leaves still hanging on, refusing to acknowledge that their purpose had been served and their time was up. The remaining canary-yellow leaves clinging to the aspen trees looked like they'd been cut from a child's vinyl rain slicker; whenever the wind kicked up, they danced madly, fluttering like butterfly wings. The air was cold, but clean, and James inhaled it with satisfaction. He could almost see the oxygen pouring out of the needles of the surrounding pine trees.

"Man, I wish the air in the city smelled like this."

Danny stopped and stuck his finger in his mouth, then held it up to test the wind. "Told ya."

"I never would've figured you for a nature lover, though, Friedman. You're more Mr. Urban Hipster guy."

"Oh, but I am a multi-faceted person, my friend. You have only begun to experience the depth and complexity that is Daniel Friedman. I'll bet you didn't know I am also an Irish dancing aficionado."

"Liar."

"Maybe. Or maybe I have an artistic side you've just never seen."

"Sure, twinkle-toes."

As they entered the woods, James heard the warning chittering of squirrels, and their quick scuffling through the dry brown leaves that covered the ground. He saw a rabbit, statue-still until they got too close, dart toward some underbrush to the side.

"This is weird," James said softly, "but I just remembered a cartoon I saw on TV when I was a kid. I don't know how it even got on a kids' show, it was so subversive. OK, picture this. It starts with realistically drawn scenes of war, grenades exploding, buildings blowing up, people getting killed. It didn't look like a regular kids' cartoon, because of the way it was drawn, realistically, maybe more like how a graphic novel is drawn. Finally, there are only two humans left on Earth, two soldiers. They both stand up from behind bushes and shoot each other dead. The cartoon goes totally silent. Then, happy music starts, and all these cute animals—rabbits, deer, foxes, like that—come slowly creeping out of hiding. They realize it's finally safe and start dancing. The rest of the cartoon showed animals living free, happy lives. I must've seen thousands of cartoons, but that one really made an impression on me."

"Maybe that's why the Seekers came to you and not me. The only cartoons I remember featured SpongeBob SquarePants."

After they'd hiked across a couple more fields, Danny said, "How do you know you can trust what they're showing you? Maybe they're really the evil ones, showing you this to try to trick you."

"Yeah, but then it still comes back to the question, why me? Why would it help evil aliens achieve their goals to trick a high school science teacher in Minnesota?"

"Why would it help the good ones to reveal all this to a high school science teacher in Minnesota?"

"I don't know!" The words exploded from James in his frustration. Then he added softly, "It doesn't make sense. None of this makes sense." He gestured at the gun Danny was carrying. "If they think I'm gonna grab one of those and go shoot the President, they're sadly mistaken."

There didn't seem to be much more they could say. They were getting nowhere. They didn't even know where they should be trying to get. Might as well just let it go and enjoy this beautiful day in the north woods.

Another mile across another meadow covered with twisting brown grass and empty milkweed pods; Danny suggested they stop and take a break. They sat down on a fallen tree trunk. Danny handed James a granola bar and chewed reflectively on his own.

"I wonder what it feels like to have an evil alien stuck in your brain," James mused. "Do you think Scofield feels it in there, or is the Evil One so completely fused with him that he can't tell any difference?"

"Even if he can't feel it, I bet his family notices a difference," Danny replied. He spoke in a high-pitched voice, imitating Scofield's wife. "Um, honey, I just asked you to pass the peas. You didn't have to throw the bowl at my head."

"Hey, Danny? I feel like an idiot, saying 'The Evil One' all the time."

Danny snorted with muffled laughter. "I know what you mean. Listen, let's make up a code name, so we can talk about it in public without getting weird looks."

"Sure, why not? Let's go by the initials, E.O. Or maybe we should name it, like Elijah, or Eddie."

"Eddie Olson! That's it."

"There's probably a whole page of Ed Olsons in the Minneapolis phone book."

"That's the beauty of it! The name Olson is like background noise in this state."

"I like it."

"So, if Eddie Olson is really stuck in Scofield, what do you think his ultimate inten—" Danny stopped in mid-sentence and put his finger to his lips. He pointed to a magnificent buck that had just stepped out from the woods at the far end of the meadow. Danny carefully positioned himself, and slowly lifted his gun, aiming. The buck lifted his head in alarm, on the brink of flight. The booming shot that broke the silence shocked James's senses.

"Yes!" Danny exulted. "I think I got him with a clean shot. You must've brought me luck, James! I haven't seen a buck like that in years! Maybe even a ten-pointer! OK, let's go get this guy. This may be the part of hunting you don't like so much."

"Danny, I'm a biology teacher. I've dissected more animals than you've ever shot."

When they got to the deer, it was down but still alive, struggling to stand up. As Danny finished him off, James looked away.

"Now we gotta get this guy back to the cabin," Danny said, as he pulled a knife and a length of rope from the backpack. "We gotta field dress it first. We're gonna make some wolves really happy today."

As James stood there gazing down on the carcass, the image that came to his mind was of the Life Force flowing from this beautiful animal and then suddenly gone, like a flashlight beam snapped off. He pictured the Earth as the Seekers had shown him, surrounded by the Life Force emanating from the planet, and thought of Hiroshima. He wondered if there was a huge gap, a void in the Life Force, when the bomb went off. Was that what they were headed for, a dead world hanging in space like a charred cinder, cold and lifeless, with no Life Force radiating from it anymore?

I've got to find a way to tell them they've got the wrong guy, James thought grimly.

CHAPTER 4

And then there was nothing—no more visions for seven weeks.

Unfortunately, the crisis with China continued to escalate, with U.S. destroyers now stationed in the South China Sea. President Scofield had all but threatened at his recent press conference to launch a nuke from a submarine if China didn't pull its troops out of Cambodia by the new year.

It was a Monday. A sense of apprehension always filled James on Mondays now. He'd avoided watching Monday Night Football, feeling ridiculous, but unable to make himself take the risk, however small.

Of course, he couldn't help thinking about the vision, but what could he do about it? He had to believe that Danny was right, that they'd sent that message out to more people than just him, that they'd given up on him, found a better person to do the job.

James sat at the dining room table and opened up his laptop. It was winter break, and he was no better than his students, he had to admit. They put off doing their homework until the last minute; he put off grading their homework as long as he could. He pulled up the reports on genetics. But giving his full attention to Robert Tolmund's mess of an explanation about recessive and dominant genes was more than he could bear. He clicked to Jennifer Alvarez's report.

That was sure to be pure poetry in comparison.

He managed to wade through ten more reports before Sara Silver's attempt to explain why she had blue eyes when both her parents had brown eyes brought him to his figurative knees. Apparently, she found spell check a waste of time, preferring instead to put all her effort into elaborating on her "blue eyes which everyone tells me are my best feeture."

He glanced over at the Christmas tree in the living room. How many Christmas cards had they received with the message "Peace on Earth" scrolled across them in elegant gold writing? Was that now impossible?

James had gone back and forth in his mind a million times: It had to have been a bad dream. A really, really vivid bad dream. That coincidentally occurred on the only two nights when the temperature in the bedroom plummeted. Right. Ultimately, try as he might to talk himself into believing that it was just a nightmare, he always failed. Because every single detail of the visions was seared into his consciousness.

His fingers hovered over the keys on his laptop, hesitating. Now that he was a little less freaked out about being contacted by aliens, with some distance from the events, curiosity was overcoming fear. It was time for some research. He typed in the Search box: "Alien Contact." His finger paused over the enter key. Did he really want to link himself with the nut jobs he knew he'd find there? No, but he had to check it out. What if other people were reporting experiences similar to his own?

Click. Over 60 million results. James scrolled down the first few. True Stories of Alien Contact. Fine, that looked like as good a place to start as any.

Twenty minutes later, James had learned that George in Wisconsin had been given an alien alphabet, which looked a lot like squiggly Chinese characters. Lydia in Arizona had been levitated out of her car on August 24, 1997 and experienced a time gap of two hours. There were signs that she had been probed. A remarkable number of people had awoken in their bedrooms to find large-headed, big-eyed aliens with thin arms starring at them, or releasing glowing yellow balls into their minds. Some of the aliens were silvery-pale, and some were glowing blue. But all the stories were completely true.

James found it disconcerting to discover that most of the people who reported a PCE—James now knew that he had had a PCE, or Personal Contact Experience, but not an OOBE, or Out of Body Experience, also quite common—most of them had had their aliens show up in the night and wake them from dreams. No doubt, these people were flakes. Flakes who had bad dreams and believed they were real and felt compelled to share them with other nuts in this vast underworld of PCE alternate reality. He also discovered that at least half of the people who'd had a PCE couldn't write a coherent sentence, much like Sara Silver. He had a feeling Sara would feel right at home on this website.

Thank God he hadn't told Emily what had happened. He'd have sounded as stupid as these people did. She would've had him committed.

He read a few more. Jake in Montana had been given a star chart by the aliens. Ah, so had Bill in Alabama. And they'd never met each other, but somehow their star charts looked similar. Well, there's proof, James thought sarcastically.

OK, how about this site: The Comprehensive Encyclopedia of Alien Life Forms. If this guy Alex really had compiled all the descriptions of aliens that people had reported throughout the world and throughout time, as he claimed, maybe there'd be something like the Seekers there. Alex was apparently a big authority on aliens, because several sites had links to this one.

James found the search box where you could put in a description of your alien, and hesitated. He was afraid he wouldn't find a match, and even more afraid that he would. He typed: "Seekers. Earth Portal. Appear when sleeping. Ride on Life Force coming from Earth. Flowing white bodies." Not much to go on, really. His finger hovered over the enter key. Then he clicked.

Five hundred thirty-seven matches. Whoa. Ten minutes into it, he realized that most of those came from the "Appear when sleeping" part, so he deleted that, and tried again. Down to one hundred sixty-two. And most of those matched "Seeker," but these aliens were seeking women to impregnate with alien sperm, apparently. OK, delete "Seeker." Twenty-eight. He read all of them. None sounded like his experience. He couldn't decide if he was relieved or not. Now the question was, should he enter his experience into Alex's database?

No. He'd had enough. James clicked on a site that sounded more scientific. Ah, yes, it was discussing SETI, the Search for Extra-Terrestrial Intelligence. An actual scientific attempt to scan space looking for signals. After all these years, SETI had come up with exactly nothing. Somehow, all those blue glowing aliens in their whirling UFOs had managed to avoid detection.

James felt himself going back to the "very powerful dream" theory. For some reason the temperature in the room had dropped significantly both times, but there were a lot more likely explanations for that than alien contact. He was sorry now he'd told Danny and hoped he wouldn't bring it up again.

James felt a hand on his arm.

"Isn't it the most beautiful tree you've ever seen?" Danielle said with admiration.

He looked over at the Christmas tree again with new eyes. That was the difference between being a child and being a grown-up, wasn't it? It was four days after Christmas. The dry tree had shed so many needles that you couldn't walk in your socks near it without poking your toe on the sharp little buggers; a layer of green coated the few opened boxes still lying under it. Ornaments had fallen off and been put back on so many times that now there was a clump of them right in the middle, and big bare spots higher up. And to Danielle, it was still magical.

Trey looked up when he heard Danielle. He'd been sitting on the couch looking at some baseball cards he'd gotten in his stocking, eagerly looking them up online to find out if he'd gotten lucky and hit a hundred-dollar card.

"Let's play Risk, huh, Dad?" he suggested.

"Risk again, tiger? Haven't we had enough of that? Why don't you go play your new video game?"

Did he really just say that? Trey looked crestfallen.

"Sorry, sport, it's just that I've got to correct my students' homework before school starts next week. Don't you guys have any homework you need to do?"

"Thanks, Dad, way to make winter break fun," Danielle said. Apparently, they were studying sarcasm in sixth grade, because she certainly was practicing it a lot lately.

James sighed. What was wrong with him? Here he had two great kids who actually wanted him to play with them, and he was shutting them out. He worked with teenagers every day. He heard what they said about their parents. Soon enough, Danielle would be complaining to her friends about him. Soon enough, she'd be shutting herself in her room and only wanting to be with, talk with, exist with her friends. Work could wait. So what if they'd played Risk three times in four days already?

Emily had objected to the game as being too violent, but James had a sentimental attachment to it. How many games of Risk had he played as a child with his sister Darlene, the prize being the winner's dishes done for a week?

"So, you think you can beat me this time?" James said. "Well, I've got a new, unstoppable plan, my friends! Set up that game board."

"All right!" Trey's eyes lit up as he ran to get the game from under the tree.

As the game moved along, James hoped that Danielle wouldn't notice that he was cutting Trey a little slack. James's yellow armies were already in control of North and South America, while Danielle's pink ones held firmly to Africa and Australia. Trey was trying to keep the continent of Asia, since it was worth the most armies, but that was a difficult task, only for seasoned pros like himself and Darlene, really. Trey's green armies were dwindling.

James passed the attacking dice to Trey. "That's it for me. I'll take my card and sit tight."

Danielle objected. "Dad, you could've attacked Trey. You're just being nice to him. Why don't you just wipe out China? President Scofield would."

As James was trying to think of an appropriate response, his phone rang. Saved by the proverbial bell. Or in this case, the ringtone rendition of "Little Red Corvette." He picked it up and looked at the screen. "Yo, dude."

"Hey," Danny responded. "So, Jenna wanted me to formally invite you guys over for New Year's Eve."

"I'll check with Emily, but I'm up for it. Unless we get a better offer, of course."

"Of course. We'll dump you if something better comes along, too."

"As I remember it, Jenna's due to give birth any day now. I don't think you're going anywhere."

"Ah, you got me there. In fact, I'd like you to do me a favor and get her up and dancing, so I can get that little tax deduction out before midnight, huh?"

"So, what're you doing now, you poor pathetic slave to the capitalist system? Personally, I'm enjoying my two-week Christmas vacation with my fourth game of Risk. These guys are ruthless."

"I'd like to tell you I'm working hard on the latest insanity my boss dumped on my desk, but I'd be lying, and I don't want to sully our friendship that way. I'm actually on level seven on that new Mars Invasion video game. I'm totally kicking alien butt here, man!"

"Well, congratulations, I guess."

"Hey," Danny said. "Speaking of aliens, any contact from the Seekers yet?"

James glanced at the kids and walked away with the phone. "No," he said in a hushed voice. "Nothing. Look, I think we should just drop it, Danny. I probably just had a really weird dream."

"Or two. When you told me about it, you believed it. You didn't think it was just a dream then."

"Anyway, it's irrelevant now. Even if, by some really long shot, it was a real experience, they appear to be done with me."

"Or just running on their own time. Maybe you're like on alien hold."

"Yeah, I guess. Anyway, all I can do is keep living my normal life.

In the meantime, Scofield is moving us closer to war every day. Even little kids know it," James said, glancing at Danielle.

"Yeah, that's the other reason I called. I got this idea for stopping Eddie Olson with a computer virus that would screw up the Pentagon computers."

"Okaaay, great," James said hesitantly. "Even if the Seekers are just a figment of my overactive imagination, this war madness needs to be stopped. But, Danny, that's way beyond what we could do."

Danny sighed. "Yeah, I suppose." Then Danny's voice lit up with excitement. "Hey, I know who could do it, though. Some teenage hacker. You know it's always the kid who sells you popcorn at the movie theater, the gawky overweight one with the pimply face, who turns out to be the one who brings half of the country's businesses to a halt with a new virus. You know a lot of smart teenagers. I bet you could find one who could infect the military's computers."

"Are you insane? Do you really think I'm going to recruit a student to commit a federal crime? Prison doesn't hold a lot of appeal for me, pal."

"Yeah, OK. Point taken."

Trey yelled from the dining room table, "Hey, Dad, get off the phone! I'm attacking you!"

"I gotta go, dude," James said. "I've got to defend North America."

CHAPTER 5

James, holding a couple of champagne bottles, and Emily, holding a tray of her famous curry crab puffs in one hand, and a bowl of warm artichoke dip in the other, stood with their son on the Friedmans' doorstep and shivered in the fifteen below zero wind chill.

"Ring the bell, will you, pal?" James said to Trey.

The door was immediately pulled open by Stewart, Danny's three-year-old son, who was obviously very eager to get this party started. He was wearing a sparkly purple foil hat that said "Happy New Year" in gold glitter, and he jumped up and down like a clown on a pogo stick.

James stepped inside, put the bottles on the foyer table and hoisted Stewart in the air. "Happy New Year, Stewart old buddy!" he said, whirling him around to his squealing delight.

Danny and Jenna appeared in the entryway. Wow, he hadn't seen Jenna for a while. On her tiny frame, the huge bulge that was her belly protruded alarmingly.

"Jenna, you look fabulous," Emily said, hugging her.

"You're sweet. I look like a hippopotamus, but thank you for saying that." Jenna brushed back her blond hair, with its perfect hundred-dollar haircut.

Danny took the champagne James held out. "Thanks. So, where's Danielle?"

James slipped off his down jacket. "She got invited to a friend's for a New Year's Eve sleepover. I tell you, hold them close and enjoy this limited time you have with them. Before you know it, they're moving out of the house and getting their own apartment."

Stewart was still jumping up and down, coming perilously close to bumping James in an area he much preferred to be a hit-free zone. He pretended to tickle Stewart, who ran halfway down the hall, turned back, and stuck his fingers in ears, wiggling them.

"Na na na, boo boo, can't catch me!"

James made a feint toward Stewart, who scurried away, giggling. Trey chased after him.

"I have to apologize for the shape the house is in," Jenna said. "We were almost done cleaning up, but not quite..."

"Honey," Danny said, before they could say anything. "James and Emily don't care if there's a few Legos laying around. Anyway, if they're gonna show up early, they get what they get, right?"

"Geez, Dan, that was polite," Jenna said.

Danny shrugged. "I don't have to be polite. They're our best friends."

Emily apologized as she handed Jenna a peace offering, the snacks. "I'm sorry we came a little early. I know you said seven, but we just couldn't wait any longer. There's so much to celebrate tonight, you know?"

"I didn't know you were so excited about our impending bambino," Danny said, patting Jenna's belly.

"Well, sure, we're happy for you," James said, "but actually Emily was referring to something a little bigger. Like world peace, you know?"

Danny and Jenna looked at him blankly. "Huh?"

"Didn't you see the news today?" Emily asked.

"No," replied Jenna. "We haven't turned on the TV all day, except for the Disney Channel. I haven't even checked my phone. We've been busy cleaning, you know, and… what news?"

The Friedman's family room reflected the mid-six-figure income the two of them pulled down, as did the huge three-car-garage house they'd bought recently in this elite western suburb. The enormous TV they were watching and the sound system that surrounded them were state of the art. The couches were expensive Italian leather, and the art on the walls and the small sculptures on the tables were original. And good, if a little too abstract for James's taste. Everything was arranged beautifully, the way Jenna liked it.

But there were touches of Danny in the room that always made James smile. On one wall hung a caricature of Danny and Jenna that had been done at the State Fair, when they were first dating. Jenna had tried to put it away in a closet, but Danny had resurrected it. Danny had dated around quite a bit before he met Jenna, five years younger than him. He'd fallen hard.

On the wall behind the bar was Danny's bumper sticker collection, at least a hundred of them tacked on the cork-covered wall. Danny loved bumper stickers: funny ones especially, but also bizarre ones, political ones, anything that struck him as interesting. But the bumper on the Dragon sported only his custom sticker. The rest were relegated to this wall.

James figured Jenna hated the bumper sticker display. But she loved Danny. This year, on the third day of Hanukkah she'd given him a bumper sticker that read, "If it's not on video, it didn't happen." Danny had been going a bit overboard shooting video since Stewart was born. So on the sixth day, Danny gave Jenna one that said, "I'm your mother. I don't want attitude, I want gratitude." He told her it was for future reference, when the kids were teenagers.

James's attention was brought back to the TV screen. Danny and Jenna were staring raptly at the two news anchors sitting behind the news desk.

Sarina George was saying, "This is indeed a historic day, Marshall. I know I've said that more than once in the past few hours, but it bears repeating."

Marshall Cantor, her co-anchor, agreed. "Indeed it does, Sarina. And coming on this particular day, as we go into a new year now with renewed hope for the future, is just very fitting. British Prime Minister John Shepherd's last-minute brokering of the peace accord was brilliant."

"I think Time magazine ought to recall all the copies of its Person of the Year issue and put John Shepherd's face on the cover. What an amazing feat he has engineered, putting together this historic peace accord." Sarina turned from Marshall and looked into the camera. "Let's look at the details of the agreement again. For that, we go to our international correspondent in London, Jessica Van Horn. Jessica, can you sum up this peace accord for our viewers?"

Jessica, standing in Trafalgar Square, said, "What it comes down to, Sarina, is really a stand-down situation. China has agreed to remove its troops from Cambodia, and the U.S. is removing half its troops from Japan in a phased pullout. They have both agreed to let the U.N. step in to provide peacekeeping troops to protect their business interests in Southeast Asia from the terrorist attacks, which have been increasing lately. Some members of Congress have expressed concern that this could leave the U.S. vulnerable to attacks from the AFAF, or Asia For Asians Front, potentially forcing Western nations out of this area of the world."

Danny leaped off the couch, cheering. "Woo hoo! Let's celebrate! This is fantastic!"

As the newscasters returned to the question of how this would affect the election next November, Danny popped the cork on the champagne. Jenna pushed herself up from the couch and got four delicate champagne glasses with twirling green stems from the bar, passing them out with a big smile.

James raised his full glass, and the others followed. "To a peaceful new year!"

"Hear, hear!"

Jenna raised her glass. "I wasn't going to drink tonight, but considering the momentousness of the occasion, I think baby here can tolerate a few sips. To John Shepherd!"

"To John Shepherd!"

Emily offered her toast. "To a better future for our children!"

"To a better future!" they all agreed.

Danny lifted his glass. "To naked women!"

The other three paused with their glasses partly raised and said as one, "Huh?"

"Well," Danny explained. "You took all the good ones already. And if we're talking about a better future, I want it to include naked women, OK?"

"To naked women!" agreed James.

"To naked men!" added Emily.

"To making love, not war!" suggested Jenna.

They all drank to that sentiment.

Suddenly the room filled with commotion as the two boys came running in. Stewart ran up to Jenna. "Hi, Mommy."

"Hi, sweetie."

He laid his head against Jenna's big belly. "Hi, baby," he said in a high-pitched voice.

"Aaaawwww," Emily said. "That's just too cute!"

"Isn't he the sweetest big brother ever?" Jenna had obviously been pushing the concept with Stewart in preparation for the real thing.

Stewart got down to business. "We want popcorn!" he yelled, jumping up and down.

"And candy!" added Trey.

"And that kids' sha-mane!" said Stewart, eliciting laughter for no reason he could see.

"And movies!" Trey ordered. "Daddy, you said this would be a fun party."

Danny laughed. "OK, kids, you guys go downstairs. We'll get your treats. What movie do you want to start with, men? How about Pizza Delivery from Planet XYZ? That's a great movie!"

"Yay!" they yelled and ran out of the room.

"C'mon, James, help me out," Danny said. "Emily, put on some happy music, OK? And you," he said, pointing a finger at Jenna, "sit down and take it easy."

Danny's kitchen was as modern as his family room. Sleek brushed stainless-steel appliances with complex electronic control panels lined the walls. As James and Danny gathered bags of chips, popcorn, gummy worms and other party food for the younger set, Danny stopped and gave James a look of dawning realization.

"Do you know what this means, man? You're off the hook! Those Seekers, whatever they were, found a better way to stop the President. Surprise, surprise. The head of a major European country is able to stop worldwide genocide better than a shlub of a guy in Minnesota."

"Thanks a lot," James said with a touch of sarcasm. "But you're right. It is a big relief. Whether what happened to me was real or just an incredibly vivid dream is irrelevant. All I've got to worry about now is figuring out how to keep my beater car running another year."

"C'mon," Danny said. "Let's get this down to the kiddies, and then let's party like it's 1999!"

The clock said 12:55. James couldn't believe it. He used to be able to party on much longer than this. He must be getting old. He looked around the family room, assessing the damage. OK, five empty wine bottles sat on the coffee table, and Jenna had switched to fizzy water after her first glass of champagne. Danny and Emily looked as wiped out as he felt.

"Well," Emily said quietly. "Trey almost made it to midnight. He really wanted to. Maybe next year."

"Thank God there's going to be a next year, now," James said.

"No shit, man," agreed Danny.

Jenna shook her head in wonder. "I can't believe they could watch three straight videos. Of course, Stewart crashed out during the second one." She paused thoughtfully. "I wonder which movies they'll look back on when they're our age and remember as the special ones. Hopefully not Pirate Pete and Toodley Toadbrains."

"Oh, it'll be worse," James said. "Trey has watched Mutant Wars: Attack of the Vampire Machines, like, ninety-two times."

Emily was thinking. "E.T. was the one that just blew me away. For years, I kind of kept my eyes open when I went through the woods near our house, hoping to run into a cute alien that would save the world and be my best friend. It was a beautiful fantasy."

Danny glanced at James; James returned a "let it go" look.

"How about Star Wars?" Danny said. "I watched those videos constantly. I wanted to be Han Solo so bad."

"Well," said Jenna, smiling and rubbing her protruding belly. "I look a lot like Jabba the Hut these days."

James glanced at Emily and saw that her eyelids were fluttering in a losing struggle to stay conscious. "Captain Solo," he said, giving Danny a mock salute, "permission to return to Star Base. We better get going, Emmy. Guess I'll have to carry Trey out to the car. That's not gonna be easy. That kid weighs fifty pounds now."

James pushed himself up off the couch, lost his balance and staggered. "Whoa," he exclaimed, catching himself.

"You're not going anywhere, guys," Jenna said firmly. "And you're for sure not taking a kid in your car at this point. As the designated sober party person here, I would like to invite you to please stay over till morning."

Emily objected. "Jenna, one of the rules my mother always taught me was, good guests go home."

"And one of the rules TV taught me was, 'Friends don't let friends drive drunk.' My rule trumps your rule."

———————

Somehow, James and Emily had managed to make their way safely downstairs to check on Trey, snuggled up so sweetly in his sleeping bag. More amazingly, they'd not only gotten all the way upstairs to the spare bedroom, they'd also rung in the New Year in the same intimate way they always had. Maybe it wasn't his longest performance, James thought just before crashing out, but it had been passionate and satisfying.

At 3:29 a.m., Emily rolled over. James was lying on his back, sleeping deeply, snoring softly. He stirred slightly, his brain disturbed, like something had clamped onto it and was holding it. He remained unconscious, but his brain was brought to an alert state; it was as though his eyes were seeing a 3-D movie.

Just as before, the shimmery planet Earth floated serenely in space, emanating Life Force. Just as before, Seekers sailed in on the Life Force, disappearing into the Earth Portal. Then, just as before, the mood turned from serene to agitated. James watched the evil Seeker get sucked into the White House, and his mind screamed in anguish and despair. He wanted to wake up, but he was being held down.

He couldn't stand this! Suddenly, he yelled out, Stop! Who are you? What do you want?

But this time Emily did not wake up and put her arms around him to comfort him. She was still asleep, and so was he.

Leave me alone! he screamed inside his head. He wanted those pictures to stop, he couldn't take it anymore. Now he was seeing the White House again, but this time jagged rays of malevolent energy shot out from the Evil One in the White House, killing every living thing that it touched. Stop! Stop! What do you want from me?

And then the terrifying vision that was playing in his brain froze, and he felt a quiver of confusion fill his mind.

Had they heard him?

Inside his head, James screamed at the alien. Why are you coming back to me now? The Evil One has been stopped. What the hell do you want with me?

The feeling of confusion remained. James felt an intense urgency to make these aliens understand that the problem had been taken care of, and even if it hadn't, that he was not someone who could stop the most powerful person on Earth.

How? How? Of course, they couldn't understand English. Goddamn, what could he do to get through to them? And then it hit him. Pictures! If they could make him see pictures in his brain, maybe—maybe—they could see pictures that he was imagining in his mind.

James tried to imagine himself standing outside at night. He pictured himself looking up at the stars and tried to imagine Seekers flowing toward him just as they'd looked in his visions. He pictured himself flailing his arms in a go-away gesture, with a negative look on his face. As he was picturing himself doing this, he thought Go away from me. Find someone better to help you.

A series of flashing colors filled his brain. He saw a blanket floating in front of him, like an incredibly intricate quilt suffused with the glow of the Life Force. Suddenly an ugly, oily splotch erupted on the quilt. It was distorting the Life Force near it just as the Evil One did. The splotch grew, oozing and covering more and more of the quilt, spitting out its dark greenish-black oily mess like a boiling mud hole. Then he saw one golden thread suddenly glowing on the quilt. It moved, weaving its way here and there across the quilt, approaching the oily splotch. Then the golden thread suddenly lifted from the quilt and rapidly wove itself into the form of himself, of James. In an instant, the golden thread unwove itself, and then plummeted onto the quilt on top of the oily splotch, completely engulfing it.

At the same time, this thought burst into James's mind with a feeling of clarity: I am the One who will stop the Evil One.

James's mind exploded in anger. After all the damage their Evil Ones had done over the centuries, all the millions of human beings they had killed, now they were worried about it and wanted him to stop it? What made it so different now, and why hadn't they cared before? Rage swamped his brain like a powerful tsunami, obliterating everything beneath it. Then, it was as if the wave retreated back into the sea, replaced by despair and confusion.

He had upset them, apparently.

And so, James deliberately pictured the worst scene of human devastation that he could think of, imagining Nazis forcing Jews into crematoriums and gassing them by the thousands, and then dumping their bodies, young and old, into mass graves. He pictured an Evil One, as the Seekers had shown him, superimposed on an image of Hitler, and then pictured this Hitler directing his air force to rain bombs on London. He imagined exploding buildings falling on terrified people. He forced himself to picture the faces of anguished, bereaved parents and children. Then he pictured the other Seekers, just as he had seen in their visions, flowing into the Earth Portal, ignoring the devastation while their Evil One created hell on Earth.

Would they understand that he was furious that they had never tried to stop their Evil Ones before? Would they be able to explain to him how they could have been so indifferent to the massive human suffering their own species had caused?

For at least a minute, seemingly random colors flashed before him. If they were trying to communicate with him, it wasn't working. Then, his mind was filled with an overwhelming sense of grief. Somehow, he had the impression that they were trying to tell him they were sorry that they hadn't stopped their Evil Ones before. If they were trying to tell him why, he wasn't catching it. But he was getting their sorrow.

Then they showed him the most terrifying pictures yet. The Evil One again was superimposed on the White House, and from it the malevolence radiated in visible rays until it flowed over the whole Earth. As Seekers were streaming toward the Earth and riding the Life Force through the Earth Portal, suddenly the Earth exploded in a fireball. The planet, and the Portal, and the Seekers, and all the Life Force, were gone. Only the stars in space remained.

James understood. They had to stop this Evil One this time, or the Portal would be destroyed.

James felt overwhelmed with despair. Please, please, don't put this on me! I can't help you! I can't prevent this tragedy. You can't put the fate on the world on me.

James felt the alien suddenly pulling away from him. Much as he wanted them out of his head, James wanted to find out as much as he could before the contact was broken. Now that he could communicate with them, he had to try to find out where they were from.

James pictured the planets and the stars. He pictured Earth, and the Seekers flowing toward it. Then he imagined the scene reversing, the aliens being pulled backward toward another planet. Where are you from? Where are you from?

If they understood, they weren't answering.

He tried another question. He pictured himself confronting the Evil One, standing in front of it, but not moving. How do I stop it? How? How? Frustration swamped him; he couldn't think of a clearer way to show it, and he was getting no response. C'mon, answer me, you idiots. Are you stonewalling me, or do you just not get it? Then the pain hit, stabbing through his head like a white-hot knife. He moaned. Was that their answer? Were they threatening him? Or was the contact actually damaging his brain?

The alien was slipping away. He didn't know why, but he felt a need to make a personal connection with it before it left. He fought through the pain and tried to form one more picture in his head: himself, with a large Seeker standing next to him. He tapped his own body and thought, James. He did this several times, and then pictured himself reaching over and tapping the alien. Who are you? Who are you? What's your name?

James felt a vibration of confusion in his mind.

But it seemed to have guessed what he was asking correctly, because James saw, superimposed on the alien's white flowing body, an incredible series of rapid flashes of colored light—a hundred shades of blue swirling around a rose and yellow center, all the colors merging and flowing, and then the sunset-colored center erupting, with silver bursts flashing in scattered patterns, and black lines zig-zagging all over. It was almost like visual music. Then he noticed with surprise that a strong odor was filling his nose. It smelled like an apple pie baking, intercut with something like the acrid smell after a gun is fired. James had the strong impression that this Seeker was telling him its name, in its own language.

The Seeker's presence was growing faint. James sensed somehow that the Portal was pulling it. He must have been picking up on the irresistible pull of the Portal that the Seeker was feeling, due to the connection between them, because for a moment James wanted nothing else but to be pulled through the Portal and into the sublime existence on the other side.

Then the connection was severed, and James woke up instantly, heart pounding like a jackhammer. He looked at Emily, still sleeping, but pulling the blankets close around her. He shivered violently, whether from the cold or the terror, he didn't know.

———————————

Danny was sleeping on the side of the bed closest to the door, thank God. Jenna lay beside him, facing away. James crept softly up to Danny. He shook him, trying not to startle him, and whispered urgently, "Danny. Danny. Wake up."

"Wha? Stewart?"

"No, it's me, James. I've got to talk to you!"

Jenna groaned. "Stewart? What's wrong?"

Danny peered through half-open eyes at James. "No, honey. It's just James. Go back to sleep."

"James?" Jenna laboriously rolled over. "What's the matter?"

"Nothing. Go back to sleep."

Sleepily, Danny sat up. James gripped Danny's arm fiercely and pulled him into the hallway.

"What's up, man?" Danny asked groggily. Then, fighting through the effects of sleep and alcohol, he noticed James's fingernails cutting into his arm, and he looked at him with alarm. "What's wrong?"

"Danny, it just happened! It just happened. Right now! C'mere!"

James urgently pulled Danny down the hall and into the spare bedroom. Once inside, he whispered, "Do you notice anything?"

Danny was suddenly wide awake. He looked around and shivered. "Yeah, it's freezing in here. Did you open a window?" He was halfway across the room to check the window when comprehension radiated over his face. "Oh, wait, that's a sign, isn't it? Holy shit! Were they really here?" Danny could barely keep his voice down, he was so excited.

"Shhhhh."

Danny inhaled deeply. "What's that smell? Why's it smell like… like apple pie? And gunshot? Were you trying to shoot them?"

James noticed Emily stirring. He wondered if whatever the aliens had done to keep him asleep had affected her, too. He pulled Danny into the hallway, shutting the door.

"See!" he said, barely able to keep the hysteria out of his voice. "That's proof. Every time they come, it gets really cold. And that smell, the Seeker just made that."

"All right, let's go turn the coffeemaker on," Danny said. "I want to hear all about it."

As Danny measured the coffee and poured the water, James paced the kitchen in agitation. If Danny experienced the same thing, then that was proof. He wasn't crazy, and he wasn't just dreaming. But then it was real. And that was worse, far worse.

Danny switched the coffee maker on. "I can't believe there were aliens in my house! God, that's unreal. Aliens, in my house! I just can't believe it. Oh man, that's unbelievable." He suddenly startled. "Oh shit, I gotta go check on the kids! They better be OK."

James looked at him bleakly. "They're OK. Those things aren't going to hurt anyone, they just…"

"They better not've touched those kids!" Danny rushed out of the room.

"…they just came to chat. Maybe next time I should offer them some coffee," he said in a strangely wooden voice.

James felt like he was going to lose contact with the floor and fly away. He opened the cupboard door and stared into it, disoriented, unable to choose which mug to take out. His mind seemed to have stalled like a flooded car engine. Finally, he stretched a trembling hand out and closed it around the nearest one. He poured himself a mugful of coffee and sat down at the kitchen counter. He tried to drink, but his hand was shaking so badly the coffee sloshed over the rim. A desperate little moan escaped his lips, and he chanted over and over in his head, Maintain control. Don't lose it.

Danny came back in and grabbed himself a mug. "They're sleeping like rocks." He looked excitedly at James. "You know, I probably sixty percent believed you when you told me all that alien shit, but now, man—one hundred damn percent!"

And then it all exploded out of James in a geyser of anger and despair. "God fucking damn it! Finally, everything was good! Finally, today we get peace! And they just can't leave it alone! They just can't let me be happy with that! Son of a goddamn fucking bitch!" He pounded the counter with his fist, knocking over his coffee.

Danny stared at him in shock. James was the only guy he knew who almost never swore.

James jumped off the stool and slammed madly around the room, smashing his fists on the cabinets and the refrigerator and the counter, spouting a stream of profanity. Danny busied himself wiping up the coffee that had spilled, giving James some space, pretending not to see the angry tears squeezing out of his eyes.

Finally, James calmed down enough to sit down. He sat, chest heaving, holding his head in his hands, moaning softly. Danny waited.

"I don't want it to be real, Danny," James said, so softly that Danny could barely hear him. Danny responded with an equally quiet voice.

"What did they show you this time? Same old thing or something new?"

"Oh, it was much more this time," James said, struggling to keep his voice steady. He looked bleakly at Danny. "I had an actual conversation with one of them. Inside my brain, while I was being held unconscious by them."

"You gotta be kidding! Oh my God. Did you ask it how they get here through space, or where they're from? Oh man, if I could ask an alien anything, what would I ask it? It's like getting to ask God whatever you wanted. That is so sweet!"

"Sweet isn't exactly the word that comes to mind, Danny. Terrifying, maybe."

"Yeah, I guess. So, you actually talked to them? Holy shit."

"It wasn't exactly a verbal conversation. They couldn't understand the words I was thinking."

"So, how'd you talk to them then?"

"Pictures. Somehow, I realized that I could communicate with them by thinking in pictures, since they'd shown me pictures in the first place to communicate with me."

"Wow. How'd you know to do that? I mean, when I'm dreaming, I'm usually less than logical, like running around with no pants on."

James sipped his coffee, trying to figure how to explain to Danny the mental state he'd been in. "It's definitely not like being in a dream state. Maybe it's like being in a coma, where people's brains may be actively working and processing information even though it looks to everyone else like they're dead to the world. But it's a different kind of coma. It felt like they were clamping onto my head and manipulating my brain energy. I think that's how they show me the visions, by manipulating my visual cortex. Like, I was in a lucid state inside my head, even though I was unconscious to the outside world. It was really weird, Danny." James winced in pain. "You got any ibuprofen? I got a killer headache."

As Danny got up to get the pain reliever from a drawer, he said with concern, "I hope they didn't mess up your brain."

"You and me both, man."

"So, in your visual conversation, did you ask them where they're from?"

"I tried to, but I didn't get an answer. I don't know if they didn't understand me, or if they didn't want to tell me. I guess I wouldn't blame them for not wanting humans to know how to find them, given our track record of wiping out other species."

"Good point."

"It was hard to think in pictures instead of words, really hard to get complicated questions across."

"Too bad you're not autistic."

"Huh?"

"Stewart has this autistic kid in his preschool class that he's become friends with. He's come over to the house a couple times. He's a pretty neat kid, actually, fun to talk to. Quirky. Anyway, I was curious, so I went to this autism website. I found out that some autistic people think in pictures instead of words."

"I wonder if I can learn how they do it. Just in case the bastards come back."

Danny gave James a sympathetic look. "So, what did you get out of your visual conversation with these bastards?"

James looked at Danny grimly. "I got the clear impression that the Evil One—Eddie, as we so innocently like to call this gross abomination—has not actually been completely stopped."

James tried to fight down the panic threatening to overwhelm him again, but his voice was shaky. "Danny, they showed me the whole goddamn world exploding in a fireball. The message I got—and I hope to God I got it wrong—is that the Earth's gonna be destroyed unless I—me, James Thompson—stop Eddie for good."

Danny looked at James with shocked eyes. "Shit. Shit, that sucks. You're serious? So, it's really all on you? They really were contacting you, specifically, after all?"

"Apparently," he said bitterly. "Oh, yeah—they also conveyed to me that they're sorry their previous evil ones messed up our world."

"Oh, man." Danny looked up at ceiling. "Hey, thanks a lot, you alien sons-of-bitches!"

James looked at his friend, the only other person in the world who shared this horrible thing with him, and anguish tore up his face. "Danny, this is crazy. What the hell do they think I can do? This is a screwed-up world full of weapons of mass destruction. And if some of our problems are caused by those shithead aliens using us—using our Life Force to get what they need, and not caring till now that they leave behind a few scumbags causing massive pain and horror—then they should fix it. They made this mess, they should fix it. Not come to me." He looked up at the ceiling, echoing Danny's gesture. "Hear that?" he yelled. "Leave me alone and fix this yourselves!"

CHAPTER 6

New Year's Day was hell. James felt like the Seekers had invaded his head last night and wouldn't get out; he could not stop thinking about what had happened.

Jenna and Emily prepared coffee and orange-cranberry muffins and eggs, and buzzed and chatted about the great peace news, and how school was going for their kids, and when would the cold snap let up, and…

Aliens. Goddamn aliens messing with my head.

"So, do you want more coffee or not, James?"

"Huh?"

"Poor baby, you're all hung over, aren't you?" Emily massaged his shoulders and kissed him on the top of his head. "Can't drink like when we were twenty, can we?"

"No. My head is killing me, actually."

Aliens. Aliens were inside my head. What did they do to it?

"I'm not surprised," Emily said. "Have you got any Tylenol around here, Jenna?"

They had to go over to his folks' house for the afternoon. As was the tradition, James and his father and his brother-in-law watched the football games, while Emily and his sister took the kids sledding. His mother busied herself fussing, as usual.

"Can I get you a pillow, J. J.?" To the rest of the world, he was James. To his family, he would always be J. J., short for James, Jr.

"Thanks, Mama, but I'm just fine. Why don't you sit down and relax for a bit?"

"Are you sure it's not too cold for sledding, Darlene?" his mother fretted.

Darlene put a reassuring hand on her mother's arm. "It'll be fine, Mama. We won't stay out too long, and Cory's dying to try his new sled. As soon as they say they're cold we'll…"

Cold. Why does it always get so cold when they come? It's like they bring space with them.

"Go! Go! Go!" His father was halfway out of his seat. "Did you see that run, J. J.? That kid should've gotten the Heisman."

"Yeah, there's no justice," agreed Darlene's husband, David. "I just hope the Vikings get him. Not likely, though."

"Nah, they'll draft for defense first, if they're smart," his father asserted in his usual authoritative voice. "The Vikings used to be famous for their defense. A purple wall no running back could get through. That classic game against Green Bay, that year when they went ten straight without a loss, it was defense…"

Loss. I am lost. No one can help me.

"No! They're throwing a flag on that? What, are those refs crazy? Did you see that?"

Aliens. Aliens. It can't be. It is. It can't be. Oh God. "Uh, yeah, they're blind."

"That's right they're blind. That was not even close to holding, and to call back a beautiful run like that, it's just a crime."

Holy Jesus, what am I going to do?

The women and children having left the house, James's mother turned her attention back to the men. "Can I get anyone some chips or a soda or something?"

"Sure, I'll take a Coke," David said.

"J. J.?"

"Oh, uh, yeah. I mean no, I'm not that hungry, thanks."

His father turned to him. "Well, you better have some of your mother's pecan pie later, or I'll never hear the end of it."

Pie, apple pie, why that smell, that was so strange. But it was really there. Danny smelled it. Nothing else could have made that smell, I didn't say anything to Danny first, he just smelled it. Aliens. God help me.

"Sure, Pop, wouldn't miss it."

He got through the day without screaming out loud uncontrollably, somehow. Pleading a hangover, James went to bed early. The knot inside his stomach, and his clenched muscles, were somehow overcome by exhaustion. He was amazed to wake up the next morning and find he'd slept all night. With no visitors in his head. Hallelujah! He felt refreshed, as if he'd just performed the hardest task of his life, but he'd done it, and now he had broken through to the other side.

Screw the Seekers.

It was the last day of winter break. James attacked it with gusto, pushing away thoughts of aliens with frenetic activity. He helped Emily take down the tree, put the decorations away, vacuum the rug. He took Trey skating, defending the net while Trey slammed pucks at him one after another. And they didn't go to the wimpy indoor Rec Center rink, oh no, they went to the flooded rink at Pine Hill Park, where it was hard to think of anything else except how cold it was and whoa, here came another puck flying at him.

For dinner, he and Emily worked together to make a fantastic stir-fry. They hadn't done that for too long, and it was nice, very nice, cooking together. He concentrated on every stroke of the knife as he cut the red peppers into exact strips.

"So, what's your New Year's resolution?" she asked as she poured the sesame oil into the sauce she was preparing.

To figure out a way of keeping aliens out of my head? To keep from going crazy? "I've been thinking we should go even more plant-based this year. So we've cut out mammals, which is fine with me, they make excellent fake meat now. And we're down to poultry maybe once a week, right? But if we really want to save the planet, like we've been talking, maybe fish only once a month, and way less dairy."

"Yeah, OK. I've been thinking the same thing. I'm probably going to buy a vegan cookbook with that gift certificate. But I can't give up cheese completely. And you know Trey can't make it without mac 'n cheese."

James laughed. "Truth, girl. So, what's yours?"

"Well…" She hesitated. "My resolution is to try to not be jealous."

"Sweetheart, you've got nothing to be jealous of. I've told you that before."

"I know, I know. But you know what, I think of all those cute young teachers you work with, especially that new English teacher, that Melinda person that I met at the holiday party, and you know…"

James took her in his arms. "Don't worry, not for a second. They've got nothing on you, baby girl. Zero."

Emily held him tightly. "Thank you," she said softly, her voice muffled against his chest. "I love you so much, you know that?"

For a moment, James thought about telling her about the alien visitations. But no, not right now. He didn't want to spoil this moment.

He kissed her passionately, then whispered in her ear, "I need you, Emily. Be here for me, OK? Always."

———

Getting back to work was a relief. Even though thoughts of the Seekers kept erupting into his consciousness whenever he had down time, even though fear of their return kept him from being able to fall asleep without a couple of hefty bourbon and sodas every night, still, work took up a lot of his thought processes.

Twenty-nine teenagers jammed into his classroom, times five periods, pretty much took all his focus. They were loud, shy, funny, scared, bold, polite, disrespectful, conventional, audacious. Some didn't want to be there, most muddled through, and a few actually were interested. They were full of pimples and full of breasts and full of swagger. They were far more aware of each other than of him. He had to work hard to keep their attention on the subject of human anatomy, rather than the anatomy of the cute boy or girl sitting at the next table.

Still, in his down time, he couldn't stop his mind from instantly filling with pounding questions and petrifying fear of the alien invasion in his head.

Driving down the freeway, he passed the billboard for the mega lottery: "Someone has to win—why not you?" Up until this moment, this billboard had always produced one response in his head: suckers! But now, he thought: I just beat trillion to one odds. I'm the freakin' alien lottery winner.

It was like he was the boy trying to hold back the waters by sticking his finger into the hole in the dike, but there were fifty holes in the wall his mind erected to hold back the alien thoughts, and he only had so many fingers.

So he decided to go on the offensive.

CHAPTER 7

When James walked into Garraty's the next Friday, Danny was already sitting at their usual table, suit jacket slung over the back of a chair, tie loosened. James stopped at the bar and got a Bergantino Winter Wheat, one of his favorite beers from a local microbrewery. He set it down on the table and reached over to flip Danny's tie, a garish thing featuring dancing bowling pins and a bowling ball with the three round finger holes making a scared face.

"Nice tie, Friedman. You've outdone yourself."

"Thanks. You're late."

"Yeah, sorry. I had to help a student after school. She's gonna flunk if she doesn't get at least a 'B' on the anatomy homework I gave them, and she just can't keep a lung straight from a liver."

"Yeah, well, she's got me beat—I can't tell my ass from your face."

"That was funny when you used it in fifth grade."

"So, was she cute?" Danny asked, sipping his beer.

"Huh?"

"The student, the girl. Was she cute?"

"She's stacked like the proverbial brick outhouse, and wears clothes a hooker would find too suggestive, but you know we teachers aren't supposed to notice things like that anymore. So if you tell anyone I said that, I'll have to kill you."

"Duly noted."

James took a long pull on his beer and added, "What I really wanted to say to that girl was, go home and put something decent on, show a little self-respect. I'll tell you one thing, Danielle's never leaving the house looking like that."

"Now the waitress there," Danny said, pointing to a perky young woman taking an order from a group of guys in matching uniforms at a table across the room. "She's a fine-looking representative of the female of the species. If I weren't married, I'd have her phone number before we left here."

"Ah, she's OK, but I like 'em a little taller, you know? With long, flowing hair. And athletic bodies."

"You just described Emily."

"She'd be happy to know that. Although she wouldn't have liked the rest of this conversation. Her New Year's resolution is to not be jealous, but she can't help it. I don't know why she's so insecure. It drives me crazy."

"Women, my friend, do not understand our basic psyche." Danny leaned back in his chair. "It is bred into the male of our species to notice and respond to attractive females. We must mate! We must spread our fantastic genes around!" Danny pounded his chest like a gorilla.

"True enough," agreed James, laughing. "But the key point that women don't understand is that although we cannot help responding to other women, we can override our biological imperative and choose not to act on it."

"Yeah, women don't give us enough credit for that." Danny drank deeply from his Guinness. "Did I tell you they've announced another reorg at work? Which means they're probably gonna dump the Focus Five project I've had my department working on for seven months."

Danny expounded on the stupidity of the corporate decision-making process at length, finally vowing that he would not give up his project without a fight.

"Good luck with all of that," James said drily, signaling the cute waitress. He ordered them some skin-on fries, and said resolutely, "OK, let's get down to it."

"The Seekers?"

"What else? I tell you, man, that last visitation has totally freaked me out. The only thing keeping me from voluntarily committing myself is that you experienced it, too—at least the after-effects, if not the direct in-brain psychedelic picture show."

"Yeah, that's really whack, them manipulating your brain. How do you know they didn't permanently mess it up?"

"That's where I'm counting on you. I might not know it. And yes, that idea has me concerned, to say the least. So please, let me know if you detect anything that makes you think my brain's been messed with."

"If you ever decide to put weed killer on your lawn, that'll be a dead giveaway."

"Hey, I'm proud of my bee-friendly, planet-friendly lawn."

"You mean dandelions?"

"Did you know that dandelions build bones better than calcium, and also cleanse the liver? Emmy and I are going to try making dandelion wine next summer."

Danny laughed. "That's perfect! Wine that simultaneously destroys and fixes your liver!"

"What I really worry about is, how do I know they won't manipulate my brain to make me do something against my will? Like what if they make me throw an Uzi in the back of my car, drive across the country to Washington, wait for President Scofield to appear at the White House door, and spray him with machine gun fire?"

"Dude, you couldn't even watch when I shot that deer."

"You noticed, huh?"

"If I see you doing stuff that's really bizarre, I'll slap you around till you come out of it."

"Thanks, I guess. Anyway, that's what I want to do today. Go on the offensive, instead of sitting around being scared and waiting for something to happen."

"I like it. The best defense is a good offense, right?"

"Something like that."

"So, I'm your right-hand man, and it's my job to watch you to make sure you're not going berserk and buying Uzis and shit."

"You got it. And I also need your brainpower. The two heads are better than one theory." James took a long, satisfying drink of beer, waiting for Danny to throw out some outrageous, but surprisingly plausible, idea. But Danny just looked at him blankly.

"OK, let me get the ball rolling here. I think it would be helpful to try to figure out as much as we can about the Seekers, based on the information I have. So, what do we know, and what can we extrapolate from that?"

"We know they appear to you when you're sleeping."

"Right. Good. So, that indicates to me that it is easier for them to manipulate my brain when I'm not in conscious control of it, and when outside stimuli are at a minimum, and I'm not using my brain to move muscles much, and so on."

"So," Danny said thoughtfully, sipping his beer for reflective aid. "OK, so maybe they can't actually manipulate your brain when you're awake. If we're lucky they couldn't make you into their puppet anyway."

"Let's hope you're right on that," James said fervently.

"Let's go back to your vision and what they looked like, or anything about them physically, you know?"

"See, I don't know if what they looked like in my vision is anything like what they look like in reality. They may have just portrayed themselves like that because they were using my brain, with its stored memories and images, and they had to work with the material they had."

"OK, but still, it's a starting point."

"Right. We should cover all ground. Well, in the visions, like I said before, the Seekers were huge, and kind of long and flowing, with lots of colors shifting rapidly over their bodies. They kind of reminded me of white jellyfish undulating in the ocean. They were sort of like spirits, too, kind of ghost-like."

"Undulating ghosts. Got it."

"Whatever they are, I know they're intelligent, conscious entities. But I can't say for sure if they had substantial bodies or not. I couldn't really distinguish a head area, so I can't tell you anything about their mouths or eyes or anything. But you'd figure they'd have to have some kind of receptors for visual stimuli, and some kind of central nervous system.

"But, see, I don't know if they're showing me themselves as they are on their home planet, or themselves as they are here on Earth. I guess I've been assuming they have same bodies here as there, but maybe not."

Danny looked thoughtful. "Yeah… Maybe, if Earth is like their heaven, their dead bodies are back on their planet, and they're just spirits here."

"Maybe. Anyway, going back to what they showed me, they were streaming through space and into the Earth Portal, like I said before, gliding in on the Life Force energy. They were not using a vehicle. Now, my brain does, of course, have a database of vehicles, so they could have shown themselves coming from their planet in a spaceship. So, either they were deliberately misleading me, or their space vehicles are so unlike anything we have that they couldn't make my brain form a picture of them, or they really do travel through space without vehicles."

"That's impossible."

"In our experience, yes. In order to do that, they'd have to not be creatures that breathed air, or anything else, for that matter. And they'd have to be able to withstand the cold, the radiation, and the vacuum of space. Seems highly unlikely that any physical bodies could do that."

"Maybe," Danny postulated, "they have physical bodies back on their home planet, but they leave their bodies behind when they travel to Earth to go through the Portal. I had a buddy in college who claimed he could do astral projection—you know, like meditate until his spiritual self was able to leave his body and travel around. He claims he went to the moon."

"Yeah, well, maybe."

"Where do you think they come from?" asked Danny.

"I've been thinking about that. Up till now, I've been assuming they come from some other solar system. But we have to consider that they may come from one of our own sun's planets."

"We've sent spacecraft to the other planets. Wouldn't we have detected them?"

"Well, yeah, we should be able to detect life on nearby planets. Our radio telescopes would pick up electromagnetic emissions from higher level beings in what one would assume would be some sort of civilization. But I'm not ruling out anything at this point, since we're dealing with so many unknowns. Maybe they have a way to mask themselves from us."

"Now you've got me thinking. It hadn't occurred to me that they might be from around here," Danny said. "But you did say they wouldn't tell you where they were from when you asked them, right?"

"Wouldn't or couldn't, I don't know."

"So, they'd be a lot more cautious about that if they were from a planet that we could actually get to, wouldn't they?"

"That makes sense. Or, maybe they come from far away and have a way to jump into our planet's atmosphere directly—you know, the mainstay of science fiction movies—wormholes, folds in the space-time continuum, like that."

"Man, the more we know, the more we don't know." Danny took a long pull on his beer. "Let's lubricate our brains."

James raised his glass. "Here's to outside-the-box thinking."

"OK, so here's one for you," Danny said. "How would these

kinds of beings communicate with each other?"

"Excellent question, my young Padawan."

Danny leaned over the table and punched James in the arm. "Hey, I ain't no wet-behind-the-ears Padawan, Yoda. We're star warriors together, man."

"My apologies, Han. That's one thing I feel pretty confident about, actually. My best guess is that they have a visual, rather than sound-based, communication system. Remember, I got the distinct impression when that alien was trying to communicate with me that it was using color and pattern to express itself. I'm kind of excited about this, I have to admit," James said, eyes lighting up. "I think I've made a really cool discovery. When they pictured themselves to me, there were colors flowing all over their white sheet-like bodies. I think that's how they talk, by using a photo-chemical process."

"That sounds really wild."

"Yeah. Some Earth creatures can do it, though. You ever seen video of an octopus rapidly—almost instantly, really— changing colors all over its body to match its surroundings? It's absolutely amazing. Maybe these Seekers are like highly-evolved octopi."

"That's a little creepy."

"And of course, that Seeker used colors to tell me its name, too. I wish you could have seen it like I did, Danny. It was like a visual symphony. Just amazing. Like this." James raised his hands and swirled the left, fingers dancing, above his balled-up right fist. "Like all these shades of blue swirling around this yellowish-rose colored blotch in the middle, and then the blotch exploded like rays of a sunset"— his right fist burst open, fingers waving out in all directions— "and then silver flashes shot everywhere"— both hands punctuated the air with rapid finger jabs— "and then this black line wove in and out, and... man, it's hard to describe, but it was astounding. And that was just the guy's name."

James took a pen out of his pocket and wrote "J-A-M-E-S" on a napkin. "Makes my name look pretty lame."

Danny looked thoughtful. "In college, I took a science fiction class, and for one assignment we had to make up a new sense that aliens might have that no animals on Earth have. I think that was the hardest paper I had to write in all four years."

"I believe it. If you were blind, would you be able to make up in your head what the sense of sight is really like? If you were deaf, could you really imagine music? I doubt it."

"So, what senses do these Seekers possess? A visual sense, clearly."

"Probably a lot more advanced than ours," James suggested.

"And what about that smell, man?" Danny said. "That I did experience."

"Right. There's got to be an olfactory sense, somehow, or that Seeker wouldn't have had any reason to create that smell."

"Yeah, and it was really there, too. It wasn't just in your brain."

"You're right. That Seeker, who I believe was present in that room, did in fact somehow release the odor when it gave me its identity. Which argues strongly for the corporal, rather than spirit, body. I'd have to say I'm tending to the theory that the way they represented themselves to me was to show themselves as they are on their planet, rather than literally showing themselves traveling to our planet. Maybe they don't want to show me their space-travel technology. Maybe they're afraid if they reveal to us how they go through space wormholes or whatever, we could get to them. Or maybe it just wasn't germane to the point they were trying to get across to me."

"Oh, wow!" Danny exclaimed.

"What?"

"I just had an idea. What if they have a force field around their bodies, something invisible that lets them travel through space without the radiation and all that shit touching them?"

"Yeah, I guess that's possible. Remotely possible."

James paused to reflect. "OK, so back to their senses. I'm guessing the sense of hearing is probably minimal or nonexistent, since they didn't try to activate sound in my brain. But the visual sense is dominant and very important. And they have some chemical sense like smell, yes."

"So, what's that leave?" Danny held up five fingers and put down three. "Taste? Do they even eat? Who knows? Probably doesn't matter much. Unless," he cackled, doing a vampire impression, "they have a taste for human blood!" He picked up a French fry dripping with ketchup and stuffed it in his mouth. "What's the fifth sense? Oh yeah, touch. Man, that makes a big difference, if they can physically touch things on Earth and, like, move them around and stuff."

"Yeah, it does. Don't know. Maybe they can, maybe not. And let's not forget, even here on Earth, there are animals that have senses we don't have, like bats have sonar echolocation. A whole lot depends on what their environment is like. If they're in water, or in thin air on mountains, or in a world with dense vegetation—that all makes a difference in which senses would predominate and be useful. Do they need to use their senses to find prey, or to avoid predators? There are a ton of factors that we just can't know."

James reached for the frics, and then paused in mid-dip as a thought struck him. "Remember that quilt they showed me, that seemed to represent me overcoming the Evil One? What I don't know is, are they showing me what they want me to do, or what I will do? Maybe they have some kind of a sense that allows them to perceive the future."

"That would be weird. So how was that again? You're the golden thread or something, you said?"

"That's me, I guess," James said, spreading his hands in a "what can I say?" gesture. "You can just address me as Your Golden Highness, Savior of the World, from now on."

"Sure, Goldie."

"Anyway, I know it's hard to believe, but having a future sense is theoretically possible. I mean, we know that because I parked on the street facing south, my car in fact will head south in the future. One thing leads to another. That's how we do our weather prediction, right? So maybe they have some highly-developed sense that lets them perceive the complexity of current events flowing inexorably into the stream of future events. You know what I'm saying?"

"I know that the fact that I'm having a beer here at Garraty's

Tavern leads inexorably to the fact that I am now gonna take a piss in Garraty's restroom."

Danny got up from the table, and left James to ponder the potential strangeness of alien life. There could be—no, surely must be—many facts about the aliens that they would not be able to deduce, because they would be totally outside human experience. James's mind was reeling, and he decided to clear it by forcing himself to concentrate on the TV over the bar.

It was 5:35, and the TV was tuned to NBC news.

The peace accord was holding, according to NBC's suave and reassuring anchorman. But some cracks were developing.

Danny returned, settling into his chair with a contented sigh, and tapped his empty glass. "My turn to pick the second-round challenge, right?"

James smiled. They had a long-standing tradition of asking an intriguing question each week, alternating who posed the question. The one who had the best answer won a beer from the other. Too often, he spent an inordinate amount of time trying to come up with a great question. But this week, it was Danny's turn. "Yeah, I think so. Bring it on."

"OK, so here's the question: If you could have any wild animal as a pet, what would it be?"

James tried to think of a great answer, since Danny had won the last four second-round challenges. But all he could think of was soft and furry. Maybe he needed comfort. "OK, I guess I say a chinchilla, since it would be so incredibly soft to pet as it sat in your lap, it would send you to bliss heaven. All your stress would just melt away." He tried to put a good face on it. "So, top that if you can."

"As a matter of fact, I think I can. A Galapagos tortoise. Because first, kids could ride on it at your child's birthday party, and your kid would be like the coolest kid ever. Second, you could paint it with Homecoming slogans and put it in front of the field at all the Westfield Homecoming games, and it would be so cool it would totally demoralize the other team. Third, they live like 150 years, so you'd never have to deal with the trauma of putting your pet to sleep." Danny grinned at James.

"Fine," James conceded, signaling the waitress. "You win."

James pointed at the TV screen. "Maybe we should consider what the Seekers say is the point of all these visions and visitations—stopping Eddie Olson."

"Right now, things are good," Danny said. "No point messing with the President if other factors, like John Shepherd and the U.N., are going to take care of the problem for us."

"I agree. But what if Scofield gets nasty again? When they showed me that quilt and me defeating Eddie, I heard—well, it's really weird, but I heard my own voice in my head distinctly saying, 'I am the One who will stop the Evil One.' It was like the message was very clearly being conveyed to me and I was understanding it."

"If they think you're The One," Danny said, making quotation marks with his fingers, "then they ought to at least tell you how you're going to do it. I mean, they could be a little more helpful here."

"No kidding."

Danny gave James a skeptical look. "I just don't trust those guys. I mean, no offense, but you, the one and only person who can save the world?"

"No offense taken, my friend. I am in complete agreement with you there."

"Maybe they're playing you. Like, they want to take out this bad guy of theirs, for whatever reason—he raped the head squid's daughter or something. But he's safely stowed inside a human body, and they can't touch humans. So, they need you to do it. But would you do it just to do some alien squids a favor? Not likely. So, they lie to you, tell you the planet's future is at stake."

"Yeah, but that begs the question again—why me? Why wouldn't they just get into the head of Scofield's chief of staff, or some disgruntled White House employee?"

"Good point."

"But you're right, we've got to question everything. For now, let's assume they're telling it to me straight. Let's say they want Eddie Olson destroyed because they believe he could ruin the world badly enough to kill off life on Earth, thereby shutting down the Life Force and their precious Portal. So, they should want to do whatever they can to help achieve that goal. If they knew how I could, or will, stop Eddie, then it's in their best interests to tell me."

"For sure," Danny agreed, "they should want to help—" and then he stopped as he saw James's eyes widen in a horrified look.

"Unless they don't want to tell me because it involves me getting killed, and they're afraid I won't do it if I know that."

"Shit."

The waitress set their fresh beers in front of them. "I've never needed a beer more than I need this one right now," James declared.

"Maybe they can only get a general idea of what's gonna happen, not the specifics," Danny suggested. "Or maybe they're so alien they can't figure how things work here, so they're just giving you the overview and expecting you to implement the plan."

"Spoken like a true manager."

"Here's what a true manager does, my friend. He manages. He controls the situation. Right now, you're not in control of this situation. They come to you whenever they choose, and you have no control over it. You know only what they allow you to know. You need to change that."

"Yeah? How?"

"Value. What is your value to them? It's the task they want you to perform. The task they need you to perform, in fact, if they are to survive. That gives you a lot of power over them. You can just say no, and what are they gonna do?"

"Kill me?"

"Well, let's assume not for now, unless we get evidence to the contrary. Anyway, if they could kill you, they could kill Scofield."

"Good point. So, what do you think I should do, Mr. M.B.A.?"

"The next time they come to you, bargain with them. Contract negotiations, if you will. What do you want from them?"

"I want to know," James said simply. "I want to know. Partly because the more knowledge we have about them, the better we may be able to fight Eddie Olson. But mostly because I've made the most amazing scientific discovery since... ever. I want to know as much about them as possible."

"Then tell them that every time they come to you, they have to answer X number of questions, or you won't work for them. And to make sure you get that opportunity, tell them they have to come to you on a regular basis, say every week."

"Are you crazy?" James exploded. "Ask them to come into my head and mess around with my brain more? How do I know that every encounter doesn't screw up my brain a little more? How do I know that the next encounter won't push me over the edge? It's not your head, Danny, it's mine."

"Yeah, I know. But how else are you gonna learn about them?"

James sat there thinking for five full minutes. Danny, for once, left him alone to think it through instead of trying to talk him through it. "You're right," he finally said. "There's no way I can turn down this opportunity. I've got to take the risk." He smiled broadly at Danny. "Maybe my father was prophetic. Maybe I will get a Nobel Prize."

CHAPTER 8

James woke up the next day to the sound of kids screaming and pounding through the house.

"Good Lord," he moaned, then rolled over to check the clock and found to his surprise that he'd slept till noon. He hadn't done that in ten years.

On his way to the kitchen, he encountered Trey tearing through the hallways.

"Whoa, slow down there, buddy!" he exclaimed, hoisting him up and giving him a good morning hug.

"Hi, Daddy."

"Hey, what're you doing here, pal?" James said in surprise, as Danny's son, Stewart, came roaring around the corner.

"Guess what? Guess what?" Stewart exclaimed, jumping up and down with excitement. "My mommy's getting my baby."

James smiled. "Oh, that's good news."

James found Emily in the kitchen, making Danielle a grilled cheese with tomato soup.

"Ah, the perfect lunch," he said to Danielle, hugging her.

"You say that every time, Daddy," she objected.

"You have to have traditions, my girl. Someday you'll be saying that to your children when they have grilled cheese and tomato soup."

"Yeah, right."

Emily greeted him with a smile and a kiss. "Good morning, sleepy head."

"Yeah, I don't know how I did that. Especially with the two cowboys tearing up the place. So, when did Stewart get here?"

"They dropped him off around nine, on the way to the hospital. Good thing. They were going to induce on Monday if Jenna hadn't gone into labor by then."

The NFC playoffs were on that afternoon. The Vikings were already out of it, thanks to that bone-headed pass that was intercepted in the end zone and run back for a touchdown last week. Still, James watched the game with some interest, unable to decide if he was rooting for or against Green Bay. On the one hand, better to have a team from their division in the Super Bowl. On the other hand, the Packers.

Trey and Stewart were building an elaborate structure with Legos. Trey was being really nice to the younger boy. He'd make a good big brother. Maybe they should have another one. No, Emily would kill him if he even brought up the idea. Trey's delivery had been really tough, and she had emphatically declared that two was enough. Danielle was sitting in a chair nearby, reading one of the Harry Potter books for the sixth or seventh time.

The domestic tranquility was broken by Stewart throwing Legos across the room and screaming, "I wanna go home! I want my mommy!"

Danielle looked up from her book, annoyed. "Daddy, can't you make them be quiet?"

"Honey, Stewart is just a little keyed up, 'cause his mom's having a baby, you know?"

Danielle returned to her book with the muttered remark, "I hope it's a girl."

"C'mere, Stewart," James said, patting the couch. "Watch how far that guy—he's called the quarterback—can throw the ball."

"My daddy can throw a ball all the way around the world," Stewart said with conviction.

"What?" yelled James. "A flag? C'mon, ref!"

Stewart jumped off the couch and stood right in front of the TV, peering intently. "I don't see a flag."

"Stewart, old buddy, can you move it, please?" James said, trying his best to hang on to his patience. "Oh, never mind. Now they're taking a timeout."

"Were they naughty?" Stewart asked. "I get time outs sometimes when I'm naughty."

While James was trying to figure how to explain football to a three-year-old, Emily's phone rang.

"I hope that's them," Danielle said.

"You and me both, sweetie," James agreed.

The big smile on Emily's face as she came into the room and switched off the TV said it all. "Let's go, Stewart! It's time to meet your new sister."

Stewart jumped up and down all the way up the hospital elevator. The kid was a human jumping bean. Then he went running off down the hospital corridor as soon as the doors opened.

"Hey, buddy!" James called after him. "You wanna see your mommy, why don't you come with us? It's this way. Here it is, room 314."

Jenna was sitting up in the bed, looking spent but happy. Danny was in the chair next to the bed, holding the baby.

"Hi, partner!" Danny said fondly to Stewart. "Say hello to your new baby sister."

Stewart looked at his dad, then ran up to Jenna and laid his head on her stomach, now much smaller, but still a round little hill. "Hi, baby," said Stewart in his sweetest voice.

Everyone laughed.

"I guess he doesn't quite get it," Jenna said.

"Stewie, this is your new sister here," said Danny. "She just came out of Mommy's body a little while ago. Be careful. Touch her very gently."

Stewart shyly touched the baby. He didn't seem to know what to make of this strange new creature in his daddy's arms.

Emily hugged Jenna lightly. "How're you feeling?"

"Very happy that I never have to do that again. Ever."

James patted Danny on the back. "Congratulations, papa. Good going, Jenna. So, what's this little cutie's name?"

Jenna smiled at Danny, who grinned at James. "Her name," he announced, "is Jaymi. J-A-Y-M-I."

"Oh, that's so cute!" Emily exclaimed.

"Yep, but it's more than just cute," Jenna said. "Danny named her after you, James."

"Oh. Oh, my God. Wow." James was rendered speechless by this unexpected gift.

"Well," Danny said, "you know I was very touched when you named Danielle after me. I'm just glad I could return the compliment."

"Thank you. But are you OK with that, Jenna? You like Jaymi for a name?"

Jenna smiled. "I think it's a beautiful name. And now that she's here, I think it's her. Look at her. She's Jaymi."

Danny took out a piece of paper from his pocket and cleared his throat. "Ode to Jaymi," he announced. Then he read, "Into our lives has come beautiful Jaymi. To name her anything else, you couldn't pay me. She's just so gorgeous, you know it might slay me. How we adore our lovely Jaymi!"

James laughed. "Don't quit your day job."

"I think that was very sweet," Emily protested. "You should put that in her baby book."

Just then Jaymi added her viewpoint, starting to fuss in that distinctive way of newborns.

"See," Danny said. "She's saying, my daddy is the best daddy in the whole world, and I'm super lucky he wrote that poem for me." The baby started crying. "Or maybe she's saying something more along the lines of, feed me." Danny stood up carefully with his daughter. "I think I'd better hand her off to the Source of All That is Good."

"C'mere, Jaymi," said Jenna, reached out. "Mommy's got some delicious milk just for you."

"I want milk, Mommy!" yelled Stewart, demanding the attention that had so unreasonably been diverted to this weird new creature.

"I'll take Stewie down to the coffee shop," Danny offered. "I could use some coffee anyway."

Emily settled into the chair Danny vacated. "I'll stay with Jenna. We've got to discuss all the nasty details—contractions, episiotomies, searing pain—you know, girl talk."

James and Danny winced. "C'mon, son," Danny said, guiding Stewart out the door. "This is no man's land."

Once out the door, Stewart ran ahead for the elevator. The boy never walked, apparently.

"You know, James," Danny said, "when I held Jaymi in my arms, I just felt this wave of protectiveness wash over me. I felt this fierce kind of love, like I'd do anything for her. There's something a little different about a daughter for a man, you know?"

"I know."

"Anyway, whatever I can do to help you take out Eddie Olson, just ask me. Anything. I've got to make the world safe for her."

Deb Kolbo Ellsworth

CHAPTER 9

"Whoa, what was that?"

A screeching tropical bird flew over Danny's head.

"I think it's cool the way birds are allowed to fly around in here like that," James said. "I almost feel like I'm in the jungle."

They were strolling through the Tropical Rainforest section of the Minnesota Zoo. Although it was snowing and twelve degrees outside, they were in T-shirts and loving it, having stowed their jackets in lockers. The air was dank and lush, a marked contrast to the bone-dry air of any other interior space in February. You could actually touch a metal railing without getting a shock. James made it a point to come here at least once a winter.

"Hey, guys, wait up!" James called to Trey and Stewart, who had run ahead to see the Komodo dragon basking on the rocks below.

"I hope Jenna's relaxing at home like she promised," Danny remarked. "She's been pretty exhausted since Jaymi was born."

James smiled. "Jaymi. Love the sound of that."

They caught up to the boys, hoping to stop and admire the largest lizard in the world, but off they ran again.

"Little boys have the attention span of gnats," James said.

Danny laughed as they followed them. "My mother says I got a 'Needs Improvement' on sitting at group time on my Kindergarten report card, and it was underlined three times. In red ink."

"You'd think a dragon might hold their interest for a while."

James was transfixed by the verdant world all around him, riotous with life, luxuriant in flowering trees and screeching monkeys and graceful flamingos. "Is it possible that Eddie could destroy all this, Danny?" he said softly. "It would be the greatest sin ever committed in the history of the universe. My God, we are so lucky to be sharing our planet with this... this cacophony of living things. We just take all this for granted," he said, waving his arms to encompass the rainforest around him. "It never even crosses the average person's mind. Go to work, pick up dinner, go to the kid's soccer game, watch the tube, and oh yeah, give profound thanks for the incredible world we are privileged to live in.

"Anyway, even if Eddie does somehow manage to start a nuclear war or something, I firmly believe that life will out. Something would survive, life would rebuild. Life is too rich and too vast and too strong to be snuffed completely. Unfortunately, it would more likely be the rats than us."

"And they're off!" said Danny.

"What's off?"

"The kids. That was pretty good. Three whole minutes in one spot."

They trailed after the boys.

"It's just possible the American democratic process might take care of my problem for me. Scofield's running neck-in-neck with Senator Hutchinson, and Governor Compton beats him by sixteen points in the latest poll."

"God, you are a wonk, aren't you?" Danny's eyes crinkled with delight. "Maybe that's how you take out Scofield," he joked. "Maybe you become a delegate to the national convention for Olivia Compton, and maybe you get interviewed by the New York Times on what the average heartland Joe thinks, and maybe your answer is so stunningly brilliant that it sweeps Scofield out of office on

Election Day."

"Yeah, that's probably the scenario," James said dryly. "I think you nailed it."

"Hey, where're the kids?" Danny said.

"I don't see them."

"There they are!" Danny pointed. "They're going through that door into the butterfly enclosure. Ten seconds more and we'd've been calling security. Damn, those little buggers are fast."

James's phone pinged as he was enjoying an ice cream cone with his son in the zoo's cafeteria. Probably Emily, checking to see when they'd get home.

But no, it was a message from a student, Abdi Noor. James had given his students his cell phone number and told them they could text if something was important. His fellow teachers thought he was crazy to do this, but so far no one had abused it. James was shocked at what he read from the boy: "Mr. Thompson, I'm really sorry to bother you, but my family is going to be deported back to Somalia. 2 of my uncles are in jail. The feds are saying my father is part of a secret terrorist cell. They think my brother is too. Sorry. I didn't know who else to ask for help. I don't know what to do."

So that was Eddie's next move, James thought grimly.

The day after James got the text, Scofield held a special news conference announcing that Homeland Security had broken up an extensive Somali terrorist ring in six states, including Minnesota. He gravely informed the American public that he'd received intel from the CIA that "Islamic-African terrorists" were working to attack Judeo-Christian democracies, especially the U.S. and Europe.

James didn't for a second believe that Abdi's family was involved in a terrorist plot. He spent all his free time trying to help Abdi's family, searching the Internet for answers, contacting government officials, going to the immigration office. But there was no way he could help them, even with the intervention of their congressional representative. Abdi, his mother, his brothers and sisters were going to be deported back to Somalia in ten days. His father and uncles, and a couple cousins, were in jail. James couldn't get Abdi's tear-stained face out of his head, weeping with fear that his father was going to be tortured and he would never see him again.

James couldn't stop thinking: If I can't even save one kid and his family from Eddie Olson, how the hell am I going to save the whole planet?

By Friday, James was a walking zombie. He was too exhausted to get up and go to the staff lounge at lunch time. He leaned back in his chair, put his feet up on his desk, and closed his eyes. In a few hours he'd be meeting Danny at Garraty's. He hoped to God talking it out with Danny would help.

But really, what could Danny say? The Seekers' vision appeared to be moving forward inexorably.

James's head nodded forward. It's like I'm on the Seekers' train, and they put me in the engineer's seat, but I don't know how to drive a train I've never been to engineers' school. The train was picking up speed the scenery was flashing by the windows so fast he could hardly see it how was he supposed to stop this train look out the window there's Earth spinning in space stars flashing by now Seekers flashing by stop this train it's going to crash—

James yelled in his mind: Stop the train!

Confusion filled his brain.

James somehow pulled his mind back from the edge of panic and realized that the aliens were back in his head contacting him. They started to show the same visuals again, but he knew that wasn't what he needed. Tell me what to do. How am I supposed to stop this guy? Help me. Random colors exploded in his brain. Hey, you alien! What do you want?

Then he remembered that he had to speak to them in pictures. He tried to picture himself confronting the Evil One. How does it happen? What do I need to do?

The weird alien blanket image now floated in James's sleeping mind. He watched the golden thread that he knew represented himself make a sharp angle and turn toward the dark green, oily splotch, which seemed to be pulsing and growing. The golden thread grew longer, spinning itself into the figure of James, as it had before. When it covered and defeated the Evil One, thousands of Seekers swirled around the golden James in a delirious dance of gratitude, colors flashing over their white bodies faster than James could distinguish them. A sweet floral scent filled his brain. A profound sense of well-being flooded his mind, as if the universe had been set right again after going off-course.

James had to make them see the truth. He pictured himself very small, standing in front of a huge figure of President Scofield, with the Evil Seeker superimposed on him. He imagined his small self pounding futilely on the foot of a powerful Scofield.

The Seekers responded with the same quilt image, but this time they showed millions of small threads pulsing and glowing, all leading to James, lifting him up over the Evil One. In his head he heard himself say, The Way comes. Somehow, he understood that although they couldn't, or wouldn't, show him what the Way was, he was surely moving toward it, enabled by many tiny intricate details that he couldn't see or know, but that would lead him to defeat the Evil One.

James felt he was supposed to say something important, but he couldn't remember what it was. Panic filled him as he feared he would blow this chance, and who knew when he would get another?

Wait, that was it. If I'm going to help you, I need to know I can have regular contact with you. Damn. How can I show you that? Then he remembered that he had practiced how to think of this request in visual terms.

James pictured himself standing with a Seeker next to him, which then went away, and then pictured the Earth rotating seven times and the Seeker reappearing next to himself. He pictured the alien going away, then pictured the sun coming up and going down seven times, and then the Seeker coming back to him. He pictured the same thing again. That had to be clear, didn't it?

There was a pause, what felt like a suspension of contact. Was the Seeker considering his request, or would it just go away? Then it felt like the alien was plugging back into his brain. He saw two shining spots of silver light float in front of him. The lights each divided into two, so that now there were four. Again they divided, with the eight lights now making the points of a floating cube. Then they divided one more time into 16 lights, with a larger cube surrounding the smaller cube. Colored lights flowed between all the 16 points and over the imaginary faces of the cubes. A feeling of pleasure and harmony filled his mind. Was that a positive answer?

James felt the Seeker begin to pull away. Who are you? He remembered how he'd asked for the Seeker's name the last time and pictured himself tapping his own body while saying his name repeatedly, and then tapping the body of the Seeker.

An image of several Seekers arrayed next to James appeared. Colors started flashing in front of James's eyes, shot through with metallic bursts and weaving patterns. He felt his mind being released.

No, wait, come back! I have to ask you so much more…

"Mr. Thompson, Mr. Thompson." Something was shaking the train. No, someone was shaking him awake.

"Mr. Thompson, fifth period's starting."

"Aw, man, what you doin'? You shoulda let him sleep, fool!"

"Ewww, what's that smell? Does someone got dog shit on their shoe?"

"Hey, why's it so cold in here? The heat go off again?"

James fought to shake off the disorientation. He stood up and shook his head.

There was a smell. The Seeker had left a distinctly foul odor.

"OK, class, settle down. Sorry, I guess I had a hard night last night, staying up late preparing enough difficult material to challenge you guys."

A few kids laughed. One smart aleck in the back row piped up. "If we're doing an experiment about dog doo, I'm outta here!"

That kid got a much bigger laugh. James smiled. "No," he said. "Actually, we're going to start our astronomy unit a little early. This one's gonna be fun, people. Now, for your first assignment, I want you to research a planet and tell me ten fascinating facts about it. Bonus points for information I don't know already."

CHAPTER 10

Danny was late. James had big news to tell him, and the guy had the nerve to be late. James watched Garraty's TV screen, showing the Gopher women's basketball game. Thank God for sports. On the news this morning before he left for school, the local Channel 4 people were doing a piece speculating on whether Gordon Cambridge would run for President after his second term as Vice President, and how that would that benefit Minnesota. The Speaker of the Minnesota House was blathering on about the jobs this would create right here at home, even though James remembered that the Speaker and Cambridge had gone eyeball to eyeball on nearly every piece of legislation when he was governor.

This was news? This was nothing. Little did those talking heads know that the real story was sitting here in Garraty's Tavern, quietly sipping a beer and planning how to bring down the head of the ticket this Minnesota-bred politician had hitched his wagon to.

"Hey, bro!" Danny punched James lightly in the shoulder.

"'Bout time you showed up! Took you long enough. I gotta tell you someth—whoa, man, I gotta tell you, that tie is over-the-top, even for you."

Danny grinned as he waggled the black tie, the tiny streetlights on the painted-on cityscape twinkling.

"If it's not electric, it doesn't work," quoted Danny. "Bumper sticker number ten." He signaled the waitress, their usual one. She gave Danny a smile and a thumbs up. He turned back to James. "So, what's up?"

"You won't believe this one, Danny! The Seekers just came to me a few hours ago—at school."

"What? They're coming into your mind when you're awake now? That's bad."

"No, no, I was asleep." James looked at Danny sheepishly. "I've hardly gotten any sleep this last week, what with working on my student's family's deportation case, so I accidentally fell asleep on my lunch break, in my classroom."

Danny frowned thoughtfully. "OK, so maybe they can only detect when you're in an unconscious state, not what setting you're in. Could your students tell they'd been there?"

James burst out laughing—not quite the reaction Danny expected. "Oh, yeah. This one left his identity smell behind. Unfortunately, his name appears to be Dog Poop."

Danny roared with laughter, pounding the table. Finally he gasped, "That is the funniest thing I've heard all week!" He wiped the tears from his eyes. "I wonder if dog shit is a prestigious odor on Planet Seeker. I'm guessing not. I'm guessing your guy drew the short straw and had to be the one to talk to you precisely because he's not Mr. Popular."

Danny did his best alien impression: "Oh no. Here comes Dog Shit again. Let's get rid of him, guys. Last time he was here I couldn't get the smell off me for a week. Let's send him to talk to that weird human guy."

As the waitress set Danny's beer down, she said, "Hey, what's so funny, you two?"

"Danny's tie," James said, still laughing.

"I don't know, I think it's kind of pretty."

They broke up laughing again. The waitress smiled at them indulgently, rather like a mother smiles at her two rambunctious but lovable sons and returned to the bar.

"Wow. I needed that," James said.

"So, why'd they come to you this time?"

"I think just to let me know the confrontation with Eddie is getting closer, evidently, and I should be vigilant. Kind of a coach's pep talk. I tried to get them to tell me what I should do, but I got nada. Either they don't know themselves, or they won't tell me, for some reason. I got the feeling they were reassuring themselves that they haven't lost me, that I'm still gonna work for them."

"Are you?"

James hesitated. "If it looks like Scofield is really gonna launch nukes or massive biological weapons or something and destroy the world, yeah, I guess so. But I really don't think those Seekers get humans very well, you know? So, I don't trust that they've got the picture for sure. I tried to tell them that I'm not a powerful person here, you know, that there's not much a high school teacher in Minnesota can do to affect the President of the United States, but I don't think they got it."

Danny took a long, satisfying drink. "I wonder if they have beer on Planet Seeker."

"I wonder how they eat, what they eat. I wonder how they reproduce. I wonder what their cellular structure is. Do they make buildings? Do they have art? What kinds of other living things do they have on their planet? I wonder a lot of things about them, but they're not giving much out."

"So, did you make the deal with them?"

"Kind of," James admitted. "It's not like I could write notes and bring them with me into my unconscious. I had a hard time remembering what exactly I was supposed to say, and I realized after I woke up I hadn't negotiated on the answering a certain number of questions thing. But I think they may have agreed to come back to me on a regular basis. They either said OK to my request to come back in a week, or they made it sixteen days. I couldn't tell. Or maybe they were just saying 'nice talking to ya, amigo'. My Seekerspeak is a little rusty."

"Why sixteen days?"

James described for Danny what the Seekers had shown him, the cube inside a cube. "Actually," James said thoughtfully, "I got the distinct impression that they consider sixteen to be the perfect number, so if they did mean sixteen days, maybe that was in order to bring good luck, or good harmony, or something. Or maybe they just use their perfect number as a phrase that means, 'absolutely, positively'. Or maybe it means something beyond my imagination. Who knows?"

"So, they're superstitious. Maybe we should find out what they think makes bad luck and use that against Eddie."

"That's a good idea," James agreed. "But I was thinking about the other aspect, the perfect number thing. If it is, why would sixteen be the perfect number? It could be the number of hours in a day's rotation of their planet, or the number of months that it takes for their planet to go around the sun in a year. Which would help us figure out what planet they're from, except we have no idea how long an hour or a month would be for them. Units of time are arbitrary constructs."

"Maybe they use a base sixteen math system," Danny suggested.

"Ah, good thought. Could be. Like the hexadecimal system we use in computing, huh?"

"Exactly. Or maybe they have sixteen fingers—eight on two hands, or four on four hands, or one on the end of sixteen tentacles." Danny wiggled his fingers at James.

"You know, I was also thinking that what they showed me might have been a representation of the four dimensions—first the two points showing one dimension, then the four points showing two dimensions, then the eight points showing three dimensions. Then the sixteen representing four dimensions, the fourth dimension being time. And you know what, if they really do have some kind of future sense that perceives what will happen, maybe they can perceive the fourth dimension in some weird way that we, obviously, can't. Maybe that's why sixteen is the perfect number to them."

"That is a really freaky idea." Danny sipped his beer reflectively and then grinned at James. "All I know is—" Danny broke into song— "one is the loneliest number."

James laughed, but then something clicked in his mind. "You're right, one is the loneliest number." He pulled out a pen and began playing with the number sixteen on his napkin. Danny watched with interest. James showed him the napkin. "Look. Let's skip one—the loneliest number—and go to two. That's what they did, they started with two rather than one, right? They didn't start with a single point, as we would, they started with a line, essentially."

"Yeah, I'm with you so far."

"So," he continued, "two is the first 'not-alone' number. What's two squared? Four. And what's four squared? Sixteen. There's a beautiful mathematical symmetry—harmony—in the number sixteen. Sixteen is a very unlonely number."

"OK, that's cool. What does it mean?"

"I don't know," James admitted. "But something is tickling at the edges of my mind."

"Don't try to think of it, just let it come to you," Danny suggested. "Tell me what else you got from this visit."

"OK, let's see. The Seeker tried to reassure me that they'd be with me, by showing me a bunch of them around an image of me. It actually did make me feel better at the time."

James let the images flow through his mind. Suddenly he snapped his fingers. "That's it! It's the two-not-one thing. Their perfect number, sixteen, is based on multiple squarings of the number two. Maybe their number system starts with two, and maybe that's because they don't have individual identities. Maybe that Seeker was telling me not just its own name, like we would, but its identity within the group. Maybe they function as a group consciousness. Like ants, maybe theirs is a totally communal society. And now that I think about it, in the visions they seem to be moving in a group, kind of flowing together. Maybe, like ants, they release the chemical smell so that their fellow ants, or Seekers, can recognize them."

"Group consciousness, huh? What if they're like The Borg?"

"Then we're dead."

Danny sipped his beer. "I need more brain fuel."

James was still putting the puzzle pieces together. "So, if they communicate with light and colors, visually, and with chemicals, maybe they can't keep any communications private. The whole group sees it or experiences it."

James slapped his palm against the table with excitement, startling Danny. "Hey, you know what else I just remembered? When they were showing me the wonderful results of Eddie's final defeat, and the picture was of all these Seekers swirling around me, all so happy and flashing colors, I smelled something then. It was an incredibly pleasant smell, and I was immediately filled with a feeling of complete well-being, like I'd hit nirvana. I wonder if the odors they release convey emotions, or maybe even influence them. So, if it's a group thing, the whole group absorbs the same chemicals and is brought into the same state, emotionally."

James's mind was racing. "Maybe they even communicate telepathically. Picture this whole gathering of Seekers, signals flowing between them all, chemicals flowing between them all, like a giant brain, in a way. Maybe you experience yourself more as one part of the whole, rather than as separate."

"But they are, James. Don't forget Eddie Olson. Some of them are very separate."

"That's right. In any system, in any life form, aberrations happen. Some of them deviate for whatever reason. Mutations, genetic combinations gone bad, environmental stress. That's probably very upsetting to the general group consciousness. They're probably happy to see those deviant ones leave their planet and head for Earth. Maybe they even exile them. We could be their Australia."

"I wonder if any Evil Ones do manage to get through the Portal and mess things up for them real bad on the other side," speculated Danny. "Not that I care. They didn't much care what those deviant alien sons-of-bitches were doing on our side."

James signaled Danny to be quiet, as the waitress approached their table.

"Can I get you anything else, guys?" she asked brightly. "It's still half price on appetizers."

"What do you think?" James asked. "I could go for some nachos. Except I'm really trying to cut down on dairy."

"Relax. Friday happy hour doesn't count." Danny smiled at the waitress. "Thanks, Jolene, we'll take a large nachos."

James sipped reflectively on his beer. "I can't believe I'm looking forward to an alien entering my brain in a couple weeks. What do you think should be my first question? I don't see any point in asking again how I should defeat Eddie. I don't think they're gonna answer that."

"I wanna know where they're coming from, but I don't think they're gonna answer that, either." Danny laughed. "Maybe you should find out what their version of a hot babe would be. Get 'em to show you a little alien porn."

"Yeah, that's exactly what I want to see," James responded drily. "I'm gonna have to think about this."

"In the meantime," Danny said as he finished his Guinness, "you can think about what your second-round challenge question is."

"Yeah, I had one, but now I think I'm changing it. OK: What famous person do you most identify with?"

Danny thought for a moment, and then responded, "Off the top of my head, I'd say Lenny Bruce. A fearless Jew who spoke the truth through cutting-edge humor."

"Yeah," James said, grinning, "I guess I can see that. If you consider photos of inadvertently funny signs to be cutting edge."

"OK," Danny conceded. "Maybe that last thing I posted online wasn't brilliant humor. Just wanted to give you a chuckle, brighten up your dreary day. If you don't like 'em, just say so."

"Oh, keep 'em coming. You're like the Michael Jordan of Internet humor. I can't stop you. I can only hope to contain you."

"So, who do you identify with?"

"Well, it just hit me as I was thinking about the fact that I have deliberately asked alien beings to interface with my brain. I'd say Marie Curie. She made amazing discoveries in radioactivity and revolutionized the fields of chemistry and physics. I would have to say that discovering the existence of extraterrestrial life is at least as revolutionary."

"True, but lots of scientists have made amazing discoveries. Why her? Why not Einstein?"

"Because she laid her life on the line for science. She died because of the radioactivity she was exposed to. I feel like I am putting myself—my body, my brain—on the line to continue trying to research this alien life that I have discovered."

"God, I've got to give this one to you," Danny said grimly as he watched the waitress bringing their nachos. "Just don't go that far, man. Seriously, don't die on me, OK?"

CHAPTER 11

James stood at his living room window, transfixed by the raging blizzard on the other side of the glass. The streetlight on the corner illuminated the blowing, whirling snow in eerie bursts, like ghosts moving through the dark night. The white swirling snow eddies reminded him of the image of the Seekers flowing through black space. Then he was struck by a startling thought. They had named the Evil One "Eddie", seemingly randomly. And yet, the word eddy meant a rotating, whirling current that's at variance with the main current in a stream. Eddie's completely at variance with the other Seekers, and damn if they don't all move like they're in the flowing current in a stream. The power of the subconscious mind—the power of the human brain working behind the scenes, as it were—never ceased to amaze him.

Then he told himself to stop thinking about the Seekers. He was sick to death of running over it all in his mind endlessly and getting nowhere.

Sometimes he could catch a glimpse of the Pedersens' porch light when the gusts of snow briefly let up, making him think of a lighthouse desperately trying to say, we're here, watch out. He knew he should get back to grading quizzes, but the consuming totality of blizzards always captivated him.

Emily called to him from downstairs. "James, it's on."

He pulled himself out of his reverie. "What? Oh, OK, I'll be right there."

James settled on the couch next to Emily. On the TV, President Scofield sat at his desk in the Oval Office. James's gut wrenched at the sight of the man. He could almost see Eddie Olson writhing around behind Scofield's eyeballs.

"My fellow Americans," Scofield began, and he sounded supremely assured and in command, the ultimate father figure. "I come to you tonight because of a grave and unprecedented threat against the United States.

"But first, I am proud to say that we dealt with the Somali terror cells decisively and thoroughly. Our intelligence operation functioned perfectly, and our military and our police forces acquitted themselves brilliantly."

Emily reached for James's hand and gave it a sympathetic squeeze. "I guess by 'perfect' he means deporting perfectly innocent families like Abdi's."

Scofield continued. "I wish that were the end of the story, that I could pat our government on the back and say, 'Job well done' and be done with it. Unfortunately, it now appears that this may be just the tip of the Islamic-African terror iceberg, if you will.

"While I am not at liberty to disclose classified details, I can tell you that Homeland Security, the CIA, and the rest of our vast and effective intelligence network are currently investigating threats in other parts of Africa, as well as Southeast Asia, and of course the Middle East.

"However, that is not enough. We cannot be complacent in the face of ever-shifting terrorist threats to our democracy and our American way of life. In fact, we are all in this together. And we need your help as well. Tonight, I am calling on every citizen of this great nation to stand up and be counted.

"Tonight, I am announcing that the United States government will be implementing what we are calling the Military Mobilization Readiness Plan. We do this with a clear understanding of the changing needs for the defense of our great country. In the 21st Century, war happens quickly. If the terrorists were to launch a coordinated, large-scale attack, we would need to be ready to respond immediately and with sufficient force to squash the armies of evil. The old Selective Service system is antiquated. It would take at least a year to implement the draft and train a sufficient number of new troops. By that time, the terrorists would have you bowing to Mecca in Birmingham.

"Under the Military Mobilization Readiness Plan, new military training facilities will be created across the country, and everyone, men and women, between the ages of 18 and 30 will be required to report one weekend a month for training, much like the National Guard on a larger scale. This way, we will have a large, trained and ready reserve fighting force available to us at a moment's notice. Some training facilities will be ready immediately, and we expect it to take approximately six months for all facilities to be operational."

James and Emily looked at each other, eyes wide with shock. "Oh my God," Emily said, "he's starting up the draft, only worse. I don't believe it."

The President continued with the details of the plan. "All eighteen to thirty-year-olds, male and female, should expect to be contacted by the Selective Service, so that you can be assigned to a training facility. If you have moved since you registered with the Selective Service, you are asked to update your information using forms available at government centers and post offices across the country, as well as online at the website address you see now at the bottom of your screen.

"I am confident that all patriotic young Americans will be happy to give up just one weekend a month to serve and protect the United States of America. In fact, just last week I received a letter from a young man in Arkansas named Allan Trinidad, asking what he could do, in the face of recent threats, to help his country. He explained that he was supporting his disabled mother, so he was not free to enlist in the military, but that he wanted to do something. Allan, thank you—this is your answer.

"My friends, we must all be like Allan. We must all do our part to protect and defend our country, the greatest country that has ever existed on this Earth. Our young people will do their part by willingly defending the United States when called to do so. But I am further asking all of our citizens to defend America with your eyes and ears. If you see or hear anything anti-American, please call our Homeland Security tip line to report it. You will see the phone number on the screen now. Please put this number in your phone now, so that you will be ready to use it when needed, whether that is next month, next year, or tomorrow. Terrorist sleeper cells could be anywhere. The Third World looks at us with jealous eyes and wants to take what we have worked so hard over the centuries to build. And if they cannot take it, they will destroy it, so we cannot have it either.

"My fellow Americans, I come before you tonight and vow that there will not be another September 11th under my watch. Nor will there be a March 29th or a June 16th, or whatever date the insidious forces of evil have chosen for the fall of America. Our intelligence tells us that September 11th was just the appetizer. It whetted the appetites of the Third World masses, who are hungry to consume America completely."

Howard Scofield stared into the camera, paused dramatically, and said firmly, "This. Will. Not. Happen.

"I expect the United States Congress to pass the Military Mobilization Readiness Act within days, confident as I am in each senator and representative's patriotism. If you are ready to defend our great country, please call or email your congresspersons by going to this website or calling this phone number, which you see now on the screen. Tell them that, by God, if you are willing to stand up for your country, they should not stand in your way. Thank you. Good night, and God bless America."

Emily switched off the TV and said grimly, "This is not good."

James was sure of one thing now. "If he's drafting an army, he's going to use it." He stood up. "I've got to get some fresh air."

James sat on the steps of his porch with the blizzard raging around him. He had not turned on the porch light. He wanted darkness. His jacket hung open, but he didn't notice. This was it, then. It was starting.

He tried to think. What now? What should he do? But his mind felt overwhelmed, as blank as the whitewashed scene before him.

He saw the snow in the yard light up and realized the door had opened behind him. Danielle sat down next to him, tucking her bare hands into her jacket pockets and shivering. "Hi, Daddy. I was looking for you everywhere. Mom said you were sitting out here?" The question in her voice conveyed skepticism that her father was a rational human being.

"Oh, hi, sweetie. Sorry. Did you need me?"

"I just wanted to say good night. Why are you out here in the middle of this snowstorm?"

"Isn't it beautiful, Danielle? We live in such an incredible world, don't we?"

Danielle looked around thoughtfully. "You're right, it is pretty, in a weird way."

They sat quietly together for a bit. James wanted Danielle to stay here with him, but he was afraid if he said anything, it would be the wrong thing, and she would go back into the warmth of the house, leaving him all alone again in the cold blank whiteness that was the world.

"It's really quiet out here, isn't it?" Danielle said softly. "Usually you hear car noises, or dogs barking, or something. But all I hear is the wind and nothing."

James smiled and put his arm around his daughter, pulling her close. "It's very peaceful, isn't it, in a weird way? Most people don't realize how beautiful a blizzard can be, at least as long as you're safe at home."

They sat together, enjoying the world stopped for a moment.

"Dad, do you think the animals like the snowstorm, too?"

"Yeah, I bet they do. I bet that rabbit family that lives under our porch is all huddled up together, just a happy bunch of fur and wriggling noses."

James wiggled Danielle's nose. She giggled with delight. "Dad, I'm kind of too old for you to do stuff like that anymore, you know."

"Oh, I hope not."

James was afraid that she would bolt inside then, but she snuggled up to him instead. Maybe out here it was OK for her to still be a little girl who needed her daddy.

"So, how's your Destination Imagination challenge going?" he ventured. "You've got the Regional tournament pretty soon, don't you? Your team gonna be ready?"

"Oh yeah. Wait till you see the cool Peace-o-matic machine we made for it! That's our technical device, me and Kari and Alisa made it, and it's really neat. It makes everyone have to say nice words to each other, even when they're thinking bad things."

"I know a few world leaders who could use that. You're pretty smart, my girl!"

"Thanks. I hope we go to State."

"I bet you do. Wanna tell me what your skit's about?"

"No, I want to surprise you. All I'll tell you is, I play a unicorn."

James smiled. He loved this child so much it hurt. He moved aside the hood on Danielle's jacket and whispered in her ear.

She hugged him. "I love you too, Daddy. Well, I better go in. Hey, do you think we'll have a snow day tomorrow?"

"I'm crossing my fingers. Good night, sleep tight, sweet dreams."

When Danielle closed the door, the darkness of the night closed in on him and sank into his core. He watched the wind-driven snow smashing into trees and tearing down branches and piling up on the cars. And he knew that he could no more stop the world's most powerful person from starting a war than he could stop this blizzard with a shovel. Danielle took the magic of the night inside with her, and James was cold and alone and profoundly depressed.

CHAPTER 12

James woke up to bright sunshine. The roar of snow blowers filled his ears. But it should have been dark, and it should have been the sound of his alarm clock that woke him up. It was a school morning. He looked at the clock. 8:30 a.m. The alarm was turned off.

Swinging his feet over the edge of the bed, he heard Emily brushing her teeth in the bathroom.

"What's up?" he asked Emily, embracing her from behind.

"Snow day. There's almost two feet of the stuff out there. The kids are thrilled, as you can imagine."

"Can't say I'm too disappointed, either."

"Well, before you get too comfy lounging about on your bonus day off, could you clear the driveway for me? I've still got to go in, if they ever get our street plowed. Those little old ladies will be sitting in their chairs waiting for seated aerobics at 10:15 sharp. Of course," she added with a laugh, "the class actually starts at 10:30, but they don't like to be late. Plus, it's arts and crafts day. We're making scented candles, with flowers pressed into the wax. Can't miss that."

———————————

James sat at the kitchen table, enjoying his second cup of coffee.

The news was all about Scofield's speech last night. The reaction was mixed, but on the whole, positive. The right wing, of course, was ecstatic, hailing his call for the MMRP as a decisive and bold strike against terrorism.

The bright sunshine washed away the despair of the previous night. By God, I'm the stealth bomber, he thought, smiling wryly at this image of himself. The secret weapon that Eddie Olson knows nothing about.

The Seekers hadn't come to him a week after the last visit, so he hoped he was right about the sixteen-day theory. If so, in three days the Seekers would be returning to him. James spent the rest of the morning working on a list of questions he should ask them, arranging them in order of priority. Number one: What are the Evil One's weaknesses? Then he tried to figure out how he could ask those questions visually, which wasn't easy.

As the day went on his mind kept coming back to the impending visit from the Seekers. While he was outside making a snowman with Trey, he found himself forming the snow into a shape that resembled the flowing Seekers. While he was watching a movie with the kids, he wondered if the Seekers had entertainment. Did they tell stories with their amazing colors? Did they have the technology to record their stories? While he was chopping the onions for the spaghetti sauce he was making for dinner, he wondered what the Seekers ate, how their bodies processed food.

Over the weekend, James could hardly think of anything else. The excitement of discovery filled him. Far from the feeling of dread that he normally associated with the aliens' nocturnal visits, he was feeling elation. He was surprised to realize that he would be disappointed if Sunday night passed with no alien connection.

Sunday evening, he stayed up late, telling Emily he had a load of tests to correct, so that she'd be asleep when he came to bed. He knew he was too keyed up to fall asleep easily, and it would be even harder if Emily were being kept awake by his tossing and turning. He reminded himself for the hundredth time that he might have gotten their message wrong, they might not even be showing up tonight. He shouldn't let himself get his hopes up like this when it all depended on the slim chance that he and an alien being had accurately communicated with each other.

He pulled out the bottle of prescription sleep medication from his bedside table drawer and popped an extra tablet. His mind was buzzing, and his body was about as unrelaxed as a human body could be as he settled into bed. A thousand thoughts about the aliens danced in his head: what kind of atmosphere does their planet have… do they form family bonds… how do they reproduce… what other life forms are there on their planet… what about plants… remember to ask about the Deviant One's vulnerabilities… how big are they… do they have skeletons… do they have circulatory systems… can they… how do they…

Images of Earth floating in space… the Life Force radiating from it in shimmering waves… James felt his mind being clamped onto, as the aliens made contact.

Hello, he thought. A small corner of James's mind registered a flicker of amazement that he was greeting these aliens like old friends. Then he remembered that he had to communicate visually, so he pictured himself smiling at the Seekers and holding out his arms to them in an open gesture.

A soothing feeling of acceptance spread through his mind, and he thought he smelled something sweet. He felt them waiting. He wasn't sure what he should do next. He remembered that he'd thought of questions to ask them but couldn't bring any to mind now.

The Seeker showed him the same quilt image again, the same golden thread and the same oily splotch. This wasn't helping. James could feel the pull of the Portal on the Seeker. He could almost feel what the Seeker was feeling, that it had traveled a great distance to achieve this passage through the Portal into its next level of existence, and it was hard to focus on anything else.

That's it. I want to know how they get here from their home world. And what happens when they get here and how do they go through the Portal?

James felt a pause as the Seeker apparently sensed the increased activity in his brain and perhaps realized he was trying to communicate with it. He wondered if the alien would be willing to give him the answers he wanted.

James pictured the Seekers flowing through space toward Earth. Is this how you get here? He then pictured the aliens on a distant planet, opening an imaginary door in space, flowing through it, and coming out of a door in space above Earth. Is this right? Is there a wormhole? Then he pictured Seekers getting into a rocket ship, blasting off from their planet, and entering the Earth's atmosphere in the rocket, from which they emerged and then flowed through the Portal, as they'd shown him. Do you use technology to get here?

He knew the Seekers couldn't understand the words he was thinking, but he hoped they could somehow pick up that he was asking questions.

There was a pause, a slight disconnect, and then a reconnection. Pictures began rolling through his sleeping but alert brain. First, he saw a monarch caterpillar crawling on a leaf. Then he saw the caterpillar hang from a stem of milkweed in that familiar J-shape. He saw it shiver and shake as its outer skin was shed for one last time and the new skin hardened into a bright green chrysalis. In this vision that the aliens were showing him, he could see inside the chrysalis as the insect broke down entirely into a gooey mess that slowly formed into a butterfly. Finally, he saw the monarch butterfly crack open the paper-thin chrysalis shell and emerge, stretching its beautiful new wings.

James was floored. Metamorphosis? Were they trying to tell him that they underwent metamorphosis, using an image familiar to him? He pictured the chrysalis with a Seeker folded up inside it, then emerging like a butterfly and shaking out its white flowing body.

A feeling of affirmation filled his brain. Yes, the Seeker was conveying to him, yes, you understand.

Then he saw Earth, from above. In the space surrounding Earth, rock-like objects appeared, racing toward the planet. As they entered the atmosphere, the outer portions of the rocks burned off. James realized that these were extremely hard shells encasing the transformed Seekers. He saw the thin shells that remained hanging in the upper atmosphere of Earth—and then they cracked. Seekers emerged from them, flowing white beings. He felt with them the sense of glorious wonder as they found themselves at the threshold of the Portal, in bodies adapted for survival in Earth's atmosphere, giddy with the Life Force flowing around and through them. Somehow he realized that, like some insects with short adult lifespans, they didn't need to eat because they would soon be drawn into the Portal.

James was stunned. How could these aliens have ever evolved to transform their bodies into something intended to survive on another planet? How could they survive the radiation of space? How did they get off their planet? How did they aim unerringly for Earth? This was a miracle of nature beyond anything he'd ever seen.

He pictured the rock-like chrysalises lifting off a distant planet and traveling through space. He pictured radiation bombarding the chrysalises, and meteors hitting them. How? How?

Again there was a pause, and he wondered if the Seeker was rummaging through his mind, trying to find a suitable image from James's experience or knowledge that would sufficiently explain this mystery. The answer, when it came, completely surprised him.

He saw himself in church, worshipping God, praying, singing, raising his arms to the glory of God. Then he saw a swirling tornado of colors, immensely vast and glorious beyond comprehension, and somehow he realized that this represented the Seekers' vision of God, as the Original Source of the Life Force. He saw this Tornado lift the chrysalises up from the planet he had pictured. It blew them through space toward Earth, surrounding them on their journey with a protective wind that blew away all radiation, all space debris, all harm.

His mind reverberated with a sense of pure joy as he saw the emergent Seekers feel the Life Force surround and engulf them. Then he saw millions of human beings, surrounded daily by the Life Force, and he knew what the Seeker was trying to tell him: you humans experience the glories of the Life Force all your lives. A feeling of transcendence filled him, and these words came into his mind: Blessed are humans truly who dwell at the threshold of the Portal.

James felt the Seeker pull away and release him. This time he awoke slowly, gently, feeling himself surrounded by the power of the Life Force. He could still feel the transcendent joy that seemed to fill every cell of his body as he experienced with the Seeker the attraction of the Portal.

No wonder the Seekers never intervened to stop their deviant ones before, he thought. They're probably so caught up in the spiritual moment that they don't even notice anything else. If I was standing at the gates of Heaven, would I be aware of the chaos and pain on the Earth I left behind?

A new thought hit James with the force of a sledgehammer. Oh my God, the gates of Heaven. Earth, our own planet, is the gate of Heaven, at least for them. Oh, my holy God, when we die, do we go through the Portal? Do we enter Heaven right here through this Earth Portal?

James was engulfed with a feeling of shame for his own species. Humans—the blessed of the universe, according to these aliens—squandered this incredible gift of abundant life every day without a second thought.

How could the Seekers have even imagined that we would destroy the sources of the Life Force so easily? How could they conceive that we would so recklessly kill off entire species, that we would even kill millions of our own kind?

James realized that the situation had to be extremely dire, if the Seekers were just now becoming aware of all the damage their evil ones did. If they were oblivious to it before, as they focused on going through the Portal, how bad did it have to be now to have gotten their attention? To be forcing them to try to stop this Evil One, when all they really wanted to do was ride that glorious Life Force through the Portal?

And they'd come to him. James Thompson. They trusted him enough to tell him about themselves, even though they had to know how vulnerable that made them to a species that would kill its own so easily. Now, for the first time, he felt compelled to stop the Evil One for the sake of the Seekers as well as for his own species. And maybe for God as well—God the Father, God the Creator, and God the Tornado. If the Earth really was the Portal to a higher existence, to nirvana perhaps, or to Heaven, then he had to defend it. □

CHAPTER 13

The teachers' lounge was buzzing when James walked in.

"Hey, Bob," he greeted the art teacher. "What's all the excitement? They give us back the free coffee?"

"You didn't watch the news this morning, did you, James?"

A cold fear clamped onto James's stomach. "No."

Several teachers were gathered around a small TV. On the screen were images of a port city on fire. Across the bottom of the screen was emblazoned: Attack in Africa.

The news anchor's voice was explaining the video footage. "These are the first images the military has released of the U.S. response to the terrorist attack in Angola. Many parts of the capital city of Luanda are on fire, as U.S. jets bombed at least twenty targets.

"The terrorist attack happened approximately four hours ago at 9:30 a.m. local Angolan time. The American embassy was attacked in a coordinated assault by three suicide bombers who entered the building strapped with explosives, followed by a truck bomb that exploded just as survivors were running out of the building, essentially leveling the embassy." The video footage changed to show scenes of destruction at the embassy: smoke, ambulances, dazed people with blood covering their faces.

The news anchor appeared onscreen. "I'm Terrance Spilcher, bringing you continuing coverage of the attack on the U.S. embassy in Angola. One of the suicide bombers appears to have been a janitor at the embassy. A co-worker had this to say about him." A black woman in a very colorful floral dress appeared onscreen, head bandaged, crying and barely able to speak. "I cannot believe it. This man I thought was fine man. He had many, many children. I know he loved them, he was working hard to provide for them, but it was so difficult, I believe. Some are saying he was paid to do this, that he did it to get money for his family. Many thousand dollars, they are saying. I don't know if I can believe that. Our friend, Maria, she was the receptionist, she was killed. I can't believe Jonas would do that for money. But maybe he had no choice. Maybe he was forced to do it. I don't know what to think." The woman broke down sobbing.

Terrance Spilcher continued. "The second suicide bomber showed the guards paperwork regarding obtaining a visa, and he did indeed have an appointment with a Mr. Alderton for that time. Apparently, he had been to the embassy the day before on business, and the guards remembered him."

A man in a security guard's uniform, his very round and dark face covered with abrasions, appeared on the screen, saying, "He was nice guy. Talked with me about his family. Said he wanted to visit relatives in the U.S. Nice guy. I had no concerns about him. You know, if I hadn't stepped away from the building to warn a young man out on the street, a demonstrator with an anti-American sign he was, to leave the area, I would be a dead man now. Praise God, I am alive to tell you about this."

Terrance Spilcher continued, "We have just learned that an American family happened to be in the embassy at the time and are now confirmed dead. They have been identified as the John Streeter family from Cleveland, Ohio. Mother, Sahara Streeter, and three children, ages twelve, eight and two."

The news anchor picked up a piece of paper. "This statement claiming responsibility for the attack was received by the Angolan government about an hour ago. It purports to be from a group calling itself the African Liberation Organization. It says, 'The bombing of the American Embassy in Angola, which the ALO planned and executed, is in response to the speech by America's fascist President Howard Scofield in which he threatens all of the third world, as he calls us. We are not the third world anymore. We are the new first world. We are the new world order. We fight in solidarity with the AFAF and our other brothers and sisters around the world. America has been warned. We demand that all American corporations and interests remove themselves from African soil, or this will just be the first attack. Africa is for the black man. The days of colonization are behind us, and we will not see them return again. We demand to see American interests in Africa begin the process of turning over their enterprises to African countries and leaving Africa within two weeks, or we will be forced to take further action.'"

Terrance Spilcher paused dramatically. "Is this the opening salvo in a new terrorist war on America, or an isolated incident? Only time will tell, but in the meantime, the results are grim."

The TV screen again blazed with explosions, gunfire, people running and screaming. Then the visuals of chaos and pain were replaced by a reporter in the White House briefing room. "We have been told the White House will be issuing a statement this morning. We are expecting Press Secretary Schraeder momentarily."

Suddenly, everyone in the pressroom stood up, as a voice said, "Ladies and gentlemen, the President of the United States."

President Scofield strode resolutely to the podium. He looked rejuvenated, oddly, like he'd lost 20 years.

The teachers' lounge was dead silent.

"I know you were expecting my press secretary, but at this time, I felt the American people needed and deserved assurances directly from their President that we are doing all we should be in the face of this despicable attack on our country. Firstly, I extend our nation's deepest condolences to the families of the Americans killed in the attack. But more than that, I extend my personal promise that their deaths will be avenged. As you have seen, I ordered our Air Force to bomb targets in the city of Luanda that are suspected of harboring anti-American rebels. Our intelligence has been watching several anti-American terror cells across Africa for some time. Although I do not want to reveal sensitive information, I can assure the American people that we are confident we have targeted this ALO terrorist group in our air strike response.

"The first contingent of American troops is now on its way to Luanda and will begin searching for the terrorist cells that are bent on America's destruction within twenty-four hours. We expect the Angolan government's full cooperation."

The President looked straight into the camera with steel-hard eyes. "As far as the terrorists' demands, the United States completely rejects them, and will not stoop to even discussing them. To the contrary, I assure you that we will do everything in our power to secure American interests and to protect American citizens in Africa. We are the most powerful country the world has ever seen, we are the greatest country the world has ever seen, and we will not let some two-bit third world terrorists bring us down. Kick us, and we won't just kick back. We will step on you. We will crush you."

———————————

James looked at his first period class, and suddenly didn't know what to say. He'd been teaching for how many years, had done this how many thousands of times? And now his mind seized up and there was nothing there.

The kids looked at him expectantly. They probably thought he had something dramatic planned and was doing this to heighten the effect.

He stood there for two long minutes, looking at them. Maybe he should just walk out. He had nothing for them anymore. Maybe he should just go home and go to bed and lie there and wait for the end.

Finally, Annie raised her hand. He made eye contact with her; that was about all he could manage.

"Uh, Mr. Thompson? Are we supposed to be giving our planet reports today?"

Thank God for students like Annie. James opened his mouth. He intended to say, yes, and would you like to go first? Instead he heard himself saying, "Yeah, we'll get to them. But let's just talk for a while first, if that's OK. I find myself rather disturbed by the news this morning. Well, more than just a little disturbed, actually. I'm terrified that we're heading into World War III, to tell you the truth. And I was just wondering what's on your minds."

He must have had a horrible look on his face, because the kids were looking back at him with dropped jaws and wide eyes. He'd better recover fast. This wasn't history class, this wasn't political science, this was plain old fact-based science, and he'd better get back to that right now. Then Laura in the third row began quietly sobbing.

The whole class waited, respecting her feelings. There were no smart remarks from the back. Teenagers could be so cruel sometimes, and so touchingly kind other times. Finally, she wiped her eyes and said haltingly, "I'm sorry, Mr. Thompson. It's just that I'm really scared, you know? 'Cause my brother's graduating in June, and he's gonna have to go to one of those Military Readiness Camps, and… and… and what if this turns into a big war and he has to go fight? I don't want him to die."

What could he say to that? Don't worry, your brother won't die? Well, he very well might. He didn't know what to say that would be of any genuine use to this poor girl, so what he said was, "Anyone else want to talk?"

A few hands went up. James signaled a boy in the back.

Darien Groveland was fierce in his response to Laura's pain, his blue eyes flashing with anger. "You should be proud if your brother goes to fight for us. I'm with President Scofield. My dad works for American Mining, and like, they've got a huge operation in Mozambique. Our military has to protect them. I'm ready to go to Africa and defend my country."

Zack Trefle was incensed. "That makes no sense, Darien!" he exclaimed. "You can't defend America anywhere except here on American soil."

"The way I see it, anywhere we got business is American soil!" Darien shot back. "Those Africans should be grateful we're over there giving them jobs and, like, teaching them democracy and all that, and instead they, like, throw it all back in our faces and attack us! America does everything for the world, and we get this bullshit back? Screw them."

"I'll tell you what America's doing for the rest of the world, Darien," Zack replied angrily. "America's causing most of the global warming that's going to hit the planet with a bigger worldwide disaster than you can possibly imagine! American industry causes the daily extinction of species from this planet. Did you know that half of the world's species will be gone within your lifetime? Those Africans are supposed to be grateful to America for giving them jobs at subsistence wages making tons of consumer goods we don't really need while in the meantime destroying their environment? Yeah, right."

There were angry words muttered in response, including more profanity. James chose to ignore the forbidden language. He noticed Alanda Williams holding her hand up. Her dark face looked angry. "Alanda?"

Alanda tapped the empathy symbol she was wearing on a chain with her long red fingernail, then gracefully moved her elegant hand into the peace sign.

"I believe you've got to have empathy to get to true peace. We've got a lot of African kids at our school, you know, Darien. You should try getting to know them. You wouldn't be so quick to want to blow their heads off."

"I got nothin' against them," Darien shot back, "as long as they realize they're in America now. They damn well better support the United States if it comes to war with their bassackward countries. They're still, like, doin' voodoo and killin' each other with all their tribal warfare. An' we try an' bring these people into the modern world, an' what do they do to thank us? Attack us! Shit, they got spears, we got nukes. They gonna know soon enough who they messin' with."

Alanda was incensed. "Are you really that ignorant, boy? What do you know about African culture? Let me educate you just a little bit. Here's one difference between Africans and Americans. They value people. We value stuff."

"They value people? That's a laugh," Darien responded. "In case you didn't notice, they just blew up a whole bunch of innocent people."

Kendra chimed in, agitated. "I'm so sick of everyone hatin' on America! They're all just jealous, and now they're trying to take what we built over there in their countries, and they think we're just gonna roll over and hand it to them? Scofield is right. It's time America kicked some ass!"

"Damn truth there, girl," agreed Darien. "I think I'm gonna sign up when I graduate in a couple years, show the rest of the world they can't be disrespecting us."

DeMarcus exploded. "Y'all'd fit in just fine in Mississippi. Why don't y'all just get a damn pickup and put a Confederate flag in the window? That's what this is really about, and you white people too dumb to know you're being played by the President!"

"That's truth, DeMarcus," agreed Alanda, standing up and addressing the class passionately. "I read on the internet this morning it was our own CIA paid those suicide bombers in Angola to do it, just to start a war. They're looking to take over Africa and turn all the black people into low-paid slaves for American big business. Don't you know what's in Angola? For your information, I just did a report on West Africa for my geography class, and I can tell you. It's oil, of course. Angola is the second largest exporter of oil in Africa. Next thing, some other so-called terrorist group will be attacking us in some other African country, and before you know it, we got World War III, just like Mr. Thompson said. Only thing is, this time we're Germany and Scofield is Hitler. He tried to wipe out the Jews, and damn if Scofield don't want to wipe out anyone with skin darker than an Italian's. You people following him like little white yapping puppies, you're all fools!" She gathered up her books and walked out.

James knew he should mark Alanda down as absent, but he knew he wouldn't.

Deb Kolbo Ellsworth

CHAPTER 14

Danny raised his empty beer glass. "Second round. What's your question?"

James pretended to think for a moment, but he was smiling inside. He'd had this one ready since last Sunday. "OK, here's one for you. What would you say is the sweetest sound in the world?"

"Hmm." Danny gazed off over the top of his glass as he reflected. "Well, the sound of a woman moaning your name as you give her sexual pleasure she didn't even know was possible is pretty damn sweet."

"Yeah, I suppose that one time it happened to you must have been pretty special."

"Man, I can't get my women to shut up. Why, you shoulda heard yo' mama the other night."

"Seriously? You're really goin' yo' mama on me?"

"Uh… no. My bad. Jews can't do the yo' mama thing. Doesn't work. Anyway, I love yo' mama. She used to give me cookies and tell me I was funny."

"Yeah, well even my mama's been known to be wrong sometimes. So, you're going with the sound of a woman's unrestrained sexual ecstasy—final answer?"

"Wait, maybe I better pick a sound I know you've heard."

James held up a large French fry in one hand, and a stubby one in the other. "Sounds like someone's got a bad case of black man envy. Have a fry," he said, flipping the small one onto Danny's plate.

"Never mind, I'm changing my answer. Miles Davis, 'Bitches Brew.'"

"Yeah, maybe. Except that's too broad. We're looking for the one, single sweetest sound in the world."

Danny's eyes lit up. "I've got it. How about the sound of your child laughing? You know how little kids do? When I make Stewie laugh uncontrollably, that is so sweet."

"Yeah," James agreed. "That is a pretty sweet sound." He paused for dramatic effect. "But I propose to you that the very sweetest sound in the world is 'thwunk'."

"Thwunk?"

"Exactly." James took a moment to swallow the last of his beer, heightening the suspense. "Thwunk is that distinctive sound the net makes when a basketball swishes through it."

"Oh, man, that is totally it! I love that sound!" Danny reached out to high-five James. "No question. I owe you a beer." Danny signaled the waitress.

"That actually came to me while I was watching the Gophers' game. That kid Luke Endmyer was draining threes left and right."

"Totally. He was on fire. The Gophers might actually make the NCAAs after all."

"Oh, yeah, they're going," James said confidently. "I make 'em for the Sweet Sixteen this year."

"Maybe. They've disappointed me too many times to get my hopes up yet."

"Man, if it weren't for basketball, I don't know what I'd do. The news is too damn bad."

"Looks like your Seeker buddies may be right. Eddie's kicking it into high gear on the highway to hell. So, when are the squids due back for a check-in? Maybe now that this African conflict started, they'll have a more concrete idea of when or how you're gonna take Eddie out. That mythical Way must be getting a lot closer now."

"Five days." James pulled a few papers out of his briefcase. "In the meantime, I thought I'd share these with you, see if they inspire any brilliant, out-of-the-box insights from your fertile mind."

"Fertile body, fertile mind, that's my motto. What you got?"

"Well, it's a long shot, but I had my students write reports on the planets. I hoped someone would come up with something that might give us a clue about where they're from, if in fact they're from somewhere in our solar system."

"Man, you should've warned me I'd be doing homework here. OK, fire away."

"Right. Keep in mind that the first four planets are rocky planets, and the next four are giant gas planets. So, starting with the first planet, Mercury. Small battered planet. Closest to the sun but has polar ice caps. That's significant because you pretty much have to have water to have life, but Mercury's a way long shot. That's all I've got. Only one person picked Mercury, and his report, which was supposed to be four pages, was two paragraphs. The first paragraph was, 'My report is about the planet Mercury.' Which he spelled, M-U-R-C-R-Y."

Danny laughed. "I'm guessing that kid's going to be studying under the great Ronald McDonald when he graduates."

"Guess I'll have to do my own research on Mercury. OK, Venus, number two. People used to hope it might have life like on Earth, but the swirling upper level clouds are poisonous—sulfuric acid. It's almost nine hundred degrees on the surface."

"So, it's just too hot for life to exist there."

"Probably, but not necessarily. They've found living organisms in super-heated thermal vents deep in the ocean, which totally surprised scientists. There's a hot new scientific theory out now that the Universe is hard-wired, if you will, to produce life. That life is a basic component of matter, sort of. So, who knows what conditions other life forms might be able to live in?"

"OK. Open mind."

"Let's see," James said, scanning the paper. "Venus rotates backwards, once every 243 Earth days, which is actually seventeen days longer than it takes to orbit the sun."

"Weird."

James shuffled through several papers, reading the yellow-highlighted areas again. Then he sat, lost in thought.

"You find something?" Danny asked.

"Yes and no." James looked at Danny with a serious expression. "No, I don't think the Seekers are from Venus. We've mapped 95% of the surface of Venus, using sophisticated radar. We know what's there, and it's not aliens.

"But Venus is kind of a harbinger of Earth's possible demise. See, Venus is the most Earth-like planet, in terms of size and density. Venus is often called Earth's sister planet. Scientists think that Venus once had abundant water, the prerequisite for life, and may have had a much more Earth-like atmosphere. But, due to a number of factors that I won't get into here, the water evaporated. Venus is the ultimate greenhouse, now. Its atmosphere is mostly carbon dioxide, and the atmospheric mass is ninety-two times as great as Earth's."

"Will that be on the test, Mr. Thompson?" Danny grinned.

"Sorry. Guess I went into teacher mode."

"No prob. It was fun to get a little taste of Professor Thompson."

"Anyway, you see my point, Danny. Venus had the potential to be another Earth, to give rise to life. But it lost out due to natural forces. But we, on the other hand, received this amazing gift, a planet with all the right conditions for life, and we're screwing it up. We humans could turn our planet into another Venus if we don't stop pumping CO_2 into the atmosphere. We might reach a tipping point where we can't turn it back. It's crazy. We might be committing mass suicide and taking most of the rest of the animals and plants with us. For being such a smart species, we're unbelievably stupid."

"I wish I could disagree."

James shuffled the Venus papers to the back of the pack and looked over the next set. "Anyway, moving on. Mars. Mars, of course, is where most early sci-fi writers placed their alien races. We know more about Mars than any other planet, since we've sent plenty of spacecraft there. The interesting thing to me is that when we finally got to Mars, when Mariner 9 set down on the surface and sent back photos, and then when the other ones, the Rovers and Curiosity and all, explored the planet, scientists were surprised at what they found. So, if we could discern so little about a close planet like Mars, that we were still surprised at what we found when we actually got there with scientific instruments, how much do we really not know about the further away planets? How much do we surmise that will turn out to be wrong?"

"So, we really can't tell anything for sure until we're up close and personal, then. You're saying just 'cause we don't see signs of life on any other planet doesn't mean it's not there."

"Sort of, in terms of viewing. Even Earth, from the flyby distance of a Voyager, you don't see signs of life. Except at night, when the lights show. But a daytime viewing, you see clouds and ocean and land masses, but you don't see the cities or the farm fields or anything. Of course, there are other ways of seeing, like radio telescopes, that should detect signs of life."

"So how do you rank Mars?"

"It's in my top two at this point. The large polar ice caps are mostly frozen water. And there are vast underground ice fields. Now, for something really cool—literally. Scientists here on Earth wanted to test Mars exploration equipment in a place that has geology similar to Mars, so they searched in these volcanic blue ice vents in Norway, right? And they found both fossilized and living microbes. They're pretty encouraged that they might find life in the ice of Mars."

"That's very interesting."

"Yeah. Also, many scientists think that Mars may have water underground, which vastly increases the chances of life there, hidden away where our instruments haven't detected it yet. Of course, they're thinking microbial life, not Seeker-type life. But who knows? Also, the soil contains nutrients vital to life—magnesium, sodium, chloride and potassium. And Mars undergoes seasonal changes, like

Earth does, and in summer its temperature may rise to 20° Centigrade. All these factors are very life-favorable.

"Plus, it's relatively close. And I mean relatively—it's still about 55 billion kilometers away at its closest point to Earth."

"Seriously? How long does it take a spaceship to get there, do you know?"

"Yeah, it's about six months, and that's going at 25,000 miles an hour. Of course, we don't know how fast the Seeker pods are traveling. And we don't know how long the Seekers can stay in a sort of suspended animation state—maybe years and years, who knows? I mean, look at those seeds they find in glacial ice that have been frozen for centuries, but still germinate under the right conditions. That blows me away. Still, if those Seekers really are traveling through space in radiation-proof cocoons, there's got to be an outside limit to how far they can come from. I wonder what percentage actually make it," James said speculatively. "If I knew, that might help us figure how far they've traveled."

Danny smiled as the waitress set the beers down. "You're a life saver, Julie. We need these. We're wrestling with some big issues here."

James shuffled papers. "OK, next one, Jupiter. Huge. A thousand Earths would fit inside it. It has a lot of moons—sixty-three, actually. Io is its only known moon with active volcanoes."

"Yeah, I've heard that the moons of Jupiter are possible for early life forms."

"That's right. Jupiter itself is basically a storm-ridden gas giant. It's Jupiter's moons we're interested in. Europa is intriguing, and it's considered the best bet for life to exist. It's covered in ice, and may have liquid water underneath that, maybe even a salty ocean. The fact that the surface remains relatively smooth, despite probable impacts from craters, suggests that there is liquid beneath the surface that flows into cracks. Did you see that IMAX film James Cameron did, *Aliens of the Deep*?"

"No."

"You should've, it was so cool. He imagined whole alien cities in the oceans on Europa, and complex creatures that humans only discover when they send a probe through the ice layer. It was an amazing movie. Anyway, I don't suppose it's going to turn out like James Cameron's fantasy, but who knows what might be living in that water, if there is water there?

"Then there's Ganymede—the largest moon in the solar system, bigger than Mercury. It's got a metallic core, liquid iron, and it has a magnetic field. It's got ice and liquid water—in fact, the internal oceans may have more water than all of Earth's oceans. It probably has a thin oxygen atmosphere." James scanned the paper. "It's pretty intriguing, actually. It all may come together into the right conditions for life. Its large subsurface salty ocean might be warm enough, being closer to the molten core. And since there are layers of rock in the interior that would come in contact with the water, the chemicals produced enhance the chances of life forming.

"The biggest issue with Jupiter's moons, or any other place we're considering that has subsurface water as the potential life habitat, is that you need an energy source. Ours is obviously the sun. Sunlight sustains all of life on Earth. Of course, things like tidal motion also generate energy, so that's the most likely source for them."

"If there's no light, how would the Seekers see the colors and the patterns they use to communicate with?"

"Excellent point. It would have to be internally generated—maybe some kind of bioluminescence. Unless there's some kind of light source that we just don't have on Earth and haven't even conceived of."

"And with Jupiter, you're getting pretty far out now, right?" Danny asked. "I mean, distance-wise."

"Yeah, it took Voyager twelve years to get there."

James sipped his beer and flipped a page. "OK, going even further out, on to Saturn. Saturn turns out to be pretty interesting, besides being beautiful. That's the planet most of the kids chose."

"Saturn's gorgeous."

"True. The rings are amazing. They're only half a mile thick, but they extend 200,000 miles from Saturn. It was funny, in Kendra's report on Saturn, she said, 'The rings are like the grooves on a phonograph record.' Then she felt the need to define phonograph record, since she apparently didn't know what it was."

Danny laughed. "Did she say it was an obsolete music transmission method now found mostly at garage sales and hipsters' apartments?"

"Yeah, something like that. Anyway, one interesting thing about the brightest ring, called the B ring, is that it gives off these crackling discharges of electricity that are at least a thousand times more powerful than lightning on Earth."

"Meaning...?"

"I'm getting to that." James scanned the paper he was holding. "Here it is. Saturn has some interesting moons, too. Titan is the second-largest moon in the solar system. Its atmosphere is nitrogen and methane. Molecules of these gases are bombarded by charged particles from Saturn's magnetic field. So that causes them to break up and combine into new molecules that settle onto Titan's surface. Get this—and I quote from Ian Taylor: 'They are the kinds of molecules that may have given rise to life on Earth. The Huygens probe showed possible methane rivers that some scientists think might harbor one-celled organisms, which might have been created when lightning or another heat source hit the rich organic stew percolating on Titan millions of years ago.' Our Seekers, of course, are not primitive life forms. Still, Titan is very interesting. However, Titan's surface is about three hundred degrees below zero."

"But we know the Seekers don't mind a little cold." Danny laughed. "Hey, maybe that's why the Seekers came to you here in Minnesota in the first place. Like the Scandinavians coming to this God-forsaken frozen wilderness in the pioneer days. It reminded them of home."

James smiled. "Oh, here's another interesting thing. Voyager picked up strange pinging noises from Saturn when it flew by."

"So, the Seekers were partying when our satellite flew by. Not smart of them."

"Now here's an exciting one. Have you heard of the moon called Enceladus?"

"No."

"You will. It's pretty small, 500 kilometers in diameter, but it could be huge in the study of astrobiology. The Cassini spacecraft discovered water-rich geysers erupting at its south pole. Plus, it found escaping internal heat, probably due to tidal activity. They speculate that huge salt-water oceans may lie beneath the icy surface. My student, Jeffrey Williams, was pretty excited to report that Wikipedia calls it an excellent possibility for harboring extraterrestrial life. NASA's going to be studying it pretty closely in the next few years, so if the Seekers are there, they better watch out."

"Ok, I'm intrigued," Danny said. "Write down how you spell that for me. I want to look up more stuff on that."

James wrote "ENCELADUS" on a napkin and passed it over to Danny. "So anyway, the next planet is Uranus. I believe every student who chose that planet did so solely based on being able to say its name in front of the class when they gave their reports. Nothing much here."

Danny laughed. "Oh, let me say it anyway, before you move on. Did you find anything of interest in Uranus?"

"Once a class clown, always a class clown."

"I beg your pardon. Now I'm the office clown. It says so on my nameplate."

"Yeah, well I'm glad you're getting the recognition you so richly deserve. Anyway, moving on to Neptune. Voyager reached Neptune in the summer of '89. Neptune's way out there. It takes 165 Earth years to go around the sun. It's a gorgeous planet, all blue. It's the last of the gas giants, made up of hydrogen, helium and methane. Who knows? Maybe that's exactly the elements life on Neptune needs. Oddly, even though Neptune is a billion miles farther from the sun, it's as warm as Uranus." James gave Danny a look and pointed his finger at him as Danny was opening his mouth. "No comments."

Danny shrugged in acquiescence. "Who me?" he said innocently, sipping his beer. "You're the one who wants to talk about how warm Uranus is."

"Let's just finish this up. It's still minus 266 in the upper atmosphere of Neptune, but it generates its own heat, unlike... uh, the seventh planet. Strongest winds in the solar system, some fifteen hundred miles per hour. Big storms. Can't see through the clouds, so who knows what's going on under them?"

"You know what you should do? The next time they contact you, say something like 'we know you're from Saturn' and see if you get a reaction. Surprise them."

"Yeah, sure, that'll work. I don't know, I think Neptune is too far away for them to be able to travel from. I just don't see how any of those alien chrysalises would survive that long of a trip through space. But of course, just 'cause the Seekers' mythology tells them that God sends them to Earth and protects them on their journey, that doesn't mean that's actually how it happens. They may still come here through some kind of weird dimensional shift or some way I can't even conceive of. I don't want to rule out anything yet."

Danny picked up the last fry on the plate between them and popped it in his mouth. "Hey, why don't you email me these notes so I can think them over? Maybe some brilliant insight will suddenly hit me."

"Sounds good. I wanna get a different point of view. The smart-ass office clown point of view."

"I wonder if the Seekers have group-consciousness clowns? 'Hey, guys, check this,' and it throws out ultraviolet and infrared in the same transmission."

"Well, they haven't struck me as the funniest of creatures so far. But then, destruction of the world isn't exactly the best topic for comedy."

Danny stood up. "I'm gonna hit the head."

James turned his attention to the news running on the TV behind the bar. The sound was turned down, but the pictures were bad enough. American soldiers patrolling the streets of Luanda. The bloody aftermath of a car bomb explosion. Citizens being rounded up. It looked like the Angolan government might be using this as an excuse to come down hard on its own dissidents.

As Danny returned to the table and sat down opposite him, James gestured at the TV. "So, where's the world-wide outcry? I mean, when we went into Iraq, there were protests all over. When we were maybe going to go against China a few months ago, the whole world was watching and praying for peace. I don't see people hitting the streets in England about this."

"I hate to say it, my friend, but no one cares about Africa. Remember Rwanda? Darfur? Etcetera, etcetera. And Scofield knows that."

"Yeah, you're right, and it pisses me off."

"I'll tell you one thing. It's Angola now, but this is going to spread to other African countries. Eddie's got a great ally in big American business. This is the opportunity they've been waiting for. Vast natural resources combined with cheap labor, and corrupt heads of state on the take, willing to look the other way as long as their palaces keep going up. It's a CEO's wet dream."

"I hate to say it, but I have to agree. What my student said about the rumors that the CIA paid those guys to bomb our own embassy? I wouldn't doubt it. There was a good letter to the editor in the paper yesterday asking how our military could have responded that quickly unless we knew about it ahead of time."

Danny pulled out his phone. "Hang on," he said, punching buttons and scrolling. "I gotta tell you what my buddy Louie posted on Facebook. There's a whole page for this, and it's already got 20,000 followers. Apparently, someone from inside the CIA claims there were memos about the terrorist attack from back in January, way before it happened."

"Seriously?"

"Exactly. It's the smoking gun."

"It's some blogger's cap gun that's smoking, that's all. They'll never be able to prove that. Do you know what Scofield's approval rating is? Something like seventy-four percent."

"Yeah," Danny agreed, "Howard's getting a free ride now. You saw what happened when that reporter asked him if the U.S. response in Angola was too extreme. He ripped into him big time, called him treasonous for giving aid and comfort to the enemy, and the hell if he was going to let that reporter or anyone else criticize him for defending our country. You saw how Congress rolled over on the Military Mobilization shit. It's an election year. You vote against that, you might as well write the ad for your opponent charging you with handing the country over to terrorists."

"What the hell can possibly derail this administration? I think Scofield's too old to get caught with his pants down."

"No man is too old to have a hot babe on the side, not if he's powerful enough."

"True, but I can't count on blind luck, or a chatty side piece, bringing him down."

"Should I give you the old, 'it's always darkest before the dawn' pep talk? I guess it's good to know what you're up against. Which in this case is ultimate power combined with stone cold ruthless evil incarnate."

"If that's your idea of a pep talk, you better never volunteer to coach one of Stewart's Little League teams. How is a schlub from Minnesota, as you once put it, going to come up with anything to combat that?"

"That's why you've got me." Danny raised his glass and clinked it against James's. "We're on to him, but he doesn't know we're on to him. Between the two of us, we'll come up with something. Hell, I'd much rather work on Project Stop Eddie Olson at the office than the Orion project. I mean, help businesses track sales of their widgets online, or save the world? Priorities, my friend, priorities."

"So, what do you suggest I ask the Seekers this time? If I can manage to keep it in mind when I'm sleeping, that is."

"We've really got to find out what Eddie's weaknesses are. Ask them to tell you everything they can about their deviant ones."

"That should be a delightful experience," James said sardonically. "If it causes me to have a mental breakdown, get me a room at the nicest insane asylum, will you? I want satin padded walls."

CHAPTER 15

James was ready for them this time. Every night before he went to sleep, he put on headphones and played a recording that said the same thing over and over: "Tell me everything you can about your deviant ones."

He told Emily it was a relaxation device. He still hadn't been able to bring himself to tell her about the alien encounters, and the longer it went on, the harder it got. Part of him hoped he could take care of the problem and then tell her about his heroics afterwards. Why worry her now?

The aliens were true to their word. Just after midnight, they entered his mind.

The pictures they showed him were disturbing. The Evil One was getting stronger, larger and more powerful. The toxic energy flowing from it radiated further, engulfing hundreds of living creatures, who succumbed in agony.

This time, James remembered what he needed to know. Tell me everything you can about your deviant ones. He pictured the Evil One here on Earth, as they showed it, and then moved it mentally backward through space to its own planet. He imagined a generic rocky planet filled with Seekers, colors shimmering and moving on their white flowing bodies. He pictured the Evil One moving among them, radiating malevolent energy in the way they'd represented it in his mind. How? Why?

The Seeker responded with visuals showing the Evil One on Earth again, growing larger and more powerful until it enveloped the entire planet with its slimy mess. James burst out in frustrated thought: No, that's not what I was asking! I know it's bad on Earth. How did it get that way? How does it operate? Why is it so evil?

He felt the Seeker who was connected to him pause, waiting for him to try again. Maybe it at least got the idea that he wanted to ask something else. He tried to calm his mind, to think of another way to ask the question.

James pictured the Seeker planet again. This time he decided to make the Seekers' environment a watery one. He pictured them swimming, flowing through the water gracefully. Then he pictured one of them going bad, turning into the Evil One. Why do they become evil?

In response, he felt a negative reaction in his mind, and then heard the word *No*. Were the Seekers learning how to translate into his own language some simple words and concepts, or was his own brain learning how to interpret what they were conveying and send it through the language center of his brain?

So, were they saying no, the deviant ones don't become evil after they become adults? Or were they just saying no, we're not going to tell you what you want to know? Well, he'd try again. This time, he pictured the aliens again in the watery world, and then pictured a tiny egg-like spot, which grew larger and larger until it was clearly a young deviant Seeker among the others. Are the deviant ones born that way?

And they responded affirmatively.

Then they showed him something he didn't expect, something more. They showed a tiny deviant Seeker, newly born, one among hundreds of normal Seekers. The group moved away from it and left it on its own. He watched it die.

Why? Why?

They showed him a small deviant one more closely. Now he could see that when the other Seekers around it displayed colors over their bodies, the little deviant one did not respond. It remained white and didn't move at all. Then he saw the Seekers release chemicals, the scents, portrayed as a murky cloud coming from their bodies and filling the water. Again, the baby Seeker did not respond. The Seekers moved away and left the baby to die.

It hit James with a shock. The deviance of the evil Seekers is simply a birth defect. They're born blind. They can't smell anything. Which means they're cut off from the group, they can't communicate. So, they abandon their genetically defective young?

James felt sick.

But he had to press on. He knew there wasn't much time before the pull of the Portal would become too strong and the Seeker would leave his mind.

He pictured a dead deviant infant, and then pictured it being encased in a chrysalis, lifting off the planet, and arriving at Earth. He pictured again the destructiveness of the Evil One. How? If they all die, how can they get here to Earth and do all that damage?

Again, he felt the negative response, and heard *No*.

The Seeker created a picture in his mind of about a hundred small deviant ones, and then made them all disappear, except one. It showed that one at the fringes of the group of normal Seekers, growing larger, and growing more distorted. It seemed to move about aimlessly, as it would if it couldn't see. It happened upon something that looked like a plant and flowed over it. When it moved on, the plant was gone. It must have eaten it. OK, James thought. Some defective young Seekers survive by chance.

The mental pictures continued. The young deviant Seeker, in its random movements, came to the edge of a large group of normal Seekers. James watched a colorful juvenile Seeker stray away from the group. The deviant one encountered it. As James watched, horrified, the deviant Seeker engulfed it with its flowing body, apparently eating it.

And you let them come here and attack us? James screamed at the Seeker in his head.

Maybe the Seeker sensed his outrage, because James's mind was filled with an overwhelming feeling of sorrow as the alien continued. Was it trying to say it was sorry? He could sense that the alien wanted to break the connection, that it was in distress and wanted to leave. He had to hurry.

James couldn't think of how to show the most important question he had to ask in mental pictures. All he could do was think the words, hoping the alien would sense his urgency and wait. I need your help, so I can know what I'm fighting against. Can you tell me any weaknesses this deviant one would have?

He tried picturing the evil Seeker trapped in Scofield's body. He pictured himself standing near him, but very small, to show that the President was powerful, and James not. He pictured himself stretching out a hand and plucking the deviant Seeker from Scofield's head. How? How?

Then, overcome with frustration at having to think of complicated concepts in simple pictures, James's mind filled with the words he wanted to say: You don't understand! We're not like you! All human beings are alone. We are born alone, we die alone. We keep our thoughts separate from each other, locked in our own minds. Your Deviant One is trapped in the body of a species that functions very well as separate individuals. It's been made stronger now!

Maybe the Seeker picked up on the meaning of the words that had exploded with such intensity in his brain. James could sense the Seeker's exhaustion; it seemed to be straining to hold the connection. He could almost feel it drawing from its final reserve of energy as it tried to respond.

James saw again the picture of the deviant one separate and isolated from the large group of colorful Seekers. He could feel the pain of the isolation. Then, the picture morphed into a human scene, the Seekers replaced by a group of humans. They showed what James had pictured: the deviant one pulsing in Scofield's brain. Scofield stood apart from the other human beings, isolated. And there stood James in the middle of the group of people, as their faces transformed into everyone he knew and cared about: family, friends, co-workers, students, church members, neighbors. A glowing, shimmering aura of Life Force surrounded each person. And all those auras were flowing together, melding into an incredibly strong, vibrant Life Force that swirled around James.

James felt a deep sense of peace come over him. The alien released the connection and pulled away from his mind. James's eyes opened slowly.

He pulled the headphones off and placed them on the bedside table. He smelled something beautiful, like sweet flowers laced with oak wood chips, and something else, a scent he didn't know. An amazing feeling of unity with other human beings filled him, as though the alien had left in his mind an impression of what it was like for them, connected always to each other. He looked at the window and was momentarily surprised by the strong light coming through a gap in the curtains, until he remembered there was a full moon.

He turned over. In the glow of the moonlight coming through the window, Emily's beautiful face looked radiant. He put his arm over her, moving close and pressing his body against hers, offering warmth to offset the cold the Seeker had left behind.

Emily's eyes opened gently. She did not seem at all surprised to find herself awake. She looked deeply into James's eyes with complete accepting love. Without a word, she began stroking his face, his arms, his chest. Slowly, tenderly, he moved his fingers through her long silky hair; softly, he traced her ears, her eyes, her nose, her mouth with one finger. Then, stunningly, he literally felt spiritual energy flowing between them, like a low-level electrical current.

They made love as if they were one person that night, in total harmony with each other, without one word being spoken. It was the most incredibly complete sexual experience James had ever had in his life.

As they drifted back to sleep in each other's arms, a fleeting thought of gratitude toward the Seekers crossed James's mind. Whatever else happened from here on out, at least he had experienced this one divine moment of pure perfect love.

James's last thought before unconsciousness took him was: I'll tell Emily about the Seekers tomorrow.

CHAPTER 16

How long could the principal drone on? This staff meeting must have been going on for over forty-five minutes, and they were only on item three on the agenda. James drained the last of the weak coffee in his paper cup and got up to put another buck in the vending machine. It still galled him that the last round of budget cuts had taken away the free coffee in the teachers' lounge.

He sat back down and tried to focus on the words flowing out of the principal's mouth like the endless Mississippi. But his mind drifted back to the incredible sexual experience of the night before, and he relived it mentally again. He wondered if Emily had been under the influence of the aliens somehow, if that scent had done something to her. He wondered if she, too, had physically felt that flow of psychic energy between their bodies.

Then he tried to figure out how he was going to tell her about the alien encounters that had been going on for the last six months in their bedroom. That would be tricky. Maybe he better make reservations at her favorite restaurant for tonight. He picked up his phone. But first he texted Danny: "Finally going to tell Emily tonight. Wish me luck."

James was brought back to reality by the collective groan coming from the assembled teachers. He heard the principal say, "...so we're asking you to spend the next two weeks teaching to the Ten Competencies tests which students must now pass in order to graduate. For example, you foreign language teachers should be working on the Appreciation of Different Cultures Competency. Each department will be receiving specific instructions on which of the ten tests they will be preparing the students for. Attached to this agenda is a schedule of departmental meetings to cover in depth the preparations for and requirements of the new tests. Admittedly, you may have to put aside your planned course of instruction, but this has to come first. You'll just have to squeeze the rest in as you can. Our job—the job the taxpayers are paying us to do—is simply to get these kids out the door with a diploma in hand. Everything else is gravy."

Great. Just great. James started mentally figuring which part of his second semester lesson plans could be chucked so he could waste his own and his students' time preparing for another test mandated by legislators who wanted to look like they were doing something for education.

"Now, moving on to the top of page two, Lunchroom Monitoring Duty. Yes, I know this isn't any teacher's favorite part of the day. Budget cuts leave us no choice. What I need to discuss today is that it has come to my attention that some of you are using this time to eat your own personal lunch. You are required to take your lunch break at your designated time."

James grimaced. This was aimed at him. He'd decided if he had to be in the lunchroom with the kids, he might as well eat his lunch with them and get to know them a little better. In fact, it was working out surprisingly well. The kids seemed to actually enjoy eating with him and conversing on an informal level. And he had no trouble keeping an eye and ear on what was happening in the cafeteria. Was there no end to bureaucratic stupidity?

The principal continued. "Next item: the band trip to Washington, D.C." He turned to a frumpy, heavyset woman sitting near the front of the room. "Bobbie, you had something you needed to bring to the group?"

Bobbie Murrow, the band director, stood up. Lord, this would add fifteen minutes to the meeting.

"Thank you, Don. Yes, things are fairly well in order. The

students will only have to miss one day of school, since our plane leaves at 11:30 on Friday morning before spring break. Students should be bringing you the blue form for making up homework, or the green form for taking tests early, should you have a test scheduled on that Friday, although I'd say that tests would be better given on that Thursday. Now, the one thing I did need to bring to this group is that we find ourselves unexpectedly looking for another chaperone, since Betty Peters is unable to accompany us, due to the sudden illness of her mother."

James's wandering mind lurched to attention. What had she said? They were looking for someone to go to Washington, D.C.?

Bobbie continued. "I realize that this is kind of last minute. But to entice you, let me say that your expenses will be paid, since we had an exceptionally strong fundraising effort from the band booster parents this year." Bobbie clapped her hands in appreciation; a smattering of teachers joined in the applause. "And, you will have the delightful opportunity to get to know these students better—especially at two a.m. when you're knocking on their hotel room door to tell them to be quiet. Ha, ha." A few teachers smiled half-heartedly.

"The highlight this year is that the band will be playing a short concert at the White House. Of course, you know that Vice President Cambridge attended Westfield High thirty-two years ago, where he was already a rising political star, being class President. I must admit, I am one who was here at that time. I know you may find it hard to believe that I go back that far. Ha, ha. Regrettably, he didn't play in the band. Nonetheless, the tour company has arranged with the White House for Vice President Cambridge to listen to our little concert, and to pose for a photo with the band afterward. I'm sure this will be a nice public relations opportunity for him. And it will certainly be a thrilling experience for our boys and girls. Especially if..." Bobbie lowered her voice dramatically. "Well, there's a possibility the President himself may attend our performance. Of course, it will depend on events of the day. But if he's available, I've been informed that he may well accompany Mr. Cambridge." She chuckled conspiratorially. "Perhaps he's seen his poll numbers in Minnesota. A nice photo on the front page of the Star Tribune might do their campaign some good. Especially if I can persuade President Scofield to make a statement supporting music education in the public schools." Bobbie sighed. "Well, I mustn't get ahead of myself."

James was stunned. My God. This has to be it! The Way, as he always thought of the events leading to his ultimate confrontation with Eddie Olson. James's hand shot up in the air.

Mason Briggs, the IB English teacher, yelled out from the back. "What're you going to play, Bobbie? The Westfield High Fight Song? Maybe they could use it to rouse up our military to fight all these supposed enemies we have!"

A few teachers laughed, but Bobbie pursed her lips in disapproval.

"No, I believe we will play a nice patriotic song, such as 'God Bless America'. So anyway, why don't you go home and talk to your spouses and get back to me by Monday, let's say, if you think you might be able to do it. Yes, James? Did you have a question?"

"No. I want to volunteer. I'd be happy to go with the band on their spring trip."

"Really? Are you sure? You don't want to talk to your wife first?"

"No. Put me down. I've always wanted to go to the White House."

CHAPTER 17

Danny intercepted James as he walked into Garraty's. "I've got the back booth today. We need privacy."

James regarded Danny suspiciously. "What's going on?"

"Just get your beer and get back there."

James reached out and flipped Danny's tie, which today featured a hand-painted Marilyn Monroe with her skirt flying up. "You know, if you want to be inconspicuous, you should try wearing more normal ties."

"Check it out." Danny pushed a little button on the back of the tie, and the sound of Marilyn's breathy voice singing "Let Me Entertain You" issued from it.

"That's a beauty, Friedman."

"Whoa," James said as he slid into the booth with his beer and regarded the huge basket of onion rings, French fries and deep-fried mushrooms on the table. "You got the Happy Hour Heart Attack Special?"

Danny picked up a giant onion ring. "According to your Seeker buddies, we're all gonna die anyway, so we might as well enjoy it."

"Don't tell Emily I'm eating these," James said as he popped one in his mouth and chewed with satisfaction.

"Speaking of, I guess you didn't tell Emily after all, huh?"

"I really was going to. Then this band trip thing came up before I had a chance. That kind of changes everything."

Danny eyes lit up with barely contained excitement. "Can you believe it? Those Seekers kept bugging you, telling you you're the one, and it looks like they were right! Man, it's like you've got this destiny to save the world. So, if you're like Luke Skywalker, I guess that makes me Han Solo."

"Why do you get to be the dashing rebel sexy guy?"

"You can't fight destiny, kid."

"Yeah, well, anyway, we're not talking about 'A long time ago in a galaxy far, far away.' We're talking about here and now."

"Unfortunately," Danny said, instantly sobering. "My nephew's on a troop carrier headed to Angola right now. My sister's going nuts, she's so scared for him. Before he left, he told me he'd been trained to use this new chemical weapon the army's developed to subdue civilians. It knocks people out and gives about 50 percent of them convulsions. He said they figure it's easier to subdue large portions of the populace and then work out who's armed and dangerous and who's friendly than to wait and see who shoots at you. But the catch is they don't know the long-term effects of this new chemical—I think he called it SBC14—on the human body. And apparently they don't much care."

"Oh my God."

"Poor Ruth. Evan was kind of a screw-up in high school, so she urged him to join the army, thinking it would straighten him out. Now she feels like she's sent him to his death."

"I suppose you've heard the latest?" James said. "I've been checking that 'Scofield Truth Probe' page. They're saying that Scofield green-lighted a secret project to develop new, worse biological weapons. AIDS and Ebola weren't devastating Africa enough, I guess. Which I wouldn't have believed six months ago, but now... well, you and I know what's really driving it. Eddie Olson's goal is to wipe out as many humans as possible, apparently. If he's figured out a way to unleash an uncontrollable deadly virus on the world, we're screwed."

Danny smashed his fist on the table in anger. "It just totally pisses me off, the way those alien bastards let their psychotic sociopathic nut-jobs come here and mess us up. But then, what would you expect from a species that practices infanticide? Too bad Eddie didn't die like he was supposed to."

"I've been thinking about that. I mean, yeah, it's horrible that they leave their disabled infants to die. But honestly, Danny, my sense is that they have a morally-ordered society—just different from ours. They're sophisticated enough to have a concept of God, right? And every single religion on Earth has a code of right and wrong. Why wouldn't they? Maybe in their view, it would be cruel to let a child live who can't communicate with the others of its group. For a group-oriented species, a life of isolation might seem worse than death. Maybe they believe Tornado God will take it through the Portal immediately, or maybe they believe it will be reborn into a seeing body. Who knows? Maybe they're a fatalistic society. What will be, will be. If it dies, it dies. If it lives, it lives.

"When they showed me what happens with the occasional deviant ones that survive, and I saw one eating a young Seeker that had strayed away from the group..." James shuddered. "That was creepy. I've been wondering if they showed me that specifically for a reason. I wonder if they were telling me that the few deviant ones who manage to absorb a normal Seeker are the ones who are then able to make the trip to the Portal, you know, because of what they take into their bodies from that normal one. Maybe they believe those few are blessed by the Tornado God to have a second chance. I don't know. I could speculate all day. I often do, in fact. It's really interesting to try to figure out these creatures."

James took a long drink, thinking about these aliens that had so captivated his science-loving heart. "Besides, I don't think any one individual matters as much in a group-consciousness society.

"Anyway," James added, "I don't know that we really have the moral high ground to stand on. Our species has perfected the art of torture, among other delights. So, I put it to you: what's worse— passive evil, just letting it happen, or active evil, doing it on purpose?"

Danny took a long pull on his beer, thinking. "They're both equally wrong. The people who just stood by and did nothing when the Holocaust happened are equally as guilty as the Nazis. If there's a hell, they're all burning together."

"Yeah, you're right. Which is why I can't just stand by and let Eddie Olson, in the person of Howard Scofield, get away with it. Knowing what I know, I have no choice."

"Good man," Danny said approvingly, sticking out his hand to bump fists.

"I just wish I knew how," James said with a grim look on his face. "Spring break's in three weeks. I've got three weeks to figure out a way to stop the most powerful person on Earth from destroying us all."

Danny grinned back at him and pulled several large, colorful pieces of paper out of his briefcase. "Don't worry, kid. You've got Han Solo backing you up. I've been thinking about this a lot since you called about the band trip. I've come up with several ideas, each of which has plusses and minuses. Look, I have charts on the likelihood of success, degree of danger, and ease of implementation for each scenario. Plus, it's all color-coded."

James picked up the top paper and read from it. "Plan A. Hide tiny knife inside phone case. Stab prez in jugular when shaking his hand." He looked at Danny incredulously. "Are you insane?"

"Well, if you look on the chart, you'll see I did rate that a two out of ten on ease of implementation."

"I'd hate to see what you rated a one."

"This is called brainstorming, man," Danny said defensively. "It's part of the CPS process—that means, Creative Problem Solving. We had a whole workshop on this at the office one day. You generate a lot of ideas, and no idea is a bad idea at the beginning of the process. The more the better. I didn't want to throw away any ideas yet, because you never know. You might be able to build on something I thought of that seemed too difficult and figure out a way to make it work."

"I know what brainstorming is, Danny. When Danielle does brainstorming with her Destination Imagination team, to try to figure out how to make an obstacle course for eggs, then no idea is a bad idea. When you're trying to figure out how to stop the leader of the free world from destroying said world, then some ideas are clearly bad ideas. That's a way bad idea."

"Yeah, you're right," Danny admitted. "I should have hit the delete button on that one."

James looked at Danny with alarm. "You don't have this on your computer at work, do you? You shouldn't have this saved on any computer, but you especially shouldn't have this saved on your computer at work."

"After I printed this out, I deleted the whole file."

"Well, you'd better figure out how to delete it off whatever backup files there are, too." James shoved the papers across the table toward Danny, suddenly feeling totally pissed off. "This isn't a game, you know."

James needed to calm his nerves. He stood up and said, "I'm gonna go use the head," and walked abruptly away.

This was crazy. He'd just had a conversation about assassinating the President of the United States. This couldn't be real. This couldn't be happening. He was James Thompson—husband, father, teacher. He was a nice guy. He didn't even like having to kill the mice which came into his house every fall, little creatures trying desperately to survive the winter like everyone else. When he was a kid, he'd constructed a little wooden box with a gangplank to capture the spiders in his house, which he released in his mother's flower garden. And he was supposed to kill someone? Those Seekers had made a terrible mistake. He couldn't do it.

He didn't think he could even go back to that booth to continue this conversation. He pushed open the bathroom door. His attention was caught by some graffiti scrawled on the wall above the urinal: "The Race War is here! All Proud White Men—be prepared! www.purewhitepeopleunite.com." Below it was the angry reply: "Shut up, you fucking white racist asshole!"

James's mind was reeling. This was getting personal, and scary.

James glanced around the tavern as he exited the bathroom, wondering if any of the normal-looking guys sitting here had written that call to arms for racial genocide.

"Hey, Michael," he called to the owner at the other end of the bar.

"Hi, James." Michael Garraty's broad face lit up with a smile of recognition. "How ya doin'?"

"Fine, more or less. But you've got some nasty racist graffiti in your bathroom. Thought you'd want to know."

Michael picked up a rag from under the bar. "Goddamn idiots," he said angrily. "I find out who's been doing this, I kick 'em outta here for good, I promise you." He stalked off to the bathroom.

White racist organizations seemed to be gaining power every day now. How soon till they were accorded legitimacy by the media as another valid viewpoint on the war on terror? How soon till they were coming after him, or his children? Was it going to come down to this for him: kill the President or see his children killed?

He was profoundly depressed as he slid into the booth across from Danny.

Danny reached over and put his hand sympathetically on James's arm. "Look, I'm not insensitive, despite what everyone thinks. I'm very, very sorry this has fallen on you. It's not fair, it's shitty, it's crazy. I understand that we're talking about something that is completely unthinkable."

"That's an understatement."

Danny looked intently at James. "Here's the way I see this. You know that question kids in college always ask each other when they're hanging around their dorm rooms late at night and feeling all philosophical? If you were alone with Hitler in a room, knowing what you know today, and you had a chance to kill him—would you?"

"Yeah. Everybody thinks they're the first ones to think of that question."

"Well, not everybody gets a chance to answer it for real. You do. You said it yourself. You're like those clergymen in Germany, right? I'm pretty sure there were some religious people who tried to assassinate Hitler, for the greater good. Of course, it's your call ultimately."

James drank half the beer before he finally spoke. "OK, what else you got on your fancy color-coded charts?"

Danny nodded. "How about hitting Eddie with a deadly, fast-acting disease, like that Ebola virus? It would be pretty ironic, knocking off Eddie Olson with a biological weapon."

"What, you have a source for the Ebola virus?"

"They're researching it at the U. I know a guy. All we have to do is figure out how you can safely carry it and transmit it to him. The beauty of this plan, as you can see on the chart, is that it has the maximum possibility of you surviving. If you can give him the Ebola virus without him knowing you're doing it, you're home safe and no one knows how he got it."

"I like the part about me surviving." James shuddered.

"Dude, I'm not sitting here alone at Garraty's for the next thirty years, crying in my beer."

"Still, we better forget that one. I'm not messing around with deadly incurable viruses. Not with students around."

"All right, we'll table it for now. Maybe we could figure out how to protect the kids. Next, Plan C. Maybe we can get him when you're touring the White House. This has the advantage of targeting Scofield even if he doesn't attend the band concert. So, you get the band kids to create a diversion. You slip off, go to Scofield's aide's office or something, and tell them you're an old friend of the veep's brother, and you're a big admirer of the prez, and you want to give him a little gift."

"What's the gift?"

"Poisoned candy."

"What's this, 'Snow White'? How'd you rate that on probability of success? I'm thinking there are too many unknowns. Would they test the candy first?"

"Maybe not, since you're just a teacher from Cambridge's hometown. Why would they suspect you?"

"These days, security's tighter than ever. But even if they didn't test it, who's to say he'd eat it? Does he like candy? Would the aide just keep the candy and pass it around to the staff? What'd you rate that one?"

Danny consulted his charts. "I rated that one a six on probability of success, but I think I'd better drop it down to a three."

"Are these in any order here?"

"No, just as they came to me."

"So why don't you give me your best shot?"

Danny looked over the charts. "OK, Plan G. This one gets a total of 24 points. It gets a nine for likelihood of success."

"OK, fire away, Han. But if this involves me flying down some White House heating shaft and relying on The Force, I'm outta here."

Danny smiled. "No, it's simple. When they take the publicity photo with Cambridge and Scofield after the concert, you make sure you stand right next to him. You have a small hypodermic hidden in your pocket."

"What's in it?"

"Snake venom. Specifically, the venom of the extremely deadly Asian Cobra. It'll paralyze his muscles, inducing a heart attack. The guy's ancient. No one will be surprised if his heart gives out."

"And you have a source for this?"

"Actually, yeah. You'd be surprised what you can get on the Internet if you follow enough links. It turns out there's a black market for deadly snake venom from Thailand. It wouldn't be easy, and it would be expensive. But I think it can be done."

"Good Lord, Danny. You are truly a man of hidden talents."

"Thank you. If we want to do it, though, we gotta move fast. It'll take a little time. But the beauty is, you can kill Scofield without anyone remotely suspecting you."

"Hey, Danny, can you do me a favor? It's hard enough thinking about myself as the Lee Harvey Oswald of our time. Could you refer to it as 'destroying Eddie' rather than 'killing President Scofield'? For one thing, you know we'd get turned in to Homeland Security in a New York minute if anyone overheard us. But mostly, I think the only way I can go through with this is if I stay focused on the point of this whole thing, which is saving the planet from Eddie Olson."

"Good call."

James downed the last of his beer. Danny signaled the waitress. "Second round's on me this time, amigo."

Danny finished off the last of the mushrooms and said, "Did you watch the Duke/Wisconsin game last night?"

"That was killer! I got the Devils all the way. Marques Jones is a sure lottery pick; I'm thinking number one. He's got moves they haven't seen yet in the NBA."

"Yeah, he's pro, but they've got no bench. It's gonna be Michigan State and Kansas. How'd you do on your bracket last night?"

"I only got one game wrong, chump, that one 15 vs. 2 upset that everyone missed. Shoulda known Syracuse would blow it, though. They always do. I picked Gonzaga to take out Arizona, and Baylor to upset North Carolina, so yeah, I'm golden. You're gonna owe me big time."

"Yeah, I'm quaking in my boots over here."

James chewed on another handful of fries. "Man, if I didn't have March Madness to distract me, I'd be suicidal. Good thing the Gophers are still in it."

"Not after tomorrow, they won't be. No way they're beating Virginia."

"I beg to differ. Hudson can shoot threes with his eyes closed, falling backwards."

James relaxed, enjoying the diversion. And especially, the support. His best friend had his back, and that meant everything. Finally, ready to go at it again, he said, "Here's how I'm trying to look at it. Scofield is already possessed by an evil alien being. He's not who he was, he's possibly not even totally human anymore. For all I know, killing Eddie would be putting him out of his misery."

"Excellent. So, should I go ahead and get the snake venom, then?"

James took a big breath. "Yeah. Do it. And hey... Listen, if anything happens to me... if I don't make it... you'll help Emily, right?"

"Yeah, of course. But don't even talk like that. You're gonna make it."

As he drank his second beer, James tried to think about anything else. It wasn't working. He slammed down the last of the beer and stood up. "I've had enough. I'm heading home. Anyway, I need some fresh air. I feel like I'm suffocating here. I gotta clear my head."

Danny stood up and slipped on his Italian leather overcoat. James put on his puffy down ski jacket and headed toward the door, while Danny was stuffing the papers back in his briefcase. Danny caught up to James outside, and they walked toward the parking ramp at the end of the block.

"Damn, it's cold." James pulled his knit cap over his ears. The March wind was blowing fiercely, bending the bare branches of the trees and scooting little pieces of paper over the icy sidewalks. Piles of dirty snow stood between the sidewalk and the street.

"At least in Washington it'll be warm and sunny," Danny pointed out. "I hate March here. It's worse than winter."

James laughed. "March is winter here, dude. You're still a New Yorker at heart, aren't you? Face it. In Minnesota, spring starts in May, runs for three beautiful weeks, and then we hit mosquito season. Last year I actually went from my furnace to my air conditioner in two days."

"The weather here sucks."

"It's lucky your dad moved your family here in July. If it'd been January, you probably wouldn't have lasted six weeks."

"And then Danielle would be named Geraldine or something, and I wouldn't be masterminding your assault on Eddie."

They were walking past a children's clothing store. James stopped abruptly and looked at his reflection in the window. "You know what I keep thinking about? Can Scofield see what those Seekers see, like that cosmic blanket they show me to represent their future stream sense, you know, like can his inner deviant seeker tap into that future sense, or does he just have normal human senses? I mean, does he know I'm the one who's gonna bring him down?"

"You know what they said about Hitler? His only distinctive feature was his intense, hypnotic eyes. Look Scofield in the eye, and maybe you'll know."

"And if I see Eddie looking back at me, and I know he knows?"

"Then laugh in his face. And make sure you, a human being standing up for your planet, is the last thing he ever sees."

CHAPTER 18

Do I ask them if I die or not? That's what it really came down to.

If the Seekers held to their sixteen-day schedule as promised, they would contact him again before he left for Washington. So, did he want to know, or not? Was it better to find out he was going to die and prepare himself for it, or was it better not to know? Of course, maybe the answer would be good news. Maybe they'd tell him he survives his encounter with the Deviant One. Wouldn't that be a relief? Then he could fly to Washington secure in the knowledge that all would go well, and he would be returning to his family as a victorious hero.

Or he'd be returning to his family in a box. God, how many times could he go back and forth on this?

When he lay down to sleep on the evening of their expected visitation, he still didn't know whether he would ask the Seeker the fateful question.

He was dreaming a strange dream about chickens being pursued by a farmer wielding a gigantic ax, in which he was simultaneously the farmer and several of the chickens. He was both a relentless, unstoppable killing force and a terrified-out-of-their-minds flock of chickens running every which way, and he lifted the enormous ax, and he screamed...

James felt his mind being seized.

Oddly, he felt a sense of relief. Hello.

James felt the alien patiently waiting. For some reason, he felt curious about this particular Seeker. He wondered what it had been told about him. Did each Seeker who contacted him pass along his knowledge to a recently-emerged Seeker, and did that one pass the information along to another—or more probably, to a group of others—before it passed through the Portal, and so on until it was time for the next contact?

He felt a benign sense of calmness and positive acceptance flowing from the waiting Seeker. I think it likes me, he thought with surprise.

But this was wasting time. He remembered the question he was wrestling with and decided right then that he had to know.

James imagined himself standing on the quilt that represented the Seekers' vision of what would happen, their future-stream sense. He pictured himself fighting with the alien-possessed President, using the golden thread as a lasso that wound round and round the evil being until it/he was completely covered. He showed himself victorious, exultantly alive while Scofield and the deviant Seeker within him lay dead at his feet.

But he had to ask it both ways. He forced himself to imagine Scofield dying, but then his own body also collapsing and dying from one last flick of the malignant rays of evil energy radiating from the evil alien. What happens? Do I die or not?

There was a pause. Did they understand him? Would they tell him if they did? Then he saw the quilt floating and saw the malignant splotch that represented the powerful deviant alien. He saw himself as the golden thread move close to it, saw the rays of malevolence shoot out toward him as he confronted it, and thought This is it. Now I will know. He steeled his mind to watch himself die and accept it.

Suddenly James's mind was filled with a symphony of colors flowing, merging, melding, bursting here and there with shots of gold or silver, with a hundred shades of green swirling and dancing around a hundred shades of red, then a hundred shades of blue racing in from the edges of his mind and lifting up the other colors in a geyser of cascading yellows, purples and oranges. Then, somehow, he knew that the strong river of deep copper reds glistening with bronze that flowed in and swirled up and around the geyser, that merged with it and yet remained distinct—was him, James. He was flowing with the river of humanity, and he—they, all together—submerged and subdued the writhing evil oily splotch.

A calm feeling of the rightness of all this filled every cell of his body. It suddenly didn't matter whether he lived or died—he was part of a far greater whole.

He felt the Seeker connecting with his own sense of harmony. And then, amazingly, he heard words in his head: *We go into Portal good happy knowing you human understanding unbreakable connection with the Way and Life Force of this blessed planet.*

James was astounded. Something strange and wonderful and frightening all at the same time was happening. The more these aliens connected with his brain, the easier the connection was becoming. Somehow, they were able to translate their language into his own for a moment, to activate his language processing center correctly. Whether they meant to, or whether it was just happening naturally, that alien just spoke to him in English words. It must have been really important, to have crossed the language barrier.

This blessed planet, it had said. The Life Force. Life. James felt something tug at his mind, something he'd been wondering about for months now. Who wanted to ask about death when he could ask about life? He wanted to know how they made babies.

James visualized himself having sex with Emily, even though a small part of his mind felt reluctant to share this intimate picture with the Seeker. Emily probably wouldn't like it. As he tried to visualize the beginning of human life, he realized with amusement—mixed with astonishment that he could be relaxed enough to find something funny while communicating with an alien being—that he was showing in his head the video he'd shown his ninth grade biology classes, of the sperm traveling up the Fallopian tube and meeting the egg, of fertilization, of the fetus growing in its mother's womb and then being born. He pictured the infant in its loving parents' arms, and then tried to mentally change that into a tiny Seeker with adult

Seekers around it. How? How do you make new life?

Oddly, the response he got was to see himself making love with Emily again, as a feeling of intense pleasure filled him. But not sexual pleasure; it was more a feeling of goodness and spirituality. He felt like the alien was trying to tell him that it was pleased that humans joined their bodies together in this beautiful way and were, at least for a moment, allowed a respite from aloneness.

Well, he was glad they approved, but that didn't answer his question. Maybe they didn't want to tell him, but he decided to try again. He pictured two Seekers, their flowing bodies pressed against each other, and then a tiny Seeker emerging from one. Is that how you reproduce?

There was a pause, a slight disconnect, and then a feeling of acceptance filled him. He had a feeling the Seeker had made the decision to trust him with this sensitive information.

He saw a large community of Seekers, colors moving rapidly over their bodies as they communicated with each other. Then he noticed one whose colors melted into one very unusual color over its whole body, but he couldn't say what the color was. First, he thought steel grayish-blue, and then he thought it was a kind of muddy yellowish-burgundy, and then he realized that it was shimmering and somehow simultaneously many colors. Then he saw another with the same color covering its whole body, and then another. Finally, there were eight Seekers all displaying the identical color, distinctive against the swirling colors of all the other Seekers. They appeared to be attracting each other and coming together.

A feeling of joy permeated his mind as the eight Seekers began glowing, and visible electrical impulses flowed between them. When they were glowing so brightly that he could barely make out their shapes, from each Seeker a small white egg emerged. The eggs converged in the center of the group and then—at the exact moment when the eggs touched each other and stuck together, he felt an ecstatic sensation of fulfillment.

Then it was like the Seeker was showing its alien version of Bio 101. He saw the elongated eggs, each with a different colored glowing center, swirl around each other. Then they floated a bit away from each other and aligned two by two, sticking to each other in pairs, the walls of the egg cells dissolving. The eggs then split across the midline, forming into two new eggs with their glowing centers now half of each color. But it didn't end there. The eggs combined two by two again in new combinations, and when they broke apart again each egg had four colors glowing within it. This happened once more, and now each egg had all eight colors glowing within.

Then the Seekers' bodies released a protective substance that surrounded the eight eggs. He watched the eggs, like bird eggs with quivering gelatinous shells, grow as the new Seekers grew within. When the baby Seekers emerged from their shells, which seemed to just dissolve at some point, hundreds of adult Seekers swirled wildly around the babies, colors flashing over their bodies so fast James couldn't see the changes. The adults' bodies released some kind of chemical, and James somehow understood that the babies were being imprinted with the community's identity—and that they were being loved unconditionally through these chemicals that permeated them all, adults and infants alike.

And then it was over. James felt the irresistible pull of the Portal for a moment, and then the Seeker released his mind.

He woke up easily, peacefully, and stared up at the ceiling, trying to remember everything he could about the encounter. A lovely odor pervaded the room—the literal smell of love, perhaps.

So, every infant is a child of, not just two parents, but eight, who are also each the child of eight. It's like each infant is a child of every member of the community. All their genetic material is so intertwined. Who would have thought? Eight individuals have to come together to create babies. I wonder what initiates the encounter. Is it just eight random Seekers who happen to be in the mood that night? Or do they have to be at a sexually receptive point in some cycle, like most animals here on Earth? Eight! Wow. Talk about group sex.

Then he shuddered. Oh my God, I think I experienced an alien orgasm. I don't know if I'm going to tell Danny about that one. But then a little smile crossed his face. Or maybe I'll just save this one till I really need something to top him.

Then his inner scientist took over. Interesting, that the orgasm happened not at the moment of the release of the sex cells, like it does for human men, but at the moment the eggs combined. Do they never ever experience individual pleasure? He compared it to human sexual experience: men and women together, reaching that ultimate moment of ecstasy, but still each in their own head, their own body. But the Seekers probably don't have two distinct sexes. That reproductive process didn't need males and females. Are they all unisex? Or are there eight sexes? What are the ramifications of that? Men are from Mars, women are from Venus, and Seekers are from…?

Suddenly the words he'd heard in his head popped back in his mind: *We go into Portal good happy knowing you human understanding unbreakable connection with the Way and Life Force of this blessed planet.* How in hell had they talked to him with real words? What's happening to my brain? Is it becoming more compatible with alien interaction, the more times they connect with me? What the hell are the rules for human-alien brain interface?

Anxiety—or maybe near panic—swept over James. God, what if my brain gets so alien-compatible that one gets stuck in it the next time, like Eddie?

James breathed deeply, trying to calm himself and to think clearly. He tried to remember the good parts, the incredible feeling of rightness and wholeness he had experienced as the copper-colored river merged with the multi-colored geyser of humanity.

Suddenly a chill came over him, and it wasn't from the cold the alien had left behind. He still didn't know, he realized. Maybe he was going to save humanity, and maybe he was going to die trying. Maybe the Seeker had avoided telling him because it didn't want him to know the awful truth. Or maybe, to a community-minded species, individual death really didn't matter.

James sat up and slipped his feet into the slippers near the bed. He knew what he had to do. If he didn't survive, he had to make sure his encounters with the Seekers did—for their sake, as well as for the benefit of the scientific community.

He pulled on his bathrobe, shivering, thinking fleetingly that if he ever got the chance to talk with them again, he should ask them why it got so cold every time they came.

Sitting down at the computer, he started a new file: "My encounters with an alien race." As he began typing out everything he could think of that he had learned or deduced about the Seekers, so that if he died his knowledge would not die with him, this thought crossed his mind: I wonder if they give posthumous Nobel prizes.

Deb Kolbo Ellsworth

CHAPTER 19

James stared at himself in the bathroom mirror. Why had he come in here? He couldn't seem to remember. He couldn't seem to focus at all.

The last week was a blur. His mind was always where it shouldn't be, never on the situation at hand. Standing in front of his class, he would falter in mid-sentence, suddenly engulfed in the vision of himself killing the President. Sitting in the auditorium at the regional Destination Imagination tournament, watching Danielle's team perform, he got lost in a feeling of despair that he might never see this wonderful child grow up. He didn't even hear the last two minutes and was brought back to reality only by the applause and cheers of the audience.

Later, when they watched the video he'd made of the performance, the last minute showed only their scenery, with no one in front of it: the action had moved, but he hadn't followed it with the camera. Danielle was so upset that he'd missed getting the ending. Emily had demanded, "What were you thinking?" "Sorry," he'd said, "we'll get it at State. Isn't it wonderful that you're going to State?" And Danielle was placated, distracted by the thrill of winning. But would he ever even know how her team did? The State Tournament was after spring break.

He watched himself in the bathroom mirror, making little jabbing motions with the toothbrush in his hand out to the side, discreet movements designed to thrust a thin needle into the President's body without anyone noticing. Oh, that's right, he'd come in here to brush his teeth. As the toothpaste foamed, he thought, I wonder if the snake venom will make him foam at the mouth.

The snake venom. The incredibly deadly snake venom that was at this moment hidden in his luggage. They'd covered everything, he hoped, including airport security. The tiny vial of venom, and the small hypodermic, were hidden inside a hollowed-out toothpaste tube, cut open and glued back together.

They had settled on this plan as the only feasible one, which meant to Danny that this had to be the Way, that Scofield was sure to show up for the concert. James was doubtful, but then Bobbie Murrow gestured to him and Shelly Friars, the other teacher chaperone, in the teachers' lounge, beckoning them to her with barely suppressed excitement. Somehow, she managed to whisper and gush at the same time. "I just heard from our tour guide, who's been in touch with Vice President Cambridge's aide, that the concert has been moved from a room inside the White House basement to the South Lawn—you know, where they hold the Easter egg roll every year? Apparently, the President is looking for a nice human-interest piece to top off the evening news. At least one major network will be there. Which virtually guarantees his attendance, unless of course some issue of national security comes up. Can you believe it? Our Westfield High School band will be performing on national TV!"

National TV. Damn. He could only hope that they would stop the cameras after the concert, that they would not be interested in televising the photo shoot afterward.

They had practiced, he and Danny, rehearsed as if for a play. Down in Danny's basement, while the boys played video games upstairs saving the world from hideous green aliens, he and Danny secretly prepared for the real thing. They'd acted it out, Danny standing in for Scofield. Practiced the photo moment with James standing on both the right and the left, so he could do it easily either way. Stand as close as possible to Scofield, syringe hidden in his palm. Wait for the moment when all eyes are forward, smiling for the photographer, no one looking at him, and just as the camera flashes, stick the needle into his body. James had practiced on a beanbag taped to Danny's thigh, how to do it swiftly and with minimal movement, how to depress the plunger immediately and pull the needle out quickly. How to palm it again like a magician, slip it into his pocket. If Scofield felt the needle going in and reacted, James was going to say, "I think a bee just stung you, Mr. President!" and he would pretend to be swatting a bee away with that hand. He practiced that line over and over till he sounded convincing.

According to their research, Scofield would feel the effects in somewhere between fifteen minutes and an hour. Presumably, he'd be back in the White House by that time. The venom produced cardiac arrest, and no one would be surprised that an old guy was having a heart attack. Or maybe they'd think he was having an allergic reaction to the bee sting. The Westfield band and its chaperones would leave for the airport, and James would dump the syringe in one of those containers for disposable needles in an airport bathroom. They'd thought of everything.

And James was scared to death. Because he knew a million things could go wrong. Maybe it would all go smoothly, perfectly, as they'd planned. More likely, someone would notice him doing it. They wouldn't kill him, because they'd want to know what he'd used on the President. Could he withstand getting beaten? He'd only have to hold out fifteen minutes. He hoped he could be a soldier. That's how he was trying to think of himself. As a soldier, an involuntary recruit in the army of humanity.

James saluted himself in the mirror, and then thought, You are going nuts. Wacko.

Emily walked in. "Oh, James, I forgot to tell you—you had a message from that woman on the reunion committee."

Reunion committee? Reunion committee? Wasn't that from his past life, when he was a normal, average guy? A guy who could brush his teeth before going to bed without flipping out? That committee hadn't met for two months, and now he could hardly bring it into his consciousness.

"What'd she want?" Try to seem normal. Try, for Emily's sake.

"She said the reservation has been confirmed to have the reunion at the Rec Center, and that any photos you can get to her to put into the twenty-year memory book, she needs by May first. And she wanted to know what rate you got from the caterer."

"Oh, yeah. Yeah, OK. I'll email her from Washington." And if I'm on trial for assassinating the President, won't that make for a hot topic of conversation at the reunion?

Emily put her arms around him from behind, circling his waist and pulling him close. "Why did you even agree to be on this high school reunion committee? You just can't say no when someone asks you for help, can you?"

Not even to aliens.

"Are you all packed?" Emily asked.

"Yeah."

"You don't sound too excited. I kind of wish you weren't going."

"Sorry. I was hoping it would be OK, since Danielle and Trey have school next week."

"Yeah, I suppose we'll manage. Too bad your spring break and theirs didn't coincide this year. But I'm kind of worried about you going to Washington. I mean, what if some terrorist nut decides to try to kill the President just when you're doing the concert?"

Like me? Me! It's goddamn me! "Don't worry. I'll be OK."

Emily gave a nervous little laugh. "I suppose I should really worry more about the cute little teenage flute players who probably have a crush on the adorable Mr. Thompson."

James turned around suddenly and swept her into his arms, leaning her back and kissing her passionately. He gave her his best Humphrey Bogart impression. "Don't worry, baby. They mean nothing to me, see? You're the only girl for me."

Emily giggled with delight, whispering into his ear, "My hero."

Suddenly he was overwhelmed by the desire to make love to his wife. He kissed her eyes and neck and mouth; he swept his hands over her lovely round ass. He grabbed her thick flowing hair roughly, and pulled her lips to his, thrusting his tongue into her mouth. He felt the arousal flooding his groin. He pressed himself against her, and said huskily, urgently, "I want to make love to you like it was our first time. I need to make love to you."

Emily lay sleeping in James's arms. He stared at the ceiling, and then looked at his clock again. It was 3:30 in the morning. Then, suddenly, he knew what he had to do. He eased his arm from under Emily carefully, and rolled out of bed.

In the living room, James first wrote the note telling Emily where to find the hidden video file, saved to the cloud. He tucked it into the notebook where he kept his passwords, hoping to God she never had to read it.

Then he settled on the couch, picked up his phone, and set it to video, switching the viewpoint so he could see himself. He looked like hell. He took a big breath and hit the record button.

"Hi, Emmy," he said slowly. "Uh… if you're watching this, it means I'm… I'm…" He faltered. His voice was shaking, and he couldn't make himself say the word. He closed his eyes, ran his hand over his face, and exhaled slowly. He tried again. "Hi, Emmy. If you're watching this, uh, it means I'm… dead." He could hardly make himself continue, but he had to.

"I'm really sorry. I tried so many times to tell you about all this. I know I should have.

"But it wouldn't have changed things. Or maybe it would have. I don't know if I could have gone and done what I guess I did do, if I'd told you. Seeing that look on your face, if you'd known I might not be coming back. I don't think I'd have been able to walk out the door.

"Did I really kill the President? I just realized, the press must be hounding you. I'm sorry to have to put you through that, baby. I suppose everyone thinks I'm a bad guy, or maybe they think I'm deranged. That would be better for you. Then they'd feel sorry for you.

"I suppose you can't believe your husband killed anyone, let alone the President. That's kind of out of my usual routine. But Emmy, believe me, I'm not crazy. I just had no choice. He was going to start

World War III. I did it for you, and for Danielle and Trey, and Cory and Sara and Jared, and Stewart and Jaymi... God, they wouldn't have had a world to grow up in.

"You're probably thinking, why me? Why did it have to be me who stopped him? But the thing is, it just fell to me. Someone had to step up to the plate, and it just turned out that I was the one.

"If it helps any, you can talk to Danny about this. I know, now you're mad that I told him and not you. But I had to talk to someone, and you know, me and Danny... Don't get mad at him for letting me go, honey. He understood that it had to be done. I know he must be hurting, too. Please, support each other."

James took another big breath and forced himself to press on with words that he didn't want to have to say. "Tell Danielle and Trey how much I love them. This will be hard for them, too. I think our health insurance covers mental health services. You should take them to a psychologist. You should go to one, too. My life insurance should pay off the house, so I figure you'll manage OK. Money-wise, that is."

Anguish tore up his face. "Emmy, I just want you to understand. I did this because I love you. I don't want to miss seeing Danielle and Trey grow up. I wanted to grow old with you, and spoil our grandchildren together, and take trips, and... Oh, hell, there just wasn't anything I could do about this. There wasn't any other way.

"I love you. I will always love you.

"I don't want to turn this camera off, because that would mean it's the end, that I'm really saying goodbye for the last time. Just remember how much I love you. Keep that tight in your heart forever."

James saw the tears streaming down his face on his phone's screen. It took two more minutes before he could bring himself to push the stop button.

CHAPTER 20

Six hours ago, James was sitting in his kitchen trying to force himself to eat something, while Danielle scurried around looking for her homework, and Trey dawdled over his cereal, Emily nagging him to hurry up and finish before the bus came. Six hours ago, James was waving goodbye to his kids as they got on the school bus. Six hours ago, Emily kissed him goodbye when Bobbie Murrow's husband pulled up to the curb to pick him up and take them to the airport. Six hours felt like sixty years.

He was on the plane to Washington, surrounded by excited, chattering band kids. When the airplane took off, James felt his past life slide away from him like the wind slipping off the plane. Now he was seated next to Bobbie, who was nattering on about something inane. "Uh huh," he said, but he had no idea to what.

"What really annoys me," continued Bobbie, oblivious to his lack of interest, "is the way everyone thinks band is a wasted class. People don't realize how much music enhances every aspect of your life. There are statistics showing that kids who take music classes in school score an average of one full grade point higher than non-music kids. I don't know why no one appreciates that. The school board has floated a plan to cut the band program in half. It's outrageous! Why not cut the football program some? But you and I both know that's never going to happen, don't we, James? Right,

James?"

James looked at Bobbie, momentarily confused, and realized he was supposed to say something. "Right."

"I know I'm right. Don's got to turn in those budget cut recommendations to the school board next month, and I don't want to be at the top of the list. Maybe I should go over his head. Maybe to the very top! We're going to see the Vice President, maybe even the President. Maybe I'll have a chance to speak with them about the importance of music programs in schools."

Bobbie's monotonous monologue blended into the droning sound of the kids talking all around him, merging with the background hum of the engine. James felt himself drifting off and was relieved. The fleeting thought that he should say something polite came and went without action. What the hell, she was probably used to people falling asleep on her while she yammered anyway. As he sank into the blessed relief of sleep, the last image in James's mind was of a road map. James's road turned away from the street his family lived on, and he knew it would never connect again. They diverged, and he would take the path that was destined for him, and they would continue on their path, their lives. His mind followed the road until it ran off the edge of the map, and he fell into oblivion.

"Hi. Guess I'm your roomie."

The portly, florid-faced man with the walrus mustache stuck out his hand and shook James's hand vigorously. "Buzz. Buzz Bergerdorf. I sell cars. If you're in the market, come by." Buzz thrust a card at James.

"James Thompson," replied James. "I sell knowledge."

Buzz looked confused, then smiled. "Oh, I get it. You're a teacher."

"That's right. I teach biology and earth science at the high school."

James continued to unpack. The hotel room was better than he'd thought it would be. Buzz was stuffing a couple of XXXL Gophers sweatshirts into a dresser drawer.

"Did you go to the U?" asked James.

"Where else?" Buzz said, and he startled James by launching into a booming rendition of the Gophers' fight song. "I played football at the U. That's where I got my nickname. Stripped their quarterback of the ball and ran sixty-five yards for the touchdown. No one could believe a big guy like me could run so fast. Someone said I made a beeline for the end zone, and someone else said yeah, just call him 'Buzz', 'cause he stung 'em like a bee. The name stuck."

James took a Gophers' sweatshirt of his own out of his suitcase. "Rah, rah, Minnesota," he said.

"Good man," Buzz said approvingly. "Tell you what. You're looking to buy a car, I'll give you the double discount. One for being a teacher at my daughter's school, and one for being a U of M alum."

"Thanks, but I'm not really..."

"Ah, listen. I'm an honest car dealer. We get a bad rap, you know. That stupid *Fargo* movie made us all look like crooks. Plus, they made everyone talk funny. We don't talk like that. We sound just like the news broadcasters."

James smiled. Buzz's Minnesota accent was so thick you could cut the broad "O's" with a butter knife. He decided not to tell the guy that *Fargo* was on his top ten list of favorite movies.

"Which one is your daughter?" he asked.

"Cammie. She plays flute."

James flashed back to Emily's comment about the cute flute players. He remembered Cammie Bergerdorf from his class last year. She couldn't stop talking. Now he understood why.

"My wife talked me into chaperoning this trip," Buzz continued. "You know teenage girls these days. We both agreed it was better for Cammie not to be alone in a hotel in a faraway city for a week. Not with her boyfriend, Devin, in the band, too. He plays drums—you know what that means."

"I'm not sure I do."

"Cammie's not thrilled that I came along, let me tell you. She thinks I'm overprotective of her, just because she's my baby. She has three older brothers. Hell, it's my job to protect her."

"Absolutely."

"You have any daughters, James?"

"Yeah, one. Danielle. She's only eleven, though."

"Oh, just you wait. You have no idea what you're in for."

Buzz picked up the band trip schedule. "So, what've they got on tap for us tonight, huh? Oh, good. Dinner at some Italian restaurant. Washington's got great food, you know, being an international city. You ever been here?" James shook his head. "Me, either. Always wanted to come here—guess that's the other reason I agreed to chaperone. I hope we get to go to a Thai restaurant. Love Thai food, the hotter the better, you know? I'll tell you another city that has great food—Miami. I won a trip there a few years ago for being top salesman of the year. I could've eaten that coconut shrimp every day. And that key lime pie. Fantastic."

Buzz looked back at the schedule. "We're supposed to make sure they're all in their rooms by eleven. You and I have to check rooms 1132 to 1140. God, they've got 'em four to a room. These kids will never go to sleep. Let's see, Cammie's in room 1117. I wonder if I could get our assignment switched so we're checking her room."

"I think you can count on Bobbie Murrow to keep a pretty close eye on the kids. I wouldn't worry."

"You don't have to worry. Your daughter's eleven. I have to worry. I better find out what room Devin's in. I hope it's one of ours."

Buzz hurried out, and James breathed a sigh of relief. The guy was going to talk his head off, and James was in no mood for small talk. He didn't need a new friend now. He felt like he was already apart from everyone, like a wide chasm had opened up: on one side, ordinary human beings living their everyday ordinary lives, and on the other side, himself, alone. It was going to be hard enough getting through the next week, pretending that everything was fine and that he was a normal person like all those people on the other side of the chasm, without having Chatty Cathy for a roommate.

James took the toothpaste box from his suitcase. No problem

getting through security. He removed the needle from inside the tube but left the tiny vial of liquid. Maybe he should practice. He imagined President Scofield standing to his right, attention focused on the photographer. He looked straight ahead, the needle hidden in his palm. He imagined the flash going off, and at that moment, discreetly jabbed the needle into Scofield's imaginary thigh and depressed the plunger.

Suddenly he was filled with rage. Rage that he had to be here, doing this. Rage that his life was being ripped away from him. Rage that he was being forced down a path he had no control over.

"Say cheese, you goddamn alien!" he said thorough gritted teeth, and then stabbed viciously at the air. "Die, you son of a bitch, die!" Over and over, smashing his pain and anger, until he slumped onto the bed, spent. Defeated. There was nothing he could do. He had to suck it up and be a soldier. I am a soldier in the army of humanity, he told himself. Maybe I was drafted—I sure as hell didn't volunteer. But I'm fighting for the human race just the same. I'm a soldier on a mission. I've got to keep focused on that.

The door opened, and Buzz was back in the room before James could do anything. Why had he been so stupid?

But Buzz just glanced at the needle and said nothing. James quietly got up and put it away in his dresser drawer.

"It's perfect," Buzz said in his booming Minnesota accent. "Devin's on our list. If Cammie's in his room, I'll know about it." He picked up the schedule again. "Looks like we've got a full day tomorrow. We're hitting the monuments on the mall, doing a concert at two in front of the Lincoln Memorial, seeing the Air and Space Museum. Great, that was at the top of my list. Oh, fantastic, we get to see the U.S. Mint on Monday. I've always wanted to see them make all that money. Wish we could take a little of that home as a souvenir. A couple mill would do, eh, James?"

James smiled halfheartedly. "Yeah."

Buzz went over to the window. "So, what's the view? Oh, this is fantastic—what a gorgeous city! I've got to take a picture for Laney."

Buzz hurried to get his phone, then held it up to show James. "Just a word of advice. I'd keep your phone in an inside jacket pocket. There's a lot of pickpockets in D.C., you know?"

Buzz seemed like the type likely to take hundreds of pictures over the next few days. But by the time they got back, the only ones that would matter would be the photos that included James. "My sweet Lord," he'd say to his wife. And the news cameras. "If only I'd known what he was going to do. He seemed like such a regular guy."

Buzz was still standing at the window, pondering. "I figure the White House is right about over there," he said, pointing. "I don't know what your politics are, James. But I can't say I'm happy about the way things have been going these last few months. Don't get me wrong—I'm as patriotic as the next guy. I enlisted in the army right out of high school, wanted to serve my country. You betcha."

Buzz paused, then resumed his monologue in a softer voice. "My uncle was in Vietnam at the end of the war. The way he tells it, I wouldn't wish that on anyone. He barely made it out. Got shot in the hand as his chopper was taking off. His best friend wasn't so lucky."

Buzz turned to James. "Back then, only the guys had to worry about getting drafted. Now they're making everyone do those training weekends—girls, too. You know, it's a lot harder when you're the father than when it's you. I'm worried about Cammie's three older brothers. I'm worried about Cammie. Hell, I'm even worried about Devin. He's a good kid, really. I don't want to see them getting drafted to fight a war in some two-bit country I can't even find on a map, you know what I mean?"

"Yes, I do, Buzz. I know exactly what you mean." Maybe I can help. I am a soldier in the army of humanity.

CHAPTER 21

The week passed in a haze of unreality. Surprisingly, James found himself grateful for his chaperoning duties. Those sixty teenagers were full of hormones and high spirits. Every time his attention wandered, some kid was pretending to push another kid into the reflecting pool, or some boy was trying to make his friends laugh by writing a dirty word on a piece of paper and sailing it over the balcony at the Congressional building, or some boy was trying to impress a girl by doing a back flip into the hotel pool, despite the NO DIVING signs. The kids were distracting, and that was getting him through it.

Even Buzz turned out to be OK. He talked so much that all James had to do was throw in the occasional "uh huh" and Buzz was happy, oblivious to James's lack of interest in the conversation.

Some parts were actually good. He really enjoyed the Natural History Museum, which he'd always wanted to see. And it was fun to watch the kids play their concert on the steps in front of the Lincoln Memorial. They collected a surprisingly large crowd of tourists, who seemed to really enjoy the performance. Well, why not? It was free entertainment. A Japanese tourist recorded the whole thing, while a little toddler danced gleefully in front of them as they played Aaron Copeland's "Rodeo." James noticed Cammie throw a quick, flirtatious smile back at Devin between songs. Devin twirled his drumsticks for her, to her giggling delight. At that moment, life almost seemed normal.

Normal, and desperately important that it continue that way. So that when they went to the Holocaust Museum, and James saw the horrifying results of a previous evil Seeker's time on Earth, he told himself that, even though no one would ever know it, he was going to stop this from happening again. So that the toddler on the Mall could grow up, and Devin and Cammie could get married, and Buzz could sell more cars. And life could go on, normal and good.

And when they visited the Vietnam Veterans Memorial Wall, as he watched Buzz search for Eugene Simpson's name, he thought, Never again. Danny's not going to have to cry at his nephew's war memorial, not if I can stop it.

The worst was at night, lying there staring at the ceiling while Buzz snored blissfully in the other bed. James's doctor had refused to renew his prescription for sleep medication anymore, suggesting that if he was still having problems, he should go to a sleep clinic to get thoroughly tested. Lying in the hotel bed, James smiled wryly in the dark, imagining himself telling his doctor that his sleep problems were caused by visitations from aliens. That would've gotten him a referral to an entirely different kind of clinic.

After two nights of very little sleep, James decided he would drug himself to sleep if he had to. He went out for a walk and picked up a bottle of whisky. He had to disguise the heavy drinking each night, pouring it discreetly into the caffeine-free Cokes he bought from the machine down the hall. But it did the trick, at least until he woke up at 4:30 a.m. with the thought immediately flooding his mind: I'm going to kill the President.

James wondered if the Seekers would pay him a nocturnal visit in these days before the Way reached its culmination. He doubted they would deviate from the sixteen-day schedule, but maybe they would feel a need to buck him up at the last moment, give him a fourth quarter pep talk. He hoped they wouldn't show. What if they disturbed Buzz? Anyway, he wasn't feeling very positive toward them at this point.

Somehow, he managed to talk every night on the phone to Emily and Danielle and Trey without breaking down. He listened to

Danielle tell him, hurt and angry, about not getting invited to a friend's birthday party, and thought, I'm not there to comfort her. It might be Emily having to comfort her, alone, through all the rest of the disappointments and heartaches that are going to come her way. He listened to Trey complain that his teacher made him stay in at recess just because he was behind in his free choice reading, and how could they call it free choice if they made you do it? He felt himself blinking back the tears when Emily told him about the old lady at Ford Creek Senior Housing who giggled like a schoolgirl when they had "beauty day" and Emily painted her fingernails with Danielle's glitter nail polish. He tried to hold on to each precious word but felt them slipping away from him. They were ghost words, made of smoke, and he couldn't hold them; the smoke swirled through his clutching fingers and was gone. He told them he went to the Air and Space Museum, and he would bring them presents, but he feared that was a lie. He said he'd better go, he'd call them tomorrow, and he hung up and closed his eyes and squeezed the pillow so tight his arms ached. I am a soldier in the army of humanity.

The night before the White House concert, Danny called. It was strangely awkward, talking to his best friend, the person he always felt the most relaxed with, feeling the gulf between them. They both knew Danny was safe at home, and James was here in Washington putting his life on the line. To break the tension, James said, "You know what bugs me, Danny? I'm a scientist, and I've made the most important discovery in centuries, maybe ever. But I've only begun to learn about these aliens. There's so much more that I want to know, and now I never will. That sucks."

"Don't talk like that, man," Danny said. "We've planned this to the smallest detail. You're going to come out of this just fine. You're going to come home. You gotta believe that. You know, if you step up to that free throw line when the game's on the line and you remember all the times you clanked it, you're gonna clank it again. But if you know you're gonna make it, you do. Swish. You're gonna swish this one, James."

"Thanks, man," James said, grateful as much for the chance to say goodbye to Danny on a positive note as for the hope Danny was trying to give him. "You hold down my place for me at Garraty's tomorrow, OK?"

CHAPTER 22

When the phone rang, it startled James. Had he actually been asleep? Buzz reached out a hand from his bed to the receiver and listened.

"Thanks," he said, his voice too loud for early morning. He hung up, sat up, and beamed at James. "That was our wake-up call. Today's the big day, roomie. It's been a long week, but it's finally Friday. Let's go. They want us all packed, with our stuff downstairs. We're checking out of here after breakfast and we're not coming back."

James shot him a startled look, but Buzz didn't notice.

"I'll go knock on the kids' doors, make sure they're up." Buzz was pulling on a robe, with far more bonhomie than the situation warranted. "Why don't you grab the first shower?"

Buzz closed the door, and James was left alone with one overwhelming thought: This might be the last day of my life. He felt like he was moving underwater as he entered the bathroom and started the shower. The water needed to be hotter. It needed to be scalding. He started to soap up, a feeling of despair spreading over him with the soapsuds. I don't want this to be happening. I don't want this to be real. I want to go home to my real life. James realized that the hot water running over his face was mixing with his tears, and he found he couldn't stop them, he was sobbing, despair overwhelming him. It's not fair, this can't be how it all ends for me, it's not fair, goddamn it, goddamn it…

Suddenly, he pounded on the shower wall with rage, furious at himself.

Goddamn it, get it together! I'm not the only one who's had to sacrifice his life. Those firefighters in New York didn't whine and cry about it when they went into the World Trade Towers. Get through this! Be strong! Do it! Be a man! Be a soldier!

There was a knock at the bathroom door.

"You OK in there?"

Oh, no. He must have been yelling. Yelling and banging on the shower walls, he realized.

"Yeah… yeah. I'm fine. Just singing."

James closed his eyes and forced himself to stand perfectly still, breathing deeply as the hot water flowed over him and encased his body in a liquid cocoon. I should take Danny's advice. Do I want to be the guy who folds under pressure, or the guy who sucks it up and does it right? Step by step he visualized himself taking out Eddie. He saw himself walking away from it, whole and safe. Then he went through the visualization again. And again. When images of failure flickered at the edge of his consciousness, he pushed them away. He imagined himself back at Garraty's, imagined clinking glasses with Danny, toasting his success. He was ready.

When James came out of the bathroom, unshaven, wearing boxers, Buzz looked at him curiously. But he only said, "Hey, you just missed a call from your wife. Hope you don't mind I answered your phone."

"No, that's OK. Did she want me to call her back?"

"No, she said she had to leave for work. She said to tell you she'll see you at the airport. Oh, and she said to tell you to wear the yellow shirt. She wants you to look good if you get on TV."

Oh my God.

"Wonder what I should wear for the cameras," Buzz said. "I understand they're gonna send a live feed to Channel 4, right?

They're gonna carry it live in Minnesota, and then it should be on the evening news, but that'll just be a thirty-second bit, I'm sure. You 'n me probably won't make the national news. What'd'ya think?"

"I dunno, we might," James said, more grimly than he intended.

Buzz looked at him curiously.

"I mean," James said, "yeah, not us. But you might see Cammie on the national news."

"Yeah, I sure hope so," Buzz said. "I'm hitting the shower. You better check on those kids in a minute, make sure they really got up."

James dressed mechanically. Socks, shirt, pants, belt, tie, sports coat. Hypodermic needle. And then Buzz came out of the bathroom unexpectedly, with a towel wrapped around his waist, and James jumped and dropped the needle. Buzz looked at it lying on the floor.

"I wondered if you were a diabetic," he said. "Doc says I'm headed that way myself, if I don't cut down on the burgers and fries." He chuckled and patted his belly. "That's asking a lot, know what I mean?" Buzz took his razor off its charger on the dresser and headed back to the bathroom, then turned around with his hand on the door handle and waved the razor at James. "You forgot to shave, by the way. You probably ought to shave for the President, eh, buddy?"

Thank God people's brains worked in such a way as to cause them to fit anomalous situations into known patterns. Of course, Buzz wouldn't think, this guy's going to kill the President. Of course, he would put what he saw into a familiar context.

James waited to hear the shower running, and then picked up the hypodermic. He stuck the end into the small bottle, drawing the venom into the syringe. He carefully shot out a drop of liquid from the tip, as doctors always did, to make sure Scofield didn't die too soon. James finished his preparations, and then went to the window and gazed out. I'm coming for you today, Eddie. You don't know it yet, but this is your last day on Earth, you son-of-a-bitch freak alien. I am a soldier in the army of humanity.

The buses dropped them off as close as they were allowed to get to the White House; James and the other chaperones helped the kids haul the instruments from there. James could see rows of chairs and music stands arranged in a semi-circle on the White House lawn, with maybe four rows of chairs arrayed in front of them. There was already a TV camera set up on a platform behind the chairs.

Then he saw the two Secret Service agents. Damn, this was it. One agent was making them put the instruments down; he was examining the cases and instruments carefully. Danny had suggested hiding the needle in a case, one of the heavy ones. "You offer to carry it, then slip the needle out while everyone's setting up." Good thing they'd gone with the other plan.

James put the case he was carrying with the other instruments. The agent looked at him and said, "You can pick this up after you go through security." James joined the line that had formed. Slowly they were making their way toward the second Secret Service agent.

James wondered if he looked as nervous as he felt. Maybe this guy would pull him out for special scrutiny just for looking suspicious. He felt like he was sweating bullets, like he was one step from breaking down and confessing.

The girl behind James was annoyed. "God, what do they think, I've got a bomb in my saxophone?"

James turned around and glared at her. "Hey. Don't even say the 'B' word around here, or you'll be watching the performance from the sidewalk."

The girl ignored James and continued complaining to her friend. "This is so lame."

The boy disagreed. "I dunno. I think it's kinda cool to be searched by the Secret Service. How many people can say that?"

"I wish I could take out the President," the girl said. "I think he's full of shit."

James wanted these stupid kids to just shut up. "Do you kids have no sense at all? Do you have no idea where we are, or how serious national security is these days?"

"Sorry, Mr. Thompson." But she wasn't. She was far more interested in talking with this cute boy than in issues of national security. James looked at the two of them, her fingers lightly playing on the boy's arm. He felt like shaking them.

"Sir? Sir, you're next. Please step forward."

James turned around. The Secret Service agent beckoned him. For a moment he almost gave in to the overwhelming impulse to turn and run away. But somehow, he made himself walk up to the agent, who waved a metal detector over his body. It beeped when it crossed James's midsection.

"Sir, please empty your pockets here," said the agent, indicating a small table next to him. James reached into his pockets and put the contents on the table. Oh God, his hands were shaking. Would the agent notice?

If he did, he must have been used to average citizens being unnerved by his sunglasses, his weapons, his unwavering alertness, like a human police dog.

The agent eyed the contents of his pockets. Cell phone. Wallet. Pocket change. Toothpaste and toothbrush, in a Ziploc bag. The agent looked at James, and he felt compelled to explain.

Through lips so dry he could hardly get enough saliva to get the words out, he said haltingly, "Uh, I know that looks weird. I wanted to brush my teeth, you know, after breakfast, so I'd have clean teeth when we met the President, you know, but we'd already packed, so I had to take it with me, so…"

"Thank you, sir," said the agent. "Let's move this along."

This time the sensor did not beep when the agent passed it over his body. James tried to keep the relief from showing.

"You can go," the agent said. James picked up his wallet, the change, his phone, and the bag with the deadly contents, fingers fumbling. He was just turning to walk away, amazed, thinking *My God, this might work*, when he heard the agent's voice.

"Sir?"

James froze. *He knows.*

James looked at the agent, waited for him to say, "Come with me."

"I'd advise you to turn off your cell phone. It wouldn't look too good if you took a call during a performance for the President."

"Oh. Right. Thanks."

"No problem." The agent turned back to the line. "Next."

———

The band members were in their chairs, tuned up and ready to play. Bobbie Murrow was standing in front of them, ready to direct the concert of her life. But the object of all those weeks of preparation was nowhere to be seen. After thirty minutes, Bobbie told the kids to hold their positions, and hurried over to one of the Secret Service agents. She returned, looking upset, to confer with the chaperones.

"I don't know what to do. That Secret Service agent said the President's been delayed. Probably a big international crisis, I suppose. He may not be able to make it. Vice President Cambridge may not be able to make it either. They don't seem to know much."

James didn't know what to feel. Relieved? Angry? Bobbie mistook the look on his face.

"I know. I can't believe it. We come all this way and stay all this time, and now the big highlight may not happen. Believe me, I'm going to have a word with the tour company when we get back."

"It's not their fault," Buzz said. "This is the President we're talking about. Things come up. Things more important than a high school band concert."

"Oh dear, what should we do?" Bobbie fretted.

"Have the kids practice again," Buzz said firmly. "Nothing else we can do. Either Cambridge shows up alone, in which case we play for him. Or they both manage to come after all, in which case these kids will play for the President. Either way, they give the performance of their lives. Even if the concert gets cancelled, worst case, we had a great band trip to Washington, D.C. Right, James?"

"Yes. Yes, you're absolutely right."

James felt the tension squeezing him like a boa constrictor. He could hardly draw air into his lungs. He stepped away from the others, closed his eyes, and prayed. Dear God, get me off this roller coaster. If I have to do it, let him come now and let me get it over with. If he's not going to come, if this isn't the Way, let me know, let Cambridge show up alone. I can't take this waiting. Please God, help me be strong. Help me be a soldier for humanity. Help me do what I have to do, for the greater good. Lord, give me strength.

———————

It took another hour for him to get an answer. An hour of pacing, while the band kids got more and more bored, sitting there with nothing to do. James let the other chaperones intervene when they started throwing wadded up paper at each other. He watched Bobbie have them run through the songs several times, while he paced. He kept his hands away from the pocket with the syringe in it.

He watched the TV cameramen chatting with each other, bored. He knew that Emily would be watching the live performance on the TV at work, probably with an audience of elderly residents. He knew that Danielle and Trey would be watching it in their classrooms, because they'd told him, with great excitement, that they'd talked their teachers into letting their classes watch it live. He knew that his folks would be watching it in their home, his childhood home. James hoped that the long delay would mean that the kids' classes would be at gym or lunch when it finally came on; that Emily would have to do something else and would miss it; that his folks would doze off, waiting. He didn't want them to see this.

A couple dozen people were sitting in the audience. He recognized Marilyn Lancaster, the representative from their congressional district, and both Minnesota senators. The others had to be their staff. Several of them had pulled out laptops and were working. Their phones were going non-stop. One woman chain-smoked. He watched Bobbie approach Senator Keller; he didn't have to hear the conversation to know what she was talking to him about. Buzz introduced himself to everyone, handing out business cards like Halloween candy.

James paced, off to the side, practicing over and over in his mind the words he would say to get next to Eddie: Mr. Vice President, I'm James Thompson. I don't know if you remember me, but I was on the basketball team at Westfield with your brother, Jack. He would then turn to Scofield. Mr. President, it's an honor to meet you. He would shake Scofield's hand, maintain his position as the photographer set up. James visualized the scene in his mind, over and over. He was concentrating so hard that he jumped when he felt a hand on his shoulder. He heard Buzz's booming voice. "Relax, my friend. Nothing we can do about it. You're kind of a type A guy, aren't you?"

Bobbie came over to consult with them. She was so frazzled she could hardly speak coherently. "I don't think the President's going to be able to make it. Oh, this will be such a disappointment for the kids. Oh my. Well, they say the Vice President is going to come anyway, now. So at least we still get to do the concert."

Relief flooded James, immediately followed by shame. Shouldn't he be disappointed that he would not be able to finish the mission to take out Eddie Olson? What kind of man was he?

And then, suddenly, it was happening. A loud voice announced, "Ladies and gentlemen, the President of the United States."

CHAPTER 23

The people in the chairs stood up. Bobbie hurried over to take her position in front of the band, signaling for their attention. They grabbed their instruments and launched quickly into "Hail to the Chief." James could see Vice President Cambridge walking side by side with President Scofield. Four Secret Service agents accompanied them, followed by several staff people.

James's mind kept reverberating with one phrase, over and over: It's really happening.

President Scofield and Vice President Cambridge stopped in front of the two centrally-located chairs, while the other people in their entourage filled in around them. They abruptly sat down, although the band hadn't finished. Bobbie was flustered. She hurried the band through the ending, directing with frantic movements. Then she turned and began the speech she'd probably rehearsed in front of a mirror twenty times.

"President Scofield, Vice President Cambridge, it is indeed a very special honor for our humble band from Westfield High School to play for you today. We bring you greetings from the people of your hometown, Mr. Cambridge. We so much appreciate your taking time out of your so very busy schedule to spend some time with us today…"

James glanced at the most powerful man in the world. Scofield was smiling insipidly, clearly not listening to a word Bobbie was saying.

Apparently, Bobbie noticed, too. Flustered, she paused, then seemed to decide to skip the next several paragraphs she'd prepared and cut to the chase. "Anyway, perhaps we should begin without any further ado. Sorry, I'm just a little nervous here." She giggled inanely. "Yes, well." She paused, pulled herself together and said with a flourish, "Mr. President, Mr. Vice President, we would like to begin with a song by that wonderful American composer, George Gershwin. We are delighted to perform 'Summertime' for your listening pleasure."

James tried to force himself to think of nothing, to concentrate only on the music. But the thoughts pushed into his mind relentlessly: images of Emily smiling at him; memories of making love with her. He remembered when he first saw Emily at the back of the church on their wedding day, so gorgeous, so breathtaking, he could hardly believe she was walking toward him, choosing him to spend the rest of her life with. He saw Danielle looking up and smiling at him as she did her homework in the evenings. He remembered Trey's excitement when he crossed home plate on his first-ever home run. Is this what they meant by your life flashing in front of your eyes? Well, damn it, he wasn't dying yet! I am a soldier in the army of humanity. What would a soldier do? Go over the battle plan in his mind, get mentally prepared.

James remembered Danny testing the venom on a little mouse, held helpless and squirming in his gloved hands. Danny had injected just a little of the venom, piercing the mouse's belly. It had been horrible watching that thing squeal, and then stiffen and die as its muscles were paralyzed.

He had a good view of Scofield, sitting there looking like a harmless old man, like someone's grandpa. Would the venom work faster on him because he was so old? Would he have to watch Scofield die?

Goddamn it, stop it. Think about the mission. He forced himself to slowly exhale and inhale. OK. He saw himself in his mind, carefully slipping the syringe into his palm as he took up his position next to Scofield, smiling for the photographer; just a little jab right as the flash went off, the one moment when everyone was sure to be looking straight ahead, and no one would be looking at him.

James must have been doing a better job of concentrating on the task he had to do than he realized, because he was surprised to hear Bobbie say, "Our last number will be 'God Bless America.'"

James looked at Scofield, and saw that even as he was smiling pleasantly, he was tearing up a bit at the patriotic hymn. The TV cameraman was moving in for a close-up. What a phony politician. Always had been. But that wasn't a reason to die, was it? Was he for sure possessed by Eddie Olson? True, the Seekers were indisputably real. But he was only surmising that Scofield was Eddie's host, based on the evidence. Really strong evidence. But what if he was wrong? Damn it, don't lose your nerve now. He's it. You know it. James looked intently at him. Could he see Eddie in his eyes, like Danny said?

"God Bless America" ended. The people in the audience were applauding politely as the band members bowed. Bobbie, flush with excitement, theatrically swept her arm toward the band, beaming and exclaiming, "Thank you! Thank you! Thank you, Mr. President, Mr. Vice President. I hope you enjoyed the performance as much as we enjoyed playing for you."

The President stood up, and everyone else followed suit. Was he giving them a standing O, or was he just impatient to get this over with? Should James move now, or would that be too conspicuous?

The photographer, a little guy who looked like a ferret, with a thin mustache lining his upper lip, hurried over to the band. "Fine, fine. We'll take the official photo now. You people in the front row, stay where you are—you're already positioned just fine, except you four in the middle, that's where the President's going to stand. You move to the ends. You people in the way back on the left side, yeah you, you come kneel in front of them. The rest of you, put down your instruments and squeeze in behind them. C'mon, move it, people."

Should he move in now? This guy was working really fast.

"OK," the photographer said when he liked what he saw, "The President and Vice President will stand here in front."

This was it. Time to suck it up and be a soldier. James had always imagined that the minds of soldiers in battle sharpened to a clear, laser-like focus. James's mind was going blank. He felt like he was moving under water, slowly, the edges of his vision blurred.

Then he bumped into Bobbie, who was inexplicably stepping between him and Scofield. She was trying to get a word in with the President, saying, "I know you are a supporter of music in the schools…" What the hell was she doing?

The photographer pushed Bobbie aside. "You, band director, go stand over there. And shut up."

James barely registered Bobbie sputtering in indignation as he moved forward. Get into position. Stand next to him. He opened his mouth, trying to force the words out of his sand-dry lips. "Mr. Vice President," he began, and the words sounded to him like they were coming from far away, "I'm James Thomps…" Suddenly he felt himself being pushed roughly aside. What? Was the Secret Service onto him?

As if from another place, the voice of the photographer penetrated his clouded mind. "Do none of you people get it? I'm in charge here. You stand where I tell you."

James looked in confusion at him, saw the sharp Adam's apple bobbing up and down his thin neck like a cork on a fishing line. Heard the man spit with irritation, "Go stand with the other chaperones over there." He felt himself being shoved away.

And so, he stood next to Buzz, who was smiling broadly, and watched the photographer take two photos, while a feeling of panic swept over him. What do I do now? What would Danny do? We didn't have a contingency plan. Hell. Danny would say, call an audible. Improvise. But finish the mission.

He heard the photographer yelling, looked toward the back, and saw a boy with his fingers stuck up like rabbit ears behind his friend's head. Same stupid wise-ass kid who'd been getting into trouble all week. "Hey, kid—keep your hands at your side or I'll have the Secret Service shoot you. All right, everyone, let's try that again. Last one. Keep your eyes wide open now. One, two, three!"

OK, now or never. James licked his lips and moved toward the

President. But already, they were turning away. No, he had to stop them. He had to do it. He heard himself calling out, choking on the words with his dry mouth.

"Mr. Vice President! Just a moment!"

Cambridge stopped, turned and looked at him with an irritated expression. Scofield stopped as well. James palmed the syringe carefully in his left hand, still in his pocket, desperately afraid he was going to stick himself, his hands were shaking so badly. He took a big breath, willed his right hand to be steady, and stretched it forward. "I'm James Thompson," he managed to say. "I, uh, I went to school with your brother, Jack. We were on the basketball team together."

He saw, as if in slow motion, everything was slowed down, Cambridge reluctantly putting out his hand. He grasped it. He saw the flicker of revulsion in his eyes as he touched James's dark skin, but it was gone in an instant, replaced by a politely friendly expression.

"Oh, yes, of course," he said.

James tried to smile, tried to look normal, as he dropped Cambridge's hand and reached out to shake Scofield's hand.

His mind went blank. What was he supposed to say? Say anything. "Uh, Mr. President, I'm happy to, uh… to meet you…"

James kept his grip tight. Don't let him go. Hang on. Say something. Why wasn't his hand coming out of his pocket? He just had to do a quick jab and it would be done, before they could stop him. In his peripheral vision he saw the Secret Service agents moving closer. Do it, do it now! "Uh, so I just wanted to say…"

President Scofield was trying to pull his hand away, giving him a look that told him he was starting to alarm the President.

Damn it, damn it. Do it.

A small corner of his mind vaguely registered that a Secret Service agent was putting his hand on his gun. Do it now! He could feel the old man trying to pull his hand away more forcibly. James's left arm slowly began lifting his hand from the pocket. Do it! Do it now!

But the agent, so well trained, stopped as he saw that James's hand was empty. Like he was watching a movie, James saw himself raise his left hand and give Scofield the peace sign.

"It's just… give peace a chance, OK?"

James suddenly noticed that the band kids near him were all watching, and he felt like he was coming back into himself, into his right mind. He didn't know where it came from, but he heard himself say, "These kids—don't make them go to Military Readiness Camps. Don't make them train for a war that you appear to be determined to start in Africa. They have their whole beautiful lives ahead of them. It's crazy, it's wrong, it makes no sense. Like I said, please—Mr. President—just give peace a chance."

James heard the applause erupting from the students around him, and to his amazement, saw many of them raise their own hands to hold up the peace sign. One girl began singing John Lennon's song. Several more voices joined her. A sax player put her instrument to her lips and started playing the tune, and a boy added his trumpet to the growing symphony.

At first President Scofield just looked confused, like he didn't know what had hit him, how this simple PR event had gone so wrong. James glanced at the chorus of teenagers, amazed himself that this was happening. When he looked back, Scofield's deeply lined face was contorted with barely contained rage, as he growled in a low voice to James, "You know nothing." Was this the true face of Eddie? Scofield turned and stalked away.

Cambridge gave James a furious look. "How dare you?" he spat at him. "How dare you, you arrogant, impudent… Just who do you think you are?" He turned and hurried to catch up with the President.

Around James, noise and celebration swirled. Sixty teenagers squealed and babbled in excitement, hugging each other, trading high-fives. Several of them said, "That was awesome, Mr. Thompson."

Then Bobbie was busy trying to round up the band members, trying to gloss over the unexpected ending that she feared would overshadow the successful performance, the greatest event of her life. "Never mind, never mind, you played beautifully, boys and girls, that's what people will see, don't worry, it was wonderful, you'll never forget it, but we have to go…" She sputtered around like a remote-control toy car, haphazardly veering this way and that.

James vaguely heard Buzz's booming voice congratulating Cammie, and then directing the kids to pack up their instruments. He closed his eyes. So, what if he told the President off? So, what if some kids gave this spontaneous, moving plea for peace? Seeing Eddie's face, he was brought back to the stark reality. He had failed the mission.

Eventually they had to move off the White House lawn. The kids, the chaperones, began lugging the instruments toward the bus. And there stood James, like a rock in the middle of a swirling river, the happy babbling stream flowing around him and past him.

Finally, the last TV cameraman, packing up his equipment, noticed him standing there alone and nudged him. "Hey, buddy, your fifteen minutes are up. Your bus is loading. Just between you and me, though—cool move on Scofield there. That took balls."

CHAPTER 24

He had to get out of there.

Emily had picked him up at the airport last night, bubbling over with excitement, thrilled that he and the band had made the nightly news. She was so proud of him. Then she filled him in on what he'd missed: the new neighbors got a dog and it barked like crazy, and Trey got an A on his history project, and her supervisor at work said she'd done an outstanding job on the field trip she'd taken the nursing home residents on to the History Center, but of course, it wasn't just history to them, it was their life, and…

James had barely spoken the whole way home, told Emily he didn't feel well, maybe he'd picked up a bug on the trip. He went to bed shortly after getting home and slept like the dead for ten straight hours.

His morning shower did nothing to make him feel alive, despite turning the heat up higher in a vain attempt to warm the cold, numb core inside him. Then, as he sat at the kitchen table staring blankly at his cup of coffee, the doorbell rang and there stood his folks, beaming at him. It was more than he could take.

"J. J.!" his father boomed, clapping him on the back. "Saw you on TV. You know you made the national news, right? You and the band, singing that song. Unbelievable!"

They blew past him like a whirlwind, on into the kitchen, the emotional force battering him. His mother set the coffee cake she'd brought on the kitchen table so she could hug him. "Oh Sweetie, we were so proud of you! Have you made coffee yet? Smells like it. Oh, I see you have some already. I'll just get Daddy a cup. Where's Emily?"

He sat at the table and watched his mother bustle about, slicing the cake, getting plates and forks and napkins, and pouring coffee. He felt drained, lifeless. He drank some coffee, saying nothing, but no one could ignore his father.

"We were so proud of you, son, your mother and I. Standing up to the President like that. Phone hasn't stopped ringing. Friends calling, neighbors calling, old church members called, your sisters called, everyone was calling to say how great it was, what you did. I guarantee you, Martin Luther King, Jr. is applauding from heaven."

Emily walked in, followed by Kirby, who searched the floor for cake crumbs. She beamed at her in-laws. "Hey, good morning. Coffee cake? Oh, that's so nice of you! This is just what James needs, I bet. He came home feeling under the weather last night." She put her arms around him. "How you feeling, honey?"

Like crap. Like goddamn worthless crap. "OK."

"That's good. You should just take it easy today." She turned to his folks. "Did you see it? James's big moment?"

"You bet!" boomed his dad. "Never been prouder of my boy!"

"We recorded it," James's mother said as she bustled over to give him another hug and a kiss on the cheek. She giggled. "We've watched it at least twenty times now, and every time, Daddy cheers when James tells it straight to the President like that. Did you get to see it yourself yet, honey? You must come over and see it soon. You should see yourself, oh my!"

Emily sat down with her coffee. "It's already on YouTube, so we could all watch now if we wanted to. We got a few crank calls here, I'm afraid. One guy said James was being disrespectful; a lady said he was an embarrassment to Minnesota. A couple of them were pretty nasty, you know, racial slurs. I won't repeat them. But mostly, it's been positive."

"Someone ought to teach those idiots a civics lesson," James's father asserted emphatically. "They never heard of free speech? We raised you right, didn't we, J. J.? Speak your mind. President needed to know that not all Americans are just going to roll over and be his lap dog."

James seized on that. "Dog."

"What?"

"Dog." James got up, grabbed the leash off the hook by the back door, and snapped it on Kirby. "I'm just gonna take him for a walk. I, uh, I think I need a little fresh air."

The snow had melted, but the lawns were brown, and the trees were still bare. James started down the sidewalk, moving slowly, ignoring the excited dog pulling on the leash. Anti-war lawn signs had sprung up on many of his neighbors' front lawns like spring tulips: "U.S. out of Africa now!" and "Oppose the Military Mobilization Readiness Law!"

James had gotten halfway down the block when he heard a car approaching from behind. The silence when the motor was turned off was broken by the sound of a car door opening and slamming shut.

"James! My man!" Danny ran up to James and clenched him in a bear hug. "Am I glad to see you!"

James regarded his best friend with strange detachment. "Oh, hi, Danny. What are you doing here?"

Danny looked at him with disbelief. "What am I doing here? Are you serious?"

"So, I guess I owe you three thousand bucks for that venom I didn't use."

"Hell, you paid that back just by stepping out that door."

The dog strained at the leash, insisting they keep moving. James didn't know what to say. How could he tell Danny how sorry he was that he had failed so badly? Failed Danny. Failed everyone.

He noticed Harlan Perkins, his eighty-year-old neighbor, come from around the side of his house, carrying a rake and waving at him. "If it isn't the man who gave the President the peace sign! Did you know you made the national news last night? That took guts, James!"

"Not really."

"Well, I was impressed. And glad you did it. Believe me, I've seen enough wars. Don't need to see another one. Enjoy your walk, fellas."

Harlan went back to his raking. When they were out of earshot of the old guy, James exploded in anguish. "Guts? Shit! I'm the most gutless wonder in the state."

"C'mon, man, don't say that."

"You know it's true, Danny. You alone on this whole planet know how true that is." James waved a hand back toward his house. "My folks are in there right now. They came over to congratulate me. My dad said he's never been prouder of me. I couldn't stand it."

"Man, I'm just glad you're here."

"I shouldn't be, Danny!" cried James. "It was like that time in Little League, that championship game, remember? Bottom of the ninth, two outs. We were down by one, had a guy on third. All I had to do was single him in. And I just stood there and watched the pitches go by, too scared to even swing. Bottom line, I lost my nerve. I failed."

"You're not a killer, man. That's the bottom line."

James looked at Danny, his eyes pleading with him to understand. "When it came down to it, even though I knew Eddie had taken him over, it was still an old guy standing there looking at me. It wasn't an alien waving tentacles at me, it was a human being. I just couldn't make myself do it."

"Honestly, man, I don't know if I could've done it either. I mean, it's easy to say I would have, standing here, but faced with the cold reality? I don't know."

"All the way home, I kept asking myself, would I have done it if our plan had worked? You know, if I could have stood next to him, and done it so no one would have seen. God, Danny, did I chicken out just because I would have been caught doing it?"

Danny gave James a look of pure compassion. "I don't think so, man. Like I said, you're not a killer."

"I finally turned my cell phone back on when we were sitting on the plane waiting to take off. I got your message a little late. So, what's your great new idea for defeating Eddie Olson?"

Danny hesitated. "Uh, I got nothing."

"Nothing?"

"No idea, no. I just said that to get you to stop. I was hoping you'd listen to the message before the concert started and abandon the plan. Listen," Danny said urgently, grabbing James by the shoulders and staring intently into his eyes. "I was watching you live on TV, dude. I went to Garraty's on my lunch hour, got them to tune it to the local station that was carrying it, sat at our table. I even ordered a beer for you and put it where you sit, superstitiously, you know? Like it would hold your place and send you luck so you'd come back. I sat there the whole time, and I wouldn't let them change back to ESPN, I kept saying you'd be on soon. How do you think I felt, man? The longer I sat there, the more I knew it was all bullshit, and chances were ninety-nine percent that I'd see you get blown away by those Secret Service agents right in front of my eyes. That concert was the longest fifteen minutes of my life, man."

Danny gave a little laugh. "You should have seen me when you gave Scofield the peace sign, dude. I was leaping around that place and cheering my fool head off. Everyone thought I was nuts."

James smiled a little at that. "Everyone at Garraty's already thinks you're nuts."

"We were idiots, James. We were just little kids playing James Bond games. God, if I'd had to watch you get killed, I'd never have been able to forgive myself."

"That's my only consolation, that Emily and the kids and my folks didn't have to see that. But, so what? I don't die now, we all die soon enough."

"Hey, it just hit me," Danny said excitedly. "Maybe that was the Way. What if you started a whole peace movement that brings down Scofield?"

James gave Danny an incredulous look. "Are you serious? What peace movement ever stopped a war, Danny? Face it. The Way came, and I booted it."

James glanced down at Kirby and noticed he'd dumped on the neighbor's lawn. For a moment, he considered just leaving it there. What the hell did it matter? Then he pulled the plastic bag out of his pocket and bent over to pick it up. As he straightened up, he held the bag of dog feces out toward Danny.

"You wanna know what I feel like now? You wanna know what I'm worth? This. This is what I'm worth."

"C'mon, man, quit saying that. Whoa." Danny pushed the bag away. "That is some pungent dog shit. Reminds me of the smell that Seeker left in your classroom that time." He laughed, clearly hoping to cheer James up, but James didn't share his amusement.

They walked past a few more houses. James felt so drained of energy he wasn't sure he could make it around the block. Just as he was about to suggest turning around, Danny said, "I wonder what Eddie Olson's signature identity smell is. Rotting garbage mixed with vomit would be appropriate."

"Yeah. Too bad I didn't pick up any distinctive odors coming from Scofield."

To James's surprise, Danny whooped with delight. "James, you're brilliant! That's it, man! That's what we need to do to get Eddie!"

"Huh?"

"We gotta find out what his identity smell is. See, it's like this. Picture yourself walking in a large crowd in a major Chinese city. No one knows you're there. All around you is the sound of Chinese. Then suddenly you hear a voice say in English, 'Hey, James Thompson.' Of course, it really grabs your attention, so you turn with a surprised look on your face to find out where it's coming from."

"OK. So?"

"So, your problem in Washington was that you couldn't positively identify Eddie. We believe he's trapped in Scofield's body, but we don't have any positive physical proof. That's our proof. The next time those Seekers come to you, ask them to release the identity smell of the Deviant One. Then you recreate it—you're a science guy, you must know how to do that—and next time you're face to face with Scofield, you release it. The shocked look on his face should tell you for sure if he's Eddie."

James erupted. "Goddamn it, Danny, shut up! There isn't going to be a next time. Don't you get it? I failed! Those Seekers are never coming back to me. I'm through!"

"Yeah, but..."

"No! No 'yeah buts.' Get it through your head—I failed. I screwed up. No, no—let me put it more accurately. I fucked up. OK? I fucked up. So just shut up and leave me alone!" James pushed Danny roughly aside and strode quickly toward his house, pulling the dog with angry jerks on the leash. He disappeared through his front door without looking back.

CHAPTER 25

James went to bed early again that night. He knew he should feel like making love with Emily after having been gone for a week. But he didn't feel anything.

His folks had mercifully left before lunch. He'd sat in the living room all day staring at the TV, watching one basketball game after another, letting Emily bring him tea and soup. The Timberwolves were on the verge of completing their best season ever. They had a good chance of winning it all this year. So what? It meant nothing.

He was afraid he should be doing a better job of faking being sick, but in fact, he looked awful. Emily kept the kids away, even though they wanted to be with their dad after he'd been gone. She'd urged him to go to bed early.

James thought he might have trouble sleeping. But at least, he told himself, he didn't have to worry about the Seekers showing up while he was asleep anymore. This actually was the sixteenth day, he realized. But there was no way they were coming now. Their future sense must be showing them a different scenario now. Probably the Earth going up in a massive fireball of nuclear war or dying from the complete devastation of the environment. Whatever, it couldn't be good. God, he couldn't think about that. He'd been right all along in telling them he wasn't the man for the job, that they didn't understand, he was no one. Why the hell couldn't they believe him?

James lay in bed and felt the weight of depression sink into him, and found he couldn't think anymore, couldn't organize his mind around any coherent thoughts. He drifted off into a blank sleep. He didn't know when Emily came to bed.

And then his blank grey dreamless sleep filled with colors, first around the edges, then coming in with swirls and flashes. He felt them seize his mind. Oh no. Oh no. This couldn't be.

What are you doing here? I failed!

James felt a calm stillness as the alien waited for him. He supposed the Seeker was waiting for a visual question from him as usual, and this infuriated him. Everything had changed, couldn't they tell? He didn't even try to think in pictures, he just screamed at them in his head: No, you can't keep doing this to me! Find someone better. I told you I couldn't do it, but you wouldn't listen to me, you bastards! You're running out of time. Get someone who can do the job before it's too late!

Maybe he had confused them, or maybe they just didn't know what else to say, so they fell back on the usual visuals. In his mind, he saw himself with the glowing golden thread surrounding him. He saw the copper-colored river again. Were these Seekers total idiots?

Then James saw the floating quilt that represented the future-stream sense. He saw that the dark green splotch had grown much larger and was throbbing, pulsating, with a sticky oily mess erupting from it and spitting onto the quilt, nearly covering it. Yes, of course, he had failed. Couldn't they see that? This was their own future-stream they were showing him, and clearly it showed that the evil Seeker was growing in strength, because he had fail... But wait. There was that golden thread, moving, weaving, coming at the huge dark mess from the right, dancing and shimmering as it tried to contain the dark splotch. The splotch spit an oily patch onto the golden thread, like a bubble bursting in a hot mud pit. The thread was covered, but then it moved again, slowly, weaving over the top. James could sense that it was damaged, ineffective. And then suddenly, all at once the golden lines flowed out from all sides of the dark mess, as if it had unexpectedly, incomprehensively gotten underneath the whole thing unnoticed, and then burst out with its radiant threads like Jack's bean stalk in the fairy tale. The golden threads rapidly wound round and round the oily splotch, tying it up completely and pulling tightly, choking the dark green abomination, which was now dramatically shrinking.

James's mind reeled. What were they doing to him? Were they trying to buck him up, to get him to try again? Were they showing what was still to happen? If they were telling him that he would still succeed, in some unexpected way, then they should help him. Goddamn it, you sons of bitches! You have to help me, then! Tell me what the Way is.

A feeling of sadness pervaded his mind. Perhaps the alien was sorry it had distressed him. But so what? He needed help, not pity.

James marshaled all his mental resources and decided to try to ask the question visually. He pictured the future-stream quilt floating, with himself as the golden thread and the disgusting oily splotch as the Deviant One. He imagined the golden thread doing just what they had shown, surprising the malignant splotch and unexpectedly enveloping it from all sides. Then he froze that mental picture in his head and projected the questioning feeling. How? How does this happen? What is the Way?

In response, the Seeker projected a picture of the quilt with thousands of tiny threads of every color rapidly lighting up at various moments and then subsiding back into the overall pattern of the quilt.

OK, so he got it that the Way is complicated, that millions of factors relate and interweave to lead to the ultimate outcome. Was the Seeker telling him that he had no choice, then? That the Way is predetermined and it's just going to happen no matter what? In that case, why did they even have to come to him in the first place, if it was just going to happen anyway? But maybe the Seekers interacting with him was part of the quilt, of the Way. God, how can I ask them such a complicated question in pictures? Free will versus determinism, as shown in a quilt. Yeah, right. Has God set it all out, and we're just following the path He laid out for us? Ah, God... maybe that's the way to show it.

James pictured the quilt in his mind again. This time he imagined the whirling Tornado they'd used to represent God, placed at the beginning of the quilt; the Tornado blew its wind onto the quilt. Then he carefully imagined certain threads glowing in sequence: red, orange, yellow, green, blue, purple, and finally his own golden thread. He imagined the same thing again in the same sequence. And again. Is God making this happen in a certain predetermined way?

He heard a word in his head: *No.* He saw the quilt with the threads glowing and then fading to a uniform quilt, and then the visual repeating but with a new pattern of glowing threads, as blue and purple glowed together and were followed by orange… dynamic… and then the pattern repeated but many threads glowed simultaneously followed by blue and purple and then silver with the orange… complicated… What was going on? He was hearing words interspersed with the visuals. He saw the quilt again, with the Tornado moving all around it and over it and under it and through it as the threads glowed, hundreds of threads lighting up and then fading… *We create the Way and the Way creates us.* The pattern was growing increasingly complicated, and more beautiful… *The Way flows through all from all with all carrying changing shaping filling being creating ever always.*

Ow, oh my God this hurts; my head hurts; what are you doing to me? A sharp pain stabbed his frontal lobes. James felt a sense of fatigue fill his mind as the Seeker began to pull away. He wanted so badly for the contact to end, but he fought through that desire. Something told him he had to hold on, to ask something else. But what was it? He couldn't think, his head hurt so much.

Just to keep the contact, he pictured himself, with a large Seeker next to him, its white body reaching out and touching his head. He visualized touching his chest several times and saying James. He touched the Seeker. Who are you?

Flashes of red, purple, gold, orange, and silver raced through James's mind in an arrangement like a piano concerto. His nose filled with a distinctive odor.

I got your smell. I smell the ocean—fish, salt, sea. It's a good smell here on Earth.

A pleased feeling filled James's mind, and the pain abated a little with the scent coming into his body. His head cleared a bit more. Then James remembered. Wait! Don't go yet! One more thing. I need to know what the identity smell of the Deviant One is.

James felt the Seeker struggling to hang on. James first imagined the Seeker next to him, then a cloud of chemicals coming from its body. He thought about the smell that he was still receiving. Then James pictured the Deviant One and imagined a cloud of chemicals coming from it. He tried to think of the most disgusting smell he knew. He remembered last summer when the dog had gotten sprayed by a skunk. He hoped the Seeker could read the signals his brain produced by the imagined smell as well as it could read his visual brain signals.

He felt the fatigue of the Seeker, as it struggled to produce one last response before the Portal took it. The picture in his mind showed the evil Seeker with the cloud of chemicals surrounding it. Then he saw the sun, and floating next to the sun, the cube within a cube. Yes, he got it! Next time. Next time, they would make the Deviant One's signature odor for him.

OK. Thank you. He tried to project a feeling of gratitude.

As he felt the Seeker pull away from him and release his mind, he heard four final words in his head: *Have heart strength surging.*

James's eyes popped open. He sat up and grabbed the battery-powered temperature sensor he'd kept on his bedside table for months. 24 degrees. He looked over at Emily and gently nudged her.

"Emmy, Emmy. Wake up."

"Huh?" she said sleepily. She looked at James. "Are you feeling worse? Do you need me to get you something?"

"Actually, yeah, I've got a splitting headache. But that's not why I woke you up."

She sat up and leaned against the headboard next to him. Then she pulled the blankets up around herself. "Geez, why is it so cold in here?"

"I'll explain. But first, do you smell anything?"

Emily sniffed the air, looking puzzled. "Yeah, I do. It smells like—like that time we stayed at that beach house in South Carolina. Like the ocean. That's weird."

James took a deep breath. "Emmy, there's something I have to tell you. I should have told you a long time ago."

Emily looked at him in alarm. "Oh, no! Oh, God, who is it? It's that cute new English teacher, isn't it? That's why you didn't want to have sex when you got back from the trip, isn't it? That's why you'd hardly look at me. God, I was so stupid. Was she a chaperone on the trip, too? Were you and she… were you…?" Emily started to cry.

"No, no, that's not it. Not at all." James's mind was reeling, hardly able to comprehend Emily's hysterical accusation, when all he could think about was the aliens he'd never told her about, the aliens that had just been in his head moments ago.

James tried again, putting his arm around her, pulling her close. "I know I should have told you sooner. But I was trying to protect you. I kept thinking that every time it happened would be the last time, that it wouldn't happen again, and I'd have no need to tell you…"

Emily was crying harder now. Between sobs, she choked out, "Then it's that woman on the reunion committee, isn't it? Or was there even really a committee? Were you just secretly meeting her every time you told me you had a meeting?"

James had to make her understand. "No, stop, please, Emmy! There's no one else. You have to believe me." He held her tight. He kissed her wet face, over and over. "I love you. I swear there's no one but you. There never will be. I promise. I love you so much."

Gradually, slowly, the sobbing subsided into little jerky gasps, the tears slowed and then stopped. She looked at him with blotchy, pleading eyes. "You're not having an affair?"

"No. I swear to God, no. Believe me, this is a lot harder to explain." James took a big breath, and plunged ahead, holding the temperature sensor for her to see. "First, look at this. Twenty-four degrees, right? OK, here's the deal. Remember that night last fall, when I woke up from a nightmare, screaming? Maybe you don't remember, but it was this cold in the room then, too. And you said you dreamt there was an intruder in the room? There was." James took a big breath and plunged ahead. "Just not a human one."

CHAPTER 26

Somehow, life went on. Somehow, even though you tried to stop an evil alien and you failed, life went on.

Somehow, you told your wife and she freaked out and finally she believed you, and life went on. That had been the longest night of James's life. What he hadn't expected was how betrayed Emily would feel. That he'd kept this huge thing from her for so long. That he'd shared it with Danny, and not her. That he hadn't trusted her.

He'd tried to explain: It was because he loved her so much, he couldn't risk losing her if she thought he was crazy. It was because he needed, absolutely needed, to have this island of stability to come home to, to keep him grounded in normal life, when the mind-boggling weirdness of the whole alien thing threatened to overwhelm him. Emily, the kids, they were the calm eye of the hurricane for him. It was because he didn't want it to be real, and if she didn't know, then at home, he could pretend it wasn't. It was because he felt protective of her. It was because, it was because... And then he'd looked at her and really saw the deep hurt, and he'd said simply, "You're right, I should have told you. Right away. I'm sorry." And they began to climb out of the bottomless pit of that night.

Somehow, you still went to your job, your kids still went to school, you made love to your wife again, and life went on.

Somehow, you signed your son up for Little League, and agreed to be his team manager again this year, because he really wanted you to, and summer was coming, and the world hadn't ended yet, and life went on. Somehow, you consoled your daughter when her Destination Imagination team lost at State because they blew their Instant Challenge, and you told her they'd do better next year, even though you were afraid there wouldn't be a next year.

It was incredible. Life on Earth was this close to ending, and yet life went on as if everything was normal. The big news last week: Scofield was sending more troops to Africa. Not just Angola, but now to South Africa as well, where there'd been another rebel attack against a U.S. corporation. People who were being paid subsistence wages to work in vast fields and large processing plants (who even knew we had such a huge operation in Africa before last week?) rioted and attacked the company's headquarters. James watched the tobacco fields burning on CNN, saw the anguished mothers carrying their small children's thin, burned bodies from the fields they'd been working in when they were set afire by the enraged mobs, and saw Eddie's hand lighting the match.

Six months ago, James hadn't even been aware that U.S. corporations had so many fingers in Africa. Now he knew that Africa was the fastest-growing part of the world for U.S. businesses, with production of everything from mining to clothing manufacturing to food and so much more. Their CEOs were united in calling for our government to protect them from the growing threat, the face of which was dark as night.

The U.S. army was engaged in "defensive" actions in two African countries, and the rest of the continent looked primed to explode in rage at the growing U.S. military presence. These military actions were not officially called war yet. Congress had only declared a resolution in support of defending U.S. interests abroad, but that apparently gave the President free rein to do as he pleased militarily.

James watched the sham of the African governments asserting their independence all over the media. They brandished empty threats and sputtered about how the American troops had better limit themselves to self-defense. Their governments declared that the troops would be ejected from their countries if their mission became one of aggression rather than protection. It was all show, staged to placate their citizens. According to many journalists, the American corporations had government officials in their pockets. Only last week James had read an article about the Minister of Defense in Kenya building a lavish personal residence, what would have been called a palace if he'd been a king. It was an ages-old story.

The real resistance was coming from the better-organized rebel groups, especially the African Liberation Organization. Scofield had done what the colonial powers had been unable to do: force Africans to look beyond tribal loyalties. People who had warred for centuries were now uniting to fight the American devil. Soon enough it would erupt into full-scale war, and Eddie Olson's lust to destroy life might be unstoppable.

Of course, the media on the left railed against American exploitation of child labor. There were exposés about the health risks to African workers, and about how American corporations were permanently damaging the environment in so many African nations. So what? America had a long history of not caring about what happened in Africa. What happens in Africa stays in Africa, James thought bitterly. Except slavery, of course. Eddie was smart in finding the one continent in the world that could burn long and hard before the rest of humanity did anything about it.

In James's classes, those students who were already eighteen now chatted with their neighbors on Monday mornings about the assault weapon they'd learned to fire at their Military Readiness Camp that weekend, casually bragging about blowing away human-looking targets, which he had no doubt were printed with dark-colored skin. James feared that in another six months he'd be reading some of their names in the Westfield Wire, the school newspaper, under the heading, "Remembering Westfield's Fallen Heroes."

Life goes on, James thought, sitting in the Perk-O-Lation Coffee Shop. It is absurd that I am sitting here attending this meeting of the Westfield High School twenty-year reunion committee, but here I am. Like it matters anymore.

James sipped his coffee and looked at the five people sitting at the table with him for the last time, thank God. He heard the staccato of Miranda's heels behind him and turned to see her hurrying back to the table, her dark brown ponytail swinging from side to side as she carried a fresh double espresso latte. Miranda had been the class President, the star of the class plays, and the editor of the yearbook. Now she was taking a leave of absence from her high-powered business job to stay home with her two young children. She was putting all that organizational energy into this committee. This would be the best Westfield High reunion ever, of that she was determined.

Miranda picked up her latte, sipped it, and smiled graciously at the group. "Thanks for all you've done, gang. I really couldn't have done it without each one of you and all the hard work you—we all—put in. All right, so this is where we're at. Everything at the Rec Center has been arranged, and we've got a good group of a dozen volunteers to decorate that morning."

Stacy looked annoyed. Stacy, the girl who'd been the subject of half the conversations in the boys' locker room. What would those gorgeous breasts feel like? Would she let you put your tongue in her mouth?

"Well," Stacy said, flipping her long blond hair back with an irritated gesture, "if anyone complains about not having it at a more upscale place, don't come to me. You know I wanted The Starlight Room at the top of the Northern Lights Hilton, Miranda."

"I know, Stacy," Miranda said, giving her an ingratiating smile. "I wish we had the budget. But you know what, your fabulous decorations will transform the place, I just know they will. It's so wonderful that you had that connection with ReImagineIt Interiors. It's going to blow people away when they enter that tropical paradise as they walk in." Miranda was gushing again. She did that a lot.

"Well," Stacy said, "I really hit it off with their head designer when they did the set for that modeling shoot I did for Mermaid Swimwear."

James sipped his coffee and regarded Stacy with amusement. Somehow, she managed to refer to her modeling career at every meeting they had.

Miranda pulled a piece of paper from her bag stuffed with reunion business. "Laura couldn't make it, but she sent this for you to see. It's the final design for the program." She passed the paper to James. Good Lord. It featured dancing Hawaiian hula girls holding exotic tropical drinks on a sunset beach. Like that had anything to do with Westfield High School in Minnesota.

Miranda continued. "You all should have gotten your invitations a few weeks ago. We've gotten a good response so far."

"Hey," James said. "That reminds me. Danny wanted me to thank you for taking his suggestion to make it casual dress."

Miranda shuddered. "Yes, well, we didn't make that decision based on Danny Friedman's fashion sense, I'm afraid. We all still remember that godawful gold lamé tuxedo he wore to prom. Still, going casual makes sense, with the tropical theme. And you can still get some pretty glittery casual clothes, am I right, Stacy?"

Stacy's eyes lit up. "Oh, absolutely. I've got these great spiky-heeled sandals, and you should see the cute little tropical dress I got, with this pink and gold sequined flamingo on it," she said, running her hands over her breasts where the flamingo would be. James smiled inwardly. If only the guys from the locker room could be here now. They'd have enough fantasy material to last them for years.

Louis took the program from James and looked at it. He was wearing a T-shirt with a CompuBoyz logo, as usual. "Girls," he said. He always called them girls. And they always gave each other a look when he did. In high school, he'd never have talked to either Miranda or Stacy. Clearly, he was enjoying this now. "Girls, tropical night at the Rec Center is perfect. This'll seem special, like being on a Caribbean cruise, which is something many people would never be able to afford. Not everyone has done as well as I have, with my own tech support company. And anyway, you know the Rec Center means a lot to our class, since we were the first to have our senior all-night party there."

Somehow James could picture Louis at the all-night party twenty years ago, parked at the roulette table and never moving.

"All right," Miranda said impatiently. "Moving on. Music. As you can see on the program, Garth was able to get Slugfest to play for us, so good job on that."

James smiled with real pleasure. "Excellent, Garth! I didn't even know they were still playing together. You've got to admire that, keeping their dream alive. Slugfest was the first concert I ever went to."

Stacy sighed. "So basically, the theme of this event is going to be, the last twenty years were an illusion, we're really still in high school?"

"Not exactly, Stacy," Louis said. "It's going to be New and Improved High School. I own CompuBoyz now. I think Melanie Schwartz will dance with me this time."

Louis stretched his hand toward James to give him a high five. What the hell. James high-fived him, just to annoy Miranda and Stacy.

"I think I need another latte," Stacy said, standing up. "Can I get you a hot chocolate, Louis?" she asked sarcastically.

It went right over his head. "My treat," he said expansively, standing up to accompany Stacy to the counter.

Miranda checked off another item on her list and looked up. "Thanks for lining up the caterer at such a fabulous price, James. I hear her food is to die for! And you're sure you can round up four reliable people who will be willing to bartend and serve drinks? For tips?"

"Yeah, no problem."

Miranda perused her list, checking off items. "So that covers entertainment, prizes, food and drink, decorations, photographer, memory book… I think we're all set."

James made a move to get up, but Miranda put her hand on his arm. "Wait a minute till they get back. I have some big news that I was saving till the end."

When Stacy and Louis sat down with their beverages, Miranda gave them all a triumphant smile. "I was just telling James that I have some very big news to share."

Louis's eyes lit up. "I hope it's that the cheerleaders are reuniting and are going to do a special cheer for us. That would be worth the price of admission right there. Do you think they could do a special cheer for my software company? You know we bankrolled a large part of this reunion."

"We are all well aware of that, Louis," Miranda said.

"C-O-M-P-U-B-O-Y-Z! Be sure to tell them it's a 'Z' at the end."

Miranda sighed. "This has nothing to do with the cheerleaders."

"Well, it's a good idea," he said defensively.

Miranda gave him a dismissive look, replaced by a brilliant smile as she beamed at the others expectantly. "You know we've all been assuming that you-know-who wouldn't come? Well... I thought I'd better give him a personal call in addition to the invitation, you know, because he might have to clear it with security or something, and so I just thought I'd give him a buzz. So, I managed to get his number, and I left a message, but I didn't really know if he even listens to his own messages or if he has someone screen them or what, you know? But guess what? I just talked to him today! He's coming!"

Stacy exclaimed, "Oh my God! Really? That's fabulous! I'm shocked."

"I know!" Miranda said, squealing with excitement like a schoolgirl.

Louis gave Stacy a leering look. "You gonna dance with your old boyfriend, Stacy?"

Stacy didn't even look at Louis. "I can't wait to tell Heidi!"

"No, you can't," Miranda said firmly. "We're not supposed to tell anyone. I got this very official telephone call from Jack Cambridge's personal Secret Service agent. He said they don't like to advertise the Vice President's brother's movements—terrorists, you know. We can't tell anyone until the day of.

"He also said this will require additional security. An advance team will be checking out the Rec Center and the surrounding area before the event. They want all doors locked from the outside, except the main entrance. They'll be checking people's purses and bags, and all packages and equipment going in. But that's really no big deal, is it, guys? I mean, Jack Cambridge is coming to our twenty-year Westfield High School reunion, right?"

The floating blanket with the dark blotchy mess and the blooming golden threads popped into James's mind, and he knew. "Son of a gun!" James said. "That's it! That's the Way!"

"Pardon me?" Miranda said.

James pulled himself together. "Oh. Nothing. Just a personal thing."

"Well, you're grinning like the Cheshire Cat."

CHAPTER 27

"When you're right, you're really right." James said to Emily as they were putting the finishing touches on the set-up in the bedroom. "It's a lot better now that you know what's going on."

"Try to remember that next time, would you please?"

James adjusted the security camera and checked the view again on the monitor. Tonight was the night, and over the last week they'd worked hard planning for it. James had arranged around the room several wide jars filled with sodium hydrogen carbonate and activated charcoal. Each of them had air-tight tops nearby to quickly contain whatever odors the Seekers released tonight. He picked up the jar next to his bedside and moved it a couple centimeters over.

"Quit futzing with those, honey," Emily said. "Relax. They're fine."

It had been James's idea to try to get a video recording of the aliens. He'd actually thought about doing it back when he first knew they'd be coming to him on a predictable basis, but he hadn't been able to figure out how to explain the camera to Emily. Now she was in on it, and it was finally happening. He'd been going to use his phone, but that was less than ideal. But good old Danny had come through again. He'd gotten hold of a very expensive high-resolution camera that would record all night long onto a storage chip. It also stamped the date and time on the video. If he ever ended up publishing his discovery, he would have the hard evidence.

James had been mentally wrestling with himself for months. The Big Question: report his findings, or keep them secret to protect the Seekers? Much as he wanted to be the one who broke the discovery of an alien civilization to the world, he was well aware of what the world might do to those aliens. If they were physical beings, he thought, they couldn't travel faster than the speed of light, which meant that they probably lived within the solar system. If that were true, we'd find them eventually. Humans didn't have a good track record of treating other species with respect, or other humans, for that matter. James was sure that if the world ever became convinced of the Seekers' existence, there would be a loud contingent pressing for preemptive destruction of the aliens before they could destroy us.

Well, whatever he ultimately decided to do with this recording, he couldn't wait to see it. The first look ever at an alien species! It was unbelievable, but it was about to happen. At least, so he hoped. He unconsciously crossed his fingers.

James adjusted the dimmer knob on the light switch on the wall again. He hoped he had the light level set right. It was a delicate balance, all the more so because he really didn't know what the parameters were. He was afraid that if the lights were too bright the Seekers wouldn't come. He had no idea if they had technology on their planet such that they would recognize, and shy away from, the video camera. He'd been experimenting with the lights all evening, using Emily as his subject, adjusting it to the lowest possible level at which he could still see her with some detail. Still, he worried that any variation from the usual darkness would keep them away.

Emily came over to him and put her arms around him. "I've got to admit, I'm really nervous. I'm glad you told me about all this, but a little part of me wishes I didn't have to know. You know what I mean?"

James stroked her hair and held her close. "Yeah, of course. A part of me wishes they'd never contacted me. It is really scary, knowing that aliens are coming into our house. I don't blame you for sending the kids over to my folks' house to sleep tonight."

"I was just afraid I'd wake up screaming and really scare them."

Emily squeezed James tighter. "OK, I admit it. I'm being an overprotective mother. I just feel better having the kids somewhere else tonight."

"That's OK. Whatever you need to do. It's only been a little over two weeks since you found out about this." Emily gave him a reproachful look. He added quickly, "I know, I'm sorry. I'm still sorry. Anyway, I'm more used to it than you are. C'mere."

James pulled Emily with him as he sat down on the bed. She snuggled next to him and he put his arms around her. "I promise you. It'll be OK. I trust them. From everything I've learned about them, everything I told you, they have no reason to harm us and every reason to want to see us survive."

"That's good."

"Emmy, I wish you could see what I've seen. I wish you could see all the colors, and the Life Force. It's unbelievably amazing. I wish I could get them to go into your head and show you, 'cause there's no way I can describe it in words."

"Oh, that's OK," Emily said. "They can stay out of my brain, thank you."

"Hey," James said, pointing at the video camera and waggling his eyebrows suggestively. "Maybe we should test out the video system. I've always wanted our own personal triple-X video."

"Uh no, that's not gonna happen." Emily jumped off the bed and ran around to the other side. James chased after her, and she giggled when he caught her and embraced her. Then she pushed him away. "Seriously. Not tonight, dear, you're about to have a headache. An alien headache."

James laughed. "Fine, have it your way. You'll regret missing this opportunity, though."

"I think it's time to take the sleeping pills."

"Thanks again for getting the prescription, honey."

"No problem. So, should I rake you over the coals again for not telling me you had a dependence on sleeping pills, or have you had enough?"

"Enough. Cheers," James said, clinking his water glass against Emily's as they downed the medication.

3:36 a.m. James was standing in front of a class of hostile tenth-graders, trying to teach them about cell mitosis, but panicked because he realized he had forgotten to prepare the lesson plan, and somehow, he could remember nothing about the subject. Suddenly everyone in the class was laughing at him. He looked down and discovered he'd forgotten to put on pants. Fortunately, at that moment a gentle blue cloud floated in front of him, covering him, and the class was drifting away in a haze of greenish-brown, and now cells were dividing in front of his eyes, giant cells, their mitochondria elongating and squiggling like eels, red eels, yellow eels, blue eels, dancing, shimmering...

He felt his mind being seized.

Hello. Thank you for coming. James felt a huge sense of relief that they'd shown up as scheduled, but for some reason he couldn't remember why. Did he want to ask them something about cells dividing?

The Seeker patiently waited. This was really odd. He couldn't come up with the question, but there had to be something he was supposed to ask. How long could they hold out like this before the Portal called this Seeker away?

Then the Seeker projected a visual, of the Deviant One with a cloud of chemicals around it.

A feeling of relief swept over James. That was it. It didn't matter that he hadn't been able to remember, because it hadn't occurred to these Seekers not to keep their word. They'd promised to give him the Deviant One's identity smell, and so they were delivering.

A strong smell entered James's nose, confusing him with an odd combination of discordant scents. They didn't go together at all. Lemon, he could catch that. Maybe mint. Something really acrid. Something else, like decaying leaves. Maybe a decaying body. What was that other odor? He couldn't place it.

He felt the Seeker pulling away. He felt relieved that the

connection was over already, and that his brain didn't hurt at all this time.

He opened his eyes. The odor in the room was strong, stronger than it had ever been before. Excited, James sat up in bed and shook Emily. He checked the clock. He checked the temperature: 29 degrees. He shook Emily again. She was hard to rouse, probably a combination of the sleeping meds and whatever the Seekers did to suppress her consciousness while they were in his brain.

James jumped up and hurried around the room, covering half of the scent-trapping dishes. In his excitement, he almost knocked one of them off the dresser. He decided to leave the others open longer, to continue receiving the chemical fallout.

He rushed back to Emily. He had to watch the recording, right now, and he knew she'd be mad if he did it without her. "Emily!" he almost shouted. "C'mon, wake up! They were here!"

Emily's eyelids fluttered up groggily. "Huh?"

"Honey, they were here! It happened! Don't you smell it?"

Emily finally dragged herself more fully awake as the powerful smell hit her. "Wow. They were here? For real? Oh my God." Her next reaction surprised James, as she started to cry.

"What's wrong?" he asked anxiously, holding her in his arms. "They didn't hurt you, did they? What's wrong, baby?"

Emily looked at James, her eyes shining, her cheeks wet with tears, and he suddenly realized they were tears of joy. "It's real. Life beyond Earth. Other beings out there. They're real."

"Yeah, it is," he said softly. "They are. It's amazing, isn't it?"

"Yes. It's wonderful."

"Hey, before the smell fades away here, I need you to try to help me figure out what it is."

"OK. I can tell you one thing—it's unbelievably disgusting." Emily took a deep sniff, then reflected thoughtfully. "This is tough. Something rotten, I think, like meat that's gone way bad. Something else I can't place. I think I'm getting a smell like when they tar the roads. Or maybe it's more like nail polish remover, but I'm not sure.

Weird, I just got a hint of mint. And lemon, maybe?"

"This one seems more complicated than the others have been," James said regretfully. "It might be tough to recreate." He got up again and covered a few more dishes. Then he turned to Emily with excitement lighting up his eyes. "Let's go watch a video!"

———————————

James's fingers fumbled with the connection. He was so excited his hands were shaking. He turned on the TV and settled down on the couch, snuggling up to Emily. "No one else in the whole world knows it, but at this very moment we are about to experience history. We are about to be the very first human beings to see an alien species from another planet. Ready?"

She grabbed his hand and squeezed it tight. "Yeah. I guess so. Ready."

James fast-forwarded the recording to the 3:15 time stamp, and they peered intently at the screen. After a few minutes of staring at nothing but their sleeping selves, Emily suddenly said, "Oh geez. I can't believe that."

"What? Did you see them? Where?"

"No, I can't believe I sleep with my mouth hanging open like that. That's gross."

"Don't worry, honey. I'm asleep, too. I can't see you. Now can we focus on the search for aliens here?"

"Right. Sure." Emily stared at the screen again. After a few more minutes, she said, "You look pretty restless. See, you're kind of moving your head around. Do you think they've contacted you? I can't see anything."

"I don't know. I think I was dreaming just before they came, so that might just be me dreaming. I don't see anything unusual in the room yet."

They stared at the murky screen.

"Look!" James exclaimed. "Look at my head. I was thrashing it back and forth and look—I just stopped and suddenly relaxed. I think something might be happening." He rewound one minute and played it again.

"Yeah, I think you're right," Emily agreed. "What's the time on it?"

James paused it at the moment his head became still. "3:36. That would be about right. But I don't see them." He pressed play, and they continued to watch.

At the 3:44 mark, they watched the sleeping James wake up and check the temperature, and then shake Emily.

"Darn it, where were they?" Emily asked. "Did you see them?"

"No," James replied in a distressed voice. "What if they're just spiritual entities? What if they have no corporeal bodies that we can capture on video?" He looked at Emily with alarm. "You do believe me, don't you?"

Emily put her arm around James. "Absolutely. I have complete faith in you. Anyway, I smelled that nasty smell too. Let's watch it again."

"OK. Maybe we should sit closer to the screen."

They moved closer and started watching from the 3:30 mark. At the 3:41 mark, James yelled "There!" He ran it back and paused it. "Look, there!" He put his finger on a spot on the TV screen near his head. "Look," he said excitedly. "See that little bit of color distortion there?"

He ran it frame by frame. "Yeah, it's definitely there! See, it's white, and then there's a little bit of color." He kept it running frame by frame. "Oh my God, look! Color flashes! There and there and there and there!" His finger poked at spots on the screen, quick tiny flashes of rainbow colors clustered in the air near their bed.

James let out a loud whoop, and leaped around the room, shouting for joy. "Yeah! Yeah!" He punched his fists in the air in jubilation. Then he grabbed Emily and whirled her around the room, laughing and yelling with exultant abandon.

"We did it! We did it!"

Emily grinned at him. "Congratulations."

"Thank you. Wow, I can't believe it. I've got 'em."

"So that was really them, those little flashes of color."

"Oh, yeah. I'm sure of it. We just need a better monitor to get a closer look at them."

The recording was continuing to play frame by frame. "Pause it!" Emily commanded.

"What?"

"Look, look at your head. You just turned it slightly. Look there at the side. It looks like a little patch of white on your forehead. Right there."

James peered at the screen. "You're right." He turned to Emily with excitement. "I think that might be the one who's connected with my brain. Whoa."

"It's really tiny."

"Yeah. No wonder we didn't spot them our first time through. We were looking for way bigger creatures."

"Yeah, I thought you told me they looked huge when you had those visions of them coming to Earth."

"Yeah, yeah they did." James shook his head and said with surprise, "I think they were trying to deke me. I think they didn't want us to know how small they are."

"Maybe. Or maybe they just don't think of themselves as small. To themselves, they're normal, you know what I mean? Like, we don't think of ourselves as small, but to a whale we are. I suppose in the ant world, they don't consider themselves small either. It's all relative."

"Yeah, you may be right. Still, I'm shocked to find out they're so tiny. This is amazing! Hey, look, there's another white spot on my head. And another one. Oh man, I think I just saw a colored spot on my ear. Let me run that back." He gasped in surprise as he watched it again. "Damn, that one might have gone into my ear. Oh man, there's three more, right there by my nose, maybe more."

"It's like you're being swarmed by alien mosquitoes. This is freaky."

"Yeah, no kidding." James picked up the remote and paused it.

"I'm counting at least fourteen on me or around me. Probably sixteen total, if I know these guys."

Emily looked at him with surprise.

At the 3:43 mark, they saw the first little white patch on James's head flash with a myriad of iridescent colors. Tiny flashes of color echoed from the others. Then the patch turned white again, and at 3:44 it lifted from James's head. The rest were all white now again. The tiny white blurs hung in the air for a moment, and then they were all gone, as if they had dissolved.

Emily turned to James. "Wow."

James sat quietly for a minute, overwhelmed, letting the miracle sink in, and then stood up. "I'm gonna go upstairs and cap the rest of those containers. Think you could make us some coffee? 'Cause there's no way I'm going back to sleep tonight." As he left the room, he turned back to Emily, eyes burning with excitement. "Can you imagine what those guys are gonna look like on Danny's huge TV?"

CHAPTER 28

James couldn't help flashing back to that New Year's Eve night—it seemed like eons ago—when they'd stood on the Friedmans' steps just like this. How innocent he'd been, standing there on the threshold of a year he couldn't have conjured up in his wildest fantasies. How could he have imagined that a few hours later aliens would talk to him in his head and tell him that he was going to be the one human being who was destined to bring down the most powerful person in the world?

Now he and Emily stood here again, and again he held a champagne bottle in his hand. But this time, they were celebrating the alien contact. And this time, Emily was holding not a plate of crab puffs, but a bag full of jars containing odors emitted by those aliens.

A line from an old song popped into James's head: "What a long strange trip it's been." It had been four nights since the Seekers' visit, and they were here to view the recording on Danny's state-of-the-art TV.

James rang the bell. Jenna opened the door, with baby Jaymi in her arms. Jaymi's face lit up with a huge grin when she saw them. James poked a finger into his namesake's tummy, tickled her gently, and said in a high-pitched voice, "Hello, little angel. I am so happy to see you, too."

"Hi guys." Jenna let out a big sigh. "Whew. Sorry, I'm still kinda freaked out about all this."

Emily put her arm around Jenna. "I know just how you feel. Listen, let's you and me go in the kitchen and get some snacks. I think we need a little girl time first. You can vent to me about them being such jerks and not telling us. I am totally with you, girl." She gave a meaningful look to James and led Jenna toward the kitchen.

When James had called Danny to tell him he'd successfully gotten video of the aliens, and wanted to watch it on Danny's TV, Danny had suggested Wednesday night, since Jenna went to her book club that night. James had had to reluctantly explain that Emily was insisting that Jenna be let in on the secret. "I'm not getting together with them for the next twenty years with all three of us knowing and Jenna in the dark," she'd said. "Danny's got to tell her. Those things came into their house. Jenna's got to know."

Danny had resisted. "She's a lot more emotional than Emily," he'd said. "I don't know what she'd do. She might throw things at me."

But James had persisted, since Emily had threatened to tell Jenna herself if Danny wouldn't. Finally, Danny had to agree. Before he'd hung up the phone, though, James left Danny with one admonition: "Don't tell her about what I almost did in Washington. That goes with you and me to the grave."

James followed Danny downstairs to the family room. "Here. This is it."

Danny took it eagerly. "I can't wait to hook this sucker up and see it!"

As he worked on the connections, James asked him, "So how'd Jenna take it?"

"At first she thought I was kidding. You know, I kind of have a joker reputation, and she was sure I was gonna say "gotcha" as soon as she said she believed me. When I finally convinced her I was serious, it was like you said. She was really pissed that I'd kept this big secret from her. I think now she's at the point that she accepts that you believe aliens have contacted you, and she respects you. I think she's still skeptical. But this should bring her around."

As he turned on the TV to check the connection, Danny added, "She can't stand Scofield either, so if we're working to bring him down and stop this African war before it turns into World War III, she's all behind that. As long as we don't get ourselves hurt, anyway. That's the one big thing she's worried about."

"Yeah, Emily too. I told her we haven't figured out what we're gonna do at the reunion yet, but it won't involve anything dangerous." James waited a beat, then added, "I hope I didn't lie to her again."

They settled down on the couch to wait for their wives, flipping through the stations. Apparently, yet again there was breaking news. Danny turned up the volume.

Over scenes of a shanty town on fire, they listened to a reporter relate the grim account: "Earlier today, rebels attacked the corporate headquarters of American Petroleum Industries in the Republic of Congo. It now appears that American Petroleum had secretly requested U.S. government military protection, fearing attacks from the African Liberation Organization, as happened recently in South Africa. A small contingent of troops appears to have been in place at the American Petroleum headquarters when rebels attacked. At this point, it seems that the American troops surprised the rebel attackers and pursued them into the slums of Pointe-Noire, the coastal city where the company is located. There are conflicting accounts of the number of casualties and the amount of property damage. However, no U.S. troops are reported killed or injured."

"Shit," Danny said. "Eddie Olson just cranked it up again."

"I just can't believe the American public's getting behind him on this."

"He doesn't seem to be bringing out the best in our country."

"Tell me about it. I just got the latest report from the Southern Poverty Law Center. White supremacist hate groups have exploded in the last few months—tripled in memberships, and new groups are springing up every day."

"Yeah, I'm getting the same news from the Anti-Defamation League."

"I didn't tell you yet what happened to us Sunday night," James said, a disturbed look on his face.

"What happened?" Jenna asked brightly, coming into the room with a big bowl of buttered popcorn, which she put down on the coffee table.

"It was awful," Emily said, shuddering as she put napkins, bowls and salt on the table. "I was so scared. But you should have seen James. He really was our hero that night."

"What happened, man?" Danny asked with concern.

"We were out for a family night, having pizza at the kids' favorite place, Pizza Paradise," James explained. "Just having a good time, when suddenly this white guy comes over to our table, and he's clearly drunk. He just starts throwing obscenities at us, the f-word, the n-word... you know how it goes. He's yelling at Emily about being a traitor to her race and yelling at me to take my bastard kids back to Africa."

"Oh my God," Jenna said, shocked. "What did you do?"

"I was so scared," Emily said. "I just couldn't believe it was happening. The guy seemed so crazy, I was afraid he was going to attack us. But James defended us. He was so great."

"What'd you do, man?" Danny asked. "You punch him out?"

"You better believe I wanted to. But my first priority was keeping the family safe. I mean, I didn't know if he was armed, right? So I just got into his space, backed him up a little, got between him and the family. Fortunately," James smiled, "I had at least six inches on him. I told him to back off and leave my family alone."

"The whole restaurant was watching," Emily added. "No one knew what to do. Except the kids, actually. They got under the table, which was really smart of them. They told me later they learned that in their active shooter drills at school."

"Oh jeez, that's freaky. So, did he back off?" asked Jenna.

"No." James looked grim. "He said I should be swinging from a noose, and he wished he could be the one to tie the rope. And then he spit in my face."

"Then you hit him?" Danny said.

"No. I took out my phone. I told him I was gonna have his sorry ass arrested for assault. The asshole just started shouting about how they should arrest me for polluting the white race. Then he pointed at Emily and called her the c-word. That's what pushed me over the edge. I shoved him pretty hard, and he hit the floor."

"Oh my god. Did the cops arrest him?" Jenna asked.

"The guy tried to get out before the cops got there, and three guys at a table near the door stood up and blocked him. They told him to sit down and wait for the cops. And he did. It was great." James laughed. "It was like the rainbow coalition of justice—a Hispanic guy, a white guy and an Asian guy."

"So that's the more or less happy ending to this scary story," Emily said. "The kids were pretty shaken up, but they saw their dad stand up to the guy and they saw other people do the same thing."

"So, do you have to press charges?" Jenna asked.

Emily looked regretful. "They took him in, but the cop called us later to tell us they let the guy go after he sobered up. They said they were sorry, but if we wanted to press charges, it probably wouldn't go anywhere. I'm pretty sure they're seeing this kind of thing happen more often lately, you know? I mean, it's just insane."

"We can hope this one guy got scared enough to not do that again, but that still leaves hundreds of other racists out there ready to go off at any time," James said.

"One cool thing," Emily added, "was that one of the police officers took Danielle and Trey's statements, too, and she was really respectful about what they said. She knew what to say to help them feel less traumatized. I can tell they're still freaked out, though. And truthfully, so am I."

"I'm so sorry, guys," Jenna said sympathetically.

"The other good thing is the manager gave us coupons for 12 free pizzas," James said, grinning.

"Screw racists. Their time is done," Danny declared emphatically. He turned to the group assembled on the couch with an eager look of anticipation in his eyes. "And now, it's time to find out how. Let's look at this video and see what we can find out about our Seeker buddies."

They watched the video once through, without pausing, so that James could get Danny and Jenna's initial impressions. He delighted in the audible gasp they let out when they first spotted a flash of color in the dim night scene.

"Holy shit!" Danny exclaimed. "Was that one of 'em? Holy shit!"

When they saw James wake up on the screen, Jenna turned to James. "I can't believe I'm saying this, but unless you went to a whole lot of trouble to make a fake video to fool me—and I can't think of one possible reason for you to do that—I'm convinced. You've got aliens coming to you. That's just totally crazy. Wow."

"This calls for a celebration," Danny said, jumping up from the couch. He passed around champagne glasses and filled them. "To James Thompson, discoverer of aliens and future Nobel prize winner!"

"I'll drink to that," James said, as the women said, "To James!"

"Now I've got one," James said, as they raised their glasses again. "To peace on Earth, and peace between planets."

"Hear, hear," they all agreed.

They watched the recording again in super slow motion. It was amazing what a difference it made viewing it on a large ultra-high-definition TV. This time, they could spot the Seekers before the colors started flashing.

James ran the recording back to the point where he believed the Seekers entered the room. "I still can't see how they get in," he said. Then he said excitedly, "There! There's a little white splotch near my head; you see it? That must be the one that makes contact with my brain."

"Oh my God, James," Jenna said. "I can't believe you just said those words so casually. If I had aliens hooking into my brain, I would so totally freak out."

"Oh, believe me, I did at first," James said. "Now I've kind of gotten used to it, in a weird way."

"Oh my God," Jenna repeated.

"OK," James said after the second viewing. "Now I want to go frame by frame, and I want us to use these." He pulled out four strong magnifying glasses and handed them around. They stood in front of the screen, ready to decipher the aliens.

Unfortunately, they'd had to set up a wide-angle shot to get as much of the room as possible, since they didn't know where the aliens would be. Even on a large screen, and even with the zoom function, it was impossible to make out details on the tiny white blobs floating in the dimly lit room.

"They look like little torn pieces of tissues floating in the air," Jenna observed. "Hardly what you see in the movies."

"You know what we should do?" Danny suggested. "We'll hook this up to my printer and print out whatever frames you want to study more closely."

"Yeah, good idea," James agreed.

They had now identified fourteen distinct Seeker entities floating in the air, near the one on James's head.

"Holy shit!" Danny suddenly yelled. "Run that back! OK, pause there." Little white blobs hung around James's head. "See those three? Right by your nostrils? Ok, run it frame by frame and watch them." As they peered at the screen, the three Seekers seemed to disappear up James's nose.

"Oh my God, honey," Emily said with concern, "it looks like you just accidentally inhaled them."

Danny burst out laughing. "Jesus Christ, bro! You just snorted aliens! That's like the most powerful blow ever! Shit, they even look like cocaine. Talk about a high!"

Jenna rapped Danny on the arm, admonishing him that this was serious.

When Danny recovered himself, James said thoughtfully, "Actually, your analogy may be better than you know. The olfactory nerve is the most direct conduit into the brain. It bypasses the blood-brain barrier. That's why cocaine is so quickly effective."

Emily looked alarmed. "So, you're telling me that these alien things might have been literally in your head? Not just on it, but in your brain? God, that's so scary."

"Yeah. Yeah, it is. But I can tell you that I feel fine. I don't feel any different. At least not yet."

They watched James slowly turn his head on the TV screen. Danny peered at the Seeker on James's head through his magnifying glass. "OK, here it goes, here comes some color. It's communicating."

"Whoa," Emily said, as her husband's dark forehead lit up with a little patch of iridescent colors, like an oil slick on water.

"I think they're replicating what your guy is saying," Danny said, pointing to the other Seekers floating onscreen. As near as their limited human eyes could make out, it did look like the others were almost instantly lighting up with the same colors that James's Seeker was producing.

"This must be when they release the smell," James said. "I wonder if they're all working together to release the chemicals that will combine into the distinctive Eddie smell. This is just before I wake up. I want to see if I can catch them leaving." James peered intently at the screen. "Man, there they go, but I can't see how. One second they're there, the next they're a fading white spot, and the next they're just gone."

"Can you see the chemicals that make the smell in the air?" Emily asked.

"I don't think so," James said, peering at the screen intently through his magnifying glass.

"Hey!" Danny exclaimed, backing away from the screen as a waking James suddenly sat up and filled the enlarged magnifying glass image with a huge eye. He blinked rapidly. "My eyes are getting buggy. I've got to take a break."

"Yeah, me too," Jenna said, sitting down on the couch. "Let's take a champagne break."

Danny stopped the playback and muted the audio as CNN came

back on. "That was by far the most mind-blowing thing I have ever experienced in my life."

"So, what are you going to do with that, James?" Jenna asked. "Are you going to bring your findings to your fellow scientists?"

"That's a very good question. I've been going back and forth on that. Fortunately, after viewing that, I realize I don't have to make that decision yet. That video of little amorphous white blobs floating in our room looks totally like a hoax. It might play well on the Paranormal Channel, but I'm not contacting any scientific journals."

"Can you imagine what it would be like to communicate visually like that?" Emily said. "You could say entire sentences in an instant, with all the possible colors and shapes and positions and movements and combinations that could happen. What an incredibly dynamic language that must be!"

"Do you have any idea how they do it, James?" Jenna asked. "How do they make all those colors appear and change so rapidly on their bodies?"

"It probably involves some kind of bioluminescence, for one thing. I'm thinking their bodies have to be covered with highly advanced cells that can instantly change colors. In Earth species, the cells are called chromatophores. They have color pigments in them that can shift around, and light-reflecting properties. Have you ever seen video of an octopus camouflaging itself against a complicated patterned background? It's stunning. They can change the colors and patterns on their skin in an instant and just blend in. These guys are like very advanced octopi."

"I can see why we've never detected these aliens," Danny said, "being so small and hard to see. Our radar's certainly not gonna notice the tiny little chrysalises, or whatever they are, coming into our atmosphere."

"Yeah," James agreed. "And who knows how long it takes until they're pulled through the Portal. Maybe they're here and then gone too quickly to be noticed."

"OK, enough show and tell," Danny said. "It's time for a little show and smell! Can we smell it? Eddie's stink, that is? You brought the jars over, right?"

"Oh yeah." James took one out of the bag and removed the cover. "Give it a sniff, tell us what you think."

"You go first, Dan," Jenna said. "I'm nervous."

Danny inhaled, and then recoiled. "Oh man, that is nasty. I don't know what it is, but I definitely don't like it."

He passed the jar to Jenna, who tentatively put her nose over it. "Eww, yuck."

"The thing is," James explained, "I've got the samples we collected, but I can't count on them lasting until I happen to meet up with Scofield, whenever that might be. I really want to try to replicate them best as possible, so I can keep a fresh, potent supply."

"It's hard to tell, man," Danny said. "It's just one big nasty."

Emily took the jar and inhaled. "The smells have blended together more," she said. "When we first smelled it, we could pick out some distinct odors. Weirdly enough, we got a hint of mint and lemon. And definitely something rotten."

"Rotten chicken," Jenna suggested.

"Moldy cheese," Danny offered. "Like Limburger."

"Well," James said. "Guess I'm just gonna have to mess around with it. I can easily put together various combinations of mints and lemon oil, and then add to it. It's gonna be trial and error, I'm afraid. Honey," he said, turning to Emily. "If we're having chicken this week, can you save the raw juices and bones and stuff so I can let them go bad?"

"Anything for you, sweetheart," she replied.

James turned to Danny. "We should make copies of this."

"Uh…" Emily sounded weird, and she had a stricken look on her face. "James," she said, shakily. "When you called Danny about coming over with this, how much did you say?"

"I dunno. Why?"

"I've been noticing some weird clicks on my phone lately… when I'm talking to you, actually. I've been meaning to ask you if you hear it. But now I'm thinking, I mean, I'm wondering… could someone be tapping your phone?"

Everyone stared at Emily for a long minute. Then Danny said, "I've got a safe deposit box. Let's put a copy in there."

"Why would the feds tap your phone?" Jenna asked. "They can't have known about any of this."

"I don't think it's about aliens," Danny said. "Ever since James gave Scofield the peace sign at that concert, ruining his little photo op event and embarrassing him on national TV, he's probably been on their watch list. You know Scofield's completely paranoid. Shit, who knows what he would order Homeland Security to do."

James exhaled loudly. "Damn."

CHAPTER 29

The final weeks of the school year dragged by even slower for James than for his clock-watching students. For them, liberation beckoned. For James, each passing day meant one more that he had survived without the feds coming after him before he could make his next attempt at taking down Eddie Olson.

Danny's got me paranoid, James thought, as he sniffed his latest attempt at replicating the deviant Seeker's distinctive odor. He set the flask down on the lab table in his classroom and looked at the clock. It was getting late. He should give it up for the day, try again tomorrow.

James was frustrated with his lack of success. The latest concoction, a mixture of oil of peppermint, lemon oil, rancid fish guts, and motor oil, was the closest he'd gotten so far. The fish definitely made a difference. It wasn't quite right, but he had to hope it would be close enough to get a reaction from the deviant Seeker within. He hoped that the fact that Eddie Olson's host body had the same relatively poor sense of smell as the rest of humans might work in his favor.

There'd been only one bright spot in the last two weeks—but that one was a supernova. James smiled, replaying the event in his mind for the hundredth time. He'd seen the Seekers up close and personal, and he had it on the hard drive.

It happened on the Seekers' last nocturnal visit with him, sixteen days after the visit he'd recorded. After discovering that the aliens were so small, James set up the surveillance camera in his bedroom to cover just the few feet around his head. It paid off big time.

James recalled the thrilling moment, watching the playback on Danny's big screen, when he saw the tiny alien settle on his head. First it floated up from the bottom of the screen, a cylindrical-shaped white creature. Then it unfolded.

"It's flat!" James had yelled in surprise. The creature, now looking rather like a tiny clothes dryer sheet with irregular edges, settled on James's head, contrasting beautifully with his dark skin. He realized that the Seekers' bodies actually looked remarkably similar to how they'd portrayed themselves in the first visions they'd given him, just miniaturized.

This time, they'd been able to see the play of colors over the Seekers' bodies in much greater detail. They watched it and rewound it five times, transported by the stunning beauty. At one point, Danny jumped up and put Beethoven on the sound system. They all agreed that it was too bad the Seekers couldn't hear, because the combination of the color symphony with Beethoven's Ninth was incredible.

Then they watched it in ultra-slow motion. From one frame to the next, yellow green glowed and then was subsumed by an iridescent rose; from one frame to the next, gold pinpricks shot out and then were gone; from one frame to the next to the next, an indigo circle collapsed on itself and vibrant sunshine yellow lines radiated from the center. They watched, fascinated, as silver and copper bands chased each other in a complex zig-zagging pattern that dissolved into a sunset peach-colored circle in an instant. In the next frame, fuzzy black lines erupted from near the edges and shot into the peach-colored circle, and in the next frame, the lines met and exploded into what looked like burning lava.

He was also able to confirm that one Seeker did float into his ear, and the three Seekers near his nostrils did go up into his nose, apparently deliberately. While it was disturbing on one level, it was also fascinating.

This recording was a gold mine, and James's notebook on the aliens was filling with nuggets. He'd added frame-by-frame printouts of the close-up recording to be analyzed carefully. And he had pages and pages of notes on each encounter, along with hypotheses based on what he'd gleaned from the aliens.

Hypothesis 31: Since no distinct body parts can be discerned on the flat Seeker bodies, even with close magnification, the necessary body parts—nerve fibers, photo receptors, chromatophores, chemical-producing cells, olfactory receptor cells, muscle fibers, and whatever else they need may be distributed evenly across the flat body. Some might be on the underside.

Hypothesis 32: Rather than having a distinct brain, they may think with their whole body via nerves distributed and connected over the flat body. Their Earth-selves may almost be one giant brain.

Hypothesis 33: Seekers probably do not consume nutrients while here in our Earth's atmosphere. They only need to live long enough to go through the Portal. Unknown: how long their Earth-based bodies can survive without eating.

Hypothesis 34: While on Earth, the Seekers need to communicate with each other, visually and chemically. Presumably, they communicate to incoming Seekers the necessity of connecting with me, and carrying on the messages about the Way, and what has been said before, and so on. This probably has to be transmitted to many consecutive arrivals to cover the sixteen-day intervals.

Hypothesis 35: The Seekers' bodies begin to disintegrate before, or as, they go through the Portal. Comparing the frame most clearly showing the Seeker's flat body before it settles on the human head with the frame most clearly showing the same Seeker's body after it rises from the human head, the latter body superimposed over the earlier body shows increased ragged edges and a 15% smaller body size. As it presumably passes through the Earth Portal, it loses size and distinction until it seems to disappear. Question: Do they pass through the Portal in groups, since they seem to have a group identity/consciousness, or as individuals?

As he cleaned up the lab, James thought about one of his earlier hypotheses, regarding how the Seekers communicate with each other chemically as well as visually. He thought it very possible that the chemical releases also served the function of bringing the group (community) into emotional convergence, as the chemicals released by each individual conveyed its emotional state and mixed with the others' chemicals. Now he wondered whether certain individuals release emotional chemicals intentionally to bring about desired emotional states?

He'd had an especially bizarre conversation with the Seekers on their most recent visit. James had been intending to ask whether they had technology. But before he could visualize anything, he felt a questioning vibration in his mind. It seemed the Seekers wanted to ask him a few questions, for a change.

The Seeker showed him humans, many hundreds of humans, of wildly varying sizes, some many times larger than others, and of all the colors in the rainbow. It was like a five-year-old had gotten out her box of crayons and decided to draw humanity.

Then he watched an alien cocoon ride in on the Life Force from space, and land in the middle of the array of colorful people. The cocoon disintegrated into a thin shell and split open. An Evil One emerged. It floated aimlessly about for a bit, and then glowed with distorted Life Force energy. The Evil One was drawn straight toward a large purple man and smashed into his brain. Then he felt a questioning sensation in his mind.

If he'd gotten it right, they were asking him what makes certain humans attractive to the aliens' evil ones. Or perhaps they wanted to know what makes our evil ones become evil in the first place, just as he had asked them for information about their deviant Seekers.

Hmm. That was an interesting question. Did he really know what factors went into creating an amoral sociopath, or a sadist who derived pleasure from hurting others?

Well, part of it was probably genetic. So, he pictured for them a baby being born from its mother's birth canal with distorted Life Force already glowing inside it.

But these ultimate human deviants, whether or not they had any genetic anomalies, were forged in the furnace of human suffering and pain, weren't they? A strong, distasteful memory flashed in his mind. He told the aliens the story of the Greenwald family, for whom he'd babysat a few times, until he couldn't stand it anymore. He imagined that horrible mother, 300 pounds of hateful menace. He remembered the day she'd come home to find a blob of applesauce on the ceiling. She'd lined all four kids up, the three boys and the little girl, and screamed at them to tell her who did it. They looked at her with terror-filled eyes and said nothing. She'd gotten out the belt and whipped those kids savagely until the five-year-old boy confessed, probably just to get her to stop. Then James remembered the day he'd watched the ten-year-old put a live snake in the road and ride his bike over it, laughing with glee as he killed it before James could stop him. He remembered that the five-year-old had told James then that his brother liked to chop the heads off baby rabbits that he caught. James pictured that scene for the aliens, too. He had no doubt that that boy would be a magnet for any deviant Seeker that came his way.

A deep sense of sadness filled his mind as the Seeker took in the information he'd shared. Then it responded with a follow-up question. It pictured for him this boy, with the distorted Life Force radiating from him, among a group of normal humans. It showed the normal humans smiling, their Life Force harmonizing with one another in color and intensity. These people then released a visible cloud of chemicals. The alien pictured the chemicals going into the deviant boy, and then showed him smiling, his Life Force becoming more normal.

The questioning feeling filled his mind. James had to tell the Seekers, No, humans cannot produce chemicals that bring the group into emotional or spiritual harmony, or that can fix seriously disturbed human beings.

But that really didn't matter. The key point was that deviant Seekers and deviant humans are two sides of the same coin. Our sociopaths are just as disconnected from the group as theirs. Maybe humans aren't chemically connected, but we are still deeply social beings who derive our greatest meaning from caring for others. That is, except for our own Deviant Ones, completely isolated in their own selves and capable only of thinking about themselves. And the worst ones, like the boy he'd babysat and his horrid mother, derived pleasure from the pain of others.

When he'd shared this insight with the Seeker, as well as he could through mental images, it had responded with understanding, and with gratitude. He didn't know what the Seekers intended to do with this knowledge, but he fervently hoped they were trying to figure out how to prevent the merging of the worst human sociopaths with the worst deviant Seekers.

And then, just before the Seeker had released his mind and left him, he'd heard these words in his head: *You human of greatest harmony.*

James brought himself out of his reverie and back to his science lab, and thought wryly, So, at least I've got that going for me. Which is nice.

As he finished cleaning up the lab, he began unconsciously humming "Amazing Grace," and then realized he was singing softly, "I once was lost, but now am found, was blind but now I see." The human mind is an amazing thing, he thought as he realized why those words had come into his head. The deviant Seekers were literally blind, but human sociopaths were just as blind to their fellow human beings.

And of course, he was once blind to the existence of the aliens. Now, his mind had been opened, and his brain had seen impossibly amazing things.

Then he remembered that the hymn had been written by an ex-slave ship captain who'd found religion and realized the great sin he had committed. And here we are again, James thought grimly, the threat from the Evil One starting with great sins being committed against the black race.

And Scofield was upping the ante every day. American troop strength in Africa was growing, and the frequency and intensity of the confrontations between African rebels and the U.S. military was increasing. James and Danny debated whether Scofield's strategy would be to provoke all-out war in Africa just before the election, or to wait till he'd secured power for another four years and then go for it.

James examined the flask he was holding. And this is somehow supposed to stop it all. Yeah, right.

His back was to the door of the classroom, so he didn't hear the man enter.

The voice was low and menacing. "Don't turn around."

James froze.

"Slowly put your hands over your head."

Oh damn, Danny was right.

"Now turn around. Nice and easy."

James turned slowly and looked at the gun pointed at him. He looked at the young man in the trench coat, and suddenly yelled, "Oh yeah?"

He ran toward his desk, ducking behind the lab stations to avoid the stream of water being shot at him from the large fluorescent green squirt gun. James dived behind his desk and emerged with a pink squirt gun of his own, blasting away with a stream of water.

"You didn't think I'd be back, did you?" yelled the man.

"I knew you'd be back, Carlos!" James retorted, as he pumped his squirt gun. "I was prepared for your insidious attack!"

"Ha! You call that prepared?" Carlos ducked behind a lab station and threw a heavy stream of water at James.

James sprinted around the room, seeking cover behind the lab stations. Carlos returned fire. As he skidded behind a lab station near the windows, Carlos's elbow knocked a covered pan from the table, spilling a half-dissected frog and its guts all over the floor. The strong smell of formalin filled the air. "Whoops," he said, while blasting James.

In another minute, they were both out of ammo, the streams from their squirt guns petering out.

James laughed heartily, put down his gun, and gave his former student a big hug.

"Man, we're soaked," he said, going over to the sink to get some paper towels. As they tried to dry themselves off, James said, "I was wondering if you'd show up this year." He grinned at Carlos. "You got the drop on me that first year after you graduated, I'll give you that. But as you've noticed, I've been prepared ever since then."

"Maybe I'll have to pull a switch, show up in January or

something."

James smiled. "So, how've you been?"

"Good. I just graduated from Gustavus. Now I'm seriously hunting for a teaching job. You know any schools looking for a physics teacher?"

"I'll keep my eyes out. I'd be happy to give you a reference."

"I owe it all to you, Mr. Thompson," Carlos said. "You totally inspired me to become a teacher."

"Well, thank you. But if you're going to be a colleague, you might as well call me James." A thought occurred to him. "Say, Carlos, how would you and a few friends like to make a little extra money?"

"Sure. I need all the money I can get at this point."

"Great. Here's the deal. I'm on the organizing committee for my twenty-year reunion. We need four people to tend bar. You'd be working for tips, but hopefully it'll pay off. I think people at reunions like to impress their old friends—and probably especially their old girlfriends—with how successful they've become. Do you think you could round up three other friends and do the job?"

"Yeah, for sure. When is it?"

"Saturday, June tenth. We'd need you by six o'clock. It's at the Rec Center."

"Oh yeah, that's right. You went to Westfield, didn't you?"

"Sure did. So, you available? You want the job?"

"Sure, Mr. Thomps—I mean, James. That sounds great."

"Give me your number. I'll text you the information." As he put his phone away, he added, trying to sound casual, "And Carlos. I may need to ask you to do a favor or two for me that night. I may want you to pour a little extra liquor in an old friend's drink, that kind of thing. You OK with that?"

"No problem."

"Thanks."

"Hey, let me get that frog mess cleaned up," Carlos offered. He wrinkled his nose at the lingering odor of formalin. "That stuff smells bad."

"That's OK, I'll get it," James said. "See you in a week."

As Carlos walked out, James cleaned up the floor and put the frog's remains back in the pan. Then he picked up the flask with the mixture he'd been working on and opened it up to smell it. But before he could put his nose to the opening, it hit him. Eddie's stink.

"Oh my God," he said softly. Hands shaking with excitement, James mixed a small bit of the preservative into the flask, shook it, and sniffed. He added a little bit more, shook it again, and tested it again. As the nasty odor assaulted his nose, he smiled with satisfaction.

Got you, you bastard.

CHAPTER 30

The Dragon pulled into the Rec Center parking lot. Danny eased it into a spot near the back, away from other vehicles. James gave Danny's truck an affectionate pat as he got out.

"Nothing like arriving in style to the big event," he said.

"You got that right, my friend." Danny clicked the lock and checked his hair in the side view mirror. "Too bad we couldn't bring the wives," he said. "Jenna could've used a glitzy night out."

"Yeah, well, I don't think a high school reunion qualifies as glitzy. I'm pretty sure Emily was relieved when I told her she wouldn't have to come, I was going to be too busy with committee duties. Anyway, I saw the list of who's coming, and Monika's definitely not on it, or Emily would've come, if only to check her out."

"No old girlfriends complicating things tonight, that's good. Of course, who knows how many girls had secret crushes on me and might want to try to spark a flame tonight."

James laughed. "You're just gonna have to break some hearts, I guess."

"You didn't fill Emily in on all the details of our top-secret mission?"

"No point in worrying her, especially if nothing happens. Let's face it, it's a long shot." James turned toward the building. "Whoa, check out that line!"

The line to get in stretched out along the whole length of the sidewalk in front of the Rec Center. A Secret Service agent was at the door, checking bags and waving a metal detector over everyone. James's mind reeled for a second, seizing up with panic as he flashed back to the band concert at the White House. Then he took a deep breath. This time, he wasn't carrying a murder weapon. This time, things would go right. It was the Way.

They joined the line. "I don't recognize half these people," Danny said.

"Half these people might be spouses," James pointed out. "Anyway, I think we've changed a bit in twenty years. Not you and me, of course, but everyone else seems to have put on pounds and taken off some hair."

"Fortunately, I'm still the same hot stud I was in high school," Danny said, flexing his arm muscles. "Like the shirt?" he asked. "I got this in Hawaii on our honeymoon."

"That is by far the wildest, gaudiest, best Hawaiian shirt I've ever seen. I particularly like the hula girls emerging from the bird of paradise flowers. That touch of glitter on the erupting volcano is pretty good, too."

"Thanks. I see you decided to go all out for the festivities."

"What do you mean? This shade of turquoise is on the edge. When I put on this Polo shirt tonight, Emily almost didn't let me go alone after all. I'm just too damn attractive in it."

As they neared the entrance, Danny turned and looked intently at James. "This is it, dude." He stuck out his fist, and they did their personal handshake. Danny gave James a satisfied nod, and they stepped forward.

The Secret Service agent waving the metal detector in front of James looked Hispanic, and when he spoke, he had an accent. "Sir," he said, as the detector beeped, "please empty your pants pockets."

James took out his wallet from his back pocket. He pulled his keys and cell phone from a side pocket on his cargo shorts. The agent picked up the phone and said, "Please do not take any photos or videos of Mr. Cambridge without his permission."

"Sure," James said, and turned to go inside.

"Wait a moment, sir," the agent said. "What's that in your pocket there?" He pointed at the bulge in the other pocket of James's shorts.

"Oh, yeah, I forgot about that," James said as he took out the bottle and showed it to the agent. The agent examined the bottle, with its black, red and gold label that read SCORCH Men's Cologne. He gave James a dubious look and handed it back without a word.

As they passed through the doors, Danny grinned at James. "Good thing he didn't spray that, or he'd really wonder about your prowess with the ladies."

"I picked this up for $5.95 at the drug store," James said. "The stuff I dumped out didn't smell a whole lot better than what I filled it with. I had to disinfect it several times to get that smell out. I made a fresh batch of Eau de Eddie yesterday. It's potent."

They picked up their nametags at the table by the door. "Hi Laura," James greeted his committee compatriot. "You did a fantastic job with these." All the alumni tags had a photo of their yearbook pictures under their names.

"Thanks. I think it'll help people remember each other."

Danny looked at his photo. "My God, I was so young, so innocent, so… so… devilishly handsome."

"Hey, there's Carlos," James said, pinning on the tag. "Let's go check out the bar situation."

As they walked across the large room, James looked around. He had to admit, the decorations were great. It was kind of fun to have a tropical paradise in Minnesota after all. People were dressed in everything from Grateful Dead T-shirts to glittery sundresses. There was a basket full of cheap, colorful metallic sunglasses on a table, which was a cool party favor, but made it harder to tell who the people were when they put them on. James grabbed a turquoise pair and stuck them on top of his head. Sounds of "I can't believe you made it!" and "You look fantastic!" mingled with the music.

"Check it out," James said to Danny, pointing to the band. "Garth actually got Slugfest to play."

Danny burst out laughing. "Wow, they don't look anything like I remember them! Look at the gut on the lead guitarist. Ah well, who cares, as long as they can play the same old songs. I'm ready to rock out tonight, dude!"

"I don't know how much rockin' we're gonna be doing. We've got to keep focused on the primary mission."

"Yeah, you're right. So, you nervous?"

"It's weird," James said thoughtfully, "but no, not really. I have a good feeling about this. This time, I feel like it's on my terms, you know? I don't know, maybe I'm just keyed up. But I honest-to-God think we're gonna get Eddie Olson tonight."

"Oh, is Ed Olson coming?"

James spun as he heard the female voice behind him. He faced Miranda. Her hair was pinned back in a bun of some sort with a tropical flower stuck in it; an orchid was pinned to the lapel of her white linen suit.

"Say, James," she said in her gushy voice, hooking her arm through his, "I think all our hard work paid off! It's a total success! Everyone loves the theme, and I think something like eighty percent of our class turned out. It's phenomenal!" She looked around. "Is your wife here?"

"No, she couldn't make it."

"Oh, too bad. I was looking forward to meeting her."

"Gee, Miranda," said Danny, in a mischievous voice. "My wife isn't here, either. Wanna dance with me later?"

"My goodness, Dan. You actually found someone willing to put up with your juvenile sense of humor?" Miranda scanned the crowd. "Oh, there's Andy. Well, enjoy yourselves tonight. Ta ta!"

Miranda hurried away, her high-heeled sandals clicking a quick staccato beat, to catch up with an attractive man in a stylish blazer.

"How could you stand being on the committee with that woman?" asked Danny. "I need a beer."

"No, you don't," James said as they approached the bar. "We've got to stay mentally alert tonight, son."

"Oh c'mon, Dad, just one. Pleeeeze?"

Carlos and his three friends wore matching tie-dyed T-shirts.

"Two Cokes, please, Carlos. Hey, no one's put a tip in yet? Let me get it started." James put a twenty-dollar bill in the empty tip jar.

Carlos grinned at him. "Thanks, boss!"

"Oh, you know we teachers are rolling in it," James joked. "I'm sure that's why you're going into the field."

Carlos laughed. "Hey, let me introduce my friends. Angela, Allison, and Quinn." James couldn't help noticing that Allison was especially hot. Carlos's friends gave him a friendly wave.

"Thanks for helping out," James said, smiling at them. "Carlos, this is Danny. He's my second-in-command. Carlos was one of my most outstanding students," James said to Danny.

James heard a cough behind him and looked around. A line had formed.

"Oh, sorry," he said to the woman behind him. No picture on the nametag, so he didn't have to worry about trying to place her.

James and Danny stepped to the side. They heard the people in the bar line talking.

"He'd better show up, after all that security," said one. "It took us fifteen minutes just to get in the door."

"I don't know why they need all that security just for Jack Cambridge," her friend complained. "Just 'cause the country's on High Terror Alert. He's not running for anything."

"I bet he makes a late entrance."

"Yeah, he always thought he was too good for anyone. He'll probably grace us with his presence for about half an hour and then leave."

Danny and James walked away, sipping the Cokes.

"What if Jack doesn't show?" Danny asked.

"He will. It's the Way."

"You're sure your phone can record long enough, right? You can use mine if you want to, you know."

James gave Danny an annoyed look. "It's fine."

"Yeah, good, good. If anyone can get Jack to reveal information about Scofield's secret plans to wipe out Africa or something, it's you. He's got to know something. This is a great plan, man! He'll be relaxed, happy to be with old friends, a little drunk. He'll talk. We're gonna nail Eddie!"

"I hope so."

"Of course, we've always got the back-up plan if the secret recording thing doesn't work."

"Yeah, I'm not so sure about that, Danny," James said hesitantly. "I still can't think of any way to get Jack to get us in to meet with Scofield. Well, definitely not me, anyway. That bridge was burned."

"I'm thinking I just tell him my family's vacationing in D.C. next month and ask it as a personal favor. You never know. Maybe that's the Way."

"Yeah, I guess it's good to keep all options open."

"Actually," Danny said, "I think I like the backup backup plan better now." He gestured toward James's cargo pocket. "We kidnap Jack, and draw Scofield to us with Jack as bait, like demand a face-to-face meeting, and whammo! You spray him with that, Eddie smells himself and Scofield's head explodes." Danny grinned broadly at James.

"Your moxie never ceases to amaze me. Sure, why not plan on kidnapping the brother of the Vice President right under the nose of the Secret Service? What could go wrong?"

————————

Jack, of course, did not show up early. But James didn't expect him to, and he wasn't worried. In fact, James marveled at how preternaturally calm he felt. Maybe this is what pro athletes meant when they said they were in the zone. He'd experienced that feeling once, at the game with Hopkins their junior year. He'd gone eight-for-eight, he'd gotten every rebound he'd jumped for, he'd known where the other team was going to pass before they did and grabbed three steals. He'd felt it flow, just flow, and it was the most glorious feeling. He was feeling the flow now.

James and Danny were sitting at a table with a couple other guys from the team, Mike and Antawn. They were both tall black men, but there the resemblance ended. Mike had a shaved head and diamonds in each ear that were twice as large as the one on Emily's engagement ring. He was making it big time as a radio deejay in Chicago, but made really serious money doing voice-overs for advertising, with a voice like deep amber maple syrup being poured over a tall stack of pancakes. Antawn had gotten more than a little pudgy over the years, sitting behind a desk at some insurance company. He'd married his high school girlfriend, and they had a son who was about to graduate from high school himself.

"Terrance is looking golden," he was bragging. "Full football scholarship offers from three schools. LaWanda thinks he should have picked Madison, but that's 'cause she can't bear to see her baby go too far from home. Boy needs to cut the apron strings. I think he was right to pick Arizona State. 'Sides that, what kid would want to be in Wisconsin when he could be playing in the warm Arizona sunshine?"

James glanced at his watch— 7:35. Still plenty of time.

Carlos came over to the table, picking up the empty plates loaded with chicken wing bones and dirty napkins. "Can I get you gentlemen something to drink?"

"Hey, what a deal," Mike said, smiling. "You know a guy on the organizing committee, you get personal service. Sure, I'll take a Surly Hell."

"Make that two," Antawn said.

"It's not what you know, it's who you know, my friend," James joked.

Suddenly, as excited buzzing erupted, everyone's attention was drawn to the other side of the room. James heard someone at the next table say, "I don't believe it—he's here!"

Jack Cambridge walked into the room.

CHAPTER 31

James had seen Jack Cambridge's picture in the paper a few times in the last couple years, but in person, he looked even better. Jack was tall, with sun-streaked light brown hair and a classically handsome, tan face. Even from across the room, James could see this was a man who spent a considerable amount of time working out at the health club. No doubt he put in a fair number of hours on the golf course, too. He exuded an aura of confidence and importance, which was enhanced by the Secret Service agent right behind him. When he smiled at the woman sitting at the table as he took his nametag from her, she was obviously star-struck. He could see her protesting that he wouldn't need a nametag, everyone knew him. But Jack pinned it on anyway, in a gesture that was either genuinely humble or calculated to seem so.

James smiled as he watched several people rush over immediately to shake his hand, talk to him, and have their picture taken with him. Not surprisingly, Miranda was among the first to greet him and gush over him. Jack looked like he schmoozed for a living, like he didn't even have to think about it. Curious, James looked around and noticed that Stacy was still over at the bar, making no move toward him. If he'd thought about it, he'd have predicted she'd play coy. Probably the right move with a guy like Jack. He'd enjoy the hunt.

8:21. James checked his watch again. Yeah, it had been close to an hour, and Jack Cambridge was still surrounded by fawning people. Someone had gotten him a drink, but he'd hardly been able to move. Jack's arm was now draped casually, possessively, over Stacy's shoulders. Stacy's husband, standing next to her, looked annoyed. James thought Jack's smile looked more pasted on now. He was beginning to worry that Jack would get bored and leave before he'd even get a chance to talk with him alone.

Danny must've been thinking the same thing. "At this rate, we're never gonna get near Jack," he said.

Antawn snorted. "Who cares? The guy was a jerk. Thought he was God's gift to women. Homecoming King don't mean shit now."

"Yeah, but he sure could shoot," Mike said.

James pictured Jack in their games, moving fluidly, swishing the ball through the net from the top of the key, the corner, anywhere. He was a natural. "You know," James said thoughtfully, "he was a different guy on the basketball court, like it was the one place he could relax."

Danny snapped his fingers. "That's it!" He stood up. "I think I saw Bobby Chen over by the buffet table. Who's ready for a little three-on-three action, men?"

Antawn broke into a wide grin. "I prefer three-on-one action—me being the one. How 'bout that hot bartender, and her friend? And maybe that one over there with the low-cut top."

Danny laughed and slapped Antawn on the back. "Dream on, big fella." He headed purposefully toward Jack.

As James watched Danny extend his hand to Jack, it dawned on him: Danny is part of the Way, too. His golden thread runs with mine, and nothing can break it. We are stronger together.

―――――――――

The game was as intense as any they'd played in high school.

Because they were wearing the nicest shirts and didn't want to sweat in them, Jack, Danny and Mike were the "skins" team. Antawn and Bobby agreed to wear their shirts—Antawn probably because he didn't want his protruding gut to contrast unfavorably with Mike's toned abs, and James was willing to sacrifice his shirt to the greater good of the Way. Because he was the Vice President's brother, Jack could persuade the maintenance man to open up the gym for them and let them play. Because Danny had suggested making this reunion casual dress three months ago, they were all, except Jack and Mike, wearing sneakers. Mike was able to persuade a buddy to loan him his Nikes. And it turned out that Jack never went anywhere without a packed gym bag thrown in the truck of the car in case he got a chance to work out.

Because it's the Way, it's all coming together.

As James took the cologne bottle out of his pocket and set it down in a corner of the gym, he thought, I am not a soldier in the army of humanity anymore. I am a player. I can play this game and I can win.

Jack sported the first genuine smile James had seen on him all night. He was having a good time, a completely natural, fine time. James guessed that didn't happen a lot for him. He could let down his guard and do what he loved best: run around and shoot a basketball through a hoop. With old friends who didn't give a rip that he was the Vice President's brother.

The men were very intense, probably sweating more than they had when they were eighteen. But they were laughing, too, feeling like 20 years had dropped away.

Bobby, who'd been point guard, was giving Antawn a hard time. "I showed you three fingers, man. How'd you forget? Three, a simple pick and roll. What you doin' shooting from 20 feet out?"

Jack laughed and tossed the ball he'd rebounded to Antawn. "Yeah, impress us, man—stuff that ball in the hole. Ain't you got no hops no more?"

Antawn bristled. "Watch this, my man!"

Then he must have thought better of it, because he passed it out to James and said, "Let's school these fools, dude."

James grabbed the ball, and before the others could react, he'd passed it out to Bobby for an easy three. The Shirts knocked bellies in a giddy display of machismo. "That's my man, the Asian Assassin himself!" Antawn crowed.

The Skins responded by upping the pace of the game. Sweat glistened on their chests as they pounded the ball up and down the floor. James watched Danny dribble down court and waited for him at the top of the key. He saw Mike open on the side but knew he didn't have to shift over to cover him. Sure enough, Danny tried to dribble around James to take the shot himself, had to switch hands, and James swiped the ball from him, passing it back to Antawn, who still hadn't crossed the half court line, for an easy jumper at the other end.

"Shit, Danny," Mike yelled in exasperation. "You're still a ball hog. Pass me the damn ball, man!"

Danny obliged, and Mike promptly faked James out, whirled around him, and laid it in. "Up by 14! We're whipping your sorry asses!"

Bobby dribbled down court and threaded it between Jack and Danny to James under the basket. He clanked the lay-up. Damn. He'd hear about this. Sure enough, here was Antawn coming back at him. "James, I can't believe the T-wolves didn't recruit you. I hear they're lookin' for water boys. Towel boys, too."

It seemed like they were kids again. James had more energy than he'd felt in years. He could go all night.

When Danny boasted, "Watch my new patented 360-reverse-angle-behind-the-back shot," and then missed the basket completely, they had to stop play because they were all laughing so hard.

Jack razzed Danny. "Who you been playing ball with since high school, dude, your grandma? You been playing in the Old Ladies League?"

James laughed. "OK, Jack, let's see what you been doing. We know you were a hot shot at UCLA. Show us what you got, man!"

Which he did. Jack proceeded to take over the game, assisted by Mike, running up the score until the Skins had a 24-point lead. Which was good, James figured. He wanted Jack to be happy. Not that he was letting him win, but still, it was OK that both of the stars from high school were teamed up together tonight. Then Jack put the capper on by sinking a three-point shot from near half court.

James whistled his admiration. "From way downtown! Forget Minneapolis, that shot was from downtown St. Paul, man!"

The Skins whooped, doing the victory dance they used to do after big wins. James had forgotten about that, but he grinned now to see them perform it with such kid-like abandon.

Antawn was having none of it. "We was just going easy on you. It's time to get a little rough, men."

The other five groaned.

"Let it go, bro," Danny said. "We'll have a rematch at our twenty-fifth reunion. You better start training tomorrow. You're gonna need five years to get in shape for that."

"Yeah? Well, maybe I'll bring my kid next time. He could shoot your lights out, chump." Antawn sucked in his stomach. Then he sighed and let it go. "Man, let's go get something to drink. I sweated a bucket out there. I'm dehydrated."

The six of them sat around the table with half-full glasses of Surly Hell. The Secret Service agent had taken a position behind Jack. Danny raised his glass.

"To old times and old friends. May the spirit of basketball never die within us, and may we never forget our teammates."

They clinked glasses.

Jack drained his beer. "God, I'm thirsty. I haven't had a Surly since the last time I was home. That tastes damn fine."

"Man, we shoulda beat you," Antawn complained. "That was a foul on that last shot."

Jack snorted. "Quit crying. Take it like a man. Anyway, you didn't lose by no two points, son, you lost by 27."

Danny waved his thumb at the agent. "Your friend with the gun's making me nervous, Cambridge. It's like you got a babysitter, man. That'd get on my nerves."

Jack looked at the agent. "Rick, will you back off, please? Christ, this isn't South Africa, it's a freakin' high school reunion!"

The agent said nothing, but he did walk away, taking up a post near a wall where he could still keep an eye on the situation. James gave Danny a small, significant smile, which conveyed: excellent move.

Antawn stood up. "I worked up an appetite. I'm gonna get me some food, dude! C'mon, Mike, they still got shrimp left."

"Don't mind if I do."

As they walked away, Danny stood up, too. "Bobby, I didn't get a chance to meet your wife yet."

Bobby smiled. "There's Talia over by the buffet. C'mon, I'll introduce you."

Jack started to stand up. "I think I'll get some chow, too."

Danny put his hand out, waving him back. "I'll send the kid over with some food. You been standing all night. Take a load off. What do you want? Ribs? Shrimp?"

Jack smiled with gratitude and sank back down. "Egg rolls and some fruit would hit the spot."

Danny was working this perfectly. As Jack turned his head and watched them walk away, James slipped his phone out of his pocket, pushed the record button, and put it on the table under his napkin. Now all he had to do was somehow get Jack to reveal top-secret information that would bring down the President. Right.

CHAPTER 32

"So, how've you been doing, man?" OK, lame beginning, but he had to start somewhere.

"Doing well, my friend, doing well. Great job, pay's excellent, and plenty of good-lookin' California women to spend the money on."

James chuckled appreciatively. OK, I've got to get him talking about his brother. Let's talk about family. He pulled out his wallet and flipped it open to a picture of his family, taken last year for the church directory.

"This is my family. My wife, Emily, and our kids, Danielle and Trey—James the third, but no one calls him that. Emily and I met in college, at the U."

"You been married that long? Shit, I don't know how you can do it with the same woman for what, fifteen years or something? Me, I need variety."

What? Was Jack insulting him, or Emily, or just being an arrogant jerk? Just because he was a big shot didn't give him the right to... And then he looked at the picture of Danielle in the photo and heard her voice in his head saying, The Peace-O-Matic machine makes everyone have to say nice words to each other, even when they're thinking bad things.

Where had that come from? The Way, the Way, it was all working together, every little thread. So, he sucked it up and said pleasantly, with a note of admiration, "Yeah, you always did have a way with the ladies."

Jack laughed. "Stacy's husband would like to punch me out. That's the dude Rick should be keeping an eye on."

"You got any kids?" James asked.

Jack's smirk disappeared instantly. "One. Ben. He's ten. His mom and me split up when he was two. She's an actress. You ever see *Make Me Scream*? She was the one who got slashed by the mutant guy with the lobster claw hand. Andrea Hooper?"

James hadn't seen it, had never heard of Andrea Hooper, but he nodded.

Jack continued. "Problem is, I'm too busy to see Ben much. I'm a partner at a top investment firm in Los Angeles. Mitchell and Dornand, you've probably heard of it. We handle the money for a lot of big stars. You wouldn't believe what Chuck DeMarco does with his cash."

Carlos, who was setting the plate of food in front of Jack, looked very impressed at what he was overhearing. James noticed that Jack seemed to appreciate Carlos's wide-eyed response. OK, a little flattery might grease the wheels.

"Impressive, very impressive. So, you actually advise Charles DeMarco, huh?"

"Nah, that's for the M.B.A. nerds there. I'm kind of like in public relations, only it's more like star relations. It's amazing how many of those big stars are interested in politics. They all want to have lunch with me. Here's my foursome for golf a couple days ago: me, Matt Blayr—who as you may know got twenty million for his last movie, and also happens to be an excellent golfer—Seth Stein, who's a studio exec at Warner Brothers, and Trent Dockery—you know, the drummer for Close Quarters? Gave Trent a few pointers, helped him take five, six strokes off his game."

James tried to look fascinated as Jack went on, dropping names and bragging about playing tennis and having drinks and going to hot

L.A. parties for his job. He wondered how the women who dated Jack made themselves sit through this litany of self-glory. Have patience, let it flow. The more he drinks, the looser his lips will get. Right now, he's dropping celebrity names. Soon, he'll be letting slip national secrets.

Finally, Jack finished regaling James with his unbelievably impressive life, and surprised James by asking, "So, what about you? What d'you do?"

"Me? I'm a teacher, at Westfield High, actually."

Jack, who was sipping his beer, did a spit take, an actual spit take. "You're shittin' me!"

"I shit you not."

"Couldn't get a job in business, huh?"

"Well, no, I actually like teaching, at least for the most part. The bureaucracy sucks, but the kids are great. Mostly, anyway." He glanced away, and noticed Danny near the buffet, talking with the three men and their wives. Good. Danny would keep them all over there. Time to go for it.

"Hey, Jack, you'll never guess what. I was in Washington in April, chaperoning Westfield's band trip. They played a concert for President Scofield and your brother. That was kind of strange, this guy I knew as a kid, and now he's a heartbeat away from ruling the free world. Especially with things so tense and knowing it's your bro sitting in on all those top-secret strategy meetings. I can't believe how scary things are now in Africa."

"Yeah, I caught it when it was on the news. Saw you give the peace sign to the Geeze-meister-in-Chief." Jack chuckled. "Way to ream him out, man. That guy's a prick."

James was encouraged. Maybe Jack supported his anti-war views.

Jack looked at James uncomfortably. "Uh, James? Look, I've always wanted to apologize… I always felt bad about the way my father treated you. It was embarrassing. Let's be honest, my dad's a fucking racist."

James's eyes widened in surprise.

"I shouldn't have let him treat you that way. This is 20 years too late, but anyway…"

James was taken aback. After a moment, he said, "That's OK. We were only kids."

Jack slammed down the rest of his beer. "So, Mr. Waters is your boss, huh? God, I hated that guy so bad."

"Mr. Waters retired ten years ago." James tried again. "Mr. Banks is still there, though. He taught political science, remember? I was just talking to him about the world situation. Things are really heating up, right?"

"Yeah, well, I don't follow politics much."

"How do you not follow politics, if your job is to wine and dine all those rich famous people and that's what they want to talk to you about?"

"You've got a lot to learn about wining and dining. They want to tell me the tax cuts for the rich should be repealed, I say, yeah, I'll pass that along to Gordon. They want to tell me tax cuts for the rich should be made permanent, I say, yeah, I'll pass that along to Gordon. And speaking of taxes, I say, we've got some great tax shelters for all that extra cash you made last year. It totally doesn't matter what my personal opinions are—which is good, since I don't have any."

James was at a loss as to where to go next. Fortunately, at that moment Carlos appeared, putting two glasses down on the table.

"A Rum and Coke, and a Surly, courtesy of your pal over there."

They looked over at Danny, who raised his beer and gave them a smile. James picked up the glass and took a long, refreshing drink. Danny was probably right. A second beer wouldn't hurt, and he needed to steady his nerves.

"How did Danny remember I used to drink Rum and Cokes?" Jack said, sipping with satisfaction. "Alcohol, man's greatest invention."

It crossed James's mind that if Jack got visibly drunk, that Secret Service guy might haul him out of there. They had to walk a fine line. He'd keep the conversation flowing while the booze worked its magic, and then try again. Fortunately, it seemed that the interest in Jack had slacked off. People were back to talking to their old friends, so maybe he would get some more time with him.

"So, Jack, I suppose you get good seats for the Lakers games, huh?"

That was all it took. Jack spent the next few minutes bragging about sitting just behind the bench, about getting to go into the locker room after the game sometimes, about running into Marcus Crowers at a party once and giving him a tip on his free throw shooting stance, which Jack noticed Marcus used in his next game.

Halfway through this recitation, James noticed Miranda heading purposefully toward them. No. But Danny was on top of it. He smoothly intercepted her and steered her away from their table. A minute later, James looked over again and almost laughed out loud. They were all on the dance floor, the men and their wives, and Danny was dancing with Miranda.

OK, Jack had finally wound down. Time to go for it again.

"Hey, Jack, did you see that movie, *Trackdown?*"

"Yeah, of course. About the suitcase nuke. The producer's one of our clients."

"So, you know how the guy knew there was a nuclear bomb in L.A., but he wasn't supposed to tell anyone? But he had to warn his daughter, and then everything got messed up. I don't know how you can stand it, knowing all these terrible national secrets, like if we're going to use nukes in Africa or something, and not being able to tell anyone."

Jack laughed scornfully. "Are you kidding? Gordon would warn his car mechanic about a bomb before he told me anything."

So, maybe the Way had come to a dead end. Or maybe, the Way was setting it up for James and Jack to become good friends, and then Jack would arrange for him to see the President, and he could whip out the scent of Eddie and cause Scofield to have a heart attack, and… Yeah, right. By that time, Africa's on fire. It's now or never.

"You're telling me you don't know secret stuff? C'mon, dude. You're important. I know you know stuff. You can tell me."

Jack looked at him with surprise, and then looked angry. "Shit, people been pumping me all night trying to find out stuff they think I know. I thought you were the one guy who didn't want something from me. Fine. You want me to give you an inside tip? Buy low, sell high. I'm gettin' outta here."

Damn, he'd pushed too hard. Jack was standing up. James put out his hand to stop him. "Hey, man, I apologize. Really, I mean it. Let me buy you a drink. We're teammates, right?"

James signaled Carlos to bring more drinks before Jack could say anything. Jack hesitated, and then sat back down. "Right. Teammates."

James, mentally heaving a huge sigh of relief, lifted his glass in a toast. "To old times. Man, some of those games were great. Like that one against Minnetonka, our senior year, when you went six for seven on threes. That was so awesome!"

"Yeah, I got written up in the paper for that game." Jack smiled, and stretched out his long frame, relaxing with the good memories. "Herb Tanako did a whole column on me. Said I had a good shot at getting Mr. Basketball. I probably would've gotten it, too, if I'd been on a better team."

"Thanks," James said sarcastically.

Jack looked at him in surprise. "No offense. You know what I mean. Our school was too small to compete against those big schools."

"Yeah, but we did, our senior year. We took out Eden Prairie, and Hopkins, too. And of course, Minnetonka."

"Damn straight." Jack smiled. "Funny, I was just watching the video of that game the other night."

James smiled too and glanced over at the agent leaning against the wall. He was talking into his cuff mike, probably with that outside agent. James hoped they weren't talking about wanting to get out of here; he imagined the man outside was probably getting pretty bit up by mosquitoes.

As he half-listened to Jack reminisce about the Minnetonka game, he noticed that Carlos was preparing to head their way with the drinks. Man, he really hoped that Rick guy wasn't noticing how much Jack was drinking.

And then he saw one of Carlos's friends, the voluptuous Allison, heading over toward the Secret Service agent. He saw her start talking to him, saw the seductive move of her hips, the flirtatious flip of her hair as she was looking at him with those gorgeous eyes and probably telling him how much she admired what he did. Telling him he was so brave, putting his life on the line. And he was going for it. Apparently, he had decided by this time that this little old high school reunion was no threat to national security, and he was probably bored as hell by now. James was filled with gratitude for Danny, who must've sent Allison over there.

As Carlos set the full glasses on the table, James said, "Man, I'm sure glad you didn't get thrown off the team. We'd've never gotten to the conference championship without you. Too bad for Shervensky, though. You were both caught drinking, weren't you?"

"Yeah. Coach kicked Shervensky off the team even though he was our third-leading scorer. There was that zero-tolerance policy, remember? Peterson stepped in to fill the hole pretty good, though. At least on offense. Guy couldn't defend his own sister."

James was genuinely curious. "How'd you get out of it? Everyone knew you were together. But nothing happened to you."

"You can probably figure. Good ol' Dad went to the principal, and that was the last anyone heard about the drinking thing."

James tried to make a joke. "What'd he do? Pay him off?"

"Uh, yeah. Money talks, man. You can't be that naïve. That's how the world works. Even in high school."

"You're serious? Waters took a bribe?"

Jack snorted scornfully. "You really are the last of the innocents, aren't you? How do you think I got into UCLA, with my bad grades? If my father hadn't made a sizable donation for the new basketball practice facility, even my three-point shooting wouldn't have gotten me in. I'd've been playing for North Dakota State."

"Yeah, but Principal Waters?"

"Money can buy anything. Anything. Money bought the election.

Money buys power. How do you think Gordon got the governorship? That's reality, bro. My family's money, my dad's connections, put me in at Mitchell and Dornand."

James was so stunned, he didn't stop to filter himself before reacting. "How can you stand it, knowing everything you've got, your dad bought for you?"

Jack stared at James for a long moment, and James thought, Oh, shit, I just totally blew it. God, I'm an idiot… and a jerk. "I'm sorry, man. That was way out of line. Forget I said that."

Jack concentrated on finishing his egg roll, and then said softly, "Of course I hate it. I've always hated it. And the worst thing is, he never lets me forget it. That time in high school, I heard him telling my mom if I got thrown off the team, I'd probably quit school, and he couldn't have an alcohol-abusing, drug-using dropout son. Gordon was thirty, he was just starting out in politics, and Dad had big hopes for him. They didn't need the scandal, he said. I'd screwed things up royally, as usual, and he'd have to fix it, as usual. As usual."

James didn't know what to say, so he just sat quietly, giving Jack space. And Jack kept talking, as if he had no choice, as if no one had ever given him the chance to be honest before. "My father is an asshole. A complete, son-of-a-bitch total asshole. He's mean to my mom, and she just takes it. He despises me, thinks he's so much better than me, so much tougher. Nothing I ever do is good enough, nothing is as good as what Gordon does. Gordon's an asshole too, but he's the golden child. I make way more money than Gordon does. Do I get credit for that? No, Gordon's going to be President someday. How the hell do you compete with that bullshit?"

Jack's expression was bitter. "I almost never go home anymore. Christmas, only for my mom."

The thought crossed James's mind that Jack probably wouldn't be saying all this if he weren't drunk. But he found himself, surprisingly, just feeling empathy for the guy, not caring anymore what state secrets he might know. How awful must his life be, this guy who seemed to have it all, who acted like he had it all, but who had nothing of real value?

"Man, I'm sorry," James said. "I mean, I think my dad's the

greatest guy in the world. I can't imagine how tough it is to have it like that with your father."

"Screw him. It's my mom I worry about. He's had so many affairs, and my mom just takes it. I'm sure he's got a piece on the side right now. OK, if I'm going to be honest, that's what broke up my marriage, too. I guess I couldn't avoid the Cambridge male curse. People probably think I'm an asshole too. But Gordon, he's worse. At least I never raped anyone. After I found out about Shaundra, man, that was it. I haven't talked to Gordon since. Shaundra didn't deserve that." Jack took another long drink, wiping his mouth crudely with the back of his hand. Jack's voice was cut with bitterness as he went on. "Fuck it. You're lucky your family didn't have money."

James couldn't believe Jack had just accused his brother of committing rape. "Who's Shaundra?"

Jack swirled his drink, lost in the past. "She was a cheerleader for the UCLA basketball team. Super cute black girl, really smart. We got to be friends. She was an international relations major, wanted to work for the state department or something. When Gordon got elected to the Senate, I got her a job in his office."

Jack took a long drink, then slammed the empty glass down on the table. "Four months later, she suddenly quits. Wouldn't talk to me. I lost touch. Then I ran into her at a bar a couple years ago. She was pretty drunk. She was so pissed at me, she just laid into me right there." Jack paused. This was clearly very painful. "Turns out my esteemed elder brother pretty much raped her. Put something in her drink, drugged her."

Jack paused, lost in painful thought. "You'd think I'd've been shocked. But that's maybe the sickest thing. I wasn't surprised. I find out my brother's a rapist, and I'm like, yeah, that fits."

James was stunned; he had no idea what to say.

Jack continued. "The only good thing, at least I know now she got her life together again. I mean, she's out of politics for good, but she's working for a non-profit now, like helping immigrants. And we're friends again. Sort of, anyway. Facebook friends. She said she's happy, and she said she knows it wasn't my fault."

"God, Jack, I'm so sorry."

"I just don't want to end up like that." Jack looked James in the eye. "You got it made, you know that? A gorgeous woman, a great marriage. I totally screwed mine up, acting just like the old man, screwing around on her and not caring. I mean, it was all consensual. I'm not Gordon, but still."

"Maybe you'll meet someone, get another chance."

"Man, being here with you guys tonight. I'd forgotten what real people are like, real friends. Everyone—and I mean everyone—in my life in L.A. is just using me, and I'm just using them. You, Mike, Antawn, you're all real. Can you believe Antawn has a kid almost old enough to go to college?"

"Yeah, that's pretty amazing. But you've got a kid. He's real."

"Yeah, he is." Jack smiled, a hazy boozy smile. "He's the best thing in my life, no doubt. I just hope I can be a better dad to him." His eyes lit up. "Angela once told me she thought I was a really great father, and he was growing up to be a good kid."

"Who's Angela?"

"She was Gordon's housekeeper. Me and Ben stayed with them once, had a D.C. vacation. It was great, just spending time together. Ben loved the Maryland crab cakes, couldn't get enough of them." Jack looked surprised by a sudden thought. "You know, it's funny, but I had the feeling Gordon was doing her."

"Was Angela black, by any chance?"

"Yeah, she was a recent immigrant, I think she may have been illegal. She had a sweet Caribbean accent I really liked. Why?"

"Nothing. It's just, some white guys get off on playing the powerful master of the helpless black girl."

"You're saying my brother likes to rape slaves?"

"Well, yeah, kind of. Sorry."

Jack groaned. "What a fucking bastard. God, I hope he doesn't get re-elected this year. Just once, I want to see him not get what he thinks he's entitled to. Just once, I want to see him fail."

James almost said, Maybe it can happen. I want to take down Scofield.

Then Jack looked at James with bleary eyes, trying to focus on him. "I don't know why I'm telling you all this. Not your problem. I guess I just don't care about covering up for him anymore, you know? Still, sorry to lay all that shit on you. You just came here to have a good time."

"That's OK," James said sympathetically. "That's what friends are for, man."

"You know," Jack said softly, his words slurring slightly. "I always liked your parents. I'll never forget the time your mom brought brownies for the whole team, after that Edina game. And your dad— you could hear him cheer louder than anyone in the arena, every game."

James smiled. "Yeah, he's never been the quiet type." He looked around the room. There were Mike and Antawn, dancing with their wives to the slow, sweet love songs of their youth. There was Danny, now back talking with Bobby and his wife at the buffet. Danny looked over and caught his eye, giving him a big grin and the thumbs-up sign.

Danny thinks I'm getting the information. But is it enough? Is this the Way? If this comes out, Scofield might just dump Cambridge and continue on to a second term anyway. We needed more. We needed something on Scofield. Son of a bitch, what should I do?

James looked back at Jack. Jack Cambridge, the man who seemed to have it all, who should have had it all, looked like the loneliest man on Earth.

Oh my God, this is going to totally screw up his life if I put this out. And for what? Maybe nothing. He's drunk. He wouldn't have told me this otherwise. I don't have the right to do this.

James cleared his throat and steeled himself to say what he had to. Knowing he was maybe blowing his second shot at the Way. The hell with it, those damn aliens would just have to find another way.

"Uh, Jack, look—I've got to tell you something." James removed the napkin, revealing his phone. "I'm really sorry."

Jack looked confused. "You want me to talk to someone?"

"Uh, no." This was so hard to say, but he had no choice. "I was recording our conversation."

"Shit, man. What? What the fuck were you doing that for?"

James felt as miserable as Jack had looked moments ago. "To be honest with you, Jack, I was doing it to try to get some secret information from you that your brother might have told you, something really bad, like torture on a large scale, or something. See, I have a very good reason to believe Scofield's going to escalate the conflicts in Africa into a terrible, huge war—that he's going to kill a lot of people and maybe use weapons that might kill us all. I was thinking maybe I could get you to reveal some terrible secret that would make Congress impeach the President. But what you told me, that's your business."

For a long minute, Jack sat there thinking, looking at James, looking away, anger passing over his face in waves. Suddenly he picked up the phone. He looked across the room. "Goddamn, I know just what the hell to do with this, man!"

James followed his gaze and saw the trashcan over by the buffet table. "Uh, please don't throw my phone away. I can just delete it. Look, I'm sorry."

And then Jack said the last words James would've expected. "Isn't that Ta'Nika Coleman standing over there?"

James looked again, and saw a tall, thin black woman with a fierce mohawk, head closely shaved on the sides, standing near the trashcan talking with a short, red-headed woman. In fact, she had her arm around her in an intimate way, and he remembered that she'd come out their senior year, in a brave and moving essay she published in the school newspaper. "Yeah, that's Ta'Nika."

"Like, wasn't she on the school newspaper or something?"

"Yeah, she was the editor."

"Do you think she still has media connections?"

James was stunned. Where was this going? "Yeah, as a matter of fact, she's an editor at the Star Tribune."

Jack spoke decisively. "Get her over here."

"Jack, you don't have to do this."

"You're wrong, man. This is exactly what I have to do. Like, it's suddenly all clear. It's time to get this monkey off my back."

And so, James found himself approaching Ta'Nika, who was wearing a T-shirt that said, "It's the FIRST amendment for a reason." He told her that he had something she'd really want to hear. Now. Intrigued, Ta'Nika followed James back to the table.

Jack looked like a different guy, a new resolve shining in his eyes. He told her he wanted to reveal something that would end his brother's political career. It was time to stop him, Jack said. Stop him before he did it to anyone else.

As Jack described his brother's assault, Ta'Nika's eyes widened in disbelief. "It's all here," he said, holding up the phone, "My words recorded and true. I'll swear to it."

"Holy shit," she said, jaw dropped in astonishment. "Jesus, Jack, I was holding off pushing you for an interview, trying to be nice letting you just enjoy the reunion, and you're sitting on this?"

Ta'Nika told Jack it would be better to be able to use Shaundra's name, to get her corroboration and consent. Jack surprised James then by saying that Shaundra had told him recently that she was thinking about going public with the story, that she thought she felt strong enough now.

All James could think was, Maybe this is the Way after all. I don't know how this takes down Scofield, but something's happening here. Those Seekers know something I don't.

And then, suddenly, Eddie snatched it all away. No, not Eddie, but Eddie's agent. Secret Service agent Rick Baker strode over and pointed to the phone in Jack's hand.

"What's this?" he demanded.

James was so startled at this sudden turn of events that he could hardly recover. "Nothing," he stammered. "It's just my phone."

"Were you recording Mr. Cambridge on this?"

"I…uh…" James stuttered.

"I'm afraid I'm going to have to check it before I can release it back to you. National Security."

Jack looked at the agent who'd been assigned to him for every trip out of the country he'd taken in the last four years. "Hey, Rick, lighten up. What the hell? We were just talking about old times, man."

Ta'Nika was incensed. "You can't do that! It's unconstitutional!"

Agent Baker looked at her with contempt. "Not according to the Freedom from Fear Act." He pointed at James. "This man threatened the President of the United States. We need to know who he's been contacting, what he's possibly planning. So yeah, lady, sue us."

Jack looked angrily at Baker. "You think James giving Howard the peace sign was threatening?"

"It doesn't matter what I think," Agent Baker said, and walked away with James's phone.

"Damn, this is really bad," James said.

Ta'Nika looked like she couldn't believe she'd just been literally handed the biggest story of the last ten years and then, moments later, had it snatched away. "Jack," she said, reaching into her purse. "I always carry a recorder with me in case I run across a story." She started to get it out of her purse.

"Don't!" James said with alarm. "If you start recording Jack, that guy'll really know something's up."

"Yeah, OK, I guess you're right. Maybe we can set something up for later. But we'll have to do it fast, before the other side can start spinning it. Could you call me from your hotel when you get back there tonight? I have a feeling they won't let me through to you. We could just record the conversation then. I could give you my number..."

No. It will never happen. She doesn't know what she's up against. Eddie will crush Jack. God, what will Eddie do if his back's against the wall?

"Yeah, I don't think they're gonna let this come out," James said. "They'll shut it down, one way or another. I don't know how yet, but they're not gonna take a chance on this hurting their reelection chances." James turned to Jack and looked him square in the eyes.

"Jack, do you trust me?"

"Shit, yeah. You're the only one who's been straight with me since I can't remember when."

"OK, then," James said firmly, making up his mind. "We've got to get out of here now. If we don't, they'll make sure you never get a chance to talk to Ta'Nika, or anyone else."

Jack started to stand up. "Yeah, you're probably right. I'm just gonna go tell Rick we're heading out with her. What can he do? I'm a free man."

James pulled him back down. "No, you're not. That guy doesn't work for you. He works for the Federal government. He's not gonna let you go anywhere."

"He can piss off," Jack said, slurring a bit as he threw an angry look at Agent Baker. Baker was talking on his cuff mike, presumably to the other agent.

"C'mon, Jack, we've got to think straight here. OK, Ta'Nika, you should get to your office. We'll find a way to get out of here. We'll meet you there. I swear."

"All right," Ta'Nika said, without hesitation. "I'll need you to put me in touch with Shaundra, too. Can you give me her number, Jack? Or, what's her last name?"

"I've just got a Facebook contact. I think I should let her know this is going down, anyway, before you talk to her. I mean, it's her choice."

Jack took out his phone, held it away from Baker's sight, and sent a message to Shaundra.

Ta'Nika handed Jack her business card. "OK, let me know when you get ahold of her. Give her my info. Here's the address of the building, my cell, my email, and my number at the paper. I gotta go tell my wife our evening has taken a serious turn."

As Ta'Nika was standing up, James said, "Listen, he won't just let you walk out of here now. Not until he finds out what you know."

She sank back down, dismayed. "Goddamn. All those articles I wrote about the erosion of freedom in the name of national security.

Now I know what I was talking about."

"There's got to be a way…" James said, thinking furiously. "All right, how about this? You go over to the buffet, look like you're just getting some food. Tell Danny we need a diversion. He'll figure something out. He's good at causing mayhem."

Ta'Nika smiled slightly. "Right. I remember. Then hopefully we can walk out in the confusion, right? Good luck, y'all."

C'mon, Danny. Come through for me. We're a team. Danny at first looked concerned at what Ta'Nika was telling him, but then his eyes lit up.

James looked at Jack. He couldn't believe what he was about to do. But it was weird, even though he was feeling nervous, he also felt confident, in control.

"Jack, you ready to move fast?"

"Absolutely."

"OK, we'll go as soon as the disruption happens."

"I don't know, man. If there's an incident, Baker'll move first to protect me. It's his goddamn job." Jack thought for a moment. "Look, I'm gonna go tell him I gotta take a piss. He knows I hate it when he follows me to the bathroom. Anyway," he laughed. "I really do need to take a leak."

"Yeah, that's good. Then when Danny throws things into high gear, I'll get out and meet you in the hallway. We'll find a way out of here, somehow."

James watched Jack approach the agent, and then leave the room. So far so good.

Then he watched Danny walk over to Carlos, slipping him some bills as he talked to him. Carlos pick up a tray full of drinks. He was walking backward, talking loudly as he went. "Yeah, yeah, I'll get those drinks to you as soon as I can! Take it easy, buddy!"

Suddenly, without warning, Carlos spun around and walked right into Miranda and Stacy, spilling the drinks all over them, the glasses falling to the floor and shattering. Their shocked screams filled the cavernous room, causing hundreds of heads to swivel toward them simultaneously. It sounded like someone had had a heart attack, they were shrieking so hysterically. A crowd quickly gathered.

James glanced at Agent Baker, who was watching the incident but hadn't left his post. Baker looked over at him. Damn. James heard Stacy screaming at Carlos. "Jesus Christ, you idiot! This dress cost $400! You better have gotten some great tips, 'cause you're paying for it, you moron!" Baker was still scanning the room. Now what?

James jumped up, hurried over to the group and said loudly, "Take it easy, Stacy. I'll go get a bunch of paper towels."

James turned and hurried out of the room like a man on a mission. Which he was.

CHAPTER 33

The hallway was lit up down to the bathrooms, but dark after that. James badly wanted to make it to the dark part. He sprinted down the hall toward Jack, waiting by the reception desk in the shadows opposite the bathrooms. Jack grabbed James and pulled him down behind the desk, motioning for him to be quiet. He heard rapid footsteps on the tile floor. James's heart was pounding wildly.

They heard the bathroom door slam open. Jack halfway stood up to run again, but James pulled him down. And thank goodness, because it had only taken Baker a few seconds to check the bathroom and come charging out again.

And then the agent stopped, just on the other side of the desk. James was sure his rapid breathing would give them away, that in another second, he'd be staring into Baker's gun. But no, Baker was talking. For a second, James thought there were other people there too. Would they be surrounded? Then he realized that Baker was talking on his cuff mike to the agent outside.

"Rivera! Lock it down! He wasn't in the bathroom… Yeah, this could just be one of Ugly Duckling's stunts. After that time in Thailand, I wouldn't put anything past him… No, no one leaves. But keep it calm. If we're lucky, he's just puking somewhere, after all he drank, and Thompson's just helping him… No, until we know

otherwise, we still have to treat this as a possible terrorist incident…
No, they can't get out, there are alarms on all the doors. Call in the
local law enforcement. We'll sweep the building… God, no, we're
not contacting Barracuda unless we have to. We'll take care of this
ourselves. He's here. He can't get out. What a goddamn loose
cannon." Agent Baker slammed his fist down on the ticket counter,
and James flinched at the sound. "Son of a bitch!"

———————

They waited till Baker was back in the ballroom. James didn't
know where they should go. His legs felt like rubber; he could hardly
stand up. They just kept moving down the hallway, till they found
themselves at the end. The big glass doors leading to the pool were in
front of them, enticing them to just push through and run for it when
the alarm went off. The snack bar was to the left; stairs leading up to
the second level were on the right.

In every movie he'd ever seen, people trying to escape kept
climbing higher and higher until they opened the door to the roof
and found themselves teetering on the edge of the building, looking
down at a drop that would kill them. Then the guys chasing them
would smash through the roof door, guns blazing. At that point, a
helicopter would descend, dangling a rope that would pull the heroes
to safety as the bad guys futilely shot at them. James didn't think the
Seekers had lined up any helicopters. They went left.

The interior of the snack bar was dark. James and Jack crouched
behind the big stainless-steel food prep table.

Jack looked around. "Maybe we shoulda gone up," he whispered.
"How're we gonna get out of here? You heard what Rick said."

"Yeah, well I used to work in the snack bar in the summers. I bet
they still keep the key for the window in the same place."

James quietly slid open a drawer and pulled out a wad of napkins.
He felt around in the drawer, then held up the key triumphantly. "I
knew it." He inserted the key into the lock at the bottom of the big
roll window through which they served the pool patrons. "Help me
slide this open."

Holding his breath, praying an alarm wouldn't go off, they slid up
the window covering as smoothly and quietly as they could. Bingo!

James looked at Jack. "Let's go."

The pool area was dark. The pool lights were still on, though, giving off an otherworldly glow as the illuminated water shifted and reflected on the lounge chairs and lifeguard stands. The eerie blueness made James think incongruously of Neptune. Suddenly, Jack shocked James by taking his phone out of his pocket and throwing it into the pool.

"What'd you do that for? Now we've got no phone."

"Exactly. That time in Thailand that Rick was talking about? I tried to duck him when I wanted to take a stripper home from a bar, and he tracked me on my phone's GPS."

"You could've just left it on that chair. You didn't have to destroy it."

"Yeah, I guess. Whatever. I can get a new one."

James's irritation with Jack was broken by the sound of sirens approaching. "Oh damn, no. We gotta go."

James was dismayed to see Jack stumble as he moved forward, grabbing a chair for balance. Damn, all that rum they'd loaded into him was now messing things up.

"Shit!" Jack said. "I can usually hold my liquor better'n this."

James looked around wildly. He didn't think Jack was in any shape to climb that tall fence. His eyes came back to the lounge chair that Jack was steadying himself on. Yeah, that might work. There was already a tall stack of chairs up against the fence. He quickly dragged a shorter stack of chairs over in front of the tall stack. Jack caught on and pulled some more chairs over. They made a third, shorter stack in front of that. The stairway to freedom. The police cars were pulling into the parking lot as they went over.

They were breathing heavily, leaning up against the concrete wall of a picnic shelter. For a heart-stopping moment after Jack hit the ground on the other side of the fence, James thought Jack had sprained his ankle or twisted his knee. But he'd gotten up, hobbled a bit, and then flashed James the thumbs-up sign with a triumphant smile.

The piercing sound of police sirens filled their heads, and they peered around the wall cautiously. Four more police cars screamed into the parking lot. They could see the Hispanic agent directing most of the cops into the building and sending some around the side to search the perimeter. The agent left one cop to guard the door, and then went into the building himself. When the doors opened, they could hear the people screaming inside. It sounded like a riot was going on.

James whispered to Jack, "Those people in there must be in a total panic. They probably think there's been a terrorist attack or something."

"Yeah. Let's go. Where's your car?"

"I don't have one."

"Say what? What'd you do, have your mommy drop you off? How can you not have a car?"

"I came over with Danny. He's got the keys in there."

"Well, shit."

Shit was right. Why hadn't the Way told him to get the keys first? Some damn Way, leaving him stranded like this. "Maybe we should just wait, see if he can get out here," James suggested. "He's pretty resourceful."

"I don't know, man. I think we should move."

James saw that the police officer on their side of the building was heading away from them. He'd be circling wider soon. Jack was right. They set off across a big field, staying close to the shadows of the trees, moving as fast as they could, heading toward Dakota Boulevard.

When he felt like they'd gotten far enough away, James stopped and looked back. The Rec Center was awash in pulsating red lights. "The more those guys have to deal with, the better. I hope the crowd in there is uncontrollable. It'll keep at least some of those cops busy."

Jack suddenly lurched off toward some bushes. James heard

violent retching. Jack emerged from the bushes wiping his mouth with a broad leaf. "If there's one thing I learned in college, it's that you feel better after you puke."

"You good to go now?"

"Yeah, man. I can take on the world now."

"That's good. Can you take on the Secret Service, the CIA, the FBI and Homeland Security?"

"No problem. I know those guys. Maybe they've got high tech toys, but they're still idiots using them. Anyway, we've got one big up on them. We know what's going on. They don't." Jack grinned. "This is gonna be fun."

―――――――――

The edge of the parking lot for the Westfield Cinema 16 abutted the big field they'd just crossed. They stood there in the shadows, trying to figure their next move.

"Why don't we just call a Lyft?" Jack suggested.

"No, no, we can't risk that. They'll get the word out to all the transportation places—cab companies, buses, ride shares. It's a pretty distinctive APB—two tall men, one black, one white, and oh yeah, one of them's the brother of the Vice President."

"I've got some cash, maybe a couple hundred. We could bribe a cabbie. A really fat tip might help him keep his mouth shut."

"I don't know, I think we're too hot. If I could just get ahold of Emily, she could pick us up and run us downtown. But you threw away your phone—yeah, I know, you had to. There just aren't pay phones around like there used to be."

"Thompson, what century do you live in? There's a phone in every pocket." Jack walked out into the parking lot, approaching a couple heading to their car. They were vehemently discussing the merits of the movie they'd just seen.

"Excuse me."

The woman startled.

"Sorry. I don't mean to bother you, but do you mind if we use your phone for just a minute? My battery's dead. My buddy here's got to call his wife." Jack gave them a dazzling smile.

The woman looked them over, considering. "Sure," she said, extending her phone. "No problem."

James quickly punched the number, turning away from the couple. "Hi, honey." He heard the anxiety in Emily's voice, asking if he was all right. "Yeah, I'm fine. You were right, though, I do need your help. I need you to pick us up at the Westfield Cinema. Pull into the back of the parking lot. I'll watch for you. But, honey, if you see any cops, just keep going, OK? Promise me."

———————————

They waited. And waited. Every second seemed like a minute, every minute seemed like ten. James continuously scanned for approaching police cars. He felt as jumpy as if he'd had six cups of coffee, but he didn't think it was all those Cokes affecting his nerves.

"Where is she? She should be here by now."

"Take it easy."

"What if someone reports suspicious characters lurking in the parking lot?"

Jack pulled out a pack of cigarettes. "Here. Take one."

"What? No, I don't smoke."

"I don't either," Jack said, lighting up. "Shit'll kill you."

"Huh?"

"I just smoke when a client wants to share a cig. I forgot I had them in my pocket, but good thing. Standing around outside 'cause you need a smoke is a great cover. Literally," he added, blowing a cloud of smoke in front of their faces.

"Oh, yeah, that's a good idea."

Jack handed the burning cigarette to James and lit another one for himself. "This'll give you something to do while you're waiting. Calm down. She'll be here."

James took a tentative puff and choked. "Guess I better not inhale," he said.

They were on their third cigarette, walking slowly up an aisle of cars toward the theater again when James spotted a couple of guys headed toward them.

"I can't stand this anymore. I've got to find out what's happening," he said to Jack. He approached the men, smiling. They returned his smile, the tips of their cigarettes glowing as they took deep drags. Fellow smokers. Brothers.

"Hey, guys, you mind if I use your phone for a minute? My battery's dead, and if I don't call the wife and tell her where I am, she'll kill me."

"Yeah, why not?" One of the men extended his phone to James. James was pleased to see Jack engage the men in conversation, so they couldn't hear him.

Emily wasn't answering her cell phone. Damn. That couldn't be good. He hoped she'd just forgotten to turn up the ringer or had buried it in the bottom of her purse, like she often did. He decided to call Danny. He knew he was taking a risk, but Danny was his man on the inside. Maybe he'd have some valuable information. Thank God Danny had made his number so easy he knew it by heart.

"This is Dan Friedman."

Oh yeah, he wouldn't recognize the caller ID. "Danny, it's me."

"Oh, hi honey! Whose phone are you calling on?"

"I'm borrowing someone's phone."

"I know. I'm really sorry I didn't call. I know I promised I'd be home, but something's happened."

"Can you talk?"

James heard Danny say to someone nearby, "Sorry, it's my wife. I gotta take this. I'll be back." Then into the phone, as he was apparently walking away, "C'mon, honey, calm down. It's not my fault. I know I said… James?"

"Yeah, yeah! What's going on?"

"Thank God! You OK?"

"Yeah. So far. What's happening there?"

"Oh man, you should see this place. It's bedlam! Everyone's freaking out, and there are hundreds of rumors circulating. They made an announcement that no one can leave. I keep trying to harass the Secret Service guys by getting people all riled up, like telling people I heard there's a bomb in the building. But now those agents are off by themselves and the cops won't let anyone get to them."

"Can you tell what they're doing, what they're up to?"

"I've been watching them. The head guy, Baker, attached ear buds to your phone, and at one point he looked like he was gonna throw up." Danny chuckled. "Must've been good, man. Anyway, then he was telling the Hispanic guy about it. They looked really grim, like they'd rather shoot themselves in the head, and then Baker pulled out his phone and made a call."

"That had to have been to either Cambridge or Scofield."

"Yeah, that's what I figure. It didn't look like the call went too well from where I was sitting."

"So, it's possible Eddie knows now," James said grimly.

"Knows what, man? What the hell was on that recording?"

James felt a tap on his shoulder. The man gestured to indicate he should finish up the call. James nodded. Then he saw Jack pull out a twenty-dollar bill and offer it to him. The guy took it. Yeah, that should cover a couple more minutes.

"It's unreal, Danny, but it's probably better if you don't know yet. You gotta be my eyes and ears inside, right?"

Danny laughed. "They told me you were a suspected terrorist who had probably kidnapped the Vice President's brother. You should have seen my acting job, man! I gave 'em that classic line about how you were always the quiet type and I never would have suspected it."

James laughed. Good old Danny.

"Hey, you be careful out there, man," Danny said. "These guys are serious. They'll shoot first and ask questions later."

"We're keeping our heads down. Can you do me a favor, though, and try calling Emily? She was supposed to pick us up twenty minutes ago, and she hasn't shown, and she didn't answer when I just called."

"Sure. Call me back in five. Listen, though, I gotta tell you the genius thing I did. That Baker guy asked me to help them out by getting a picture of you from the photographer and taking it out to the police officer at the door so they could put it out, you know, like on an APB. So, I picked a random photo of a guy who looks nothing like you. With any luck, they're looking for the wrong guy."

It was fifteen excruciating minutes till another movie let out and they could find someone to bum a phone from. This time, Jack just outright offered a twenty. They were closer to the theater than James liked, but a phone was a phone.

Danny answered on the first ring. "James?"

"Did you get ahold of Emily?"

"Sort of. Look, don't freak out…"

"Oh my God! Is Emily OK?"

"I think so."

"What d'you mean, you think so?"

"When I couldn't get Emily's cell, I called your house phone. Good thing you're still retro enough to have a land line."

"Danny! Emily?"

"Right. She managed to let me know that there was a cop sitting in your living room with her."

"Oh shit!"

"Yeah, don't worry. She'll be OK. Listen, she said something weird about wanting to see a movie at the Westfield theater next week. Does that mean something to you?"

"Yeah, that's where we are. She was going to pick us up. Damn, damn, damn!"

"Hey, I can do it, man! I'm in the Dragon right now, not that far."

"Huh? You're not at the Rec Center?"

"No. See, when they were talking to Antawn, I realized it was only a matter of time till they figured out that I'm your best friend, not just a basketball buddy from the past. I didn't want to be interrogated, if you know what I mean, or held as a material witness, or whatever the hell they do to best friends of known terrorists.

"I figured it was time to get out of there. I went to the cop at the door and told him I'd remembered that you'd left your jacket in my car, and if they wanted it so a dog could get your scent, I could get it."

"Smart. So, you're OK?"

"Yeah. I took off. Good thing we had to park in the back of the lot, as it turned out. Didn't turn on my lights till I was down the street."

"OK, good. We'll be at the back of the parking lot."

"OK. We're still gonna nail Eddie, buddy."

Danny hung up. James updated Jack.

"Too bad about your wife, but I guess we're back on track again." Jack looked around. "I seriously gotta take a piss. Those Rum and Cokes are running right through me."

"Where're you going?" James said in alarm, as Jack started off toward the brightly lit buildings. "Wait, can't you just use the bushes?"

"Nah, I want some coffee." Jack pointed to the coffee shop near the movie theater. "I need to clear my head."

"Hey, I don't think that's a good…" But Jack was gone. Damn. What should he do now?

Three minutes later, the question was answered. James saw two police cars pull into the parking lot, lights and sirens off. One headed toward the back, shining lights around the parked cars, searching. The other drew up in front of the theater. One officer jumped out and hurried into the theater. His partner stepped out and scanned the area in front.

James ducked down behind a car. This didn't look random. Damn, Danny, don't pull in.

Then James forgot about Danny. Jack was coming out of the coffee shop, carrying two cups of coffee. He tried to send mental vibes Jack's way. See the cop. Turn around. Go back.

But Jack hadn't looked up yet. He was concentrating on trying to carry two full cups of hot coffee. All that cop had to do was turn his head, as he surely would at any moment.

James stepped out of the shadows and yelled, waving his arms. "Officer! Officer!"

Then, as the police officer turned and headed toward James, James experienced a sudden shock of recognition. He knew this guy. He was the liaison officer at the high school. And he was very young. Maybe, just maybe, the Way was still working.

"Officer Thorton! Hi! So, this is what you do in the summer. You know, you're the best liaison officer the high school's ever had. The kids really relate to you." James's thought was simple—keep him occupied while Jack got away. Jack was the key. "So, what's harder to deal with, huh, criminals or tenth graders?" James tried very hard to chuckle naturally.

"Thanks for saying that, Mr. Thompson. I do try hard to relate to the kids. But, well… this is really weird, but you're wanted. I mean, the FBI's saying you're a terrorist."

"What're you talking about?"

"I know, it sounds crazy. But look," he said, holding out his phone with James's picture on it. "Everyone's looking for you. Something about the Vice President's brother being kidnapped by terrorists."

The shock of seeing his picture, his wanted picture, was almost more than James could handle. And then he noticed that Jack was still approaching. Didn't he see what was happening? Go, go, turn around, get out of here!

"What? That's crazy! Will, you know me. They must have me confused with a different James Thompson. It's a common name. For God's sake, I'm a teacher. I'm not a terrorist."

"Yeah, I know. Makes no sense. But I'm still gonna have to ask you to come in with me. You can get it all straightened out at the station."

"C'mon, Will. I'll get this taken care of in the morning. You have my word."

"I'm sorry, Mr. Thompson. I really have to take you in. Anyway, it's for your own protection. You're lucky it was me. If any other cop had seen you, you might be dead."

James saw the hand reach out to tap Officer Thorton on the shoulder. Oh my God. He heard the voice.

"Officer?"

Will Thorton turned around, and Jack immediately decked him with a hard punch to the chin. Thorton crashed into the side of a parked car and crumbled to the ground. James could do nothing but stand there, staring in shock.

Jack was exultant. "I punched out a cop! God, I've always wanted to do that!"

James dropped to the ground and put his hand on the officer's chest, his ear near the man's mouth. "It's OK! Thank God, he's breathing. He's alive."

Jack was scanning the area. "We're OK, no one saw that. But that cop car back there is getting closer. We gotta go."

James looked up at Jack, shock and anger mixed on his face. "What the hell did you do that for? I know this guy. He works at the high school, Jack. He's a good guy. Oh, man, I'm gonna have to buy him a cup of coffee every day next year to make this up to him!"

Jack picked up the coffee cups he'd set down. He put one down near the unconscious cop.

"There. That can be your first payback cup." Jack chugged half the coffee from the other cup, then dropped it, coffee running out and staining the pavement near the cop like blood at a crime scene. "Now can we go, man?"

Maybe it was something in Jack's tone, maybe it was seeing him gulp scalding hot coffee. James snapped out of his shocked state, and they ran, crouching between the parked cars.

CHAPTER 34

It only took them a couple of minutes to get to a nearby neighborhood and the relative cover of dark alleys. James felt slightly ridiculous running from the shadow of one garage to another, like he was an actor on a second-rate cop show on TV. And then a police car cruised past the alley, suddenly shining its blinding searchlight in their direction. James's breath caught in his throat as they quickly pressed their bodies against a garage door, hoping the door frame would conceal them. The police car moved on and James let out a ragged gasp.

"Shit, that was close," Jack said.

James took another big breath of air, blowing it out slowly to steady himself.

They ran for ten blocks, but James knew this wasn't nearly enough distance. The area would be flooded with police cars at any moment. It occurred to James that they had upped the ante. Now he was a dangerous federal fugitive who had just assaulted a police officer. They would assume he wasn't going to surrender peacefully. Not to mention, he was black. They would shoot to kill, 100% certainty. Then another thought hit him.

"Damn!" he said, stopping.

"What?"

"I'm so stupid. How did I not notice?"

"What?"

"My shirt. Our clothes. That wanted picture of me that Will showed me—it was from the reunion tonight. It showed me in this turquoise shirt. We gotta change clothes."

"OK. Is there a store nearby? We're still pretty close to the commercial stuff on Dakota Boulevard, right?"

"No, that's no good."

"Don't worry," Jack said. "I can pay for it."

James couldn't help feeling a surge of annoyance at Jack's assumption that he couldn't afford to buy a shirt, but he let it go. "No, I mean nothing's gonna be open at this time of night. Maybe in Los Angeles, but not here. So, where can we get new shirts?"

"If this were a movie, the hero guys would find a clothesline full of clothes in someone's back yard," Jack offered.

"Well, it's not a movie, and it's not 1950. People actually use machines to dry their clothes now, even here in backwater Minnesota." James snapped his fingers. "That's it, though. What street are we at?" He peered at the street sign. "Spruce. That's good. If we head back to the main drag, I think there's a laundromat right around here."

James was right. Maybe the Way was still working, he thought, as he gazed at the Super Clean 24-Hour Laundromat across the street. They could see into the brightly lit interior through the large picture window. One woman was sitting in a molded red plastic chair, reading a book. So good, maybe she hadn't seen any news reports. It looked like there were several dryers going, so maybe some people had thrown their stuff in and then gone to the bar on the corner to make the wait more pleasant.

"I don't feel good about stealing someone's clothes," James admitted. "I mean, I know we have to, but I don't like it."

"Oh yeah. I forgot you were a preacher's kid. Would it make you feel better if I left a hundred bucks in the dryer?"

"Well yeah, actually. Thanks."

James thought about how they should do this. "OK, so we just need to stroll in, like we've just come back from the Happy Loon bar there to get our clothes. Hopefully we'll find a couple shirts we can use. Or maybe you'd better just go in yourself, and I'll wait out here. She might get scared with two guys coming in, especially me."

"What, 'cause you're black?"

"Yeah."

"You serious?"

"That's reality, Jack. Especially lately."

"Shit, I'm sick of this stupid bullshit. Who the hell cares if she gets scared? That's her problem, not ours. Come in and pick out a shirt you like, man."

They were just about to step out onto the brightly lit boulevard when two police cars came screaming down the street, lights flashing. They waited another minute and then decided to go for it. James's heart was pounding wildly as they pushed open the door. Any police officer cruising Dakota now would spot them through the big window in a heartbeat.

Unexpectedly, the young woman looked at them and smiled. "Hi," she said, her pierced eyebrows rising invitingly. Jeez, was she looking to pick someone up, being here alone in this place at this time of night?

"Hi."

Jack moved toward the back, saying, "I'll check our stuff, man."

James sat down near the girl, reluctantly, and turned his back to the window. It was the best he could do. At least he could distract her from watching what Jack was doing.

"Something's going on," she said. "That's like the sixth cop car that's gone by in the last few minutes."

"Really?"

"Yeah. So, you guys are late-night laundry freaks too, huh? It's the best, isn't it? Like, you meet such interesting people. And you can

303

always get a machine, right?"

"Yeah." His brain was frozen. He couldn't think of anything to say, but he had to say something. "Uh, what're you reading?"

"This book about how to be a conscientious objector," she replied, showing him the cover. "I'm trying to stay out of the army. Otherwise, I'm going to Canada. Or Australia. Or maybe Fiji. You know?"

"Yeah, I do. Good for you. You shouldn't get yourself killed so some corporate CEO can get richer. Listen, there's a good website you can go to that'll help you stay out of the military. Do you have a piece of paper?" He wrote down the web address for her, while thinking, I'm being hunted by every cop within twenty miles. What am I doing?

The girl was looking at the paper as Jack breezed past him, saying, "The stuff wasn't dry. C'mon."

"Well, good luck," James said. Jack was already out the door. James thought he'd seen some clothing in his hand, but he'd gone by so fast, he figured the girl might not have noticed.

"See you around," she said.

James turned at the door. "Don't let 'em get you."

They sprinted across the wide boulevard and back to the comfort of the dark neighborhood side streets. Jack held out a pink shirt with white stripes and a white collar and said, "I think this'll fit you."

James just caught himself from bursting out laughing. "Danny'd be proud," he said, as he removed the Polo shirt and slipped on the new one. Jack was putting his head through the neck of a tight black T-shirt with a Led Zeppelin album cover pictured on the front.

"OK," James said, "That's better. Let's throw these in that garbage can over there."

"Now what?" Jack asked.

"I don't know." James stood there, thinking furiously but coming up with nothing.

Jack grabbed his arm. "Look." He pointed to an open garage. Someone had forgotten to put their garage door down.

"Maybe they left their keys in the car," Jack said hopefully as they headed toward the garage.

"First shirts, now cars," James muttered to himself.

Jack entered the garage and opened the car door. James winced as the car light came on. Jack's muffled voice came from inside the car. "No luck."

Jack emerged from the car, holding something.

They stepped back outside, and Jack handed him the prize he'd found. "This was on the passenger seat."

James turned on the phone. "Awesome, whoever's phone this is didn't put a password on it."

"Idiot. Who knows when someone might steal your phone and use it."

"Indeed. OK, we're good. I'll call Danny."

"No, wait. They might have been tapping Danny's phone, right? That might be why they sent those two cop cars into the movie theater parking lot."

"Oh, man, that's so messed up. You think they could do that so fast?" James shuddered, and then recovered himself. "Maybe we should call Ta'Nika first." Then he hesitated. "Wait, what if they're tapping her phone, too? I don't know, maybe they'd have to get a warrant to tap a newspaper's phone. I'll just have to be careful what I say."

It rang twice. C'mon, be there. It rang again. Damn, now what do we—

"This is Ta'Nika Coleman."

"Ta'Nika! It's James."

"James! Are you with Jack? Are you OK?"

"We're good. So far, anyway. We got out of there all right, amazingly. But we're kind of on the run from the cops now. Are you at your office?"

"Yeah. Doing the preliminaries. We're ready to go as soon as I can talk to Shaundra. Did she answer Jack's message yet?"

"I don't know, he doesn't have his phone anymore. We're borrowing this one. I guess Jack's gotta try to connect with her on Facebook again. God, I didn't even think about that till just now. I'm kind of overloaded, you know what I'm saying? Anyway, I'm trying to think how to tell you someplace you could pick us up, so they won't know what I'm talking about, in case they're tapping your phone."

"They better not be. That would be highly illegal."

"Yeah, well, you know Homeland Security trumps everything these days. So…"

"Let's assume they already know I'm at the office, then. If I come get you, what's to keep them from following me?"

"Yeah you're right. In fact, I'd probably better disconnect now before they trace this. Can they do that?"

"Got me. They can on TV. Listen, maybe you better not come here after all, although my boss wants to talk to Jack to confirm this. He's on his way in now. I don't have to tell you it's the biggest story of the year. I know he'd prefer to talk to Jack in person, but maybe it would be OK over the phone. Just call from someplace safe when you can. And have Jack's friend call me. If he can't get her, we may have to go with what we've got for now, update it when we can talk to Shaundra. We don't want to lose this. Hey, James—be careful." She hung up.

James stood there, thinking hard about options, until Jack brought him back from his thoughts. "So, what now?"

"I don't know. My folks? No, they never hear the phone at night. I know, my sister! No, wait, they're on vacation. Anyway, you've got to talk to Shaundra. That's priority number one." James handed Jack the phone. "Why don't you use this to get on Facebook and see if she answered you."

A few minutes later, Jack looked up. "No, nothing yet. I sent another message. I'll keep the phone, so I can get it if she calls me. I gave her this number."

"Good, good. I still can't think of anyone to call, though. Ta'Nika said we should just stay hidden and not try to get to her office. But I

wonder if she just said that in case they were listening. Anyway, the editor-in-chief or the publisher or whoever, really wants to talk to you before they release this story."

"Wherever we go, we can't stay here. Let's just steal this car, man. This is our best shot. I can sneak in there and find the keys without anyone hearing me."

James doubted that. "Even if you could, the guy would hear us starting the car. He'd report it stolen and the cops would pick us up in three minutes."

"We could push it out into the alley first."

"No, he still might discover it was gone a minute after we left."

"Guess you'd better try Danny then. We'll just have to hope they're not tapping him yet," Jack said.

"Wait. No. I've got a better idea." James's eyes lit up. "They've got tons of high-tech tools to find us. They rely too much on technology. That's their Achilles' heel." James pointed to the bicycles at the back of the garage. "We've got to go low tech."

The bike path went straight from the western suburb into downtown. It was wide, it was paved, it was secluded, and James knew it like the back of his hand. He'd ridden it many times, and he felt confident now as they rode silently by the light of the full moon. The path followed the train tracks on one side, and on the other side there were groves of trees most of the way. Sometimes they passed people's back yards and the backs of apartment buildings and schools and businesses. They didn't see a car moving or another person.

The path curved, and they were passing by Cedar Lake, the moon and stars reflecting off its dark surface like flecks of silver in a shiny black granite slab. It was so peaceful, they could almost forget the danger they were in. James felt himself relax for the first time since he'd run down that dark hallway at the Rec Center over two hours ago.

James looked at Jack and smiled. "We're flying in under the radar, Jack."

"Me an' Karen Shipman used to ride our bikes on this path to

Cedar Lake and make out at Hidden Beach, on nights just like this."

"A night like this could almost make you forget the winters here. Look at that, Jack." He pointed ahead as they rounded a bend. The brilliant skyline of Minneapolis was framed by the trees on either side of the path. It was breathtakingly beautiful. He always loved it when he came around this curve and the skyline suddenly came into view. But he'd never seen it at night before, shining with thousands of lights, as though a patch of the star-studded sky had been put under a microscope and enlarged.

James chuckled. "I feel like Dorothy with her pals on the yellow brick road, when they first see Emerald City."

Jack looked at James. "So, what'd you think I was going to do back there at the theater when you were talking to that cop? Why were you so shocked when I hit him?"

"I was just trying to keep him from spotting you. I thought you'd hide. Escape. Not almost kill a really nice guy who I happen to know is getting married soon."

"Ah, he'll just have a bad headache. I wouldn't've just left you, man. We're teammates, right?"

"Right. I guess we're in this together."

They rode in silence. James wondered what Eddie was up to. On a serene summer night like this, the balmy air caressing his face as they rode, crickets and frogs by the lake raising up the Hallelujah Chorus of Nature, it was hard to believe that such evil was at work. But it is, it is, you know it. Keep focused.

James found himself needing to get in touch with a higher power. Oh Lord God, he prayed, I believe you are guiding me now. I ask you to continue to guide me on this journey, to let me feel your divine strength. You have given us this wonderful gift of life in all its abundance, here and throughout the Universe. Lord, please help me defend it. Please be with me as I complete this task.

They had a few more miles to go. He looked over at Jack, gliding silently next to him, and decided maybe he wasn't the jerk everyone thought he was. He'd gotten a raw deal in his family situation, that was for sure. How bad would it mess you up to grow up with a father who abused your mother, who favored a brother who turned out to be a rapist?

"You know, Jack, maybe you should volunteer to coach your kid's basketball team. You'd get to see him more. Plus, it's fun. I coached Trey's tee-ball team, and it was the most fun I had in a long time." He laughed softly. "I always thought of baseball as a simple game, till I tried to teach it to a bunch of four-year-olds."

Jack gave him a dubious look but seemed to be considering it.

"Maybe that's not a half bad idea," he said after a couple minutes. "I actually wanted to be a coach when I got out of college. That's what I would've done if I'd had a choice."

"You didn't have a choice?"

"It didn't seem like it at the time. You might have something there, though. Ben's pretty good. He can already shoot over me."

"Guess he inherited your shooter's touch."

Jack smiled. "Yeah, I guess he did."

After a few more minutes of silent pedaling, Jack said hesitantly, "Uh, can I ask you something?"

"Yeah, sure."

"Do you run into racism often?"

"You asking for real? OK. Day to day, going through my usual routine, it's not bad. But it's always in the back of my mind, every time I step out my door. Have I been stopped for DWB? Yes. I always put my seatbelt on. I always avoid eye contact with a cop who's driving by, 'cause if I draw his attention, chances are good he'll turn around and stop me. Lots of times, it's subtle—the look you get, the moment's hesitation. The store manager keeping a closer eye on you, that kind of thing. Lately, though, it's definitely gotten more overt, more out there. Look, I hate to say it, but you've lived a very privileged life, Jack. You have never for a second had to worry that when you walk into a bank to ask for a loan, they won't give you their best service. You are the default, man."

"What do you mean, it's my fault?"

"No, not your fault. Default," James explained. "See, I have this theory that there are default settings in people's minds. Middle-class white male is the standard default. It's what everyone assumes you are unless proven otherwise. So if I call up the bank and tell them I want a second mortgage, and make an appointment to talk to them about it, then when I walk in, I know I'm probably going to see the guy pause—hesitate just a bit—as he resets the image he had in his mind of me before he met me. Unless, of course, he—or she—happens to be black. See, I was doing it myself, thinking of the bank guy as the default white male."

"Shit, that must be weird. How do you not want to punch those people out?"

"It's just reality. I gotta admit, though, when Emily's talking to someone at a party, and I walk up, and she introduces me as her husband, occasionally I get that double-take, and yeah, I do kind of want to punch them out. But like my daddy always says, if Jesus can turn the other cheek, so can you. Anyway, lots of people experience it, not just me. Like, Christian is the default religion. Danny's always finding that people just assume he's Christian, especially in this state. They'll start talking about Christmas or something and just assume he celebrates it. And then when they find out he's Jewish, they usually go, oh, excuse me for not being politically correct. I should have said the holidays," James said, perfectly imitating the sarcastic undertone people often used.

James glanced at Jack. "You can figure what most people's default setting for criminal is." He waved. "That would be me. You wanna play the default game? Let's say I tell you a crew is coming over to fix the roof. What do you picture?"

"Hispanic men."

"I say we're going to my son's school to meet his first-grade teacher."

"Woman. Either young woman or old grandmother type."

"Kid who wins the national spelling bee."

"Asian kid."

"You got it. But it's changing, you know, even here in Minnesota. Trey's Kindergarten teacher was a man from Venezuela. Trey thought he was the coolest guy ever. I really believe that the default mechanism in people's brains just won't work anymore in a few years. I believe—I hope—that by the time Danielle gets married, no one will be surprised if he's from India or Canada or Japan, if he's blond and blue-eyed or black as the night."

"Even if he's a she?"

James laughed. "Judging from the number of posters of the latest teen heartthrob up on her walls—what's his name, Brian something—I think I'm safe in saying it'll be a male."

"Brian Grant. He starred in the movie, *The Prince of Brooklyn*. We're investing his millions for him. Kid's a jerk. Don't tell Danielle."

"Hey, can I ask you something?" James said.

"Yeah, sure."

"Why aren't you a racist, like your father?"

"That's simple. Experience. When I was on the team and hanging out with all you guys, I found out you're just like everyone else. What I mean is, you're all just who you are—you're James, and Antawn's Antawn, and Mike's Mike. You're just regular guys. You know what I mean?"

"Yeah, I do."

"So, then I basically realized that my father was full of shit. Of course, that wasn't the first time that thought occurred to me." He grinned.

The city lights were so bright they were washing out the stars now. When they rode under the Highway 94 overpass, James stopped his bike. "We're getting pretty close to downtown. Check the phone, see if Shaundra's answered you yet."

Jack's face lit up. "Yes! God, I thought she'd probably freak out, but she did reply!" He read the message. "OK, so she is freaking out. But she says she's pretty sure she wants to go through with it. But she only wants to do it through me. She won't talk to Ta'Nika unless I'm there, too."

"Excellent! So, OK, we're going in."

"I'll call Ta'Nika."

311

"Let's hold off for now. I don't want to tip anyone off, not when we're this close."

"Hey, check it out." Jack pointed toward some bushes, smiling. James spotted the two bodies entwined. Young love. Then he heard a female voice, and she wasn't happy, she was crying, and then suddenly she jumped up and yelled, "I don't care! I don't want you to join the Army! I don't want you to go to Africa! Just don't leave me, OK?" She started sobbing again, and the boy stood up and wrapped his arms around her.

James got back on the bike. "Let's go do this," he said grimly.

CHAPTER 35

The trail ended in another mile. They ditched the bikes behind some bushes. "We're gonna have to go on foot in the streets," James said. "Bikes are conspicuous. We gotta be super careful. I'm thinking if we go down Hennepin Avenue, there should still be plenty of nightlife out. Hopefully we can just blend in with the crowds. That might be safer than being all alone on the street, where they might spot us easier, you know?"

Jack grinned at him. "I'll go you one better. I assume Minneapolis is still the gay capitol of the Midwest. Cops ain't lookin' for two gay guys, are they?"

———————————

Never in a million years would James have imagined himself strolling down Hennepin Avenue arm in arm with the brother of the Vice President of the United States. Before they stepped out on the street, Jack ran his fingers through his hair to throw it forward over his eyes. James unbuttoned his shirt to the navel, blessing God or the Way or whatever for handing him a pink and white striped shirt to complete the disguise. And no one saw them for who they were at all. Either people looked away from them in distaste, or they smiled at them but saw nothing more than a gay couple.

James had been floored that Jack had even suggested this. He would have pegged him as too macho. But when he'd asked Jack if he could really do that, could pull off acting gay without it bothering him, Jack had just laughed. "Get real, man," he'd said. "I've gotten to know so many gay people in Hollywood you wouldn't believe it. It's no big deal, Thompson. Lighten up."

They were several blocks down Hennepin Avenue, just about to pass the Moose and Goose Saloon, when a cop suddenly came around the corner heading toward them. Damn. To turn around now might look suspicious; the cop might stop them just to find out why they were avoiding him.

"Let's go in," Jack whispered to James. As they turned to go through the door being held open by a guy coming out of the bar, Jack turned his face to James, away from the cop, and pretended to be whispering lover's words into his ear. The cop didn't give them more than a glance.

"This was a brilliant idea," James said as they stepped inside.

The Moose and Goose was dark, crowded and noisy. James glanced around as they waited for the cop to get further down the street before venturing outside again. Strobe lights were flashing near the dance floor, illuminating the gyrating men's bodies with vivid green, blue and red light.

"Lucky this turned out to be a gay bar," James said.

"Guess your default setting for 'bar' is more like The Touchdown sports bar, huh?" Jack looked around. "I could use a drink."

"Are you kidding?"

"No, I think it would steady my nerves."

"Forget it, Jack."

A short, rather pudgy man put his hand on Jack's arm. "I'll buy you a drink."

"He's with me," James said firmly. "And he doesn't need a drink."

"OK, fine." The man held up his hands in the gesture of surrender, taking a step back.

James turned his attention back to Jack. "We can probably go in a minute."

The short guy's voice intruded on them again. "You look familiar," he said to Jack. "You been in here before?"

"No, I'm from out of town."

Then, just as James was about to suggest they get moving, the man snapped his fingers. "I got it! You're Jack Cambridge, aren't you? Don't deny it," he said, as Jack was opening his mouth to do just that. "I'm a political junkie. Like totally. Oh my God, I don't believe it! What the hell are you doing here? I mean, I guess I know why you're in here, but why here in Minneapolis? You back home visiting family?"

Jack stared at the man, apparently unable to think of what to say. James was thinking wildly, hoping their cover wasn't blown. He sure couldn't have the guy yelling to his friends to come over and meet the Vice President's brother. But before he could think of anything, the man continued. "Don't worry, I'm not going to out you. Even though lots of politicians have openly gay relatives these days. But that's your business. I'm guessing your brother wouldn't be too hot on you coming out, am I right? He's the darling of FOX News, right?"

"You got that right," Jack responded.

The guy winked at Jack, then continued, "Second question is, what the hell is going on in Washington? I don't mean to offend you, but Scofield is totally insane. All I can say is, good thing I didn't pass the physical, or I'd be going to those bullshit Military Readiness Camps right now getting trained to kill people I got no reason to kill. It's bullshit, man. No offense."

Thank you, Lord, James thought. "I'm so glad to hear you say that," he said to the man. "I'm James. And you are...?"

"Adam."

James stuck out his hand and shook Adam's hand. "Glad to meet you, Adam," James said, then leaned in closer and spoke in a conspiratorial whisper. "As it happens, Jack and I are on a covert mission working against the war. Jack has some inside information that we need to get to the media. It's gonna blow the whole thing wide open. You got a car here?"

"Yeah." Adam's eyes glittered with interest. The political junkie was hooked.

"Can you give us a ride to the Star Tribune building?"

"Are you serious? This is for real?"

Jack raised his hand as if taking an oath. "I swear to God, Adam. This is dead serious."

"Wow. Listen," he said, turning to James. "If you'll take my picture with Jack Cambridge," he said, handing James his phone, "I'll drop you at the front door."

James hesitated, but decided it was worth the risk. "Yeah, OK, why not? But you've got to promise not to put this online before the news hits tomorrow."

Adam raised his hand in a Boy Scout salute. "On my honor," he said.

James had to move back a few steps to get them both in the picture, since Jack towered over the beaming Adam. As he handed the phone back, he said impatiently, "So, let's get going, huh?"

"I gotta get my car from the valet," Adam said. "I'll meet you out front. Look for a cherry red Toyota hybrid Camry." He started to leave, then turned around. "This is for real, right? You're not just trying to lose me? This isn't a joke?"

"C'mon, Adam," Jack said, his tone both intimate and utterly serious. "We need you, man."

"OK, give me your number, just in case I need it," Adam said brazenly. "Here's mine. Call me." He held out his phone so Jack could read the number.

Jack shrugged. "Sure, man, why not?"

Adam looked thrilled as his phone rang. He answered coyly, "Hello? Who's calling?"

James had to smile, imagining Adam's dismay when he found out he had the number of some dude in Westfield.

As Adam turned to go, Jack said, "I'm gonna hit the head, as long as we got a couple minutes."

"Yeah, I guess I will, too," James said.

Adam grinned and wagged a finger mischievously at them. "I don't really think it's gonna take me that much time to get my car."

"Huh?" James said.

"Don't get me wrong, I get it," Adam continued. "I know danger is a turn-on. No one knows that better than me."

Jack looked slightly irritated. "Jesus, Adam, get your mind out of the gutter. We're just gonna take a piss, then we'll be right out."

"Whatever," Adam said breezily as he walked away.

They fought their way through the crowd towards the bathroom at the back. James made it a point to get in and out as fast as possible, which amused Jack, and made James feel annoyed at himself. Then, as James was waiting for Jack to come out, he saw the cop come in the entrance—the same cop who'd passed them on the street. Damn it. He was clearly looking down at his phone, possibly at their photos, and then scanning the crowd.

James hurried back into the bathroom, and grabbed Jack, who was drying his hands in the air dryer.

"Hey, what the hell—"

"C'mon, we gotta go!" James said urgently. "That cop's here."

They looked around the back hallway for another way out. There was an emergency exit at the end of the hall. James hesitated, but Jack said, "I don't think it'll go off, it's just for show," and pushed it open. A screeching alarm went off.

"Fuck!" Jack yelled as they pounded down the back steps.

The alley was mostly dark, and they randomly turned right at the bottom of the stairs and ran flat out. James's heart was pounding so hard he could hardly hear anything else. He looked back as they reached the end of the alley and saw the cop at the top of the stairs. As they reached the street, they heard a shot.

"Sonofabitch, he's shooting at us!" Jack yelled, shocked and angry, as they turned the corner.

They were both in good shape, thank God, hopefully putting

some distance between them and the cop. James risked a glance back, couldn't see the cop, but that didn't mean he wasn't still following them, he had to be calling for backup…

James gestured to the right, and they turned down Nicollet Avenue. All he could think was to get some people between his body and the cop, maybe get lost in the crowd. He nearly tripped over a chair he didn't see at an outdoor café, stumbled forward but kept his balance. They were running so fast, zigzagging in and out and around people who were strolling and laughing and crowding the sidewalk and were oblivious and all it took was one opening, one clean shot…

"Look!" Jack shouted, pointing toward the next intersection. The light rail train had just stopped and was letting off passengers. They sprinted for it as fast as they could, and just made it through the doors before they closed.

James was panting as they collapsed on a seat. Had the cop seen them get on? God, he hoped not.

"Which way are we going?" Jack asked, breathing hard. The answer came at the next stop, as the doors opened and a melodious woman's voice said, "Warehouse District." A large crowd of very drunk people, mostly women, got on. The young women were giggling uncontrollably. One of them was wearing some kind of bridal veil, but her dress, as well as those of her friends, was hardly a wedding dress, unless this was a hooker's wedding. Then he remembered, the Warehouse District was Party Central for bachelorette parties these days. As the train started up again, one of the women lost her balance and landed on his lap. "Oops," she said with a giggle. "Hey, you guys wanna party with us?"

"Uh, no thanks. Here, you guys sit down," James said, as he and Jack took seats further from the girls. He turned to Jack. "Looks like we're going the wrong way. We're heading to Target Field. That's the last stop, and then it goes back. So, we could just stay on, and get off not far from the Strib building."

"Yeah, maybe. But that cop's probably called for backup by now, and what if they start searching this train? I feel like a sitting duck right now. I can't believe that idiot was shooting at us," Jack said angrily. "Doesn't he know who I am?"

"I was running while black, you know. He was probably just trying to scare us. And it worked. I've never been so scared in my life."

Just then they heard the tune for the theme from some old TV Western. James looked expectantly at the young girls for someone to answer her phone, wondering why a twenty-something girl would choose "Rawhide" for her ringtone. When it played again, it dawned on him what it was.

"That's your phone," he said to Jack.

"Target Field," said the lovely woman's voice over the loudspeaker.

As the doors slid open, Jack said, "Hey, Adam, calm down, man. Look, we ran into a situation. We're getting off the light rail at the Twins' stadium right now. Pick us up. We need you, man. Don't fail us."

Adam pulled his gleaming red Toyota up to the curb on 7th Street, around the corner from the newspaper building. "Hey," he said as they got out. "You can't give me a hint what this is all about?"

"With any luck, you'll be reading the whole story tomorrow," James said as he got out. "Thanks for the help. You're a national hero."

"Yeah, thanks, man," Jack said, reaching back into the car to shake Adam's hand. The thought crossed James's mind that Adam probably wouldn't wash that hand for a week.

"Good luck," Adam said as he pulled away.

James worried that they didn't have much time now. If the cops contacted the feds to tell them they'd been sighted downtown, they could be showing up here any minute. Jack cautiously stuck his head around the corner, then pulled it back and whispered, "It looks OK."

James looked around the corner. The street was quiet. Too quiet. He smiled briefly at his little joke, wondering how he could think of something funny at a time like this, but he was suspicious. He scanned the area and was dismayed to see the police car parked further down the street. Then he saw the officer through the glass front of the building.

"There's a cop in the lobby waiting for us," he whispered.

"Shit."

"Jack, I've got to ask you, are you still willing to go through with this? I mean, for me this is all about stopping Scofield from getting re-elected and getting us into a huge war. But for you, this is personal. It's gonna tear your family apart. Gordon might be prosecuted, he might even go to jail. You don't know what it's gonna do to your mother."

"Yeah, that's the only thing that's bothering me. But Gordon's got to pay for what he did." He looked at James with angry resolve. "Let's do it."

"OK, good. The question is, how're we gonna get in there?"

"I'll call Ta'Nika, she'll get us in. There's got to be a back door." Jack pushed the redial button.

Ta'Nika told them she'd meet them around back at the loading dock. Then, as they were starting back that way, the phone rang. It was Ta'Nika, telling them it was no good, the guy in the warehouse had been told by the cop not to let anyone come in that way, and to let him know if anyone tried.

James thought again, but only one answer kept coming. It had to come down to this. There was no other way. This was the Way. Me and Danny. It comes down to me and Danny. It all comes together right here, right now, all those threads in that future-sense quilt.

"Give me the phone," he said. He had to make this quick. Please, be OK, please don't be at a police station, please be there…

"Hi."

Thank God! "Danny! You OK?"

"Yeah, I'm good. You?"

"Yeah. Listen, we need your help. You remember Plan C for the band trip, the Snow White plan? I need you to be the band kids. Got it?"

"Yeah, I got it. Where?"

"At the place where Tony H works." Tony Holmes was an

occasional sports columnist for the paper, whose misguided opinions Danny enjoyed skewering. Danny always called him "Tony H." Hopefully if the feds were listening, they wouldn't know what that meant.

"OK. I'm on it. Plan C in five minutes. Good luck, buddy."

"Same to you, my friend."

James disconnected and handed the phone back to Jack. "OK, I think this is our best shot. Danny's gonna create a diversion, so we can get into the building."

"What's he gonna do?"

"I don't know. It'll be good, though. This is kind of a specialty for him. You missed what he did earlier this evening, but it was brilliant. We'll have to get the whole story from him later, when this is all over."

They waited, just on the other side of the entrance to the newspaper building, hidden in a brick alcove deep in the shadows. C'mon Danny, work your magic. Let's see a little mayhem here.

It was eerily quiet in the downtown business area, away from the entertainment district. James could hear his own heavy breathing.

Then, abruptly, the silence was broken by the sound of a car engine roaring, growing rapidly louder. James turned his head; it sounded like it was coming from behind them. They heard a screeching sound, tires squealing, the motor revved to high speed, and suddenly Danny's truck blasted out of 6th Street onto 3rd Avenue. James watching in horror as Danny turned sharply left, wildly out of control, and smashed head on into the front of the Hennepin County parking ramp. The sickening, unmistakable sounds of an accident—the bang of the impact, the glass shattering—filled the night. The truck's horn was blaring, it wouldn't stop. The image of Danny slumped against the steering wheel seared James's mind.

Oh, Jesus, Danny, no…

They heard the cop burst out of the door, calling for an ambulance as he was running across the street, saying there was an accident, probably a drunk driver.

Danny, no…

James felt Jack pulling on his arm, whispering urgently, "C'mon, man! We gotta go now!"

James ran with Jack; out of the corner of his eye he could see the cop leaning into the cab of Danny's truck. Jack grabbed the door just before it closed, and James forced himself to turn away from his best friend.

CHAPTER 36

There was a guard at the lobby desk. He looked at them quizzically. "What happened out there?"

"Accident," Jack said quickly. James's head was still swimming; he couldn't seem to pull together a coherent thought, let alone speak. Jack said calmly but urgently, "We need to see Ta'Nika Coleman. She's expecting us."

The guard looked them up and down. "Those federal agents that called, they said I was supposed to hold you if you showed up." For one tense moment, no one moved. Then the guard pointed to the elevators. "Third floor."

"Thanks," Jack said. As they headed across the lobby, Jack turned back. "You won't mention this to that cop, right? We're breaking the biggest story of the last twenty years."

The guard gave them a thumbs-up gesture. "That's what Ta'Nika said."

When the elevator doors opened on the third floor, James and Jack stepped out into a large open room. There were at least forty or fifty desks, some in cubicles and some out in the open. Only a few people were actually at the desks working this late at night; most of the computer monitors had screensaver animations running. A couple people were at the window, looking down at the street below.

Ta'Nika spotted James and Jack right away, and hurried over, surprising them as she stretched out her long arms and pulled them into a hug. "Thank God you made it. I thought that might have been you in that crash out there. How'd you get past the cop?"

James felt sick. Jack shrugged his shoulders.

"Anyway, it doesn't matter right now," Ta'Nika continued, leading them over to her cubicle. "The important thing is we've got to get this story out ASAP. This has got to be the craziest night of my life. I can't wait to hear what happened to you, once we're done here."

On the cubicle's wall was a nameplate: TA'NIKA COLEMAN, A-1 EDITOR. Ta'Nika sat down at her desk, gesturing to her computer screen. "I've written up a draft, based on what you told me, Jack, but I'll need to talk to your friend to finalize it."

James felt a wave of disgust run through him as he saw the photo of Vice President Cambridge on the monitor.

Jack took the phone from James and brought up the Facebook message with Shaundra's number.

Ta'Nika turned to James. "Sit down," she said, indicating the chair next to her. "You look dead on your feet."

"I'm just gonna go see what's happening out there," he said. He could see Danny's truck from the window. It looked like the cop was tending to Danny, but not doing CPR or anything that would indicate Danny was seriously hurt. He hoped he was right.

Ta'Nika walked over to James. "That looks bad. So, I've got a call in to our publisher. I actually pulled him off a yacht on Lake Minnetonka." She smiled. "That was kind of fun. I filled him in, and he's salivating, let me tell you. He's given it preliminary approval, but this story is so huge, of course, that he wants to come in and personally read it and talk with Jack. Get all those ducks lined up. Only thing is, I don't know if we've got time to line up those little duckies."

James finally found his voice. "I don't think so. A cop spotted us downtown. I'm surprised the FBI or Homeland Security hasn't shown up here already."

"Still, we could save it and get it out later, as long as we have it. I should probably wait for Mr. Atkinson."

Jack's voice grabbed their attention. "Shaundra, hi. It's me, Jack. Long time since we talked, huh? So, uh, so how are you doing?"

They hurried back to Ta'Nika's desk. Jack sounded really nervous.

"Yeah, I know this is weird. Really weird. ... Yeah, I mean, I really appreciate your talking to me. ... No, no, I promise. It's your call. If you don't want to go through with it, I won't say another word about it to anyone, ever."

James could hardly breathe, waiting for the answer from this stranger, who had no idea the fate of the world might be hanging on her decision.

"I know, it's weird after all this time. Like I said in the text, more stuff has come up. He may have done the same thing to his housekeeper in D.C. So, like, maybe there are more women. ... I know, that's what's been holding me back, my mom would be heartbroken. Look, I know you'd have to really put yourself out there and tell the whole world this really personal thing. I'll back you up. If you want to press charges, I'll testify for you. All I'm trying to say is, I've got your back. I want to make it up to you." Jack gave them a distressed look and mouthed, "She's crying."

God, how awful, James was thinking, at the same time he was thinking impatiently, C'mon, get on with it, we don't have time.

Jack made a sympathetic sound to whatever Shaundra said, then responded, "I'm just like, he shouldn't get away with it anymore. He's done." Then, Shaundra must have asked about Ta'Nika. "She's cool. I've known her since high school. I trust her. She's a good person, she's honest, she's real."

There was a long pause. Was Shaundra speaking, or thinking? Come on, Shaundra. Come on. Do the right thing. And then, massive relief as he heard Jack say thanks and hand the phone over to Ta'Nika.

"Hi, Shaundra, this is Ta'Nika. Listen, I know how really hard this must be for you. Jack told me you'd already been thinking about coming forward with this, so I really appreciate that you've decided to do this now. What you're doing is important."

Ta'Nika listened to Shaundra's response, and then said, "I'm going to put you on speakerphone, so I can type while you're talking. I'm also going to be recording this for accuracy. Is that OK with you?" Ta'Nika was taking out the recording device she had shown them earlier and putting it next to the phone. "OK, whenever you're ready."

They heard Shaundra's voice, at first tentative and wavering, but then picking up strength, as she told the story and answered Ta'Nika's questions. They had to wait while she cried, but she recovered and said, "OK, I can keep going."

My God, I can't believe this is the Vice President she's talking about. This is crazy. Of course, it was an old story, powerful men forcing themselves on women. But now it was real; he knew the guy personally.

"Thanks," Ta'Nika said, as Shaundra finished. "You are amazingly strong, Shaundra. It's going to get tougher for you once this comes out, but I really believe you'll be able to handle it. You are a remarkable woman. If I were you, I'd call your friends and your family right away, because the press is going to be on your doorstep in the morning. You're going to want your people to hear it from you first. I hope they can be there for you, help you get through this."

"Yeah," Shaundra said, "I've got good support here. I already told most of them a few years ago, and they know I was thinking about going public. Thanks."

"Good luck. And Shaundra, you probably want to contact a lawyer tomorrow too. You're going up against some powerful people. You're gonna need some power on your side, too."

"Oh my God. OK." They could all hear her take a deep breath. "Ta'Nika? Thanks for believing me." Shaundra hung up.

Ta'Nika rapidly typed for a few minutes, and then said, "OK, I'm going to send this to the other people here on the floor, so they can check it, too. I don't want any mistakes." Ta'Nika stood up and said loudly, "People! I'm sending you the piece I told you about. Get right back to me on it, please!"

Ta'Nika sat back down, pulled up a menu on her computer screen, and clicked a few times. She looked at James, remarking, "OK, it's ready to go, formatted and everything, so they should be able to get it back to me in less than five..." She paused, finger hovering above the enter key, as the sound of a wailing siren filled the air, immersing them in the high-pitched scream as it stopped outside their building. "Oh my God, they're here." She looked at James with alarm. "What should I do?"

"It's an ambulance," a guy said from across the room, looking out the window. "They're here for that accident. You want someone to go down and get a picture, Ta'Nika?"

James moaned, putting his head in his hands. Danny. He sent a quick prayer: Please let Danny be all right, please God.

"What a night," Ta'Nika said. She looked up and saw a young woman standing on the other side of her partition. "Kathy, send George down to..." Ta'Nika faltered in mid-sentence. James looked up and saw why. The woman's face was frozen in a dropped-jaw, wide-eyed caricature of horror.

Ta'Nika swiveled her chair around, and James and Jack turned with her. They found themselves staring at the guns of Agents Baker and Rivera, advancing rapidly toward them. Rivera kept his gun leveled at the three of them. Baker was holding out his badge and yelling at the stunned people in the newsroom.

"Federal agents! All of you, clear the room immediately!"

No one argued. They hurried out, looking both confused and terrified. James hoped they would call the cops when they left the room, and then realized that wouldn't help. These were the cops. The highest level cops.

Agent Baker turned to face them. "Ta'Nika Coleman, you are forbidden to reveal anything you have learned this evening. It is all classified material under the National Freedom from Fear Act."

Ta'Nika was incensed. "You can't do that! You shutting down the press is more of a threat to our national security than anything else. We have the right to publish this story."

"We can let the lawyers argue that. I am under direct orders from the President of the United States. Now step away from the computer. Go sit over there," Baker said, indicating a chair that Agent Rivera had pulled away from another desk.

Ta'Nika eyed their guns and shakily stood up. James and Jack remained frozen near her desk, Agent Rivera's gun never wavering from its lock on James's chest.

Baker turned his attention back to them. "James Thompson, you are charged with committing a terrorist act against the United States of America."

Jack looked righteously pissed off. "Hey, Rick. What terrorist act? Me an' James just wanted to slip out and have a little fun. I wanted to see some of my old hangouts without you guys trailin' me around."

"Mr. Thompson, you're under arrest." Baker noticed the bulge in James's shorts pocket and pointed to it. "I want you to remove what's in your pocket very slowly."

James carefully put his hand in his pocket, and very slowly pulled the cologne bottle out, showing it to the agent.

"Put it on the desk," Baker instructed.

James couldn't believe he had come this far, and it was all being pulled out from under him. An image of Danny dead, himself in prison, and world war raging flashed in his head. This couldn't be how it ended. What about the Way? A feeling of rage toward the Seekers engulfed him. Where are you, you alien sons-of-bitches?

Ding! What? For a brief, bizarre moment James thought the Seekers had actually heard him and were going to materialize in the room. Then he saw the others turn and look toward the foyer, all except Agent Rivera, who never took his eye, or his gun, off James. The elevator doors opened, and two Secret Service agents emerged, guns held ready.

"It's secure."

Two armed men in camouflage moved quickly out of the elevator. Then, James was stunned to see Morris Gastineau, the CIA chief, step out. What was he doing here?

And then Vice President Cambridge emerged.

CHAPTER 37

Oh my God, this can't be happening. The image of the future-stream that the aliens had shown him flashed in his mind. That dark, evil splotch looked like it had triumphed. But then those golden threads had suddenly shot out everywhere, overwhelming it. Looking at Cambridge now, exuding power, surrounded by all those guns, James thought, They got it all wrong.

Gordon Cambridge strode into the room with icy fury. He swept his gaze over the newsroom, and then commanded, "Morris, this is a classified situation. Have your men disable the security cameras."

One of the men in camouflage, he must have been a Special Ops agent, aimed his gun at the security cameras on each side of the room and shot them out.

Ta'Nika let out a scream of shock.

James suddenly remembered that it was Cambridge who'd gotten Gastineau the CIA directorship in the first place. They were old buddies from college or something.

Rick Baker cleared his throat. "Mister Vice President, the situation has been contained. Nothing has been released yet."

Vice President Cambridge's eyes bored into him, his voice shaking with anger. "You two are the worst excuse for Secret Service agents I have ever seen. There should never have been a situation. Somehow, Agent Baker, my brother managed to walk away from you tonight with a man intent on bringing down our government. You and that taco-eating fool over there are incompetent idiots. You will pay the price for creating this mess, believe me."

Wow, James thought—somewhat oddly given the gravity of the situation—Jack was right. He is a class-A bastard. He glanced at Jack and saw that he was staring off to the side, stone-faced.

Vice President Cambridge continued. "Mr. Baker, I'll take that recording."

"It's in a safe place, sir," Baker replied.

Cambridge looked furious. "You and I will go get it as soon as we're finished here." Then Cambridge turned his head, looked at Jack, and said with a sneer, "Oh, hello baby bro. Fancy meeting you here." When Jack didn't respond, he said, "Still not talking to me, I guess. You're cutting me to the quick."

Morris Gastineau gave Ta'Nika a contemptuous look. "You're Ta'Nika Coleman, I presume?" She nodded slowly. "Miss Coleman, you're about to get a lesson in modern journalism. Perhaps you should have gotten the story straight before putting your money down on a drunk and a woman with a personal grudge. The story that's coming out tomorrow is far more interesting—about how an African terrorist group right here in the Twin Cities, led by this traitor masquerading as a teacher of impressionable teenagers, abducted the brother of the Vice President right from his high school reunion, and how our brave defenders of freedom thwarted them. Plus, it has the lovely touch of the Vice President flying to his brother's side. You know, if it can happen to the Vice President's brother, it can happen to anyone. And how would you feel, Mr. and Mrs. John Q. Public, if your child were abducted by terrorists right in your own hometown?

"Oh, I should tell you, Miss Coleman, your publisher is waiting downstairs. He was not in the least happy to hear how you've been duped by this terrorist group." The nasty smirk that Gastineau gave Ta'Nika made James want to punch him in the mouth. "If you still have a job here after tonight, I'd suggest you do a poll in a week or so on this administration's approval rating. I'm predicting we top ninety percent. Isn't it just deliciously ironic? Your actions tonight are going to seal the President's victory in November. Oh, and another thing, Miss Coleman—anything you think you know from tonight—speak one word of it, and you will be prosecuted for libel, at the very least. And we will win, do not doubt that. Your career will be ruined. So, I'd suggest you keep your baseless allegations to yourself."

Baker spoke up. "I have already apprised Miss Coleman of her legal obligations under the Freedom from Fear Act, sir."

Vice President Cambridge practically spat at Baker. "Shut up, you idiot, and let a professional handle this." He turned his attention to James.

"I remember you," he said slowly, his voice dripping with contempt. "You're the peace nut from that ridiculous band concert. You caused us some problems, did you know that? I'm glad I have the chance to finally even the score."

James forced himself to look straight at Cambridge, and what he saw took his breath away. There was pure stone-cold hatred in his eyes, unleavened by any trace of humanity. Look him in the eye, Danny said, and maybe you'll know.

And James knew. Knew the truth in a sickening instant. The floor shifted beneath him, and he nearly fell over as a wave of vertigo washed over him. There stood Eddie Olson.

CHAPTER 38

"Morris," Cambridge commanded. "Have your men take the terrorist away. They know what to do with him, I believe."

Oh, holy God, they're going to torture me, they're going to kill me. James felt panic flood him, he didn't know what to do, he didn't know how to stop this, it was Cambridge, Eddie was Cambridge, oh God…

But as the Special Ops men moved toward James, Agent Baker intervened. "I'll take him into custody, Mister Vice President," he said, and James had the strange feeling Baker was trying to protect him.

"Agent Baker, you are relieved of duty," Cambridge said coldly. "If you can't even ferret out the leader of the African terrorist movement in America when he's right under your nose, you're clearly useless."

James's mind was whirling as the puzzle pieces spun together—Cambridge pulling the strings behind the scenes, Cambridge in collusion with Gastineau to start a war in Africa, Cambridge the racist possessed by an evil Seeker, wanting to kill, to destroy life, to kill black people, to destroy the African continent, it all made sense…

"Sir," Agent Rivera intervened. "We were in the process of…"

Suddenly, James heard Danny's voice in his head: Don't forget the backup backup plan. Relief filled James, washing away the mind-numbing terror that had swamped him. Danny was still with him.

As the others turned to look at Rivera, James carefully worked the stopper out of the top of the cologne bottle, making as little movement as possible.

"Don't you get it, amigo?" Cambridge was saying contemptuously. "Am I going too fast for you? You're fired, too." He turned to Gastineau. "How do you say, 'incompetent fool' in Spanish?"

Cambridge turned back to James and waved his hand dismissively. "Take that mess away."

Jack finally looked at his brother. "Gordon, stop, he didn't have anything to do with this." Cambridge ignored him.

Oh my God, this is it. James's legs felt like rubber; he wasn't sure he could walk on them. And then James realized that he could use the fear that he must be showing to his advantage. He gasped and let his body sway, as if his legs were giving out. He reached out for the desk to catch himself, knocking off the coffee mug that was near the edge, and letting the bottle with Eddie's stink fall to the floor with it. Everyone froze momentarily.

Then Cambridge laughed derisively. "I think he just shat his pants. Take that scared little boy away."

As the special ops men moved forward again, Jack said loudly, "Don't touch him."

Cambridge turned toward him. "Jackson," he said coldly. "Shut up and let the grown-ups handle this."

Jack glared at his brother. "He's my friend. Leave him alone."

"Some things never change. You're drunk and you're stupid and you have terrible taste in friends. And now you need your family to bail you out of a mess again."

"Fuck you."

Part of James's mind was riveted on the exchange between two brothers who hated each other, and part was wondering when anyone else would notice the horrible smell that was now spreading in the room.

Suddenly Jack was screaming. "Jesus Christ, Gordon! We both know he's not a terrorist and he didn't kidnap me! We both know the truth, don't we? You raped my friend! That's what this is all about! You raped her, you goddamn sonofabitch!"

"You've got it all wrong. She was begging me for it." Cambridge turned to Ta'Nika. "Every black woman wants a big white dick inside her, am I right? Am I right, sister?"

Ta'Nika stared straight ahead and didn't respond.

Cambridge spoke with chilling detachment. "Jackie boy, you need help. See, you think I don't care about you, but I do. In fact, I know of a very secure, very effective addiction treatment center in upstate New York. I can get you in tonight." He turned to one of his own agents. "Agent Fristner, escort my brother down to our vehicle."

"Go to hell!" Jack screamed, vaulting over the desk and running further into the pressroom, screaming like a madman.

"Stop him!" Cambridge yelled.

The Vice President's two agents went after Jack, who was wildly ripping everything he could grab off desks—photos, candy jars, pens, reams of paper—and flinging them at the agents, while screaming at them: "Stay away from me, you assholes!"

Gastineau turned to the two special ops guys. "Go help them," he ordered.

And then James realized that everyone in the room had their eyes riveted on Jack, who was going berserk. He leaned over to Ta'Nika's computer and hit the enter key.

Then he looked at Cambridge. No one else was watching, so James was the only one to see his body suddenly stiffen and his eyes roll back in his head.

Oh my God, I think it's actually working. I think Eddie just caught his own stench. Now— will it make things better, or worse?

James looked back into the newsroom and saw that the agents had finally caught Jack and restrained him. He was fighting them, resisting with a lifetime of built-up anger.

As they worked to haul a struggling Jack back to the front of the room, James looked again at Cambridge. His face was studded with beads of sweat. He could almost see the war going on in the nerves of his brain between the newly-awakened alien and his own human self. He imagined the wild electrical impulses smashing into each other, short-circuiting his brain. A shudder ran over Cambridge's entire body as he fought to regain control. Cambridge locked eyes with Jack, whose arms were pinned behind him.

The look Jack gave him was bitter. "I still know what I know."

Cambridge practically spat at him. "Shut up." James noticed a bit of drool running from the side of his mouth. The beads of sweat were dripping off his jaw.

He's coming unhinged.

Cambridge shuddered again as he tried to maintain control.

"What's that disgusting smell?" Gastineau suddenly interjected, wrinkling his nose.

A strange strangled gagging sound came from Cambridge. His hands were shaking badly. "I am ordering... this newspaper..." he gasped, "shut down until all files... can be purged of... treasonous materials." A string of drool plopped onto his chest.

Gastineau exchanged an alarmed look with Agent Fristner.

"I'm afraid it's too late for that," James said, amazed at how strong his voice sounded. Everyone looked at him in surprise. "The truth is already out."

James waved his arm to indicate the room. Glowing on all the computer monitors on every desk was the mockup of the front page of the Star Tribune. The large headline blared, "V. P. CAMBRIDGE ACCUSED OF RAPE."

Cambridge's face drained of color. "That's impossible."

"Oh, no, it's very possible," James said smoothly. He couldn't believe how serene he felt. Like he was in the zone again. He indicated Ta'Nika. "She sent the story to the Star Tribune Online just before you got here. Looks like it just went live."

Ta'Nika spoke up. "He's right. I'd say we got a big scoop." She smiled at Cambridge, twisting the knife.

Gordon Cambridge stood with his mouth hanging open. Then, it was like his veneer of humanity suddenly peeled away like cheap varnish. His face turned red as he shrieked furiously, "Get that nigger out of here and shoot him!"

As the Special Ops agents moved toward him, Agent Baker stepped in front of James. "No, sir, I'm sorry, but that's not going to happen." Agent Rivera moved to stand next to Baker.

Cambridge was beside himself with rage. His arms were flailing wildly, and spit was flying out of his mouth as he shrieked, "If they don't move, shoot them!"

Everyone was stunned, frozen. The Special Ops men looked questioningly at Gastineau. He shook his head at them, no, behind Cambridge's back. The thought crossed James's mind that maybe Gastineau had seen a glimpse of Eddie before.

Cambridge looked wildly from one agent to the next. "Hasn't anyone got the balls to shoot a traitor?" he screeched.

James looked him in the eye, coolly. "Mr. Cambridge, no one is going to shoot you here. You're entitled to a fair trial, just like every other citizen."

Cambridge stared at him for several seconds, mouth open but unable to get any words out. Then he made a horrible retching sound, vomited, and started spasming convulsively, his eyes rolling back as he nearly fell to the floor. Morris Gastineau moved quickly to catch him, calling for the other men to help him. They braced Cambridge on each side.

"Let's get him out of here," Gastineau said urgently. "He needs a doctor." The men tried to get Cambridge to move, but he seemed to be resisting. His eyes darted wildly from one person to the next, and an anxious moaning sound was coming from his slack mouth. Then he spoke in a bizarre half-human voice: "Should have died long ago." He moaned. "Got to kill it." Before anyone knew what was happening, he grabbed the hand of the Special Ops agent near him who was holding a gun and pointed it toward himself. One shot went off, just missing his head.

"Let's go now!" Gastineau yelled.

Cambridge collapsed, not resisting as they moved again toward the elevator. But as the doors opened, he suddenly stopped and turned. He struggled to focus on Jack. "You are not my brother," he said bitterly.

"That ship sailed long ago, bro," Jack replied softly, as the elevator doors closed.

For a moment, everyone was quiet, unable to process what had just happened. Agents Baker and Rivera dropped into chairs, looking shell-shocked. James half expected the elevator doors to open and Cambridge to leap out and spray them with gunfire. But when another minute passed, and nothing happened, James closed his eyes and thought with relief, It's finally over. We won. We did it.

Then Ta'Nika threw a quick look at Baker and Rivera and jumped up from the chair. She hurried over to her computer and began typing furiously. With a dramatic flourish, she hit the last key and turned back to James with a big grin.

"All right, I just sent this out for real. They're going to be checking the Internet to see what we wrote as soon as they can, so it'd better be there. James, you were brilliant! I can't believe you bluffed the Vice President."

James noticed a small smile cross Agent Rivera's face when he heard this.

James looked at Jack, who looked stunned. "Gordon's a sick man, Jack. I mean literally sick."

Baker walked over to Jack and put his hand on his back. "Son, you deserved better than this. I hope things work out for you. You know your life's gonna be hell for a while, don't you? Maybe I can help keep the press off your back."

"You just got fired, Rick, remember?"

"I could use a temporary job as a personal bodyguard. Anyway, I kinda feel like I owe you."

Jack smiled weakly.

"Oh, and here," Baker added, taking James's phone out of his pocket and handing it back to him.

James was stunned. So, Baker was bluffing Cambridge, too. Unreal.

Just then, the elevator pinged again. They all turned apprehensively as the doors opened.

"Mr. Housewright!" Ta'Nika exclaimed.

"Alright, what did I miss?" Then the publisher broke into a huge grin and waved his phone. "I've got the photos right here! I got them taking the Vice President out! I was in the lobby. He was a mess. I don't think they even saw me." He handed his phone to Ta'Nika and rubbed his palms together eagerly. "Fill me in, Ta'Nika! But first, get these pictures out. We've got the goddamn exclusive story of the century!"

As they sat down at Ta'Nika's desk and began conferring, Agent Rivera spoke up. "I suppose we ought to let those people at the reunion go home. I'll give them a call."

"I'll call the Homeland guys," Baker said. "Fill them in."

He turned to James. "I'll call the cop at your house, too, Mr. Thompson. Then you can talk to your wife."

"Oh my God, Emily!" James imagined her sitting at home for the last several hours, terrified, not knowing what had happened to him.

"Oh, Mr. Thompson," Baker added. "Your buddy out there, in the truck?"

James froze, unable to breathe.

"Last I saw, he was alive, but he looked pretty bad. Hopefully they got him to the hospital in time. He was a pistol, that friend of yours."

CHAPTER 39

James walked down the hospital corridor, flashing back on the last time he'd been here, when he'd met his namesake, Jaymi. That seemed like ages ago. And now he was headed to see little Jaymi's dad, who'd nearly been taken away from her before she could even say his name. Danny'd been this close to snuffing out, one little current removed from that stream of Life Force that James now knew flowed from this planet. Danny, his comrade in arms. The one person who'd been with him every step of the way since that day in Garraty's when he'd told this fantastic tale, and his friend hadn't blinked.

James knocked tentatively on the door to room 418, dreading seeing Danny's bandaged and mangled body lying there. He opened it slowly.

Danny looked as bad as James had imagined—head bandaged, face bruised, swollen, and cut. His whole torso was wrapped in bandages. He had a cast on his right arm and tubes coming out of his left hand, attached to a bag that James hoped was dripping pain relief into Danny's system. Even so, seeing Danny alive filled James with such joy that he broke out in a wide grin. "Dude, you're a mess!"

"Yeah, I've been prettier."

James laughed and moved to stand next to the bed, hand resting lightly on Danny's sore shoulder. "How you feeling?"

"Like Muhammad Ali's punching bag. But it could've been worse, so I'm not complaining."

"That's an understatement. You remember the day when Jaymi was born, when you said you'd do anything to protect her? I never thought that meant smashing the Dragon head-on into a wall at full speed."

Danny smiled weakly. "Yeah, well, a man's gotta do what a man's gotta do. So, what's the big surprise you couldn't tell me over the phone? You getting the Congressional Medal of Honor?"

James pulled up a chair near the bed and paused for dramatic effect. "We were a little off on the Eddie Olson thing. Turns out he was stuck in Cambridge."

James hoped to see Danny's eyes bug out and his jaw drop. He was not disappointed.

"Say what? OK, fill me in, man. Every detail. What happened up there?"

So James told the story, the most amazing story of his life. He was enjoying being the one with the spell-binding tale for once, maybe even laid it on a little thick at the part where the Special Ops guys were inches away from taking him out and shooting him in the back alley. When he came to the part where he coolly put down the Vice President to his face, Danny whistled in admiration. "Balls of steel!"

"That's me."

"Holy shit," Danny said with alarm. "Do you realize if you'd gone through with the plan in Washington, you'd have actually put Eddie into the most powerful position in the world instead of taking him out of it?"

"Yeah, that thought has crossed my mind."

"But you didn't, Mr. Nice Guy, so all's well that ends well." Danny smiled with satisfaction. "Cool that the Eddie stink actually worked."

"Yeah. Against all odds, you actually had an excellent idea there. I wonder if the effect wore off when he got away from the smell, or if he's permanently deranged now?"

Danny held out a remote control with his left hand, pointing it at the TV mounted near the ceiling. "Check it out."

The TV was tuned to CNN. The sounds of reporters shouting questions filled the room. A press spokesperson was standing outside United Lutheran Hospital in downtown Minneapolis, where Gordon Cambridge had been taken. She looked totally beleaguered.

"Was Mr. Cambridge's heart attack caused by the revelations which appeared in the press today?"

"Is Vice President Cambridge expected to recover sufficiently to remain on the ticket?"

"What's President Scofield going to do? Are you expecting him to come here to see the Vice President?"

"Is President Scofield going to dump him from the ticket?"

"The New York Post has dubbed Cambridge 'The Creep Veep.' Can you comment on that?"

The press spokesperson finally said, "We have no further comment at this time. We will update you as to Mr. Cambridge's medical condition later today." She turned and walked back into the hospital.

CNN cut back to the anchors at the news desk. "The woman who made the allegations, Shaundra Williams, has not spoken to the press yet. But we have word that she will make a statement sometime this afternoon," the male anchor said. "Elisa, do we know anything further about the involvement of the Vice President's brother, Jackson Cambridge?"

"One of the most astonishing things about this whole situation is that Jack Cambridge has said that he backs up Shaundra Williams' allegations. The Star Tribune quotes him as saying Shaundra told him about this several years ago. Apparently, they were friends at UCLA. He said, and I quote, 'Shaundra wasn't ready to come forward until recently. I told her I would support her whenever she felt ready. At the time, I didn't know why she quit her position in my brother's office, and when I found out, several years later, I was horrified.'"

The female co-anchor turned to her partner. "John, I just don't think there's any precedent for this. Jack Cambridge was in Minneapolis for a high school reunion yesterday, but at this point we don't know if he's still in the city. Sources say he may have gone to his family home, to be with his parents in this difficult time. We do have confirmation that Jack was at the Star Tribune building last night, where Vice President Cambridge experienced his heart attack. Sources say that an unidentified black man was at the newspaper office with Jack Cambridge. We are trying to determine his identity."

"We're in uncharted territory, Elisa." John turned to the camera. "Events and revelations are unfolding at a dizzying rate. Stay tuned to CNN for all the latest."

Danny muted the TV and turned to James. "So, Mr. Unidentified Black Man. What're you gonna say when they identify you and want your story?"

"Damn, I don't know," James responded with dismay. "I'm not gonna betray Jack, that's for sure. I guess whatever he decides to tell the press, I'll back him up. Our conversation at the Rec Center stays private. So does our little adventure getting to Ta'Nika's office."

"Oh, yeah, man, I gotta to hear all about that, too." Danny's eyes glittered with excitement.

"You, I'll tell. You and Emily. That's it. And I'm sure not gonna be talking to the press about little green men—or more accurately, little white flowing Seekers. But there's even more. Jack thinks Gordon forced his immigrant housekeeper to have sex, too. I gotta figure more women will be coming forward now. Guys like that, they don't stop at one or two. I guess I better talk to Jack so we can agree on what we say. I'm thinking, keep it simple. Give a simple statement to the press and stick with it—Jack shared with me, as his friend, some information that he felt it was time the country knew about, and he asked me to come with him to give him moral support when he went to the newspaper office. Maybe I should throw in that it was a difficult decision for Jack and the press should leave him alone."

"Yeah, that'll work," Danny said sarcastically as he unmuted the TV.

The male anchor was saying, "In the latest twist in this increasingly bizarre tale, key members of Vice President Cambridge's own party issued a statement moments ago calling for his immediate resignation. Clearly they are afraid of his taking all their candidates down in flames in the coming election."

The female anchor nodded. "If I may be permitted a war analogy—which I think is fitting—it's like a grenade went off and now the mangled arm must be quickly amputated. Assuming that this scandal doesn't take down the President as well, insiders are speculating that President Scofield will turn to Senator Caroline Garcia of New Mexico. She is known for…"

Danny muted the TV again. "Damn, Eddie's up the proverbial shit creek."

"You know, the Seekers kept telling me the Way would come to me. Who'd've figured the Way would turn out to be this way?"

"Yeah. I was still kinda hoping aliens would drop out of the sky and blast Eddie with lasers."

James burst out with a big laugh. Then he turned to his bandaged friend, suddenly serious. "But you know what, Danny? You know what really means the most to me?"

"That you saved the world for our children?"

"Well, sure, that. But what I was going to say was, that you stuck by me from the beginning. I'd have never gotten through this without you. You are truly the best friend a man could ever have."

"Likewise."

James thrust out his right hand toward Danny, gently moving through their handshake routine with Danny's hand sticking out of the cast, barely able to move. The gesture had never meant so much.

"Man, Danny. That was really brave, what you did, crazy brave, crashing the Dragon like that. Putting your life on the line. And it worked, it got us in there, and the rest is history. Of course," James continued, "you realize you might have been able to accomplish the same diversionary success simply by running naked through the Minneapolis streets in front of that cop."

"Man, I wish I'd thought of that last night! Well, you know what they say. Hiney sight is 20/20!"

James groaned and laughed at the same time. "How can you come up with such a bad pun while under the influence of pain medication?"

"I think it's precisely because of the meds, my friend. My mind is sliding like a greased pig right now. No impediments. In fact, don't take anything I say seriously."

"Duly noted."

"Actually, I take that back. I've got to say something serious here, for once in my life. Maybe I never said this before, but one thing I've always admired about you is you're a stand-up kind of guy. I'll never forget that day in seventh grade, when those guys were harassing that short kid, Curtis something, who always wore those lime-green sweats, you remember? The kid who still carried a Big Rig lunchbox? It was in the cafeteria, they were threatening to dump his food on him, and no one was doing anything about it. But you stood up and defended him. You do the right thing. That takes a lot more guts than people realize."

"Well, thanks, but a lot of people do the right thing."

"Maybe. But you did right by Jack. That's why the Way came through you."

"Man. Poor Jack. About the only good thing is that Baker said he'd make sure any charges against us get dropped. He didn't figure it would be too hard to persuade the local cops not to press charges against the Vice President's brother, even if he did assault a police officer."

"How's Baker gonna do that? I thought he got fired."

"Maybe, maybe not. Those guys are probably so preoccupied with bigger problems right now, I doubt anyone remembers Cambridge fired them. Or takes it seriously, if they do, since he was obviously incapacitated."

"Wonder if Baker could get my reckless driving charge dropped. My insurance is gonna go through the roof."

"Maybe. It's worth a shot. Did they charge you with DWI?"

"Nah, they tested me, and I was under the legal limit, thank God. So, it could've been worse. I guess if I have to pay a fine and higher insurance rates for a while, it's worth it. For saving the world, you know. Not a bad trade-off."

"Not bad at all."

Danny looked thoughtfully at James. "You think we'll ever completely figure out the Seekers?"

"I think we'll be sitting in our rockers on the porch at the old folks' home arguing about where they come from."

Danny laughed, and then winced at the pain. "Ow. I cracked a few ribs. It hurts to laugh."

"Ouch," James said in sympathy. He stood up. "I guess I better get going. You need to rest. I gotta go pick up those bikes we ditched last night before someone finds them. I'm hoping I can drop them and the cell phone at the guy's house without running into him. If I'm lucky, his garage door will still be up, and he won't even have noticed they were missing yet."

"Good luck on that."

"When's Jenna coming?" James asked.

"She was here all night. She went home to sleep a few hours ago, but she'll probably be back soon. Just as well she didn't run into you here. She's pretty pissed at both of us."

"She'll get over it. You're a hero, you know."

"Yeah, well she was pretty freaked out last night."

"I was pretty freaked out myself when I saw you crash right in front of my eyes."

Suddenly Danny grinned. "I can't believe you deked the Vice President of the United States!"

"Hey, how do you think I score half my points on you? Fake right, go left. It's fundamental basketball, my friend."

"God, I wish I'd been there."

James smiled at him. "You were, Danny, you were."

CHAPTER 40

James passed through the kitchen on his way to the back yard, stopping to get a glass of iced tea from the fridge. He smiled with satisfaction as he looked at the August calendar they'd just flipped to. Four weeks with nothing more written in the days' squares than "neighborhood block party" on the first Tuesday, and "Cory's birthday party—Darlene's 3:00" on the 24th. He hadn't even written in the back-to-school teacher orientation week at the end of the month. He'd think about that later. Right now, he needed his chill time.

The fallout from that night in early June had been unrelentingly for weeks. The media called every day, and they came knocking on his door, despite his unwavering answer: "My statement is as follows—I am a friend of Jack Cambridge. In the course of a conversation we had at our high school reunion, Jack shared with me some damaging information about his brother, Vice President Cambridge. He said he had come to the conclusion that the country had a right to know this information. Jack Cambridge made the decision to help his friend, Shaundra Williams, bring this to the media, and I assisted him as his friend. That is all I have to say."

Even when the press found out about the lockdown at the Rec Center and interviewed people who were there, and then wanted his reaction; even when they asked him if he was a sympathizer with

African liberation groups, or if he was a terrorist himself, he kept his cool and held his ground. He'd sent Antawn a text of appreciation after he saw him interviewed on Channel 4, saying indignantly, "Man, y'all are racist! If Jack had left with a white guy, you think they would've locked us down? You think you'd be asking me if a white guy was a terrorist? It's bullshit. Everyone there knew we played hoops that night, man! In the gym. Me 'n Jack and James and all of us, we was teammates. That means something, you understand? Those feds overreacted, like they always do when there's a black man involved. Y'all get out of my face, man!"

He couldn't believe the number of reporters who managed to get his cell phone number. He deleted the messages they left without listening to them; he deleted their texts without reading them. He refused to relent and change his phone number.

Emily was excited when The Today Show was after him, dangling a trip to New York. She insisted that his heroics should be recognized and celebrated.

But James had promised Jack that the details of that night were strictly between them. Several national magazines offered large sums of money for his inside story; they finally pushed too hard when one of them played the guilt card. "Teachers don't make good money, James. We all know that. You gonna look your little girl in the eye in a few years and tell her you don't have enough money to send her to college, because you were too scared to tell the truth about what happened that night?" James just blew up at the guy, shocking himself with the ferocity of his response.

No question, his nerves were on edge. He thought he'd be done with the whole thing once the Way was accomplished. He wasn't. At night, he found himself back in the newspaper office in his dreams. Sometimes, Cambridge's face morphed into an evil Seeker, leering at him, as men in camouflage, their faces covered with ski masks, dragged him away. More often, he had long dreams: he and Jack were running in the dark, hiding wherever, but the Secret Service men—always with dark glasses—would find them, and they'd run and hide in a dumpster, and the Secret Service would find them, and they'd get away and hide in someone's garage, and the Secret Service would find them, and on and on, and they could never get away. He usually awoke with a scream at the part where guns fired at him.

Of course, it had been worse for Shaundra. She was hounded by the press relentlessly. The right-wing media painted her as a liar, an attention-seeker. Until two more women came forward. And then they found Angela, the housekeeper. She'd been deported and must have figured she had nothing more to lose by telling the truth.

During the long days of June and early July, James anxiously read the newspaper and watched the news, wanting to make sure that the Way had finally been achieved. Yes, Eddie Olson was definitively stopped, but could the events the evil Seeker had set in motion be stopped as well, or was it too late?

James was thrilled when, after Ta'Nika's exposé of Gastineau's role in the events that Saturday night, Congress began an investigation into Morris Gastineau's leadership of the CIA and the allegations that the agency secretly provoked the war in Africa.

But the best indication for James that Eddie's attempt to destroy humanity had been thwarted was that President Scofield, reacting to the thirty-point drop in his poll numbers, promised to start pulling troops from Africa within two months. And he went along with Congress when they voted to suspend the Military Mobilization Readiness camps pending further study. Africa had been relatively calm so far, thank God.

He couldn't ask the Seekers if the world really was safe again, because they hadn't come back to him. He took that as the answer: they didn't need him anymore, since the Way had been accomplished and things looked good in their future-stream sense. In a way, he was relieved; but in another way, oddly, he missed them. He assumed they were blithely sailing through the Portal again, oblivious to humans once more.

Assuring himself every day as he read the paper that he really had defeated the deviant alien was one step in the process of dealing with this huge thing that had happened to him. The biggest step came the second weekend of July, when James was complaining to Emily again about the how the media just wasn't letting up on him. "Then let's get away," she said. "You don't work in the summer. I can take time off. Let's ditch them."

They went camping in the Rocky Mountains. The kids climbed up and down the rocky hills and played in the streams, and he climbed steep paths up gorgeous mountainsides, the strenuous exercise purging his mind of disturbing thoughts. He and Emily sat together in meadows overflowing with jubilantly colorful mountain flowers, breathing deeply of the pure air, watching the occasional hawk riding the wind from the mountaintops into the valley. It was like deep meditation for his soul. Emily told him he was a hero for saving all this beautiful life, this precious Earth. Maybe the whole world didn't know just how much of a hero he was, but she did.

And then, the definitive end of the Evil One. Gordon Cambridge committed suicide just before they got back from Colorado. The press crawled all over him for his reaction, but again, he kept it simple, made the same statement every time. "I'm sorry for the family's loss." And he was sorry, for Jack's mother. But Eddie had destroyed Gordon long before the gun did its work, and he couldn't forget that Gordon was the kind of person who had attracted ultimate evil in the first place. Mostly, he felt glad that Shaundra wouldn't have to testify in court now.

Fortunately, the world and the news moved on fairly quickly, once Gordon Cambridge was in the ground. After all, it was an election year.

As he turned to leave the kitchen, the TV caught his attention. How many times had he said to the kids, "It's not a sin to turn off the TV"? For all the good it did. Here it was, blasting out some inane cartoon, and no one in the room. He picked up the controller to turn off the satellite, hesitated, then flipped to CNN. It featured election coverage, as usual.

"Fresh off the nomination, Olivia Compton enjoys a 27-point lead over President Scofield in the latest polls. Governor Compton is scheduled to speak at rallies today in Ohio and Georgia, while her running mate, Senator Abraham Miller, will be addressing the NAACP. Senator Miller, of course, was the head of the Jewish Anti-Defamation League before being elected to the Senate, and he has a long history of fighting for the rights of minorities. On the other side of the campaign trail…" James turned it off.

Today the lawn was mowed, the kids were over at friends' houses, and the hammock was calling his name. He decided to go back to the living room for that sports car magazine he'd picked up. A guy could dream.

He picked up his phone and saw he had a message from Jack. "Hey, Thompson. How ya doin'? I suppose you've seen enough on TV to know what's going on with me. I wanted to let you know I'm OK, 'cause you probably saw that the investment firm cut me loose, and I figure you feel guilty for screwing up my life."

James winced. Jack continued, "Anyway, you didn't, so just chill on that, OK? I've made some good investments myself; I'm not hurting." Jack chuckled. "Believe it or not, someone actually asked me if I wanted to run for state office. Shit. I'd be a dogcatcher before I'd do that. But—you're gonna like this, dude—I'm seriously thinking of getting my teaching license so I can coach high school basketball. Although I may not have to do that, 'cause UCLA is talking to me about an assistant coaching job. But that's on the down low, so don't be talking to the media about that, huh?"

There was a pause, and then Jack's voice came on hesitantly. "Uh, about Gordon's suicide. I'm not gonna talk to the press about it, but after what we went through together that night, I guess I can talk to you. See, the weird thing is I don't feel bad about it. I don't feel anything about it." Another pause. "Anyway, the other reason I was calling is I'm gonna take Ben on a fishing trip to northern Minnesota next week, so I wanna stop by on our way through. I hope you got a hoop in your driveway, man, 'cause me 'n Ben wanna take on you and your kid. Give me a call. Later."

James would call him back tonight. It would be good to see Jack again. But right now, he had a date with a hammock.

As he stretched out, he thought, This is the definition of a perfect day.

The sky was a brilliant blue, the clouds gorgeous giant white mountains, like they were designed for a movie set in heaven. The flower garden was incredible, a riot of yellow lilies and deep blue larkspur and orange cosmos. Butterflies floated from one flower to the next, putting the exclamation mark on the glory of this summer day. James could almost see the rays of the Life Force flowing from the butterflies, and the flowers, and the trees, and that cardinal sitting on the branch of the oak tree towering over him, and everything else in this lush, vibrant corner of Earth that was his own.

The last sound he heard was the distant roar of someone's lawnmower, summer's white noise. He drifted off, completely content. He was dreaming: hiking in the mountains, Emily beside him. They came to a tall waterfall, and he pulled her to him. They began making love, lying in a vast mountain valley covered with wildflowers. His dreaming mind vaguely noticed that the flowers around them were starting to shimmer. The colors became more intense and filled the air with vibrant purples and golds and deep reds and greens. Emily disappeared. He felt his mind being grasped.

He saw the first vision they showed him, of the Earth suspended in space, stars glittering around it like the lights on a Christmas tree, and then the Life Force flowing off it, and the Seekers streaming into the Earth, disappearing into the dark shimmering Portal.

In his mind, James said, Why are you here now? I did what you asked of me.

He saw himself as the gigantic golden-threaded man, with millions of little Seekers whirling around him, almost like they were dancing. A feeling of profound gratitude filled his mind. So, they wanted to thank him. Fine. My pleasure. Glad it's over.

There was a hesitation, and then he heard a voice: *Implore you. Warn you.*

What?

The vision that filled his mind was chilling. He saw humans burning forests all over the planet, the blazing inferno visible from space as the Seekers emerged from their cocoons and watched. He saw humans dumping poison into the oceans, saw the color change from blue to a sick yellowish brown. He saw humans slaughtering animals—apes, whales, frogs, birds, elephants, bears, so many species—by the millions, carcasses piling up on the Earth in great rotting heaps. He saw the Life Force flicker, shrink, fade to a shadow. A tremendous feeling of despair filled his mind, of the horror and the wrongness of all this.

Somehow, he understood. The Seeker was telling him that they now realized that humans were capable of destroying their own planet, incomprehensible as that might have been.

He saw the Earth, with its weakened Life Force, shimmer as it transformed into the Portal. But the Portal was a pale grey, and the Seekers who came to it were not able to pass through.

Then he saw the ultimate horror. Millions upon millions of Seekers materialized in the skies above the Earth; millions upon millions of Seekers descended and landed each on a human being and were absorbed into the brains of those humans. Then he saw the Life Force drain from the humans, as they collapsed and died.

Oh my God, that can't be real! What are you telling me? James screamed at the alien in his head. You can't do that! You're going to kill us? Who are you to decide to wipe out millions of people? We are human beings!

The alien apparently picked up on his extreme distress, because he was filled with sadness as he heard words in his head: *Sacrifice. Save Portal.*

James saw, among the millions of dead bodies, other humans still alive. He saw a few Seekers floating in the air. He saw the planet revived, vibrant, alive with healthy oceans and forests, mountains and tundra, teeming with animals. He knew what they were telling him: if they thought humans were close to destroying the world, they would be forced to sacrifice, themselves as well as humans, to save it.

Or were they telling him that this was going to happen? Did that awful future-sense quilt show this devastation coming? Is that what they were warning him about? He was their hero, so they were warning him? For what? So he could save himself, save his family? No! James mentally screamed at the alien, frantic to get it to understand him. That's not what I want! Don't do it, don't destroy my people. You can't! These are innocents! Please, if it gets bad, give us a chance to find a way to stop it. I'm begging you. Please.

James was panicked, desperately trying to think of a way to visualize this for them so they'd get it, but his mind was frozen.

Then they sent a response, perhaps understanding his anguish at the sight of millions of his fellow human beings being murdered. He saw the future-sense quilt floating. He saw many individual threads light up and fade, flashing silver, emerald green, ruby red, and at the center of the quilt lay the devastated Earth. But then that faded away, and the quilt flashed new colors, different threads lighting and glowing. The Earth now lay centered on the quilt in all its lush vibrant glory, Life Force streaming abundantly from it. And he heard these words in his head: *Humans choose own fate.* Pain shot through his head as he heard the words. Whatever they were doing to manipulate the language area of his brain, it hurt. But he was willing to take it if he could get answers, assurances.

James felt blankness in his mind where the alien had been. But he hadn't felt it pull away and break the connection. Was the alien thinking? Had James made it understand that it would be wrong to wipe out large numbers of humans, as wrong as what the Evil Ones did? He felt a small glimmer of hope that they would listen to their human hero.

He felt the Seeker reconnect. Pain stabbed through his head again as he heard words: *Wishing gift you.* My God, what kind of gift could they possibly give him? The thought occurred to him that maybe they could somehow implant in his brain the future sense, so that he could anticipate humans turning again toward great evil and try to stop it. But would he even want to know the future? No, that wasn't likely anyway. Probably they'd just shower him with some scent that would make him feel better, try to take away the fear of humanity being nearly wiped out by them. Well, it wouldn't work.

He felt the Seeker muster its strength and worried fleetingly about what would cause it to need such strength, what were they going to do…? The pain split his brain with blinding force. He heard these words: *Sharing you oldest greatest stories called Primary.*

The pain faded from James's head and a feeling of deep peace saturated him. He saw endless nothingness, darker than black.

Then an enormous whirling tornado was suddenly there, but it was like it had always been there; he just hadn't seen it. Millions of stars were flung out from the center of the tornado. He saw space, not as we see it in our telescopes, but all of it, the vastness incomprehensible and yet clear, stars and galaxies glittering and stretching on and on forever.

Now out of the center of the tornado blew the sun, our sun, blindingly bright and glorious. Then the planets flew out of the tornado, blown by its powerful wind into orbit around the sun.

Color exploded in James's head, a swirling symphony of such joy and pure beauty that he was overwhelmed with awe. James heard words again, such a long string of words that it should have taken his head apart in pain, but he felt nothing but serenity. *The Greatest One is only thing in all Space and Time that is alone unto Itself and is One Not Many, because It is All in One.* He realized that this was the Creed of the Seekers, the single most important sentence in their colorful language.

The story, their Primary story, their Genesis, went on. He saw seeds spewing from the tornado, blowing through space on the divine wind. Some landed on Earth, and some landed on what he realized was the Seekers' home planet. He saw their home planet but could not identify which one it was.

He watched the seeds sprout on the Seekers' planet, and even though the seeds looked identical, many forms of life grew from them: dozens of plants—long waving plants sending out hundreds of tendrils; tiny glowing lichen-like things stuck to the rocks; and twisting yellow balls of string-like fuzz. And creatures also grew from the seeds—Seekers, of course, but also creatures scurrying over rocks with thousands of tiny legs protruding from jelly-blob bodies; giant torpedo-shaped creatures with huge fan-like wings—or fins—propelling them; iridescent round globes that darted up-down-sideways so fast he couldn't follow them… He couldn't tell if they were moving through water or air. Oh, it was so amazing! He fought to imprint these images on his memory. But then it was gone, and he saw Earth.

The same seeds fell on Earth: a barren, volcanic Earth from eons ago. And from the seeds grew all life on Earth, riotous in its variety—countless species of plants and animals growing and flashing before him like a movie on super fast-forward speed.

James saw the Life Force flowing from the planet. But then, astoundingly, the viewpoint changed, and he saw Earth from the Seekers' planet. It was a small spot amongst the stars, but glowing and shimmering with the Life Force, such that it rivaled the sun in its intensity; it was the most compelling thing in the heavens, a beacon for all life in the Universe. He could feel the pull of the Life Force even from that place.

The scene changed back to primitive Earth. He saw early humans, small and ape-like, skulking in bushes, hiding in caves. Then the cocoons of the Seekers appeared in the skies above them, although the primitive humans didn't notice.

As the Seekers moved through the Portal, he saw their bodies disintegrating, being shed. Tiny bits and pieces of their bodies fell like snow on the primitive humans, as well as on other life forms. But unlike the other animals, the humans were clearly receptive to alien debris, absorbing the particles into their bodies.

And now the humans were changing from primitive primates into Homo Sapiens; now they were banding together in communities, hunting and growing food cooperatively. They absorbed more of the Seekers' shed bodies, and now they were speaking languages. As they absorbed even more particles, they built cities; they absorbed more, and made art.

James was stunned.

At the same time that he was watching humans transformed, he saw the Earth in its early stages, with a weak Life Force radiating from it. At first the transition through the Portal appeared to be difficult, and many Seekers didn't make it. But as innumerable Seekers moved through the Portal, millennia upon millennia, humans grew in intelligence and self-awareness. As they became creatures capable of building the Sistine Chapel and then painting the ceiling in magnificent beauty and filling it with glorious music, the Life Force grew ever more vibrant and strong. The Seekers rode in on the strengthened Life Force and passed through the Portal more and more easily, in harmony with the complex Life Force emanating from human beings, as well as the multitude of other living creatures.

The pictures faded away.

James's mind flooded with one word: Symbiosis.

The strong sense of contentment he felt told him that the Seekers were pleased that he understood their meaning. James felt his heart racing and knew somehow that tears were flowing down his face.

James felt the pull of the Portal through his connection with the Seeker. As the Seeker was leaving, he heard final words of parting, and knew that he would not hear from the Seekers again. *Wishing you*

James life touching other humans and fulfillment of the Portal. For the briefest of moments, James thought he glimpsed the other side of the Portal, dazzling in a brilliance that was more than he could endure.

James gasped and opened his eyes. A strong smell of oranges and something like maple syrup filled the air. He shivered violently, spasms wracking his body. Even though it was a hot summer day, he was freezing. But he knew it wasn't just the cold that the Seekers produced that was making him shake uncontrollably.

James looked up into the brilliant blue sky. He raised a trembling hand, his index and middle fingers forming a V, which he held up toward the clouds. "Peace," he said softly—but whether in supplication or in warning, even he didn't know.

ACKNOWLEDGEMENTS AND THANKS

Thank you to my brother-in-law, Ron Bergantine, for consulting with me on being a high school science teacher, and on hunting.

Thank you to Pam Huey for giving me a tour of the Star Tribune newsroom.

And thank you a million times over to my very supportive husband, and best reader, Mike.

ABOUT THE AUTHOR

Deb Kolbo Ellsworth lives in St. Louis Park, Minnesota, just outside of Minneapolis. She is a teacher, and is the co-author of a parenting book, *Your Amazing Preschooler: How You Can Have the Same Capable, Confident and Cooperative Child at Home That Teachers Have at School.* Deb spends her spare time promoting The Empathy Symbol (EmpathySymbol.com), which she created many years ago, and which is now being used around the world to express the core value of empathy. She is also a Challenge Master for Minnesota Destination Imagination. Deb graduated from Gustavus Adolphus College and received an M.A. in psychology from the University of Denver. She and her husband, Mike, have three wonderful sons—Zack, Devin and Alex.

www.ingramcontent.com/pod-product-compliance
Lightning Source LLC
Chambersburg PA
CBHW062006170626
46813CB00001B/53